MAGGOTS
SCREAMING!

MAX BOOTH III

Ghoulish Books
an imprint of Perpetual Motion Machine Publishing
Cibolo, Texas

Maggots Screaming!

ISBN: 978-1-943720-68-2

www.GhoulishBooks.com
www.PerpetualPublishing.com

Cover Art by Corinne Halbert
Title Text by Zach Chapman
Back Cover Art by Luke Spooner

ALSO BY MAX BOOTH III

For Jack, who helped me begin this book.
And Frank, who helped me finish it.

THIS IS THE story of how we found you.

Maybe you already know it. There's no telling what's in that head of yours. More than likely you know more than I ever will, and that's okay, I don't need to know everything. Some things aren't meant to be known. Some things *can't* be known, no matter how hard you try to understand them. I wish Dad could have figured that out sooner. I wish so many things. It's about the only thing I *can* do, where we are now. Wish things. Wishes that will never come true. No matter how loud I scream at the sky. Nobody is listening. Nobody worth a damn, anyway. And that's okay, too.

But here is what I do know.

It started with a finger.

Poking out of the dirt in Mom's garden. Like a flower composed of flesh.

Pointing directly at the sun.

The sun in Texas is different than the suns in other states. In Texas, the sun can't be ignored. In Texas, the sun controls everything, living and dead. In Texas the sun is a hero and the sun is a villain. It's a mad scientist holding an entire state hostage. In Texas we ask the sun permission before we do anything, because if we don't, we know the consequences will be dire. So it made sense, that the mysterious object—*the finger*—sprouting from the dirt would be worshipping the same burning star everybody here worships. Anything else would have been considered blasphemy.

I noticed it first.

MAX BOOTH III

My shovel made contact as I attempted to dig up the desecrated hibiscus. I thought maybe it was another root. They'd proven tricky to dig around, even after Dad moistened the earth with a hose. Some of the roots I'd managed to splinter by driving the tip of the shovel down with all my strength. By then, blisters had already started forming on my fingers, and I was secretly looking forward to squeezing them until they burst. There's something thrilling about that clear juice trickling down your palm afterward. Is it always in you, waiting for the right blister to make its escape? I don't think it's pus. Pus is thicker, and more yellow—plus it has that smell to it . . . the kind that makes you feel like maybe there's an unknown disease percolating somewhere inside you.

I nudged the thing sticking out of the ground with my toe, testing how firm of a hold the earth had on it, and the object bent forward—like a metallic mailbox flag.

"What is that?" I asked.

Behind me, raking bush debris into a trash can, Dad said, "What's what?"

"*That.*" I dropped the shovel and pointed at the thing sticking out of the ground. "What *is* it?"

"It's nothing," he said, then stared a little longer, then kneeled in the wet dirt and touched it. "Where did this come from? Did you put it here?"

"I didn't do anything. I just found it."

He lay on his stomach, pressing his face inches from the object, studying it from various angles, whispering, "What the fuck?" over and over. Almost like he was hypnotized by our discovery, like he would've kept repeating the same question for the rest of his life if left undisturbed.

I shouted his name and he jerked away from the object. His eyes were wild with an emotion I couldn't understand.

"What is it?" I asked again, and this time I didn't want to know the answer.

But he told me anyway.

4

MAGGOTS SCREAMING!

The finger led to more fingers, which led to a hand, which led to a wrist, which led to an arm.

Guess where the arm led.

Dad relieved me of shovel duty. As he worked, I hovered over him a little too closely, watching the hole widen, only semi-aware of the spade swinging back inches from my face, of the rogue clumps of dirt flinging haphazardly. If I got hit in the crossfire, the pain would have been worth it. There was a body in our yard and I was going to absorb every detail, no matter the cost.

The only reason Dad decided to make this garden our weekend project was because of Mom's boyfriend. His name's Miguel, but if you ask Dad what his name is, he's liable to tell you it's, "That fuckin' traitor piece of shit cocksucker."

You see, Miguel and Dad used to be friends. Them and this other guy, this kind of *weird* guy named Andy. The three of them did everything together. I never had much of a problem with Miguel. Andy, though, he always came off as a little spooky, but he had this great dog named Comrade, so sometimes him coming over wasn't as bad as it could've been.

I remember one time, when I was much younger, they took me on a fishing trip. Not like the kinda fishing trip you see in movies. We didn't own a boat or nothin' fancy like that. But there's this bridge outside the limits of Guadalupe County. Nothing you can drive on or anything. A little rickety bridge with a roof cover. It connects one end of a bike trail to another. Under the bridge is a small river, or a lake, or a stream, maybe. I don't know the difference between them. Dad's told me before but sometimes when

5

people tell me things it's like they get deleted from my brain before I have a chance to latch on to any of the words.

It's a little tricky, but if you're careful and maintain the right balance you can maneuver yourself below the bridge and sit on the big rocks next to the water. Dad and Miguel and Andy used to do it as kids, I guess, and still did as adults. I would always beg them to take me. I guess eventually my begging wore them down and they brought me along. Nearly fell and broke my ankle trying to get to the fishing spot. Dad had to keep grabbing my arm to help me stay standing. He didn't seem annoyed about it, though. More like it made him feel good to be saving me over and over. Like it made him feel useful. Sometimes people need to feel like that, I've discovered. Otherwise they start wondering what they're even doing here.

Once we got down there, him and Miguel and Andy cracked open the cooler and drank every can of beer floating in the melted ice. I drank two cans of Big Red they'd brought along specifically for me. Before we called it quits, I'd end up catching a catfish. I wanted to take it home with us, but Dad said they never took fish home, they were strictly catch-and-release fishermen, that they didn't know the first thing about properly preparing fish. "C'mon, Max," Miguel had said, "it's the boy's first catch. You gotta preserve the moment somehow, don'tcha?" And I guess the guilt trip worked its charm over Dad, since he sighed and helped me trap the catfish in the cooler.

When we got home, the fish was no longer moving. Dad wrestled its awkward, lifeless body into a plastic bag and stuck it in the freezer until he could figure out what to do with it, and I went off to play Xbox. A little while later, Mom returned from the grocery store. She opened the freezer, saw the bag Dad had left there, and picked it up. "What's this?" she asked us, and that was when the bag started moving. My fish hadn't died, after all. She shrieked and whipped the bag against the wall and now it was for-real dead. We threw it away instead of eating it since none of us knew how to cook it and plus we were all secretly terrified it was somehow still alive, even though no one would admit it aloud.

Two years later, Mom and Dad were getting divorced, and a couple months after that Mom and Miguel started dating. Now Dad and Miguel don't talk to each other, and Dad's always in a bad mood.

On the Friday we found you, Dad was in one of the worst moods I'd ever seen him in. It was his weekend to have me, according to the courts, and I guess Mom and Miguel got the dates mixed up somehow, because they'd planned this big weekend getaway down in Corpus Christi. Miguel had rented a cabin near the beach and everything. Apparently he couldn't get his deposit reimbursed on it and the rental place refused to reschedule us, so it had to be *this* weekend. Mom either forgot or intentionally neglected to tell Dad until late Thursday night. The following morning, bright and early, Dad was banging on our door, face tomato-red.

"You are *not* taking *my* son on *my* weekend," he'd practically screamed once Mom opened the door, still half-asleep. I could hear them arguing from my bedroom. The whole neighborhood could hear them. The whole planet.

One time, at a friend's birthday party, this squirrel fell out of a tree and broke its legs. It went crazy and crawled around the front yard trying to attack us. My friend's mom called the police station and they sent out a cop and the cop walked up to us with a real big grin on his face and said, "Watch this, kiddos," then shot the squirrel in the face and it exploded all over the grass, painted the green this terrible red. Everybody started screaming and crying and my friend's mom tried reassuring us the cop had done the humane thing, that the squirrel needed to be put out of its misery.

I suddenly couldn't stop thinking about that birthday party while listening to Dad and Mom argue out on the front porch. Dad was screaming like that squirrel had been screaming. Consumed by rage. I got scared someone would call a cop to come put him out of his misery, too. If this continued much longer, what choice would anyone have?

I wondered if he'd be the same cop, and if he'd be wearing the same satisfied smile as he executed my father.

"Dylan has been talking about this trip all week," Mom was saying when I tiptoed down the hallway. "Do you really want to break his little heart just because of . . . what? Your ego can't handle him having fun without you?"

"It's not about my *ego*," Dad said. I peeked around the edge of the hallway and spied on their argument. Dad on one side of the screen door, Mom on the other. "It's about the *agreement*. You had him last weekend, did you not? Am I crazy? Did I imagine that?"

"No."

"Then that must mean this weekend is *my* weekend, right? Is that not the agreement we came to in a *court* of *law*?" He sighed and paced around the front porch, rubbing his hands through his hair. "What good's an agreement if it can be broken at the slightest inconvenience? Why bother making one in the first place, huh? You say it's just this one time you need him on my weekend, but what about my *next* weekend? What happens when you need him then, too? Don't you think I need him just as much as you? Don't you think I miss him something fierce? You break the agreement now and who knows what unfolds? You might not realize it yet, but this is your attempt to steal him away from me forever. This is you planting a seed that spouts the tree with me no longer in his life."

"Max, you're being ridiculous. If Miguel hadn't put down the deposit already, it wouldn't—"

He shoved a finger against the screen door, inches from her face, like he was trying to penetrate her skull with telekinesis. "Don't you dare mention that motherfucker's name to me. Goddamn you. Goddamn both of you."

I thought about the squirrel and how quickly its

sickness had ruined a perfectly good birthday party, then stepped forward into the living room. "It's okay, Mom. I want to go with Dad, anyway."

She gave me a look like I was acting just as ridiculous as my father, and I never felt more connected to him. "Dylan, be quiet, you don't know what you're talking about."

"Yes I do. I want to go with him."

She always said that—*you don't know what you're talking about*—whenever I contradicted her in some way, and it made my blood boil. Like Dad's blood was boiling out on the porch, like it'd *been* boiling since she texted him that we'd be down in Corpus this weekend—shoot, his blood had done been boiling much longer than that, probably since at least the divorce, and certainly once Miguel started dating Mom. Whose blood wouldn't look like a witch's cauldron at that point?

She shook her head, not believing the betrayal coming out of my mouth. "You're coming with us, and that's final."

"You heard what he said," Dad said, gesturing down at me. "Even he doesn't want to go, and still you're trying to violate the court order? What kinda mother are you, prying a son from his father for no good reason? No good reason at *all*. You oughta be *ashamed*."

Instead of responding, she just sighed there on our side of the screen door. I could feel her surrendering next to me and a sickness blossomed in my stomach. Of course I would have preferred to join her and Miguel on our little getaway. She was right—I'd been looking forward to the trip all week. But couldn't she see what this would do to my father? Couldn't she predict the possible consequences that might unfold due to this violation? As I had hid in the hallway listening to them fight, an infinite amount of timelines spanned in my mind: one where we left for Corpus, and Dad went home and drank himself into a coma, the kinda coma a person never woke up from; one where he followed us to Corpus and waited until we were asleep, then abducted me in the night and burned the cabin to the ground with Mom and Miguel still inside it; one where Dad didn't have the patience to wait and allowed his rage to consume him whole out here in Mom's front yard; and so on, and so on. Going with him instead of Mom and Miguel seemed like the only logical method of preventing the unthinkable. To be fair, I did not consider my father a violent man. He had never hit Mom and, to the best of my memory, light spankings when I was younger had been the only times he'd ever laid hands on me. Yes, he often got angry, but that didn't qualify him as a murderer. Everybody gets mad. Rage is in human DNA just as love and hunger and sadness is. And sometimes rage gets out of control. Sometimes you can't help it. Squirrels are considered cute and adorable, but sometimes they go mad and try to kill everything in their path and the only way to stop them is to call a cop to come blow their brains out. If a squirrel can do that, then—under the correct set of circumstances—so could my father.

I didn't understand why Mom couldn't see that.

"You'll be there until Monday," she told me as I gathered my belongings. Dad was waiting out in his truck, trying to cool off with the AC. No way in hell would she have allowed him to enter her new house. Especially not after the tantrum he'd thrown on the porch. "We won't be able to come pick you up if you get bored. You know that, right?"

"Yes, Mom," I said, refusing to look at her as I shoved a fistful of clothes in my bag. "I know."

"I just don't understand why you suddenly don't want to come to Corpus with us. All week long you've done nothing but talk about that beach, and now you don't care? What happened?"

I crammed one last comic book in my backpack and zipped it up, then slung it over my shoulders. I finally looked at her and noticed a single tear struggling to remain contained in the corner of her eye. "Because it's not fair to Dad."

"So what?" she said, whispering now so he didn't somehow overhear us from his truck outside. "Since when has he ever been fair with us?"

"*Mom* . . . it's his weekend. We should have never planned this trip for his weekend."

"It was a mistake," she said, and I didn't know if I believed her.

"Well, what do you always say about mistakes?" I asked her, and when I stepped forward she stepped back. "Don't you always say own up to them?"

"Yes, but . . . ?"

"I don't want to hurt his feelings," I told her, whispering again. "I know you don't care about that, but I do. He's still *my* dad."

Her mouth opened and closed for a brief, cartoonish second, then she sat at the edge of my bed with her hands folded in her lap. "Okay, I'm sorry." She sucked in a breath. "I wasn't thinking about it that way, and I apologize."

"Thank you."

"If you want to go with your dad, you can go with your dad."

I hugged her and she squeezed me like she'd never see me again. I tried to squirm away but her grip was impenetrable.

"I love you, Dylan," she whispered into my ear.

"I love you, too," I told her.

The screen door banged shut from the living room and I shot out of her embrace like I had something to feel ashamed about. Miguel's voice rang out down the hallway: "Hello? Y'all know Max's sitting out front?" He poked his head around my doorframe with a puzzled expression written all over his face. "I tried to say hi but he wouldn't roll down his window."

As we were pulling out of the driveway, Mom told me not to spend the whole weekend in front of the TV, and I lied and told her I wouldn't. Infinite screen time was one of the few perks of sleeping over at Dad's since the divorce. We often stayed up past midnight eating greasy pizza and watching action movies from his childhood. "They don't make them like they used to, I'll tell you that," he'd mumble next to me on the couch, usually around the midway point of a six-pack, both of us illuminated by the glow of his little television set. Not the big one we used to have there. Mom took that with us when we moved out. Now it remains in our new living room, where we barely use it. Apparently staring at the screen long enough rots your brain. She also smokes two packs of cigarettes a day, so sometimes I wonder if she's the best person to be giving health advice. Honestly, she should've left the TV with Dad. At least at his place it would've been properly loved.

Either way, those parting words of hers as we backed out of the driveway, they latched onto Dad like a leech. "'Don't spend the whole weekend in front of the TV'?" He mimicked her voice as if she were a bird in the process of being pecked alive by a much larger predator. "The hell was she trying to imply, anyway?" He nudged me with his shoulder and glanced away from the road. "What've you two been talking about? You telling her all we do is watch TV?"

I shook my head. "I haven't been telling her anything."

"You saying we don't play together? That I don't take you places?"

"I never said that."

"Last time you came over, didn't we play mini golf?"

I nodded. "We did. At the pizza place with the movie theater."

"And did you tell her about that?"

"What?"

"Did you tell her I took you mini golfing?"

"I don't remember."

"You don't remember?" His face got all screwed up as

he looked at me again, and my whole body tensed, silently begging he'd return his gaze to the road before getting us in an accident. "I take you out, spend my good hard-earned money on a place like mini golf, and you don't even tell your mom about it?"

"I didn't say I didn't tell her. I just don't remember. That was a long time ago."

"Dylan, it's been two weeks."

I sucked in a breath, hating the interrogation. "Maybe I did tell her."

"Well, you either did or you didn't."

"I think I did."

"And what did she say about that?"

"She said it was nice."

He jerked his head so suddenly I thought he was going to swerve the truck into a tree. "*Nice?* What kinda response is that? Is it *nice* for a father to take care of his son now? Like I don't always? What else did she say?"

"Dad, I don't remember."

He shook his head, mumbling something, more in conversation with himself than anyone else. "*Nice.* Jesus Christ. I'll show her *nice.*"

He was starting to unsettle me a little. The way his brain worked sometimes when it came to Mom, he could fixate on the tiniest details and obsess over them for the rest of the night trying to pry more information from me.

I cleared my throat and tried to change the subject. "So, what do you want to do today?"

"Well, god forbid we spend time together watching TV."

"We could continue our *Simpsons* marathon. Or play *Zombies Ate My Neighbors*. It's not a big deal."

"Wouldn't want to be a terrible father or anything."

"You're not a terrible father."

He glanced down at me again and smiled. "Thanks. That means a lot."

"You're a great dad," I told him. "The best dad I know."

His smile spread wider and he returned his eyes to the

road just in time to see a red light and slammed on the brakes. We sat there watching traffic pass in front of us, neither of us saying a word. A truck with a lawn care company name stenciled across the driver's side door took its sweet time crossing the road. A trailer was hitched to the back of it, storing an assortment of mowers and weedwhackers and other lawn equipment.

Dad let out a laugh once the truck was out of sight.

"What's funny?" I asked, not liking the way he sounded.

"Your mom doesn't want you watching TV, that's fine, no problem. I just thought of a great father-son project we could do together. Something I've been meaning to take care of since she moved out. Why not today, right? Why not?"

When I was younger, a baby really, barely old enough to form coherent memories, Mom planted a garden in the back yard. A little patch of life next to our tall wooden perimeter fence, twenty feet wide, six feet long, consisting of four boxwood hedges along the fence, followed by a morning glory, a hibiscus, a lantana, then two Texas sages on either side. Most thirteen-year-old boys don't know the names of plants. None of my friends would've been able to name any of them. I probably wouldn't have publicly admitted to possessing this knowledge, either—at least not at school. But I could certainly remember Mom talking about the plants when we used to live at Dad's house. They were her pride and joy. I remember going out and helping her water them. I remember posing in front of the hibiscus as it bloomed so Mom could take plenty of photos to post on Facebook. The hibiscus was her favorite. "The very definition of beautiful," she once said about it, who knows how many years ago, then pinched my cheek and added, "Just like you."

Maggots Screaming!

I protested when Dad first revealed his plan. "That's Mom's garden. We can't kill it."

He shook his head, smiling. "Ah, but that's exactly why we *should* kill it—don't you see?"

"No."

We were standing out on the back patio. Across the yard, against the fence, was Mom's garden. The idea of removing it seemed like a sin. I felt guilty merely entertaining the idea and prayed Mom never found out about this conversation.

Dad did not try to shield his impatience as he rubbed between his eyes. "Think of it like this, okay? Mom and I are never getting back together, right?"

"I don't know."

"Oh, c'mon, you don't know? Yeah you do. We all know. It's not happening."

"Okay."

"Sorry to break it to you, kiddo. But your mom . . . she's a lot happier without me. I don't like it, but it doesn't matter what I like. Facts are facts. We tried to make it work and I failed, or she failed, or maybe we were never meant to be together in the first place. Who knows? Maybe the only reason we were ever supposed to meet, the whole point of fate pinning us in the same room, was to squeeze you outta my dick, right? Well, mission accomplished, I guess!"

"Dad!" I shouted, grimacing and laughing at the same time. I stepped away from him, out of the shade next to the door and deeper into the yard. Sweat generated the instant the sun made contact with my flesh. It was supposed to get up to 105 degrees at some point that day and I was not looking forward to it.

He scratched his head, watching my retreat with curiosity. "What I'm trying to say is there has been a separation, and everybody seems to be on board with the separation except for me. Mom has moved on. You seem okay with it."

"I'm not—"

He held up his hand, palm-out. "It's fine. You oughta be okay with it. What other choice do you got, right? And I guess the same question oughta be directed toward myself. What other choice do *I* got? Not much. I could sit at home every day and get drunk and sad and try to think of a way to win her back, or I could finally grow a pair and move on. It's been . . . what, two years now?" He paused as a fresh sadness morphed his face. "Wow. Holy shit. Two years, huh? Okay." He scratched his cheek, lost in his thoughts, then spit in the grass and pointed at the garden. "Your mom was able to move on. That's fine. She has a new house. She has a new boyfriend. She has friends. She has you practically whenever she wants you. But me? I got what? I got the house. Sure. But that's only because it belonged to my own mom—your grandmother. Obviously she wasn't gonna take that, too. But what does that mean? It means every day, I wake up and the first thing I see out the window is . . . is . . . is *that* . . . those dead flowers that ain't ever gonna blossom again . . . just like me and your mom, right? We ain't ever gonna blossom again either, are we? This . . . what? This *metaphor* laughing at me every day I get dressed for work. Or is that an *analogy?* Whatever. You know what I'm talkin' about. She's gone but her footprints are everywhere, and I ain't ever gonna get past this until I erase them somehow and figure out a way to start fresh." He clamped a hand around my shoulder. A little too hard. I tried not to wince. "And that's where I need your help, son. If I do this alone . . . I'm afraid I'm not strong enough. But with you by my side? It'll almost be like we're forming a new kinda bond, something that lasts forever, no matter what. Because you know what we'll do after digging up your mom's old plants? We'll take a drive on down to Lowe's and pick out a new garden together, one you and I will plant, as father and son." He smiled, getting lost in his own fantasy. "This way, every morning when I get ready to make my deliveries, I won't be forced to think about your mom—I'll be reminded of the quality time we spent together this weekend—a weekend nobody will ever be able to take away from us—and maybe life won't be so goddamn miserable. Doesn't that sound nice?"

What it takes to destroy a garden: gloves, a hedge trimmer, bypass loppers, a rake, and a shovel. Also, empty trash cans and plenty of water—water to stay hydrated and water to moisten the dirt. Maybe other methods exist, but this is the way my dad taught me on the Friday that we found you. The Friday that changed everything.

My reluctance to kill something Mom had planted faded as soon as Dad gave me permission to use the hedge trimmer, which was probably the next best thing to an actual chainsaw. Mom would not have allowed me within six feet of the hedge trimmer. But Dad, on the other hand, giggled and told me to go wild. "Just don't cut your fuckin' arm off," he said. "Imagine the kinda shit your mother would give me if she came back from Corpus and you was without an arm. Good god, I'd never hear the end of it!"

"I won't cut my arm off," I promised him.

"Attaboy." He patted me on the shoulder and showed me how to handle the hedge trimmer. I'd imagined operating the machine would've been far more complicated than what the reality ended up being. The trickiest part was getting it started. Using one hand you had to grip the handle, inch your thumb up and slide a safety guard forward, then squeeze the trigger before letting the safety guard fall into place. Dad could do it no problem since he had giant hands. My thumb barely reached the safety guard, and the whole machine was heavier than he made it out to be and I had to hold it up with two hands otherwise the weight would sag my arm down, which seemed like a pretty surefire way to mutilate one of my legs. But once I got it going, things were peachy as long as I didn't stop squeezing the trigger—which I had to do every thirty seconds or so to give my hand a break from the hedge trimmer's jerky vibrations.

The plants were mostly dead. It had not rained in several weeks, if not months, and Dad clearly hadn't been watering them. As I trimmed away at the wild bushes, Dad brought out his stereo and hooked it up to the outlet on the outside of the house next to the patio. Within seconds one of his beloved Black Sabbath CDs started blaring in the back yard. The one with that Iron Man song on it that I like so much. I don't know what it's called. It's about Iron Man but it's really not. At least not the one I know about. That's what Dad always said, but I don't know if he knew for real or was trying to give me a hard time.

With the music blaring loud enough to irritate the neighbors, he scooped up the bypass loppers from the grass and started snipping off any branches too thick for the hedge trimmers to eat through. Every time he snapped the handles together, he let out an exaggerated karate-movie grunt and screwed up his face so he looked like he had delivered a great deadly blow to one of our many enemies. Maneuvering the hedge trimmer proved to be slightly more difficult while giggling at Dad's antics, but somehow I managed not to drop it on my foot or cut my arm off, which I had already vowed not do under any circumstances. If possible, I intended to keep my promise.

I loved it when he acted goofy like this. It reminded me of how things used to be before everything changed, before Mom fell out of love with him and decided we would live somewhere else. When I was younger, his silliness would make her laugh just as much as it would for me—but in those months before they informed me of the impending divorce, I noticed a change unfold. Dad's jokes got less frequent, yes, but when he *did* try to play around with us,

Mom wouldn't smile like she used to smile. Instead she seemed annoyed. It got to a point where the mere sound of his voice provoked a negative reaction. When they finally told me their plans, I was not surprised—but that didn't mean it hurt any less.

It was good to see him acting silly again, even if we *were* destroying Mom's garden.

After cutting the bushes down to their stumps, we raked the fallen branches and leaves into a trash can and surveyed our progress. We'd been working for a little over an hour at this point and both of us were drenched with sweat. The sun had not given us a break even for a second. I was reminded of the many times I'd cooked fire ants with a magnifying glass and reckoned this was some form of revenge. I deserved nothing less than for my flesh to burst into flames.

"Now what?" I asked, panting.

"Next we gotta dig up those stumps." He was panting just as hard. "Gonna be a pain in the ass, I'm guessin'. It being a drought and all."

"Because the ground's dry?"

"Exactamundo." He scratched his chin and calmly paced around the desecrated garden. "It's lookin' pretty good, though, ain't it?"

"I can't believe it's gone," I said, trying not to frown and failing.

The frown turned out to be contagious. He clapped me between my shoulders the way fathers clap their sons in TV shows. "What did I say, huh? Tomorrow, you and me are gonna stock up at Lowe's, get ourselves a brand-new garden. Something real special, right?"

"Okay."

"What kinda plants you thinkin' we oughta get?"

The thought of what we would replace Mom's garden with had not occurred to me until then. "Maybe something that can grow food?" I said. "Like tomatoes or something?"

"Oh," Dad said, glancing at the stumps, "you're thinking about one of *those* kinds of gardens."

"We don't have to," I said, slumping my head. "It's just an idea. We can do whatever."

He grinned. "You know, I love myself some tomatoes."

The talk of tomatoes made us realize how hungry we'd gotten during our workout. Somehow it was already past noon. Dad got out the hose and laid the end in the middle of the soil and partially twisted the nozzle so a small portion of water trickled out.

"We don't get it wet, we ain't ever gonna get those stumps out, trust me," he said, leading me across the yard and through the back door. We took turns washing our hands at the kitchen sink then piled into his pickup and headed down the street to Whataburger.

Along the way we listened to another Black Sabbath CD. Windows down, volume cranked. Cars next to us stared like we were lunatics. Like they were afraid of us. Like they envied us. The music was uncomfortably loud and, as a result, it targeted a spotlight on us, which made me feel embarrassed and thrilled and terrified all at once. I didn't want anybody to look at us, yet at the same time yearned for the world to know we existed.

I got my usual: the grilled cheese meal with a Coke and chocolate chip cookie. Dad got a patty melt. We returned to his house and ate at the kitchen table. I split my cookie with him and he gave me some of his onion rings. He liked to dip onion rings in bleu cheese dressing and often encouraged me to give it a try, but I refused. Just the smell of bleu cheese held the potential to ruin my appetite. No way was I going to allow some of it in my mouth.

Look—if you think I'm delaying the inevitable, you are correct.

This Whataburger was our last normal meal together before everything got crazy.

Before we unearthed what could not be reburied.

MAGGOTS SCREAMING!

Before we found you.

But what's the point in telling you about that kind of stuff?

That's not what you want to hear.

Is it?

After we finished eating, neither of us had the energy to resume our yard work. I suggested we surrender and watch *The Simpsons* for a while, but Dad shook his head and said we'd never get up again if we sat on the couch, which was a fair point, so we played a game of gin rummy at the kitchen table then chugged a bunch of water and forced ourselves outside.

My stomach dragged. It felt like I'd swallowed a ship anchor. The desire to nap intensified until I could focus on little more. Dad nudged me along and told me next time we'd eat only salads if Whataburger was going to affect me so badly. I wanted to tell him I'd never seen him eat a salad in his life, but he was sensitive about his weight even if he acted like he wasn't.

We forgot to move the hose after picking up lunch. The earth had transformed into a small quagmire. Dad groaned and made a comment about next month's water bill. We stood over the black water overflowing into the grass. It all looked strangely beautiful, the destruction of earth and merging of garden and yard. I could have remained in place watching all day, all night, forever—long after the water flooded our yard, after it swallowed me whole along with everything else in the neighborhood—somehow, I would still be watching.

Then Dad said, "I read somewhere it's impossible to drown yourself." He licked his lips, steadying his thoughts. "Like, if you're in the bathtub and you try forcing your head down in the water? Nothing's gonna happen. Your . . . what do you call 'em? Your internal *reflexes* kick in, and whether you wanna live or not, they don't give you much choice."

"Oh," I said, nodding along thoughtfully, "okay."

"That's why, if you really wanna drown, what you gotta do is find a bridge that extends over a lake or river."

"Like the one you and Miguel used to go fishing at?" I asked, and immediately regretted uttering his name.

Except, instead of getting mad or sad like I expected, he grinned. "Exactly. You get a bridge like that, tie several bricks to both of your feet, then jump off the side. Gravity will take care of the rest, and it won't matter one lick how much your reflexes try to fight the inevitable."

I shuffled my feet and tried to think about how to respond to something like that. Nothing came to mind. I scooped up the shovel and asked him if he wanted me to start digging.

"Yeah," he said, excited, "let's do this."

The first body we found was Dad's.

We didn't recognize him at first, there being so much dirt on his face and all. Plus, we were too overcome with the shock that comes with discovering there's a body buried in your back yard to really assign any identity to the person.

You were the second body, but again, it took us a bit to piece it together. At first it looked like a slightly smaller copy of the first body. Which wasn't far from the truth.

Dad dug faster, more frantic. Neither of us verbally acknowledged our discovery. The bodies were laid out side by side, shoulder to shoulder, spanning the width of the garden. On the left was Dad, then you, and the body on the right, the one that made our brains finally click and accept the reality of the situation?

"Oh my god," Dad said, dropping to his knees at the edge of the hole.

"Mom?" I whispered, too afraid to get any closer.

But it was her. It couldn't be anybody else. Which

meant the other two bodies—you and the larger one—they had to be us. Dad and me.

All three of us, together again.

Like some kind of family.

The bodies were naked. You and the other two. Maybe that was another reason it took me so long to recognize y'all. How often does a thirteen-year-old boy think about his parents without any clothes on? Yet there they were, in the garden grave, everything out for me to see. Not just them but also you, or me, or both of us, however you want to think about it. All of the things that got me sad when standing in front of a mirror within the privacy of the bathroom were now displayed out under the sun. If I hadn't been paralyzed with confusion, I would have fetched a blanket from inside the house to cover up your shriveled genitals. Instead I sat on the grass, Indian-style, waiting for Dad to react in a way that would confirm we were hallucinating or this was only a dream or what*ever*—anything to convince me none of this was real. I didn't start crying until after he started, then neither of us could stop.

Eventually we exhausted ourselves of tears. The Black Sabbath album had long expired in the CD player. The only noises present in the back yard were our noses sniffling snot and cicadas buzzing in some unknowable place. After a while, even the sun had decided to pack it in. Nothing wanted any part of whatever this was. We were alone, forced to deal with it ourselves.

The bodies appeared less threatening without the sun irradiating their flesh—less real, almost, easier to convince ourselves you belonged in some dream reality separate from our own.

"Okay," Dad said, rubbing his face, "let's go."

He reached down and helped me stand, then led me through the back door. The house felt different.

Insignificant. How could anywhere else ever be as important as our yard? I already yearned to return outside and visit the mysterious garden grave. Idling around the kitchen only seemed like an unnecessary distraction.

Dad had his cell phone out, dialing a number.

"Are you calling the police?" I asked, and he looked at me like I was crazy.

"Your mother."

"Why?"

Again, that same look. He pointed at the door. "I need to make sure she's okay."

He paced around the kitchen with the cell phone pressed against the side of his head. I got a glass of ice water and sat at the table. His anxiety was contagious and before long my legs couldn't stop bouncing up and down.

"C'mon, c'mon, c'mon," he was mumbling, waiting for someone to answer. Then he lit up. "*Lori*. Hey. It's me. I just wanted to—no, everything's fine, yeah, everything's good—we just haven't heard anything from y'all and wanted—yes, uh-huh—we wanted to make sure y'all got there okay and everything. You know. Just to check up or whatever." He clicked his tongue, listening to her talk. "No, he's already asleep. It's not that early. C'mon, what did you want me to do? We had a long day. What do you mean, doing what? Father-and-son activities, that's what. Yeah, I'll have him call you in the morning. Calm down. Shit. You're the one who didn't think to call beforehand. Now you're tryin' to act like it's my fault or something. Excuse me for checking up on you. Next time I won't bother."

He hung up but it was unclear which one of them had gotten to the END CALL button first. By the sound of things, it was likely a draw. "Jesus," he said, "what is *wrong* with that woman?"

"Dad," I said, the rim of the water glass rubbing against my lips, "what are we gonna do?"

He stopped and glanced down at me like he was shocked I was still in the kitchen with him. "What do you mean?"

I nodded at the back door. "What are we—"

He waved the question away. "No way am I prepared to answer something like that right now."

"Shouldn't we call someone?"

"Someone like who?" Dad snickered. "The law?"

I shrugged. It didn't seem like such a bad idea.

He sat at the kitchen table across from me, all jittery. "What do you think's gonna happen if we do that?"

"If we call—"

He nodded, impatient. "Yes. If we call the law."

"I—I don't know. They'll—they'll help?"

"Help?"

"Yes?"

"Okay, that's fair," he said, then raised his pointer finger, "but what, exactly, do you think we need *help* with?"

I didn't understand why he was being so obnoxious. It seemed so clear in my head, but any time I tried to open my mouth all I'd do is stutter and trip over my own words. After a few failed attempts I gave up and pointed at the door again, hoping that would be enough of an explanation.

Dad leaned against his kitchen chair and lightly drummed his fingers along the table. "Okay, Dylan, let's think about this."

"Okay," I said, unsure why he assumed I hadn't already been thinking about it. What else could I possibly have been thinking about?

"Let's pretend those bodies outside are normal bodies and there's nothing out of the ordinary about them. Let's pretend they're not . . . well, you know."

"Us?"

"Those bodies . . . they're fresh. They haven't decomposed or anything like that. We get the law down here, nobody's gonna believe that some previous occupant of this house might be responsible. Whoever buried them out there, it happened recently. You understand what I'm saying?"

"They aren't old."

"Exactly, they're *fresh* deaths. Fresh enough that the law will require some kinda explanation from me better than, 'I just found 'em here, officer, I swear to gawd.' This here's my property, and with me having a rap sheet, shit's already not exactly in my favor. But again, that's all pretending everything's normal, that we've found . . . regular bodies. We didn't find *regular* bodies, though, did we?"

I shook my head.

"Dylan," he said, leaning forward, "I need you to do me a favor, okay? I need you to tell me *exactly* what you saw out there in that hole. I gotta figure out whether or not you and I saw the same thing or if I'm losin' my mind or . . . or . . . or whatever the fuck. You know what I mean?"

"Yes."

"So? What did you see?"

"It was us."

"I'm gonna need you to be a little more specific."

"You . . . me . . . and . . . and . . . " I couldn't finish it.

"And your mother?"

"Are they really us?"

He shrugged. "Dylan, I know about as much as you do right now." He sat at the table, thinking, then got up to brew a pot of coffee. It was late in the evening at this point. I'd never seen him drink anything at night besides beer.

"Why wouldn't you let Mom talk to me?"

"What?"

"You told her I was asleep already and I couldn't talk on the phone."

"I thought maybe you'd tell her about what we found out there."

"Why can't she know? She's out there, too."

He shook his head and faced me again. Behind him, coffee dripped into an empty carafe. "I don't think there's any reason to bother her, do you? She's on vacation, right?"

"Yes, but . . . "

MAGGOTS SCREAMING!

"And what would she really do, anyway? She wouldn't know any more than we do. Telling her this early would only scare her, and there's no point in scaring your mom unless we absolutely have to, don't you think?"

"Okay."

"Once we know more about what's going on, then yes, of course I'll tell her. But right now . . . I think it's probably smart if we just kept this between me and you. Our own little secret. What do you say?"

"Yes," I said, secretly liking how much he was trusting me about something this significant. "Just me and you."

"Great!" he said, clapping his hands and grinning. "Now, how about a glass of chocolate milk? We got a long night ahead of us."

We each took a bathroom break, then rendezvoused at the kitchen table. Dad with a cup of coffee, and myself with a glass of chocolate milk. He'd sprayed whipped cream in mine, as an extra little treat. It tasted so good, for a second I forgot about the garden grave in our back yard.

Then Dad said, "Did you notice they're the same age as we are?"

"What?" I said.

"The bodies. They weren't . . . younger versions of ourselves, or anything. That boy out there in the hole is also thirteen years old, just like you. Their physiques, their ages, it's like all three of them are parallel with ourselves. That's how any one of us would have looked if, this very morning, we decided fuck it and stripped naked and crawled into a random grave. But does that make it weirder, or somehow *less* weird?"

"Maybe it's . . . " I didn't know how to finish the sentence. He looked at me, hopeful, waiting for my idea, so I said the first thing that came to mind. "Maybe they're zombies?"

"If they were zombies, don't you think they would have tried eating our brains by now? And besides, what kinda zombies you know about look exactly like other people?"

"I don't know."

"No zombies I ever heard of, I'll tell you that."

We sat at the kitchen table for a while, uncertain of what to say or do. Dad poured us more coffee and chocolate milk. Second helpings did not come with whipped cream on top.

"This has to be some kinda prank," he finally said. "Those bodies . . . " He shook his head. "Someone's gotta be fuckin' with us."

"Who?" I said. "Why?"

He scratched his chin, thinking it over. "Plenty of crazy sons of bitches out there with sick senses of humor. Hell, I betcha they ain't even real corpses."

"What are they, then?"

"Fakes, I imagine."

"Like mannequins?"

He shrugged. "Shit, could be. I sure as hell didn't touch 'em—did you?"

I told him I hadn't, which he already knew.

"As far as we know, they could be made outta plastic, and we've been in here playing with our dicks and freaking ourselves out for no reason." He chugged the rest of his coffee and told me to wait inside.

"Why can't I come with?" I asked, despite the thought of seeing you again making me feel sick. I'm sorry to admit that but it's the truth. I was scared.

"It's past your bedtime," Dad said, which was the last time someone ever told me that.

Twenty minutes passed and he still hadn't returned. I got bored of sitting at the table so I got up and washed our cups at the sink. I didn't know if he was done with his coffee or not, but around this time of year you couldn't leave any unclean dishes out too long without generating an ant colony. Plus, chocolate milk tends to stain the bottoms of glasses, and I didn't feel like getting yelled at about something so trivial—especially compared to what was happening out in our back yard.

I climbed on the kitchen counter and pressed my face against the window, peering out into the night. Dad's cell phone flashlight was visible near the garden. I thought I could see him knelt in the grave, but it was too dark to make out any solid shapes. I got paranoid he would turn around and catch me peeping, so I jumped down to the floor.

I certainly wasn't going to sleep any time soon, so I started wandering around the house that used to be my house. Maybe it was *still* my house. I don't know. Dad sometimes got annoyed with me whenever I referred to this place as "your house" and Mom's place as "my house". He said I had grown up here for the first decade of my life and nothing would ever change that. Which made sense, but sometimes it got tricky in my head, since most of my stuff was at Mom's new house, and I slept there on school nights. Did I ever stop living at Dad's house or has a part of me stayed there forever?

I thought about you buried outside and shivered.

In the wooden doorframe connecting the kitchen to the living room, Mom had catalogued my height over the years with a pencil. The last line hit below where my chin stuck out now, marking how tall I'd been a little over two years ago, right before everything changed. People talk about life-changing moments all the time and I figure divorce is one of the big ones in that category. Sometimes I thought about Mom and Dad getting married and wondered if they knew, even then, that their futures would eventually no longer align. There was no way. Would they have proceeded to live together for however many years, wasting time they could have spent with someone else? Did they regret ever getting married in the first place? I wondered if they would have stayed together as long as they did if I'd never been born. Had my existence been some form of glue preventing them from separating? And, if so, what had happened to make that glue come undone? Had I somehow *failed* them?

I wished I could've called her right then. Just to hear her voice. To make sure she was okay. But I didn't have a cell phone. I'd asked for one many times. Practically *begged*. Neither of my parents thought I was old enough, despite nearly everybody else in my class having one. Probably one of the few things they could still mutually agree on.

After they divorced, nothing was ever the same again. A knife got wedged into reality and split it down the middle. Most of the time I stayed on one side of the divide, living a normal life with my mom. Going to school. Hanging out with my friends. But, a couple days a month, I dipped across the line and spent some time in Reality B, the timeline where I lived with my dad in the old house. We played video games and watched movies and ate greasy fast food. Sometimes he got drunk and cried about how much he missed Mom, but most of the time we had fun.

I'd never seen my dad cry until the divorce. I didn't think dads *could* cry. The divorce had broken something inside him. Meanwhile, it seemed to have *fixed* something inside my mom. I'd never seen her happier now that we lived alone. Sometimes she got stressed about money but nothing too crazy. Dad never seemed like a bad guy but something about him made her unhappy. I didn't understand what the big deal was. Maybe I never would.

I rubbed my finger against the pencil mark on the doorframe and wondered if she had known it would be the last time she'd ever measure my height in this house. A part of me would remain that height forever. Like a ghost unable to grow any taller.

I felt the pressure of the divorce before the effects

started hitting. Kind of like when you're standing in the bath tub and you close your eyes and let the shower head spray you directly in the face and the water gets in your nose and mouth and you keep letting it hit you as hard as it can, almost like it's a game, seeing how long you can last before turning away. You can feel that pressure building and building against your face, in your ears, inside your head, and you know something has to be done before it's too late, and you know sooner or later you won't be able to turn your head in time, that the water will drown your lungs and dissolve your brain and there won't be anything you can do about it, and you know that's exactly what makes it all so freakin' exciting.

I felt a similar pressure building in the kitchen as I waited for my dad to return from outside. Whatever we had discovered out there in Mom's garden, it was another one of those life-changing events.

And this time, a lot more than just my dad would get broken in the process.

By the time Dad returned I had started wondering what would happen if he never came back, if he walked outside and simply disappeared in the garden grave. Maybe it was some kind of portal that could transport people to alternate dimensions, and he had abandoned me here on boring Earth to visit a new, more exciting reality.

But of course he didn't leave me. The door creaked open and he stepped into the kitchen, looking more confused than the last time I saw him.

"Well?" I said. "What happened?"

He ignored me and grabbed his washed coffee mug from the dish drainer and sat at the kitchen table. He gripped the handle like it was full of liquid. His hands were trembling.

"Dad?" I touched his shoulder and he flinched.

"What?"

I pointed at the door. "Are they real?"

"Oh." He raised the empty coffee mug with both hands and pressed it to his lips, hesitating, then lowered it to the table. "I think maybe I'm in over my head here, boy."

"What are we going to do?"

"I gotta call someone."

"Mom?"

"Best to leave her out of this mess."

"The police?"

He laughed. "What did I already say about that nonsense?"

"Then who?"

He scratched his head, thinking it over, then started digging through his jeans pocket for his cell phone. "Andy might know what to do."

"Oh."

I never cared much for Andy. My mom once told me he was a bit "off his rocker" which was her way of politely describing him as "batshit crazy". Before the divorce, Andy and Dad and Miguel all fished together, got drunk in our living room during basketball games, went out bowling—they were practically inseparable. Then Miguel betrayed Dad and, as consequence, disbanded the trio. Dad hadn't spoken to Miguel since. I wasn't sure exactly what Andy's role was in all of this, but I saw him hanging out more with Miguel lately than Dad. Sometimes I feared Dad didn't have any friends left. Maybe I was the only person he had left. No wonder he freaked out so much when he found out about this Corpus Christi getaway.

Dad stepped out on the backyard patio to call Andy. I pressed my ear against the window and eavesdropped the best I could:

"Hey. Yeah, it's me. Listen, I—no, I'm not calling about that, I don't give a shit—man, listen, okay? Would you fuckin' listen? I got something going on over here. Something . . . freaky. I don't know what to do. I can't tell you over the phone. It's the kinda thing you won't believe unless you see it with your own two eyes. Yeah, right now, man. This shit can't wait. Trust me. Okay. Thank you. Seriously."

I scrambled away from the window as he returned to the kitchen. He gave me a look like he knew fully well I'd been eavesdropping. "Andy's on the way."

"What is he gonna do?"

He sighed, stuffing his cell phone in his pocket. "I don't know. Maybe he's heard about something like this happening before. In one of his books or podcasts or whatever."

"I'm scared, Dad."

He nodded. "You'd be crazy not to be. Now come on. We gotta find some clothes."

"What for?"

"Shit, I ain't letting that nutjob see your mom in her birthday suit. She'd never forgive me."

Dragging three corpses out of a grave proved to be more difficult than either of us anticipated.

You were, of course, the easiest. Dad was able to pick you up without my help and carry you to the patio. I trailed behind with his phone flashlight app helping guide the path. He set your body down on the concrete and went off to fetch the hose from the side of the house, leaving me about half a minute to stand over your corpse without any supervision. I didn't know what to expect to feel. I'd stared at my own naked body in the mirror plenty of times. But this was different. It felt less like I was looking at *myself* and more like I was looking at *someone else*. You weren't a reflection in the mirror. With a reflection there was some comfort in knowing that if I moved, then so would the reflection. It wasn't like that with you. If I moved, you wouldn't do a single thing. You were dead—and, as far as I knew, I was very much alive.

So what the hell *were* you?

To be honest, I still haven't quite figured that out. Maybe one day you'll tell me. I ain't counting on it, though.

Someone else maybe wasn't the best way to describe you, either.

Never once did I view you as a stranger.

Sometimes, after spending a long day playing outside, later in the night a person might discover a mysterious bruise somewhere on their flesh and have no memory of how it might have been obtained, yet there's no question about whether or not the bruise was a part of them now, albeit temporarily. That's similar to how I was feeling while standing above you. The *Where did you come from?* question was prominent in my mind, but at the same time I had already arrived at a bizarre peace with your existence, somehow understanding you were always meant to be here. Except I doubted your presence would be as brief as a bruise.

Dad returned with the hose and sprayed the dirt off your corpse. After the front side was mostly clean, I helped roll you over so Dad could spray your backside. I expected your flesh to feel cold. That's what movies said about dead bodies. They were always cold. But you were warm. Maybe the earth naturally heated you in your garden grave. I don't know. After most of the dirt was gone, Dad carried you into the living room where we'd already laid out three sets of clothes. I usually didn't keep any extra clothes at this house anymore, so it was fortunate on my part that I'd packed enough to last several days, otherwise I don't know what we would have dressed you in.

Although Dad had been able to bring you inside without any help, he found a greater struggle when it came to getting you dressed. I had to hold up your arms and wrestle them into a blue Bart Simpson T-shirt that had DON'T HAVE A COW, MAN printed along the front of it. Once it had been one of my favorite shirts. When it slid onto your body I knew I would never have the courage to wear it again, yet I felt a strange calmness about it. Seeing the shirt on you wasn't the same as giving it to another person. I didn't feel as if I had *lost* the shirt. Instead it was like I was extending the ownership to another part of me.

I just realized, even now, you have that same shirt on. For some reason, neither of us had ever thought to change your clothes after the night we removed you from the garden. I'm sorry about that. I hope you don't mind too much. If it's any consolation, I doubt I'll ever get to change my clothes again, either. Not now.

After we dressed you in my extra basketball shorts and DON'T HAVE A COW, MAN T-shirt we went outside and fetched Mom's corpse. Both of us hesitated over the garden grave before leaning down. I don't know what was going through Dad's mind as we looked at her body and I don't know what was going through mine, either. If I did know I probably wouldn't tell you, anyway.

Aside from occasional late-night private browser searches on my iPad, she was the only other naked woman I'd ever seen. Certainly the only one not digitized on a screen. Everybody sees their mom naked when they're younger, usually at an age where we don't remember much about it. Eventually there comes a time where that's no longer considered appropriate. I don't know what age, exactly, you aren't supposed to see your mom naked anymore, but I have a pretty good feeling thirteen is well past the cutoff date.

She didn't look dead. That was the thing. None of y'all looked dead. Not yet, at least, not in that perfect moment before we took you out of the garden grave and set in motion the things that were to come. I don't know what I assumed a dead person would look like but certainly not like what we found in the back yard. You guys looked . . . alive? At the very least, asleep. But there was no way you were alive. Not after being buried for who knows how long. *Alive* isn't the right way to describe it, either. Subtract you and the other two bodies' likenesses, and there would have been something undeniably . . . *off*. Even when regular human beings are asleep, they are not perfectly still. And y'all, down in that garden grave? Might as well have been statues.

The moon was out by then and the pale flesh of Mom's corpse glowed against it. Her body reminded me of a "dropped item" you could retrieve in a video game. Something like *Minecraft* or whatever. Her outline was highlighted in the darkness, as if to ensure we didn't overlook her. Her eyes were closed. So was her mouth. I couldn't stop staring at the areas on her no boy is ever supposed to stare at on their mother. Her breasts possessed a terrifying magnetism to them. I wanted to cry. Suddenly it seemed like a bad idea to remove her. She looked so content in the hole, as if she'd been born to live there. Disrupting her from this bizarre death slumber felt blasphemous.

"Dad, I—"

"You get her feet," Dad said, and the decision was made. He grabbed her by each wrist and I wrapped my arms around her ankles and together we lifted the corpse of my mother out of the hole. Dad didn't have much of an issue on his end, but I struggled. Bush and plant debris littered most of our back yard, so on top of carrying a dead body we also had to maneuver around various objects impossible to see in the darkness. At one point I tripped over the unearthed stump of a Texas sage and nearly dropped her, but somehow managed to maintain my balance. My grip tightened around her legs, pressing down against her warm skin, then I got paranoid I was hurting her and loosened my fingers. I knew she was dead but that didn't stop me from caring about her.

We laid her body out along the concrete and Dad hosed off the dirt, then we brought her inside. He couldn't find any of Mom's clothes from when we used to live here. Instead he slipped on a black San Antonio Spurs jersey over her—DUNCAN, #21—my dad's favorite. He didn't need my help this time, thankfully. I couldn't bear to touch her again. The sweatpants he gave her were too big, but it wasn't like there would be much walking around in her future.

I desperately wanted to call and hear her voice again. I knew Dad already checked up but I needed some kind of personal reassurance that whatever this was in our living room, it wasn't *my* mom, at least not the mom I knew and loved. Yet, looking at the corpse on Dad's couch, I couldn't help but feel love for her. It did not take long for me to start thinking of her as *Mom,* too. My brain was scrambled and couldn't comprehend anything it was processing.

In any case, I did not call her. I knew Dad would tell me no, that if we both called in the same night to "check up" it would seem suspicious. Although I wasn't so sure it would be a bad idea to update her on what was going on here. Maybe she would have a better understanding of the situation and know how to deal with it. In a battle of intelligence between my mom and dad, the winner would've been unquestionable. But I also understood why Dad wanted to hide it. This was not . . . a normal discovery we had made. Look at how both of us had cried above the hole, unable to understand what we were witnessing. Obviously we didn't want my mom to experience a similar emotional wreckage. Not unless it became absolutely critical to involve her—and even then, maybe we could avoid it.

"Okay," Dad said, twisting his spine sideways in an attempt to crack it, "let's go get—the last one."

He'd paused while talking, interrupted himself, but I know what he was originally going to say.

Me.

Let's go get *me.*

Unsurprisingly, he was the heaviest of the bunch. We couldn't lift him for long and settled on dragging the body through the back yard. I tried not to stare at his penis as it flopped against his inner thighs, but I don't think there's much point in hiding these kinds of things from you. You wanted the story, the whole story, and this is part of it. In the beginning we dragged the three of you out of the garden, and it was messy, and ugly, and by the time we had everybody inside and dressed we were exhausted as hell yet in no way prepared to sleep any time soon. How does a person sleep during such ghoulish circumstances? The idea sounded ridiculous.

Dad dressed his dead self in another pair of sweatpants and that was it.

"No shirt?" I asked.

He paused, looking over his corpse's exposed gut and sagging breasts, and frowned. "Nah, fuck it."

The three of you were propped up, side-by-side, on the couch together. Y'all just about looked like a regular family. If we'd taken a photo to preserve the memory, I bet we could've fooled plenty of folks into thinking you were alive. Sleepy, maybe, but alive.

Despite knowing Andy was on the way, we still screamed when the door knocked. Silence had percolated so long between us in the aftermath of dressing our corpses, that for a second it was like we'd forgotten the concept of noise entirely.

"What's that?" I whispered, jumping so hard I nearly spilled my glass of water.

Dad widened his eyes, mouth agape, presenting a similar feeling of fear and confusion, then—slowly—his face relaxed. "It's gotta be Andy. Who else?"

"The police?" I said, an immense wave of guilt washing over me. Like we'd committed some kind of crime by removing the bodies, like we were responsible for you being there in the first place. Like we had done something *wrong*.

Dad froze at my suggestion, giving me a paranoid look

like I'd read his mind. He waved me off and said, "What business would they have here, huh?" and took off for the living room without waiting on my response. Which was a relief, because I don't think he would've particularly cared much for what I had to say.

I could smell the liquor as soon as Dad opened the door. Dad grimaced and flinched away, then said, "Jesus, how much have you had tonight?"

Andy laughed, feigning offense. "It's every American's right to drink within the confines of his own home, ain't it?"

Andy's black and white heeler, Comrade, slipped in through the door without waiting for an invitation. I knelt and braced myself for her embrace. Comrade loved attention—especially attention from me. While I didn't care much for Andy, one perk of his presence was his dog, who accompanied him wherever he went, usually sans leash.

Comrade headed for my open arms, big dumb smile across her face, then abruptly changed course and went for someone else.

You.

She went for you.

You and not me.

This was probably the first time I found myself feeling jealous of you.

She stood on her hind legs against the couch and started sniffing your lap, curious about what new oddity had been introduced to our house since her last visit.

Andy took Comrade's lead and stepped past Dad, despite Dad holding his hand up to stop him. "Now, wait a second," he tried saying, not to much success.

"Wait a second nothin'." Andy belched. "You call and drag me outta my drinkin' chair, I ain't waitin' no goddamn anything."

Andy made it to the center of the living room and stopped, cocking his head the way people do when they've stepped in dog shit and only first realize it once the scent hits their nose. Only . . . you and the other two bodies, you didn't have a smell. At least not yet. But believe me. It would come. And, when it did, it would never leave again.

Even now.

It's still here, isn't it?

Slowly—enough time for several mississippis to pass—he turned toward the couch.

Toward the corpse family.

A glacier could've melted before he finally said something. Dad and I stood on opposite sides of him—staring, waiting—hoping for some semblance of confirmation on our sanity.

"Hmm," he said after a while, "now what's this shit right here?"

Dad cleared his throat. "Well, man, that's what I wanted your opinion on."

Andy chuckled, taking turns glancing at Living Dad and Dead Dad. "My opinion? Shit. My *opinion* is I've ain't had nowhere *near* enough to drink."

Dad tried bringing him into the kitchen so he could explain things, but Andy refused to take his eyes off you guys. Same with Comrade. She seemed to love you far greater than she ever loved me. That's the thing with the dead, I've learned. They will always be more important than the living. The dead have accomplished something that every living person is terrified of facing. They've done the impossible. They've died.

"Those are cool as shit," Andy said. "How'd you make them? Or was it a special order kinda thing?" He messed around with his pony tail sticking out through his black baseball cap. On the front of the hat, in large white text, followed by a single period, it read:

40

OBEY.

"I . . . I didn't make these," Dad said.

"You know," Andy said, "Dan—Dan as in our *coworker* Dan—once tried going through one of those speciality websites. I ever tell you about that? Funny as shit. Evidently there's this website, it can mold a fleshlight outta just about anything." He stopped and glanced over at me. "You know what a fleshlight is, right?"

"Uh," I said.

"C'mon, man," Dad said.

"You're how old?" he asked me. "I assume you've started jerking off, right?"

"Uh," I said again.

He nodded. "Yeah, you've started jerking off. I can tell by your face."

"Andy!" Dad said.

"What? Look at how red his cheeks just got. Face the facts, buddy. Your son jerks off." He laughed and returned his attention toward me. "Anyway. A fleshlight is just a kinda tool you can stick your pecker in. Buy them at any pedestrian sex shop. Maybe ask your dad to go in for you, though. Sex shops don't take too kindly to kids. Most of 'em, anyhow."

"Oh," I said, "okay."

"Remind me again why you're teaching Dylan about fleshlights," Dad said.

"Because what I'm about to say about Dan wouldn't have made any sense without the right context already in place."

"What *about* Dan?"

"Well, he found out about one of those websites, like I was saying, and he gets the bright idea that maybe they can make a fleshlight out of his wife's ass. Which, I mean, it ain't a bad idea. You've seen Dan's wife, right? Shit, if I had an ass like that I'd never stop touching it, I don't care how weird it'd look."

"Andy—" Dad tried cutting him off again, but it was no use. Once Andy got started on one of his anecdotes, there was no stopping him until he was finished. The situation didn't matter. Not even if there were three dead bodies co-existing in the room. With Andy, all you guys seemed to do was increase the size of his audience.

"Anyway," Andy said, "the thing with this website is, in order for them to even *get* to work, first they need a . . . what do you call it? A mold *encasing* of the object in question. And they're not located anywhere near Texas, so you gotta, like, mail the shit in—right? Of course Dan doesn't want his wife to know about any of this weird pervy shit. This has gotta be his own secret little plaything. So what does this fuckin' lunatic do? He waits until she's sound asleep—then, like, very carefully he pulls down their blanket and somehow undresses her, and . . . like, some kinda motherfuckin' *ass* ninja, starts applying the mold shit, hoping like hell she don't wake up, but of course she wakes up. That shit is cold as fuck. Starts freaking out, screaming, I mean hell, it's the middle of the goddamn night, how do you think *you'd* react? You ever have something cold and wet suddenly touch your flesh while sleeping? She pissed the bed. Of *course* she pissed the bed. Completely destroyed those goddamn sheets. Dan tried explaining himself but that only made things worse. I hear they're getting a divorce. Which is a bummer, but those kinda things are sometimes inevitable, as you well know. Anyway. What company did y'all use for these . . . uh, things?"

Looking at my dad, it was clear he already deeply regretted getting Andy involved in our mess.

"We found them," he said, doing a terrible job of subduing his impatience.

"Found them?" Andy said. "What are you talking about?"

"In the back yard," I whispered, and they both swiveled their heads toward me, as if they'd forgotten I was in the room.

"The back yard?" Andy echoed, then looked to my dad for confirmation, but he was too dumbstruck to respond, so I did it for him.

"We were digging up my mom's old garden, and . . . they were there, in the ground."

Despite the obvious horror of the situation, I felt weirdly cool about getting to explain to someone else what was going on. Almost like an adult.

"Bullshit," was all Andy said.

Dad nodded. "I think someone's trying to pull something on us."

"What do you mean? Someone like who?"

He thought it over and shrugged. "I don't know. Some kinda prankster dickhead with nothing better to do."

"For what reason, though?" Andy asked.

And Dad threw his arms up, at a loss. "For . . . for the purposes of being a piece of shit. How should I know?"

"You really found them in the ground?"

"That's what he said, ain't it?" Dad said, referring to me—including me as an equal, another puzzled investigator assigned to the impossible corpses mystery.

"How deep?" Andy asked, scratching the trailer trash stubble across his chin.

"Deeper than the plants, I'll tell ya that."

Andy had a half smirk across his face, like he hadn't stopped suspecting *we* were the ones playing a prank on *him*. Which, I suppose, was fair. These weren't exactly the most ordinary of circumstances. Even Dad and I hadn't fully accepted this new reality yet.

Hesitating, Andy joined Comrade over by the couch and reached toward my mother's corpse. He softly caressed her cheek, letting out a subtle gasp, then touched the side of her neck. Checking for a pulse. Had Dad already done that on your bodies? I didn't think so. How sure were we that y'all were definitely dead, right? Why *wouldn't* we assume, though? Buried in the ground like that. What else could you have been?

The way Andy jumped, however, pretty much cemented our assumptions. He wouldn't have reacted like that to someone who was alive. Or to some Halloween trickery. People were displayed out along our couch. Real people. Dead people.

"Comrade," Andy said, tone serious, "get down. Now."

She ignored her master's commands and continued exploring your scents. I hoped you were enjoying yourself. What I would have given right then, to switch positions with you, to feel the unconditional love of a great dog.

"Comrade! C'mon! Get!" Andy grabbed her chain collar and pulled her off your lap. No dog has ever liked me with such enthusiasm. With such intensity. I couldn't believe it.

Andy pointed at the three of you like he was making an accusation. "What . . . what . . . what *is* this? Goddammit, what *is* this?"

"You think they're real?" Dad asked, and from the sound of his voice I couldn't decide what answer he might've been hoping to receive.

"If they ain't, someone sure as shit sunk a helluva lotta cash in 'em." He took a good look at Mom's corpse again, then started inspecting you and Dead Dad, once in a while glancing at me and Living Dad. Comparing us.

"What are you doing?" Dad said.

"Wait a second," Andy said, shaking his head, pointing at Dead Mom. "Where's Lori, huh? Where'd she go in all of this?"

Dad tried to respond but instead backpedaled and started trembling.

Andy matched his retreat with a step forward. "There's two of both of ya but only one of her. Where's the other Lori? What's going on here?"

"What are you trying to say?"

"What did you do to her?"

"What did I do to who? *Lori?* What are you *talking* about?"

"Where is she?"

"She's in Corpus with Miguel, you dickbrain. Fuck you for thinking otherwise."

Andy kept checking you and Dad's corpse, searching for some missed flaw or giveaway confessing that you weren't the same as Mom's body. Then he turned and stared at me. Really stared. I was standing in the same spot across the living room. Hadn't moved or nothing. Waiting to see how this was all gonna play out.

"Is there anything you wanna tell me, Dylan?" he said. "Anything your daddy might be neglecting to share?"

"Dude, what the fuck?" Dad said.

Andy ignored him and kept his attention trained on me. "Would you prefer you and I step outside and have ourselves a little chat, just the two of us?"

I shook my head. "My mom's on vacation. We . . . we found them outside," I said, pointing directly at you. "All three of them."

Another pause from Andy. Going over my words in his head like he was swigging around mouthwash. Then he spun back to Dad. "Why did you call *me* about this?"

Dad shrugged. "I figured . . . if anybody might have some inclination about what's going on here, it'd be you."

"You haven't talked to me in about a year, man. All of a sudden we're friends again?"

Dad sighed, rubbing his temple. "We don't need to get into that right now."

"Who says you get to decide what we get into when? An hour ago I was home getting a good buzz on. Now you've dragged me over here into some fuckin' . . . what the *hell* is all this, anyway? What the *hell* is goin' on? What the fuck?" He marched over to Dead Dad and slapped his pale shoulder. "This is you." Then he gestured at Living Dad. "And that's also you. How the fuck is that fair?"

"You telling me you've never read or heard about something like this happening before?" Dad asked.

"I mean . . . " Andy took a deep breath. "The only secrets from the government we even know about are because people got sloppy somewhere. The amount of shit nobody knows, that they've managed to keep hidden, that's where shit's gonna get real fuckin' weird. Wouldn't surprise me in the least if some perverted corpse doppelgänger conspiracy was floating around somewhere among their files."

"So you think this might have something to do with the government?"

Andy chuckled. "Shit, pardner, how many times I gotta say it? It's always the government—even when it ain't."

I didn't know what he meant by that—and, judging by Dad's facial expression, he didn't either.

"Have you called anybody else about this?" Andy said. "I know you ain't dumb enough to have gotten the cops involved . . . right?"

"Of course not," Dad said, offended. "What do you take me for?"

"I gotta ask, don't I? We don't talk in how long? Who knows which ways you've changed."

"It hasn't been that long, for Christ's sake. And besides, we're Facebook friends, ain't we?"

"So what? I'm also Facebook friends with my cousin's husband, Greg, and I fuckin' *hate* that guy. He's such an asshole. Always ever postin' about *The Office*. Yeah, Greg, we already know it's good. Pick a new show, you piece of shit."

" . . . What?"

"All I'm sayin' is you act like I'm the one dating your ex-wife."

"No, but you're still friends with the son of a bitch dating her, though."

It was almost humorous, how much petty bickering the two of 'em were doing while standing in the same room with three corpses. Neither possessed the slightest idea of how to handle the matter at hand, so they'd sought momentary refuge opening old wounds. Eventually, thankfully, they abandoned these past grudges and returned to the couch. They stood over the bodies, real serious, while I rubbed the top of Comrade's head. She'd finally come to me. Then Andy giggled.

"The hell's so funny?" Dad said.

Andy leaned over Dead Dad and gave one of his hairy breasts a little jiggle. "Your man boobs are hilarious."

I tried not to also laugh and failed. Dad noticed my betrayal. The look on his face was heartbreaking. I wanted to crawl out into our backyard garden grave and hide. Disappear within the obscurity of dirt.

"Don't touch that," Dad said to him, which only made Andy give the nipple a tougher tug.

"Why?" Andy said. "It's not like you can feel it or anything." He stopped and released my dead father's breast, then turned to us. "Wait, *can* you?"

"Can I *what*?"

"Maybe it's like some sort of voodoo doll or some shit. Whatever I do to *this* body, you also feel."

"I don't think that's quite how this works."

"Works? Like you know how this *works*. As I recall, you're the one who called *me*." He slapped Dead Dad across the face and his body slightly adjusted before settling on the couch.

"Hey!" Dad shouted.

Andy spun around, excited. "Did ya feel that?"

"No, I already told you I—"

Andy didn't wait for Dad to finish his response. He bounced over to you and backhanded your cheek. Your head jerked to the side. For a second I believed that I'd felt the slap land upon my own cheek, but I suspect it was merely the shock of witnessing my face get assaulted from an outsider's point of view.

"Hey!" Dad shouted. "Don't hit my son."

Andy demonstrated an *ah-ha!* gesture. "So you admit it?"

"Admit *what*?"

"That he's your son?" Andy said, talking about *you*, not me.

"I don't know *what* he is yet, but I reckon you shouldn't go around slapping kids, dead or alive *or* . . . or . . . or something else."

"Something else like what?" I asked, reminding them again that I was in the room.

"I don't know," Dad said. "Ain't that what we're here trying to figure out?"

"Exactly," Andy said, and proceeded to slap you across the face again.

"Goddammit!" Dad shouted. "Stop doing that!"

Andy laughed and backed away, hands up in surrender. Comrade tried charging forward and taking her master's place in front of your lap, but I restrained her—out of protection of your well-being or my own selfishness, I couldn't tell which. Maybe the two feelings could co-exist, side by side. It didn't matter much, anyway. Nobody else was paying attention to me by then. You and the rest of your grotesque corpse family had managed to successfully commandeer the spotlight, and you hadn't even *done* anything. Sitting there on the couch, being dead. Y'all just about made me sick.

We had to take a break from dead bodies for a while. It was past midnight but that didn't stop Dad from brewing a new pot of coffee. Andy preferred booze. Somehow Dad convinced him caffeine would be a more appropriate beverage choice for the kind of situation we all found ourselves in. Reluctantly, he agreed, but promised to act real grumpy about the whole thing, which we had already expected anyway. We sat around the kitchen table drinking coffee, each silently daring the others to speak first. Well, *they* were drinking coffee. I had a glass of ice water, although I'd originally requested another helping of chocolate milk. Dad told me no way, that too much dairy could destroy my stomach. "Imagine how your mom would react," he'd said, as if she wouldn't have much bigger fish to worry about than my stomach being upset.

With one hand I played around with my glass of water and with the other I continued gripping Comrade's collar. She was determined to break free and love on you. You were suddenly her favorite person, and I would have been perfectly content if I never saw you again.

"Okay," Andy said, tapping his fingers along the brim of his Buc-ee's coffee mug. "If we're gonna stop messin' around and get to the bottom of this, we best start strategizing."

"Why would they be here?" Dad said, running his hands through his hair. "Where could they have come from?"

I shivered and folded my arms across my chest. It had quite suddenly gotten unbearably cold in this kitchen. Comrade made a subtle growl as I dragged her closer to my lap. "Are they really . . . us?"

Andy smacked his lips together. "Might be a little premature to make a conclusion like that. But hell, at this point, anything's a possibility."

"Are you sure they're real?" Dad asked.

Andy shook his head. "I ain't sure of any goddamn thing." He drummed the table for a second, exhaling dramatically. "You ever see a dead body before?"

"No. Of course not."

"What do you mean, *of course not*? People die every day. Hell, man, since I got here tonight probably a thousand poor sons of bitches have dropped dead all around the world, and even that's a wee bit of an underestimation."

"What?" I said, voice cracking. "Is that true?"

Andy nodded, proud of educating me about something. "Over one hundred and fifty thousand people die every day. That's a fuckin' fact. Most from heart disease bullshit, yeah, but you also got plenty of malaria cases, too. Parkinson's Disease. Road injuries. Hippo attacks. Even *heat* gets its share of kills in per day, and I'm not talking about the movie, bucko."

"What movie?" I asked, and Andy grimaced.

"That still doesn't mean I've seen a dead body before," Dad said. "Wait, have *you*?"

"Not in person, at least. But pics? Videos? You betcher ass I've seen videos. Fella, I've seen videos that'd make your asshole leap outta your throat."

"I . . . what . . . what does that even mean?"

Andy thought it over, then shrugged. "I don't know. But it sounded cool, didn't it?" Neither of us responded, so he wiped his face and continued. "The point is . . . no, I ain't ever seen one up close before, but out of the three of us here, I absolutely got the most experience—which is why you called me up in the first place, despite ghosting me for however many fuckin' months, and—"

"Ghosting?" Dad said.

"Yeah, what about it? People say it. I've heard them."

"What are you talking about?"

Andy sighed and begged me to rescue him. "Dylan, you wanna tell your obsolete father what *ghosting* means?"

"I don't know what it means, either," I admitted.

"Holy hell," he said. "It's like talking to a family of Neanderthals or something." His face distorted after that last remark. A real light-bulb-going-off-in-your-head epiphany. "Wait a second."

"For what?" Dad said, still annoyed about not knowing what *ghosting* meant.

"That ain't such a far-fetched idea . . . is it?" Andy stood from the table and started pacing around the kitchen, which only succeeded in exciting the dog. Her collar dug into my fingers as I tightened my grip.

"*What* idea?" Dad said.

"*Neanderthals.* Ain't you listening to a word I've been saying? Goddamn *cavemen,* baby! Motherfuckin' Fred Flintstone and Bamm-Bamm and shit."

"You think . . . those bodies out there are cavemen?"

Dad asked the question like he couldn't tell if Andy was screwing with him or not. But of course Andy was being serious. It wasn't that crazy of an idea. At least no crazier than anything else we'd come up with tonight, which hadn't accounted for much. Unless you'd recently learned about Neanderthals in the previous school year, like I had.

"No," I said, testing the volume of my voice, trying to match the other two men, "it can't be Neanderthals."

Andy looked at me with pure outrage. "And why the hell not?"

"Neanderthals . . . they don't look like how we look." I hugged my chest again, shivering. "They're smaller. Their bones aren't as evolved."

Comrade wrestled out of my grip and took off for the living room. Nobody but me seemed to notice or care.

"He raises a valid point," Dad said. "And besides, them being cavemen, that don't explain anything. Why would they look exactly like us, and what kinda goddamn insane coincidence would land them in our back yard?" He also wrapped his arms around himself and glanced around the kitchen, perhaps searching for the cause of the room's sudden temperature shift. "Goddamn, Dylan, did you fuck around with the AC again? You know how expensive that can get."

I shook my head and told him I hadn't touched it.

Andy laughed. Gave us another look like we were pulling something on him. "What're you guys talking about? You're really that cold?"

"What?" Dad said. "You ain't?"

"It's hot as balls in this house."

It was then that I noticed the beads of sweat dripping down Andy's face.

"You've also been drinking tonight," Dad said, calming my unannounced paranoia. He got up and approached the thermostat on the wall between the kitchen and living room. Leaned forward and squinted for a couple seconds, then said, "What the hell?"

"What?" Andy and I said in unison.

"Says it's seventy-nine in the house."

"That feels about right," Andy said, taking off his **OBEY.** cap and rubbing his sweaty hair. "I told ya. Hot as balls."

"Damn contraption must be busted or somethin'," Dad said under his breath, then sat at the table. He looked utterly exhausted and I felt about the same. Could you blame us? We'd both gotten up super early that morning. Let me remind you this was the same day Dad barged over to Mom's and threw a fit about our Corpus Christi trip. So much had happened since then and neither one of us had so much as napped. No wonder we were freezing.

"You guys ever hear about what happened to Paul McCartney? Like, what *really* happened?" Andy asked us. "Supposedly, back in the sixties, he died in a car crash. Like, it was *rough*. Dude got fuckin' decapitated and everything. This was right before *Sgt. Pepper*. But instead of reporting his death to the public, he was simply replaced with a lookalike."

"A *lookalike*?" Dad said.

"Yeah, like, the winner of a legit lookalike contest. People *auditioned*."

"That cannot be true."

"Who's Paul McCartney?" I asked.

"Just some music asshole," Andy said.

"Why wouldn't they report it?" Dad asked. "That doesn't make any sense."

"Because, man, don't you get how big they were back then? The whole fuckin' stupid country would have died from grief. So they replaced him. Even bragged about it in their goddamn lyrics. Dude, go listen to the end of 'Strawberry Fields Forever' and it'll blow your mind. Lennon straight-up admits to burying Paul. 'Cranberry sauce' my ass."

"What does this have to do with anything?"

"What do you mean, what does it have to do with . . . ?

Max, buddy, in case you ain't noticed, this house is crawling with lookalikes."

"Yeah, but come on. These weren't winners of a lookalike contest."

"Well, they sure as fuck ain't *losers* of a lookalike contest, either," Andy said, glancing at the doorway leading into the living room. "Have y'all considered time travel yet?"

"Time travel?"

He shrugged. "Sure. Why not? This could definitely be time travel, right?"

"But they look like they're the same age as we are now," Dad said. "Wouldn't they be older looking if they came from the future?"

"Unless they traveled from another dimension. Like, a bizarro version of our own reality."

"How do we figure out if something like that happened?"

"I guess you'd have to ask them."

"Oh, okay," Dad said. "I'll take that idea under consideration, thanks."

"You know," Andy said, "the thing I don't get, is if they're real bodies, and they're *actually* dead, then how come they ain't, ya know, all rotten and shit? They might as well be in-store displays. No corpse has ever been more *pristine* than the three y'all got in the other room."

"So then they're not real?" Dad said, a manic mixture of relief and disappointment in his tone.

"I didn't say that, now did I?" Andy smacked his lips, thinking things over. "Maybe their lack of wear and tear just, what, implies they only recently died? That their deaths . . . it ain't so much ancient history but breaking news?"

Dad yawned and rubbed his eyes. "What are you suggesting?"

"I think we gotta cut one of 'em open, see what's going on inside. If they got real organs or what."

"What else would be in there?" I asked, not wanting to hear his answer, but I got it anyway.

"Who knows? If they ain't human, *real* human, then it could be anything beyond the flesh, right? Robot shit like gears and wires. Or weird alien tentacle crap. We haven't even begun to speculate aliens, have we? Shit. They could definitely be aliens."

"*Aliens*?" I said, rubbing my cold cheeks and trying to warm them.

Andy nodded. "Aliens, yeah, for sure. Or maybe we open one of them up and find . . . hell, I don't know, *nothing*. Maybe they're just hollow inside. Or a buncha . . . what's that shit called, you find it inside walls? Fiberglass insulation. What would that mean? No clue. But it could be there. We won't know shit until we take a peek, right? So then why don't we go take a peek?"

He got up and started rifling through the kitchen drawers.

"What are you doing?" Dad asked. He stood, but instead of joining Andy by the kitchen sink, he ventured over to a coat rack and tossed on a hoodie.

"Trying to find something sharp enough to cut through flesh."

"I think maybe we need to talk about this a little more."

Andy pulled out a large butcher's knife and grinned at Dad. "What's there left to talk about? We can speculate all goddamn night and it ain't gonna get us any closer to solving this mystery. *Action* is what's required! Lights . . . camera . . . *action*, baby, *action!*"

He took off for the living room. Dad followed, stuffing his hands in his jacket pockets. I surveyed the coat rack and realized I no longer had a jacket here. All of my cold weather clothes were at Mom's house. What reason would I have needed to bring a jacket this weekend? It was the middle of July, *in Texas*. Few places on this earth reached hotter temperatures than a Texas summer. A cold night like tonight usually didn't happen until closer to

MAGGOTS SCREAMING!

November. Dad was right. Something must've been broken on our thermostat.

There was an old denim jacket on the rack, underneath several other coats. Something Dad used to wear when he was younger, and thinner. It was big on me, but small enough to not look too cartoonish. I slipped it on and raced into the living room, hoping I hadn't missed anything. Moving fast proved to be surprisingly difficult. My shins ached, as if I'd recently exercised. But, thinking about it further, I *had* recently exercised. Digging up an old garden wasn't exactly a walk in the park. It'd been tough. And then we'd transported three heavy corpses . . .

I wondered how other kids in my class were spending their summer vacation.

Dad and Andy were standing in front of the couch trying to decide which one of you they'd cut open. Comrade had given up trying to sniff you and had instead curled up across your lap and had already fallen into a peaceful sleep. I didn't understand why she'd chosen you when you weren't even trying to pet her. I would have petted her all night and told her what a good girl she was but she didn't care, she didn't want me, she only wanted you.

So be it.

You could have her then.

Wasn't like she was my dog, anyway.

"No way in hell you're touching the boy," Dad said.

"Agreed," Andy said. "Even if he's dead, I'm sure the punishment's much more severe when it comes to desecrating a child compared to a full-grown adult."

Dad gestured to Mom's body. "Her."

"No way," Andy said.

"Why not?"

"Because she's the only one who ain't here."

"Exactly."

"Meaning she's the only one who I'm not sure is *anywhere else.*"

"Oh come on."

"Eileen?"

"I did not kill my ex-wife."

Andy ignored Dad's last comment and side-stepped in front of Dead Dad's body. "Besides, this one already has his shirt off."

Dad sighed, defeated. "Only a little cut."

"Why?" Andy asked, snickering. "You afraid it's gonna hurt?"

"I don't know what to expect, do you?"

Andy thought about it, then shrugged and leaned forward, probably trying to determine the best spot of skin to puncture. Viewing this inspection from across the living room, I realized a change had occurred on the three bodies. Your flesh had paled significantly since the last time we were in here. You'd all lost the pinkish pigmentation found on most white people, at least the ones in my family.

"They look different," I said. My lips were freezing and made the act of talking incredibly annoying, but a new detail like this couldn't go unannounced.

"What are you talking about?" Andy said, glancing over his shoulder at me, one hand gripping our butcher's knife.

"No," Dad said, "he's right. Look at their coloring." He picked up Mom's arm then dropped it. "Holy shit, they're cold."

Confused, Andy grabbed Dead Dad's arm. "Well, they're dead. Of course they're cold."

"But they weren't cold earlier," Dad said. "They were warm. Maybe a little hot."

"Further proves my theory that they only recently died," Andy said. "And besides, have you looked at yourself lately? When was the last time you got any sun?"

"What are you talking about?" Dad said. "I spent all goddamn day outside."

But Andy wasn't joking. Dad's flesh was about as pale as his deceased counterpart. Suddenly nervous, I rolled up one of the sleeves on Dad's denim jacket, then glanced down at my forearm and confirmed my suspicions. I let the sleeve fall back without showing anybody. If they wanted to see how pale I'd gotten, I'm sure all they had to do was take a good look at my face.

"Must be the AC," Dad said, sounding like he was trying to convince himself more than anyone else. "I'm telling you. Something broke in it. Lowered the temp until it froze over or something. You weren't so boozed up, you'd feel exactly what I'm talking about."

Andy slowly shook his head. "Hot. As. Balls."

"Then explain why both me and Dylan can feel it?"

"I don't know," Andy said. "Maybe it's got something to do with the fact that you two also got a pair of zombie twins in the house with ya. Take a look around, pardner. When it comes to my glorious likeness, I'm one of a kind." He winked and made a little kissy face. "We need to at least see if these guys can bleed."

"Do corpses bleed?" Dad asked, which was a question I'd never considered in my brief life.

"Good question," Andy said, lifting Dead Dad's arm. "Let's find out."

He pressed the blade into his pale flesh, then waited a second. Nothing happened. He dug it in slightly deeper and a thin line of blood emerged from the hole. It did not come out in a steady stream like how people bled in movies but instead like tear drops dripping from a person's eye sockets. Like the wound was crying.

Andy let go of Dead Dad's arm and stepped back. "All right, so we know they can bleed."

"How come there's only a little bit?" I asked.

"His heart is no longer functioning, if it ever even *was* functioning," Andy said. "Meaning there's nothing working the pumps."

"Pumps?"

"That's right. What we're seeing, I think, is the leftovers. Like when you take a piss and give your pecker a good shake but still manage to spill a little drippage on your boxers."

"You know a lot about this stuff," Dad said, rubbing his jaw and wincing.

Andy belched. "I mean, I know *some* shit, but I'm mostly making some logical guesses here."

"Do you think we should still cut one of them open? Like all the way open?"

"Yeah, but maybe in the morning. I'm beat."

Dad yawned. "You can stay here if you want. Save you a drive."

"Will they be okay?" I asked, realizing how tight my jaw had gotten. Forming words proved far more painful than I could have ever anticipated. "Are we just gonna leave them here until morning?"

"Well, we sure as hell aren't gonna drag them back to the garden," Dad said. He tried to crack his neck and moaned. I could relate, as my neck was also feeling stiff. I never wanted to work outside again after today. Physical labor had destroyed us.

In the end, we decided to throw a sheet over you and the other two bodies. If we were freezing, who knew how cold you guys must've been this whole time. Andy let Comrade outside to pee, and she wasted zero time in returning to the couch, this time curling up on the carpet next to your feet. I considered grabbing her collar and dragging her down the hallway to my room, but it was no use trying to force someone to love you. Dad had learned that the hard way with Mom. Once someone decided they were done with you, there was no changing their mind about it.

The first time I found out about death, really understood the finality of it, I don't know how old I was. Mom and Dad were still together. I don't know where they were, though. Maybe inside. Not me. I was out in the front yard playing golf.

MAGGOTS SCREAMING!

Playing golf like how a little kid plays golf. I owned a plastic red golf club and several plastic red balls and sometimes I would slap them around the front yard. I wasn't strong enough to achieve much distance with my swings, so there was never any danger of accidentally hitting passing traffic or a neighbor's window.

Much like the back yard, we also had plenty of bushes in the front of our house. These bushes were taller and more spread out, giving a boy my size plenty of room to explore. On the day in question, I remember hitting one of my balls into these bushes. From across the yard I watched the leaves swallow its cratered red plastic and felt an immediate sense of dread at the possibility of never seeing it again. I rushed into the bushes and searched everywhere, and just when I was beginning to surrender to the inevitability of failure, there it was—*my ball!*—half-hidden under a fallen leaf.

And, next to the leaf, something else.

A frog.

Staring up at me, curious about this gigantic creature he'd caught trespassing in his bushes. Leaving me to suspect maybe he wasn't real, that he was just a statue or something, but then I noticed the subtle movements in his throat and stomach. The kind of breathing motions universally associated with frogs.

We were both looking at each other, as if daring the other to move first.

I've thought about this day a lot since it happened. I'll tell you that. It's never far from my memory. From my conscience. And, despite that, I don't quite understand what made me do what I did. I can't remember—or maybe I *refuse* to remember—what sparked the idea, or how something so violent could have originated in my head to begin with, but it happened and I can't pretend it didn't.

I lifted my plastic golf club and swung. Lightly at first, testing how it'd feel. The frog didn't like this new disturbance. It tried to leap away. That's when things got out of hand. I followed. I swung harder, faster. At some point I was screaming. The frog died long before I stopped hitting it.

In the heat of the moment, I did not feel bad. I'd never felt greater. Killing that frog had been one of the most exciting moments of my life. Up until we found you in the garden, anyway.

The excitement didn't last. Seconds after dropping the club and inspecting the frog's ruptured body, a new feeling consumed me.

Guilt.

I don't know how to describe guilt. If you've never felt it, then consider yourself lucky. It's like you've taken a big bite out of pure poison and everything inside of you gets a nasty taste of it. For a while, nothing can bring you joy. The reminder of what you've done wrong looms over like a storm cloud refusing to part and all you want to do is reverse your actions. You'd do anything to *take it back* but it's too late, there's no undoing what's been done.

That's how I felt in those bushes, staring down at the frog I'd murdered. No matter how long I looked at it, nothing changed. I thought for sure maybe it would suddenly get tired of being so still and hop up on its legs and return to its family. But of course that didn't happen. The frog stayed dead. After a while I didn't know what else to do so I collected my golf toys and went inside and curled up on the couch and watched TV with my parents until I finally fell asleep, and that night and the night after and the night after that I dreamed about frogs and nothing else.

I woke up screaming.

The previous night—or, earlier that morning, depending on how you want to look at things—I remembered collapsing in bed, sore and exhausted, then I was awake again, this time consumed by agony.

MAGGOTS SCREAMING!

In recent years I'd often woken to a similar sensation. Charley horses, growing pains, whatever. A natural part of getting older, my mom had told me. Everybody gets them. I understand that. But this . . . this was something different. Never before had I woken to a charley horse spasming throughout every inch of my body. Usually they target one specific area, like my thighs or calves. But not this. Head to toe, nothing but torment. My face ached. The louder I screamed, the worse it hurt, which only resulted in more screaming, followed by more pain.

Somewhere in the house, my father was screaming just as loud.

I tried to get out of bed and failed. My limbs refused to follow simple directions. Everything was stiff. And cold. So freakin' cold. I managed to wiggle a couple inches to the side and nearly passed out from the pain. I tried to scream for help but nothing I said sounded like real words. It was like an invisible weight had crushed me against the mattress and now I was slowly suffocating.

My bedroom door swung open. With immense willpower I turned my head toward the entrance, expecting to find my dad and instead only seeing Andy. Behind him, down the hallway, Dad hadn't stopped screaming.

"Hell's going on in here?" he said, half-asleep, half-terrified.

"*Hurts! Hurts! Everything hurts!*" I shouted, powering my voice through a raw throat.

Andy flipped on my bedroom light and leaned over my bed. His eyes widened the more he looked at me. "Holy shit," was all he said, and backed up against my bookcase, knocking over several old Goosebumps books my parents had bought me years ago at a library discount sale.

"What?" I mumbled, lips unbearably heavy. "*What?*"

Andy pointed at me, arm trembling, and stuttered several times before finally forming a coherent sentence: "You look like hell, boy."

He took out his cell phone and turned on the camera

app, then switched to the frontward lens and turned it toward me so I could take a look at myself. My lips were blue, discolored. Freezing. I was freezing. And I was pale, yes, paler than I ever thought could be possible, but also, somehow, at the same time . . . shiny? Like someone had polished my flesh while I was asleep, added a slick sheen to the front of my body.

I say the *front* of my body for a reason.

When Andy helped me sit up, and noticed a new feature behind my neck, he nearly dropped me. "What the hell . . . ?" he said, pulling back my T-shirt and revealing more of my shoulders. I was left with no choice but to wait while he continued inspecting me and speculate on what could be causing such an animated reaction. "*What the fuck?*"

"What? What? *What?*" I screamed.

The way he had me propped up was almost cartoonish. For whatever reason my limbs refused to bend, including my spine—despite Andy's added assistance. So I couldn't sit up, not how he wanted me to, at least. He had to slide me half-off the mattress and half-on his lap, like he was puppeteering a malfunctioning ventriloquist's doll. But to see more of my back, he ended up kind of tossing me on the mattress, face-first, and rolling up my shirt.

Behind me all I could hear was him muttering, "Holy shit," and, "What the fuck?" over and over.

"*See,*" I whispered, every bone in my body aching simultaneously. "*Let me see.*"

His camera app made a flashing noise and he propped the phone in front of my face, showing me a bizarre bluish-purple marble texture. It took me entirely too long to realize it was a photo of my own back.

After that, I started screaming much louder.

The pain no longer seemed to matter that much.

MAGGOTS SCREAMING!

Dad was experiencing similar issues, we soon discovered. Andy left me in my bedroom to go investigate the other noises of agony emitting throughout the house, then returned to inform me of the bad news: "Looks like your dad's also fucked up."

The pain coursing through me was too great for me to register what he meant. "What's wrong?" I managed to ask.

All Andy could do was shrug. "Hell if I know. Both y'all are stiff as hell and white as ghosts. You'd think you two were the ones who was dead."

And, just like that, Andy stopped talking and I stopped screaming and we looked at each other, a new realization digging into our brains.

The answer was so obvious it was almost stupid.

Andy let out a sigh and lightly kicked his boot against the door frame, then said, "Ah, dang."

It took some doing, but Andy dragged the both of us to the living room. Every time one of our limbs were forced into motion we'd let out another cry. Neither of us could bend any part of our bodies. It was like something had locked us in place and then threw away the key. Andy tried to prop us up on chairs but the man only had so much energy left in him. He abandoned this objective and settled for laying us on the carpet, in the middle of the room. After contemplating, he ran off down the hallway and returned with two pillows, which he wedged under our heads.

"There," he said, clapping his hands together as if they'd somehow accumulated dust during our transportation. Then he stood above us, waiting for something to happen, and we lay beneath him also waiting for something to happen.

Nothing happened.

Every time I tried to move, another explosion of pain burst through me. Same thing with Dad, only inches away.

63

We were paralyzed but nothing was numb. We could feel everything.

Bodies are strange entities. I've always found the operation of limbs quite mysterious. That somehow, just by *thinking about it*, I can make my arms and legs do whatever I want. By sending invisible signals from my brain, I can walk forward or backward or decide to jump or dance or do the splits. Nothing on my body moves unless I tell it to move, and I don't know *how* I deliver these messages, not fully. It's a low-key form of telekinesis that nobody ever seems to talk about. We all have magic inside us and we utilize it every second we are alive. And sometimes, when we're dead. It's a subtle magic that we all take for granted until we no longer have it.

Like that early Saturday morning, sprawled out on the living room carpet, parallel to my equally-paralyzed father. No matter how loud I screamed orders inside my head, my limbs refused to obey. My body had gone on strike but it didn't seem to have a list of demands. It didn't want anything except to be left alone, which was the one thing I refused to allow it.

Andy paced around us, in a circle, muttering, "Okay, okay, okay," over and over, at a loss for what to do. If Dad and I had been able to speak coherently, I sincerely doubt we would have contributed anything more productive. Last night, before our sudden paralysis, we hadn't known what to do—and now? We knew even less.

From the corner of my eye I could detect a sudden motion of white. Andy had pulled the sheet off the couch, exposing you and the other two corpses to the living room once again. And, although I could not see you with my head facing the ceiling, it was easy enough to tell the three of you had also undergone somewhat of a transformation during the middle of the night. Otherwise Andy wouldn't have said, "Ah, fuck," seconds after uncovering the couch and resumed his frantic pacing.

Next to me Dad kept whisper-screaming, "Dil! Dil! Dil!"

And I kept whisper-screaming back, "What! What! What!"

But he only followed my response up with more, "Dil! Dil! Dil!"

Andy paused above us, lunacy in his eyes. "Would you two shut the fuck up for a second? I'm trying to think here, for crying out loud."

Which was exactly what Dad and I were doing—crying out loud, I mean.

We did not quiet down. If anything, we got louder. Andy threw up his hands and told us he couldn't handle this kind of noise, then stomped off to the kitchen. Cabinets opened and closed. Ice shuffled out of the freezer. A liquid poured into a glass. I didn't need Dad to tell me what was already obvious: Andy was making himself a drink, a drink with alcohol involved. I also didn't need to ask Andy *why?* to know what he'd say: *If I'm gonna solve this little mystery, I'm-a need to get good and drunk first.* And, considering Dad currently couldn't stop him—given that he was, ya know, *paralyzed*—why not give it a try?

I don't know how much time passed before he returned. When your body is completely consumed by pain, seconds quickly translate into hours. But he did come back, and when his face reappeared above us, his expression seemed much more confident than the last time we saw him.

"Okay," he said, "so this is the situation—as far as I can see it, anyway. Something happened while you were sleeping. I don't know what. But now y'all can't move worth a damn. I can't, uh, bend you—which is . . . like, what the hell, right? And those fellas over there," he pointed to the couch, "they're in the same boat as y'all. Except they're already bent, like in sitting positions, and I can't seem to straighten them out. I try any harder and I'm afraid of breaking them in half. And your skin. Both you two and those . . . corpses. You got that ghost paleness going on. You know what I'm talking about. Watch any movie set in a morgue. That's how pale you guys are. Except for your backs. I don't know what's going on there but both of your backs are this weird bluish-purple. That same color is on the corpses, too, but not in the same place as you. They got it, like, under their thighs, on their feet. The best theory I've been able to come up with is maybe it's because you two were lying on your backs and those guys have been sitting up all night. I read somewhere once, that when a dead body decomposes, gravity collects all the blood in a person and drags it down to the lowest point. Which, I guess, would make sense . . . if you two was dead, which you clearly are not. So what the hell, right?"

Then he paused, thinking the situation over. The gears were turning in his head about something. He kneeled over Dad for a second, gasped, then maneuvered over me and pressed first his hand over my chest and then his ear. Followed by another gasp.

"*What?*" Dad managed to say.

"Uhhh," Andy replied.

"*What, goddammit, what?*"

"Your goddamn hearts ain't beating."

"*What?*"

"YOUR GODDAMN HEARTS AIN'T BEATING."

"*Shut up.*"

"It's the truth, motherfucker. Why would I lie about something like that?" He started pacing around us again, fooling with his hat, then stopped and said, "Okay, I need another drink," and took off for the kitchen. More ice cubes fell into a glass, then another helping of liquor.

As we waited for him to return, someone else decided to finally join our little living room party: Comrade. And this time, much to my shock, she did not want anything to do with you. She went straight to me, like she'd always done before you decided to move into our house. I hoped like hell you were witnessing this. I prayed you felt every ounce of jealously I'd experienced the previous night.

Maybe she detected how much pain I was experiencing

and had come to help make everything better. She started sniffing and licking my left arm, which tickled, but in a good way. I tried to laugh but couldn't remember how to make the sound with my mouth. Then the tickling evolved into something more violent, and I realized much too late that she wasn't only licking my arm—she was biting it.

Eating it.

The scream that emitted from between my lips prompted Andy to come sprinting into the living room.

"Comrade!" he shouted. "No! Bad girl! Bad!" He grabbed Comrade's collar and dragged her away from me and my body jerked to the side. She hadn't released my arm from her mouth. "Comrade!" Andy shouted again. "No! Bad!" More wrestling commenced and Andy finally got my arm free of his dog's teeth.

I found myself feeling grateful that I couldn't look down and see what kind of damage had been inflicted upon me during Comrade's mangling session. It was probably for the best, especially after hearing Andy gasp afterward.

"Ah shit," he said, "I'm sorry, kid, I'm so sorry."

Beside us, Dad was losing his mind. He had no idea what was going on but surely had picked up on the fact that I'd just gone through something a little traumatic.

"Let me go lock her up in the bathroom or something," Andy said. "I don't know what the hell her problem is."

Footsteps vibrated against the carpet as he dragged Comrade down the hallway. It was amazing how much sound I'd started detecting with my ears so close to the floor. Any little motion could project their own vibration. Like my father, trying his damnedest to get up and help me. He'd managed to rock his body in subtle movements, but I'd managed to hear him. I interpreted these movements as a good sign, one that implied our paralysis would only be temporary.

Andy returned to the living room and apologized again about Comrade's behavior. "But don't worry," he said, "she's not getting out of that bathroom any time soon.

Fuckin' crazy-ass dog." He checked our hearts again and shook his head. "Y'all's shit still ain't beating. I don't know what to say."

"*Help*," Dad said.

"Help how? You want me to call an ambulance or something? I can do that, sure, but I'm using *your* phone and the moment I hang up the call I'm getting the hell out of here." Standing above us, he gestured at the couch, despite the fact that we couldn't turn our heads. "I don't know if any of y'all have noticed, but this whole setup here looks suspicious as a motherfucker."

"*No*," Dad croaked out.

"Hell," Andy said, "maybe your hearts *are* beating. Ain't like I'm some kind of expert. Just because I don't hear shit, that don't mean anything. Not really. I wish we had one of those listening doohickeys that nurses got. Like with the metal headphones and shit. You can hear anything with one of those."

He sat in the recliner. I didn't need to see him to know that. The chair had always made a distinct sound whenever someone surrendered their weight between the arm rests. A little squeak, followed by a prolonged creak as it rocked with its new guest.

I could tell by the sound of his voice that Andy was starting to get sleepy again, despite everything going on. It wasn't like he could feel the pain Dad and I were experiencing. Plus he was drunk again, or at least on the right path.

"I know y'all can't talk," Andy was saying, "so I'll go ahead and do the talkin' for all three of us."

Next to me, I swear to god I heard Dad laugh.

If Andy heard him, he chose to ignore it. "Let's say whatever's going on here *does* involve the government, which . . . c'mon, seems pretty fuckin' likely to me, don't you think? So let's say it *is* them. That they . . . that they what? That they're conducting some sorta bizarre experiment on y'all. What happens once we call for an ambulance then? Several possibilities cross my mind. One, an ambulance never comes. If the government is behind all this shit then you betcher ass they got wires hooked up on your phone, which means they probably intend on somehow interrupting any nine-one-one calls and impersonating emergency dispatchers through their own phone line. An ambulance might show up, sure, but I sincerely doubt an actual paramedic will be behind the wheel. They might even be dressed in the usual paramedic getup, but so what? You think a government official can't take a trip to Party City, get themselves all kinds of cheap disguises? Then what happens? Well, shit, that's the easy part to guess. They load you and the boy and whatever the hell these bodies on the couch are into the back of their fake-as-shit ambulance and transport y'all to some secret facility surrounded by barbed wire fences. And, as for me? I'm fuckin' dead meat is what I am, pardner. I'm what you'd call a *witness*, and when it comes to spooky government conspiracy bullshit, there's no such thing as a witness, at least not one with a very long lifespan. They'd either kill me right here in the house or pretend like they was simply taking me in for questioning, but I know full well what kinda perverted macabre rodeo they're up there running, and it sure as shit ain't one I intend on stepping into any time soon, not without putting up one hell of a fight first."

Andy paused. Ice rubbed against ice as he took another sip of his drink. Down the hallway, Comrade scratched at the door and whined. She was desperate to continue eating me.

"But that's assuming the government is keeping tabs on everything going on here tonight. Honestly, I'm surprised they haven't already barged through the front door. You were real smart earlier, Max, how cryptic and shit you were when you spoke to me on the phone. Way to use that smooth brain of yours. But still. You have to imagine if they're going through all the trouble of implanting body-double corpses or *whatever the fuck* this is, they'd have also installed some pretty high-tech security cameras to watch over their property. I feel fairly confident in ruling out cameras. Unless . . . well, shit, I don't know . . . unless this is all part of the experiment. Unless they're sitting back and waiting to see how the three of us *react* to this weird-ass discovery. Probably up at Randolph right now, watching us through their little security monitors, eating popcorn and jerking each other off." His voice got louder, like he was yelling at the hypothetical cameras. "*I hear movie theater butter works as a real nice lubricant, you sick demented fucks!*"

He laughed and drank more of his booze. I guess it was technically *Dad's* booze, but whatever. Wasn't like Dad was in much of a position to reclaim it.

"Okay," Andy continued, "let's say this shit *ain't* the work of Uncle Sam, and it's something completely unrelated. When the ambulance arrives and takes the *briefest* of assessments of this situation, who do you think they're gonna call? You think something this strange falls under local jurisdiction? Hell nah. They're ringing up the nearest *X-Files*, *Men in Black* motherfuckers they can find and telling them to get their asses over here pronto. And then, once again, you lot end up in a secret bunker to get experimented on for the rest of time, and I'm tossed in some unmarked grave. There's no way around it. Calling nine-one-one . . . I don't see how it's gonna help much. If your hearts are already stopped, then shit, that means you're what? A coupla zombies? No nurse is gonna know how to handle some weird-ass supernatural zombie bullshit. And if your hearts *are* still beating, and I'm just deaf, then fuck it, why not wait this out a little bit longer? Maybe this issue will somehow resolve itself, right? I mean, hell, sometimes things work themselves out without any outside interference. You get a scratch, do you rush to the hospital, or do you apply a little water and soap and wait for it to scab over and heal all on its lonesome?"

MAGGOTS SCREAMING!

If I could have talked right then, I would have pointed out that this situation required something more significant than a scab. It was probably a good thing I couldn't talk, though, because he would have asked what it required if not a scab, and I have no idea what I would have said. Considering how much everything hurt, I would've most likely suggested death as the only suitable medicine. *Put me out of my misery,* I would've begged, all the while wondering if death was a possibility at that point. If I was already dead, could I die again? And, if so, what the hell would that mean?

So, yeah, it was a good thing I couldn't talk.

Some thoughts, they're better off unspoken.

Andy fell asleep not too long after that. His snores were loud and wet. I found myself at first annoyed listening to him sleep, and then jealous, then quickly back to annoyed. Sleepiness hit me like Comrade scratching at the bathroom door, whining to be let out, and I was positive if I could only close my eyes it would finally find me. But I couldn't close them. At some point during all the commotion, my eyelids had also grown stiff, an action I could hardly believe possible despite personally experiencing more than enough evidence there on the living room floor. My eyelids were stuck at the top of my eyes, like curtains jammed in a window, refusing to lower no matter how hard I struggled. My eyes became unbearably dry, and I could do nothing except lie on the carpet and let it happen, hoping someone would notice and help me. If only Andy would have snapped awake and used his fingers to pull down my eyelids, I would've never asked for anything again. Cancel all future birthdays and Christmases. This was the only gift I'd ever want. But he remained asleep, his snores dragging on longer and wetter and more disgusting by the minute, and I remained awake, staring at the ceiling and wondering if I concentrated hard enough whether or not I could trigger hidden telekinetic abilities to collapse the roof on top of us all.

The house did not cave in. In fact, nothing at all happened for several hours. I was awake for all of it, consumed by this relentless pain worming its way through my body, my eyes becoming drier with each passing second. After so long the act of screaming felt too boring, so I gave up, surrendered to the agony. You'd think I would have gotten used to the sensation. That's what I was hoping would happen, at least. But did it? Well, I think you already know the answer to that.

Then the flies showed up.

Their arrival seemed to change everything. I went from being forced to wait on the floor, paralyzed, until Andy woke up, to being forced to wait on the floor while several dozen flies swarmed around my face, landing on my cheek, buzzing into my ears. I decided to take up the art of screaming again once the flies tried squeezing between my lips.

Next to me Dad was also screaming—or, *attempting* to scream. He sounded muffled, restrained. The flies weren't just after me. They were trying to infiltrate both of us. The screaming didn't scare them away like it was intended. I felt a rattling against my teeth, then a bizarre tickle in my throat. The flies were inside me and there was nothing I could do to stop them because stupid Andy was somehow still asleep and I couldn't move, not one miserable limb. I was trapped in my own flesh as the flies explored my insides, and I wished more than anything for the roof to collapse and kill us all, truly obliterate our existences from this nonsensical world. But of course the roof didn't fall, and I remained motionless as more flies landed on my exposed eyeballs, erasing my vision with their squirmy black bodies, their incessant buzzing drowning out all other sound—Dad's screaming, Andy's snoring—and, for a spell, flies were all I knew.

Maggots Screaming!

Until something hard smacked me in the face, knocking my head to the side and scaring away the swarm of flies that had momentarily conquered my body. Andy stood above me, asking if I was okay, grabbing my arms and dragging me across the floor, and I slapped him away, told him I was fine, told him he was hurting me, he was squeezing my arms too hard, and I wiggled free from his grip and stood up, so tired, so utterly exhausted, and Andy stared at me in shock and I didn't understand why he was reacting like that until I realized *holy crap* I was standing I was moving I was talking, and down on the floor Dad was also slowly climbing to his feet, dazed, spitting out dead flies, which made me realize I could also spit again, and I put this rediscovered ability to good use, but no matter how many flies I expelled from my mouth I was convinced there was at least one more somewhere inside me, hanging on for dear life—buzzing.

THE STIFFNESS IN our limbs finally loosened, but we still had a heck of a time controlling our bodies, at least compared to before we dug up Mom's old garden. The act of walking turned into what I imagine stepping through quicksand must feel like, although—in retrospect—I don't think I've ever encountered actual quicksand in my whole life, which I guess isn't saying much, considering my age, but I also don't think I've ever *met* anybody who has personally witnessed quicksand. Of course, it's not like I've ever *asked* anybody about it, either, so I suppose it's entirely possible many people in my life have quicksand experience and they've never spoken to me about it. Personally, if I'd discovered a pool of quicksand, I suspect I would never shut up about it. That doesn't mean it doesn't exist. Look at you and the situation we all found ourselves in that weekend Mom and Miguel went to Corpus Christi. Nobody ever told me one day I could potentially find a dead clone of myself buried in our back yard. There was no preparation. No school drills. One day it just happened, and maybe it'd happened to other people before me, and they'd simply chosen to keep it to themselves. Considering what happened after we regained function of our limbs, I can absolutely understand why someone wouldn't want to talk about it.

Out of everything on our bodies, it wasn't our limbs that we experienced the most trouble with—but our eyelids. During our inexplicable period of paralysis, we'd forgotten how to open and close them. Which meant they mostly remained open for long stretches of time without us realizing it. Our eyes became unbearably dry to the point that it pained us to *see*. After Andy freaked out and made us look into a mirror, I learned a particularly dry eyeball can transform over time. Which is what happened. The white part of our eyes took on a strange reddish-brown discoloration.

A couple years ago, my mom itched her eye too hard during allergy season and it opened up this vibrant red scratch line that quickly spread to the entire eye. *Bloodshot* is how she described it. The injury lasted a couple weeks before healing, but while it was there, every time I looked at her eye I wanted to vomit. I didn't realize how lucky I'd had it back then, how bad it could get.

"The other eyes don't look like this," Andy told us, after inspecting you and your dead companions. "But their eyes have been shut the whole time—I think? Yeah, they haven't been open, have they?"

Dad shook his head no, unable to look away from the bathroom mirror. We'd sent Comrade out to the back yard now that it was morning. After being cooped up all night in one room, she'd probably stored up enough urine to fill up the garden grave we'd dug.

"They feel like sponges," I said, sitting on the closed toilet. "I can't stand it."

"Another thing," Andy said. "The flies, they've found the other bodies. I can keep swatting them away, but they just come right back when I stop moving."

"No shit," Dad whispered, taking the thoughts out of my head and turning them into words. We were facing the same issue. Any time we grew too still, another swarm of flies would find us, designating our flesh as improvised landing pads, eager to find ways into our various orifices. They could smell something on us that, at that point, we were too afraid to admit. Most folks would have categorized this mindset as *denial*, and they wouldn't have been wrong.

Andy licked his lips, tapping his fingers against the bathroom doorframe. "So, I know what we all said last night about keeping this stuff to ourselves, but I think maybe the situation has changed a little bit, don't you?"

"What are you saying?" Dad asked, opening the mirror and digging through the medicine cabinet.

"I'm saying I think we oughta take a trip down to the hospital."

"No," Dad said without hesitation. "Not yet."

Andy's face got all screwed-up looking. "Well, why not?"

"I can fix this," he said, and a stream of thick yellow liquid dripped out of his mouth.

"What the fuck?" Andy stepped away, grimacing.

Dad wiped his chin and continued browsing the medicine cabinet. "Sorry."

"What *was* that?"

"I don't know."

I suddenly became acutely aware of a liquid building up in my own mouth. I stood off the toilet, lifted the lid, and parted my lips. A helping of the same thick yellow substance dripped into the bowl. It didn't feel like I was regurgitating. There was no applied *pressure* to my stomach, or anything like that. It was more like drool, the way it sometimes builds up in your mouth while you're asleep. It felt . . . *natural,* in an utterly terrifying way. Like this yellow substance had *always* lived in my mouth and I'd somehow never noticed until then. Which only got my mind racing faster, wondering what else had been residing inside me all this time without announcing its presence.

The human body is an unsolvable puzzle.

The more you explore it, the less it makes sense.

Dad found what he'd been searching for: a bottle of eye drops. He studied the directions, then frowned. "I didn't know this stuff could expire."

"How old is it?" I asked.

"Couple years past its prime."

I didn't need him to explain his intentions. Our dryness was a mutual dryness. If anything, I was disappointed I hadn't thought of it first. "Will it hurt us?"

Dad chuckled. "Take a look at us. You think it really

matters at this point?" He twisted off the lid and squirted a few drops in each eye, then moaned in a sick relief. "Oh, gawd, that's the spot. Yessir, I'll take another, don't mind if I do." He applied another two drops.

"What about me?" I asked, resisting the alien urge to tackle him and pry it from his hands.

"Hold your horses," Dad said, motioning for me to sit on the toilet, which I did. He didn't have to tell me to keep my eyes open wide since they already were. Each drop felt like a miracle. I never wanted them to stop, but of course they did, and I begged Dad for a couple more, they were a little dry, please, one more drop was all I needed, maybe two, or three.

"If we use them all now, what will we do later?" Dad said, and I know he made a good point, but I didn't care about later. *Later* felt like a fantasy. There was only *right now* and *right now* I wanted more drops—and not just a couple. I wanted him to pour the whole bottle into my eyes. I didn't care about the consequences. Consequences were for people who weren't actively decomposing.

"I'm sorry to be the one to break this to you," Andy said to Dad, "but a couple eye drops ain't gonna fix the bigger issue at hand here."

Dad ground his teeth together and applied a couple more drops, then stuffed the bottle in his pocket and pushed his way out of the bathroom. Andy and I followed closely behind.

"What's the plan then?" Andy said. "Might help if you kept me in the loop, considerin' you was the one who called me over here and all."

We stopped walking once we were standing in front of the couch. Andy hadn't been exaggerating. Your entire face was covered with flies. I waved my hand at them and they only flew away for a second before returning. Maybe I should have been a better person and tried harder to save you from being probed. I guess, at the time, I was thinking better you than me. Like you wouldn't have done the same thing if our positions had been reversed. Like you wouldn't have also let the flies feast on my insides.

"They reek," Dad said.

"I don't know if you've noticed this," Andy said, "but y'all don't smell like rainbows and unicorn farts, either."

Dad hesitated, then sniffed himself and grimaced. I didn't smell too great, either.

"Something . . . weird is happening," Andy said. "Some kind of . . . I don't know, voodoo shit, or something."

Dad nodded, pointing at the corpses. "This whole thing started after we took them out of the grave."

"The grave?"

"Or the garden, or whatever the fuck you wanna call it." Another stream of yellow juice drooled out of Dad's mouth. This time he didn't bother to wipe it clean. "So what I'm thinking is, what if we put them back? Place them where they were when we found them, cover 'em up with dirt again, maybe everything goes back the way it was."

"I mean," Andy said, "that's a better idea than what I was gonna suggest."

"The hospital?" I said.

"You're goddamn right. Step one foot in one of those cesspools and you're liable to end up in some government freezer, being experimented on by assholes with Smith and Johnson for last names. I don't know what I was thinking. I guess y'all just spooked me a little."

I remained quiet, too afraid to argue that maybe a hospital *was* the best option. I didn't want to hurt their feelings by suggesting they were in over their heads. Even if I *had* said something, I sincerely doubt they would've listened to me. Maybe this is me trying to justify my silence. Maybe I didn't want to go to the hospital, either.

As it turns out, it's difficult to perform manual labor when you're already dead. Mobility may have returned to our limbs, but that didn't mean they were exactly *productive*. We couldn't hold on to anything for any real length of time before losing our grip. And forget about *pulling* anything. Dad and I each took an ankle from Dead Dad and tried to get him off the couch, and the only thing we succeeded in was upsetting the flies around Dead Dad's face.

"Goddammit," Andy said. "Am I gonna really have to do all of this myself?"

Dad held up his hands, opening and closing them. "I don't know what's going on. I can't . . . they aren't *working* right."

"Well, this sucks," Andy said, circling the room and studying the three of you on the couch. "This really sucks."

"Quit your bitchin'," Dad said. "At least you ain't the one dead."

"Quit my bitchin'?" Andy said, offended. "Last time I checked, *you* was the one who called *me* for help, not the other way around."

"Are we dead?" I asked. My lips stung when I moved them, chapped beyond belief. I already knew the answer, and so did he, but I wanted to hear him say it. I wanted audible confirmation of the obvious truth.

Dad stared at me, then shrugged. "I don't know."

"Okay," I said, because I didn't know what else to say, then I turned away from them and hobbled down the hall. I closed my bedroom door and sat on my bed and tried to cry but my eyes were too dry to form any tears and Dad still had the bottle of drops concealed somewhere in his pocket. So I sat there at the edge of the mattress and imagined I was crying, which was somehow sadder. Down the hallway I could hear Dad and Andy attempting to move you and the other two corpses. They were struggling, just as we had struggled to bring you inside the previous night. Except we didn't have flies to fight yesterday. Now the whole house seemed like a public playground for flying insects.

I was not stupid. I knew why the flies were there. They were there for you. They were there for me. If I paused long enough, they'd find the courage to land on my face again. I tried to keep moving my hands around my head, but it was exhausting. I was so tired. All I wanted to do was sleep but the dead can't sleep and that's what I was, right? *Dead.* So what choice did I have but to sit on my bed and wait for something new to happen? What do dead people do in their coffins? They wait. They wait and they wait and they wait. And then they wait some more.

Except my situation was different. I wasn't locked in a coffin. I could get up and move around. Which are things the dead are not supposed to do. It goes against everything we understand to be true in the universe. So what did that make me, exactly? What did that make any of us?

I opened my walk-in closet—mostly reserved for boxes of old toys from my childhood—and examined myself in the long narrow mirror hanging against the door. I already knew how pale my skin had gotten, but seeing it again startled me. All the color in my flesh had fled. Like it was scared of me. Like it hated me. Where does color go when you can no longer see it? Does it exist, somewhere, like a forgotten ghost—or does it simply fade away forever?

A chunk of flesh was missing from my left arm, on my inner elbow. It didn't hurt like it looked like it should hurt. The only reason I noticed the injury was because of the mirror inspection, otherwise I might have never paid any attention to it. I feared my body was already deteriorating, but after closer study, I remembered how desperately Comrade had tried feasting on my arm earlier that morning. She'd really sunk her teeth into me. Had Andy noticed exactly how much damage she'd inflicted? If so, he hadn't bothered letting me know—which was maybe for the best. Now that I saw my arm in its current state, there wasn't much I could exactly do about it. A band-aid would look pretty pathetic slapped over such a gaping wound. And besides, it wasn't like it was bleeding or anything. The hole was dried out, like an empty grave.

I hoped Comrade had enjoyed what little of me she'd managed to tear away.

I stuck my right index finger into the wound on my left arm and wiggled it around a little. There was an unexpected warmth. A pleasantness. I debated fitting my entire hand into the hole, but was terrified I would succeed. What would I do then? I would be left with little choice but to continue sliding my arm in, deeper and deeper, until it was time to force my face into the wound, then the rest of my body, like a snake eating its own tail, or a thirteen-year-old boy crawling into his own flesh.

When I pulled my finger out of my wound, I discovered a small white fleck stuck to the tip of my nail. Probably something from the carpet, I figured. Must've gotten mixed into my wound when I was paralyzed in the living room. I decided it wasn't anything to get worked up about and flicked it off my finger.

Of course, I now know that I was wrong, it wasn't carpet litter or anything that innocent, but I wouldn't figure that out for a little while.

Not until they started hatching.

Later, I found Dad and Andy sitting at the kitchen table again. Andy was out of breath, doubled over and wheezing. Face and hands and clothes covered in dirt. Dad was filthy, too, but he didn't seem to have so much as worked up a sweat. The bottle of artificial tears was on the table between them. It looked empty.

"Did you use it all?" I asked. I tried to tighten my hands into fists but my fingers disobeyed and got all twisted with each other, forming a pathetic contortion that wouldn't do much good to anybody.

"Relax," Dad said. "I saved you a little."

I plucked the bottle from the table without asking permission, tilted my head, and held it over my eyes, squeezing with desperation. A single drop fell from the tip, and missed my eye. It hit my forehead and rolled into my hair.

"One drop?" I said. "Only one drop?"

Dad shrugged. "I didn't see you out there helping. It's hard work, you know. Dries a man out."

"Well, what am I supposed to do, then?"

Again, another shrug. I would've punched him if my hands remembered how to form fists. I don't care if he was my dad or not. Once you were dead, stuff like that no longer mattered as much. The only thing I truly cared about right then was getting more artificial tears. Any other issues could be addressed after my eyes were no longer so dry. It was impossible to think when you were looking out of two unused sponges.

"Hell, I don't know," Dad said, then gestured at the sink. "Why don't you get a wet washcloth? I gotta figure out everything or what?"

I considered yelling something at him so I could get the last word in, but the act of opening and closing my mouth had already thoroughly exhausted me, so I turned away and fetched a clean washcloth from one of the drawers, soaked it under the faucet, and laid it across my eyes like it was a mask. The coldness blasted a jolt of energy through me. I quickly ran it under the faucet again and slapped it over my face, spine leaning against the sink, head tilted, enjoying the water as it bled into my eyes.

"Did you do it?" I asked without moving from what I'd decided was the perfect way to stand.

"Did we bury them? Shit yeah we buried them." Andy coughed, out of breath. "Well, I mean, *I* buried them. Your dad mostly stood around and watched."

"I told you," Dad said, voice low, annoyed. "I couldn't grip the goddamn shovel."

Although I was blinded by the washcloth, I could hear the flies as they approached. At a certain point their buzzing started sounding like a machine, like an engine.

They would never give up. I could keep swiping at them but it'd only be a temporary solution, like covering a bullet hole with a band-aid. I let them crawl on my face, trying to make myself content with their legs tickling my cheeks, my ears, my lips, but I couldn't do it, it all felt so . . . *wrong,* so unnatural. I shook my head and they fled the scene. But not too far away. The buzzing was somewhere in the kitchen. Waiting for me to let down my guard again.

"How long do we have to wait?" I asked. I said the words quickly, terrified a fly would take advantage of my vulnerability and sneak into my mouth. "How long until things get normal again?"

"Why do you think we know any more than you?" Dad said. "Goddamn . . . fuckin' . . . flies . . . "

"They ain't botherin' me none," Andy said.

"*They ain't botherin' me none,*" Dad said, mimicking him. "No shit they ain't botherin' you. No one ever thought they were."

"You know, you're acting like a real jerk today."

"Don't you think I got plenty justification? I mean, *shit.* Don't you think I got all the justification in the world?"

"All I'm saying is, last night I drop everything and come help you. You and I ain't talked in how long. You ghost me—don't fuckin' laugh—you *ghost me*...and now you're actin' like none of the past year ever happened. Like you ain't been a jerk at work whenever we cross paths, like you ain't being a jerk right now, even after I just spent half the day burying your dead family for you."

"They ain't my family."

"Well then whose are they?"

I removed the washcloth from my face. It'd already lost its moistness. Something Andy said inspired a new concern, something none of us had voiced yet. "What about Mom?"

Dad swatted a cloud of flies away and said, "What *about* Mom?"

"Do you think . . . what's happening to us . . . it's happening to her, too?" I almost didn't want to say it. As if by just asking the question would make it true.

"No, don't be ridiculous," Dad said, almost too quickly, then he paused, thought about it a little longer. "Shit, I don't know."

"We need to call her," I said.

Dad nodded. If it was possible to get any paler, he probably would've.

"If she's like you guys," Andy said, "what are we going to do?"

Dad ignored the question and dug out his cell phone, dialed Mom's number, then held it against his ear. Waiting. Waiting. He sighed. "Hey, it's me. Call me back when you get a chance. Thanks." He set the phone on the table and folded his arms across his chest.

"No answer?" Andy said.

Dad tried to laugh, but it sounded painful. "What was your first clue?"

"See?" Andy said. "There you go, bein' a goddamn jerk again, for no good reason."

"You're right. I'm sorry." He swatted at another cloud of flies. "But come on. Look at this shit from my perspective and try to understand why I might be reacting all irritated, irrational as it might seem."

"I *get* that, Max, I *do*. That still don't give you any right to treat me like I ain't been here all night and day trying to help you."

Dad remained quiet, and I wondered if he was ever gonna say anything at all, then he stood and swung at several flies that refused to give him space. He didn't hit any of them. They only moved away a couple feet and then returned, somehow closer to him than before he'd tried to kill them with his fist.

"Where's Comrade?" I asked, and Andy nodded at the back door. I hobbled across the kitchen and peeked through the window, spotting Comrade sitting in front of the re-covered garden grave, staring at the dirt, not moving, like she was in deep concentration. I couldn't help but wonder what her little dog brain was thinking about all this. If she found it strange that there were suddenly two versions of Dad and me, or that one version had buried the other version like they were tasty bones—which, in a way, is exactly what you were, or I guess *are*—bones, that is. Tasty, though, that ain't for me to decide. Did any of that make a lick of sense to Comrade, or was she as puzzled as the rest of us?

"She ain't pissing on the grave, is she?" Dad called from the kitchen table, and I shook my head.

"What's it matter to you where my pooch does her business?" Andy said.

"Call me superstitious, but I don't think it's the best idea to desecrate . . . whatever the hell that is out there. Look what happened once we took them out. Who the hell knows what kinda fucked up hoodoo voodoo bullshit would befall us should your dog's urine trickle down there."

"Okay, I see your point," Andy said. He waved me aside and opened the back door. "Comrade, getcher ass in here." Comrade remained seated in front of the garden grave. *Watching* the dirt isn't an apt enough description for what she was doing. More like *worshipping*. Like someone at church in deep prayer. "Comrade, goddammit, getcher ass inside! Now!" Andy shouted again, then made a clicking sound with his mouth, and Comrade snapped out of her daze, broke away from the grave and ran into the kitchen.

Andy shut the door and leaned against it, cracking his neck and studying the two of us. "Well, any difference yet?"

Dad shrugged. "I don't know. How do I look?"

"Like shit."

"What about you, Dylan?" Dad asked.

But I was too busy trying to push Comrade away. She wasn't biting or getting violent or anything like that, but she had definitely taken too strong of an interest in my scent, and kept pushing her snout against my crotch, sniffing with an uncomfortable determination.

"Comrade!" Andy shouted. "Get away from him!"

She refused to listen, and Andy cursed under his breath, then dragged her away by the collar.

"She can smell the dead on me," I whispered, trying to make sense of everything.

"Maybe we gotta give it a little bit more time," Dad said. "When we took them out of the grave, the . . . the *curse?* Whatever the fuck. It didn't happen instantaneously, right?"

"How do you know it didn't?" Andy said. "Just because it took you a while to notice doesn't mean it hadn't already been working its mojo on you. Do you know how long a dead person takes to start showing symptoms that they're dead? Because I sure as hell don't."

"We ain't dead, goddammit, we ain't—that's impossible, okay? So stop saying it," Dad said, shaking his head, looking like he didn't believe a single word coming out of his mouth. "Dead people can't . . . they can't do what we're doing, okay? They can't walk around. They certainly can't fuckin' talk, now can they?"

"Then what are you?" Andy said.

Dad stared off into the distance, searching for some unreachable answer, then said, "Something else."

"We need supplies," Dad said a little while later, and Andy laughed, asked what that had to do with him. "Well, in case you've missed it, I ain't exactly in the right state to go shopping."

"Bullshit," Andy said. "I've seen way grosser fuckers than you shamblin' through Wally World."

"C'mon, man, you gonna do it or not?"

Andy thought about it, then exhaled. "Hell, it'd do me some good to get out of this stinky-ass house awhile, anyway." He tossed the rest of his coffee in the sink. "What do you want?"

"Eye drops," I said, interrupting my father from saying the same thing. "Lots and lots of eye drops."

Dad nodded. "What he said. Plus, I don't know. Just browse around. We need medical shit."

Andy raised his brow, amused. "Medical shit?"

"Well, I ain't no expert, am I? Yeah. Medical shit. Bandages and Peroxide. You know. Stuff that's gonna help us with...with whatever the fuck's happening to us."

"How is it you don't have any bandages?"

"Lori took them, when she moved out."

"That was over two years ago."

"Yeah, and?"

"And you haven't thought to buy any more?"

Dad scrunched his face up, frustrated, and waved at a new cloud of approaching flies. "I haven't *needed* them until now, okay?"

Andy held up his hands, laughing. "Okay, shit, calm down. I'll also pick you up some tampons while I'm out."

"Oh, fuck off," Dad said, then betrayed himself with a smirk.

"You gonna give me any money or what?" Andy asked. "Because I'm broke as shit until payday."

Dad nodded, then collected his wallet from the kitchen counter area reserved for car keys, loose change, and unwanted mints from Sonic. He pulled out several twenty-dollar bills and handed them to Andy, then said, "Under any circumstances, do not forget the eye drops."

Andy folded the cash into his jean pocket and said, "I'll see what I can do."

Thirty seconds after he walked out the front door, Dad turned to me and said, "Now we just gotta hope he doesn't pass a bar on the way there."

With Andy gone, there was nobody to stop Comrade from resuming her investigation. She had never listened to my dad, not even when he was alive. Once upon a time she'd obeyed my orders. Stopped something when I told her to stop. Sat when I told her to sit. But things had changed since the last time she visited. I didn't smell like she was used to me smelling. I was something different. Something too impossible to ignore. She didn't seem to view me as a threat. More like food, or a fun toy. If I remained still and let her sniff me too long, she'd get gutsy and try taking a chomp out of me again. But if I kept petting her and pushing her mouth away every once in a while, she resisted the urge to tear apart my flesh, and for that I was thankful.

"How are you feeling?" Dad asked. We were seated across from each other at the kitchen table, playing a game of gin rummy. Two glasses of water sweated on the wood, making some of the cards damp. Neither of us had so much as sipped from our drinks, despite our mouths feeling as dry as our eyes. I'd tried taking a sip earlier, but ended up having to spit it out after realizing I no longer remembered how to swallow. I imagine something similar had also happened to Dad, which would explain our sudden shared aversion to inserting anything else in our mouths.

"Not great," I said.

And he cocked his head at me, curious. "Did you just say grape?"

I sighed. Accusing me of saying "grape" whenever I said "great" was one of his favorite stupid jokes. "No, Dad, I did not just say grape."

"Because, if you want grapes, I could text Andy, ask him to pick some up while he's at the store."

"I don't want any grapes, Dad."

"Okay, just checking."

I set down my cards and rubbed my stomach, which had gotten incredibly bloated throughout the morning. "I don't feel good, Dad."

"I know. I'm sorry. Me neither, buddy." He rubbed his own stomach. "You also got issues down there?"

"It's like I have to poop," I said.

"Have you tried?"

"I can't."

He nodded, looking hopeless. "Yeah, me neither."

"Are we really dead?"

"I don't know. I don't think so. But maybe." He set down his cards, too, then held up his glass of water and gave it a little sniff. He grimaced and returned it to the table without drinking any of it. We sat in silence for a while, rubbing our individual stomachs, fighting off Comrade from getting too brave, staring off into space and getting lost in our thoughts.

Then a massive, undeniable fart ripped through the kitchen.

If not for the vibration that shot through my chair, I would have accused Dad of letting loose. But no. It definitely came from me. So did the next dozen or so, one after another, in long, drawn-out eruptions. Meanwhile, my stomach—bloated beyond belief—would not stop rumbling. The sudden farts seemed to egg it on, both my ass and stomach working together to make as much repulsive noise as possible.

Dad stared at me with absolute horror, but only for a moment, as it didn't take long for gas to reach his own exit point. Then his face turned to shock, then a confused amusement as the both of us—together, as father and son—filled the kitchen with our flatulence.

"Well," Dad said, fighting back a giggle, "I'm glad Andy isn't here, at least."

Between us, Comrade sat on the floor with her head cocked, studying our behavior with curiosity. Which of course only made me laugh harder. The more I laughed, the more my body shifted, which prompted additional bursts of gas to escape me—now, not only from my butt, but also through my mouth. Loud, wet belches shot out between laughs.

An awful taste overwhelmed my senses. Something similar to rotten eggs.

MAGGOTS SCREAMING!

I stopped laughing. So did Dad. He'd started burping, too. Neither of us could stop. Something in my stomach felt alive. The spasms got stronger and more frequent. Like my insides were pulsating. It was *painful,* which came as a surprise, since I was sure I could no longer feel anything— after all, I hadn't noticed Comrade's biting activity on my arm until inspecting myself in a mirror. But this was different. This was *internal.* Deep in my gut. In my organs.

Something was wrong. Something was seriously wrong. I fell out of my chair and glanced across the floor and noticed Dad was also there, curled up on his side, arms wrapped around his stomach, a yellow liquid dripping from the corner of his lips, where his tongue drooped out. The same substance coming out of my mouth, too. Flooding my lungs and forming a puddle on the kitchen tile.

Comrade approached, cautious, and started licking up the liquid next to my face. It must've tasted good because instead of recoiling she licked faster, then moved on to my mouth, where my own tongue drooped out between my lips, but I pushed her away and moaned something close to, "No, get away!"

She backed off, standing between us, and started barking. The kind of barking she sometimes does when you're taking too long to pet her. It was her *impatient* bark. Impatient for what, though? Her chance to eat us?

I hugged my stomach again and it felt impossibly fat. Same with Dad's stomach. He'd always been a big man, but never *that* big. Our bodies were swelling with excess gas. And his skin. His skin had changed. It was no longer so pale but a bizarre, discolored green. The word "zombie" never sounded more appropriate.

Above us, on the kitchen table, Dad's cell phone started ringing.

We looked at each other, both of our eyes grotesquely wide, like they were bulging from the sockets, sharing a moment of bleak recognition.

Groaning, Dad pushed himself into a sitting position, then reached up on the table and felt around, blindly, until retrieving his phone. He answered it and attempted to press the device against his ear, but his whole body was shaking, especially his limbs. Then he groaned again and dropped the phone so he could clutch his gut and fall on his side. The phone landed between us, face-up. Closer to Dad. He gambled removing one arm from his stomach, which was something I didn't have the courage to do right then. Slowly he extended his arm out, hand trembling, and poked the SPEAKER button on his phone, and the voice of Mom's boyfriend drowned the room.

"—hear you, Max. Are you there? Something's happened—I can't hear you. Hello? Hello?"

"*I'm here,*" Dad managed to coherently moan, and I had never been more impressed with my father.

"Oh, okay, good, good," Miguel said, out of breath on the other line. "So, listen, you and I gotta talk—uh, Dylan isn't nearby, is he? Go somewhere he can't overhear us. It's about his—it's about Lori. Something's happened to her."

The spasm in my stomach got stronger.

"*What?*" Dad said.

"We think maybe she's come down with some sort of bug. We're at the local hospital, here in Corpus—the medical center?—and things are . . . nobody really knows what's going on with her. Never in my goddamn life have I seen so many doctors confused. They just wheeled her away to a private room on the top floor since she won't stop screaming. I had to come outside for a minute, gather my thoughts, smoke a cigarette. I don't . . . I'm sorry to call you like this, man, but I'm scared, and I thought you oughta know. Tell Dylan however you think is best. I don't—are you still there?"

"Yes."

"She don't look too good, Max. I've never seen anybody look like this before in their life."

"It's okay," Dad said, face strained with obvious pain.

MAGGOTS SCREAMING!

"What are you talking about?" Miguel said. "This shit's about as far from okay as it can get."

"I'm . . . I'm gonna fix it. Tell her I'm gonna fix it."

Wind rattled against my dad's speakers. Wind from Corpus. Finally Miguel said, "Look, I'm gonna go back up and see how she's doing. I'll let you know when we find something out. But I don't see us getting home by Sunday night, not at this rate." He paused, waiting for Dad to say something, but Dad was too busy hugging his stomach and—by the looks of his face—trying not to scream again. "Okay, well. I'm gonna go. The signal inside this place is dogshit, so text me if you have any questions and I'll try to answer them next time I step out for a smoke."

The call disconnected.

Slowly, Dad and I managed to stand from the floor. It looked like Dad was smuggling a basketball under his shirt. Glancing down displayed a similar sight with my own gut. So tight I feared it might pop. Unable to resist, I gave my stomach a small poke, which triggered another long, uncontrollable fart, followed by something wet trickling down my leg.

Without saying another word, I hurried to the bathroom, locked the door, and removed my soiled pants, along with my jacket and T-shirt. I stuffed my clothing (except for the jacket) into the tiny trash can next to the counter and plopped on the toilet, nude. I hadn't pooped my pants since the first grade.

I stood in front of the mirror and frowned. My stomach had gotten bigger. Bloated beyond belief. The discolored green had spread down my body. I tried convincing myself this was a good thing, that it was better to have *some* kind of color than none at all, which had been the case earlier in the day, but c'mon, one look at me in that mirror said everything I needed to know. None of this was *good*. None of this was remotely close to *good*.

Like Dad in the kitchen, my eyes also seemed to be bulging from their sockets. And my tongue. It kept drooping out of my mouth, like it had a mind of its own. I looked like a cartoon character. Like one of the old cartoons from when my dad was a kid. *Looney Tunes* or the *Animaniacs*. In cartoons, bodies don't have to make sense. The animators can manipulate their characters however they want. And that's exactly what it felt like was happening here: someone manipulating my body. But for what reason? Someone else's sick entertainment?

There was something else I noticed in the mirror, of course. Something I'm sure you're well familiar with.

On my arm, where Comrade had bitten into me. She'd left behind an open wound. Last time I'd inspected it, the gash was empty, dried out. But now there was something different. There was something inside my wound. Something . . . *moving?*

I broke my stare from the mirror and glanced down at my arm, raising it to get a better look, rotating it toward my face. If I was still capable of breathing I would have sucked in a breath and held it. An unnerving whiteness had grown in my arm. For a moment I thought I was looking at my actual bone. But bones . . . bones don't writhe, do they? No, this was something else.

Something alive.

The things in my arm were small and numerous. Like little pieces of rice. With my uninjured right arm, I trembled and reached toward it, not wanting to touch it but at the same time not wanting to do *anything else* besides touch it. The responsible thing to do would have probably been to leave it alone, not to agitate it any further, but some things you simply cannot ignore, especially when they're inside your body. Especially when they're mobile.

Especially when they're eating your flesh.

Because that's what they were doing. We know that now, don't we? What was in my arm wound. Honestly, Dad and I should have anticipated something like this happening much sooner, considering how we'd "woken up" earlier that morning drowning in flies.

MAGGOTS SCREAMING!

And what do flies leave?
Eggs.
Which hatch into what?
Which hatch into what?
w h i c h   h a t c h   i n t o   w h a t ?

The first maggot I pulled out of my arm did not want to leave. It clung to my exposed muscle like a kid being dropped off for their first day of kindergarten. It wanted to stay within the safety of my warmth. I tugged harder and it came free and I felt bad, like I'd done something wrong. I held the insect up to face-level, pinching one end with the tips of my thumb and index fingers and letting the rest of the minuscule body hang, like how you'd examine a booger. And it wiggled, desperate to prove it was alive, to show off its uncanny abilities. And I held it there and I watched it demonstrate what it could do, and then I dropped it in the sink and turned the faucet on and drowned it. After it was dead I tried to fit my arm under the sink, but the basin wasn't deep enough to position the wound correctly, so I fled to the shower and turned it on as hot as it would allow and blasted the water directly into the gash Comrade had created with her teeth. Maggots fell out of me in huge chunks, landing on my feet and wriggling between my toes before being carried away toward the drain, only they didn't disappear like I'd hoped they would. There was too many of them. Instead they clogged the holes and water started filling the tub. The water turned dark and sick. Not just from the maggots but from the various yellowish liquids slowly dripping out of my other orifices—my mouth, yes, but also my anus, my *penis,* everywhere. I wanted to collapse into the blackening water and drown with the maggots, but feared my lungs were already expired, so what would be the point? I turned off the water and stepped out, but kept the shower curtain shut, concealing the mess I'd created in the tub. My arm wound was once again maggot-free. I wondered how long it'd take for them to find me—how much time would pass before my body would once again be altered in some mystifying, grotesque nature? I did not want to find out, but of course I did.

I tiptoed out of the bathroom with a towel wrapped around my waist. Dad was fortunately nowhere in the kitchen. I managed to sneak through the house and down the hallway into my bedroom without running into him. I put on my last pair of clean clothes. They barely fit me, thanks to how much my body had bloated throughout the day. I'd only packed two sets, three including the clothes I'd left Mom's house wearing. We'd dressed you in the rest of my clothes—the basketball shorts and DON'T HAVE A COW, MAN shirt. If I pooped my pants again or made some type of other mess, I didn't know what I'd do.

When I returned to the kitchen, Dad was sitting at the table again, and I noticed he'd also changed clothes. Which made sense. Our bodies seemed to be operating in tandem. When something peculiar happened to one of us, it was a pretty sure bet it'd hit the other person soon after if not simultaneously.

We shared a moment of eye contact where neither of us said anything. What was there to say? We'd defecated ourselves. The fact that we'd both done it made the situation less humiliating, but it still happened, all the same, and we made an unspoken pact never to acknowledge the incident.

Dad stood from the table and hugged me and I hugged him and we remained like that for quite some time. Comrade kept trying to sniff at us and Dad and I would take turns lightly kicking her away, but between her and the flies, it was beginning to become quite clear that we would never be left alone again.

MAGGOTS SCREAMING!

Just when we'd concluded Andy had no intention of ever returning, we heard his truck pull up outside the house. The engine was loud enough to rattle the neighborhood. The moment he turned onto our street, Comrade went nuts and pawed at the front door, which was probably the most excited anybody had ever been to see Andy. As far as I knew, he'd never married or been in a serious relationship. If he had any family at all, I'd never heard anybody talk about them. Dad and Miguel were his closest friends, and after Miguel started dating Mom, the friendship soured, at least with Dad. Over the last year or so, I'd seen Andy socializing with Miguel, but this weekend was the first time him and Dad shared more than a couple sentences together, far as I knew. They all worked together at UPS, but it wasn't like they all drove the same truck or anything. Must've been easy for Dad to avoid crossing paths with any of them. In his eyes, Miguel had committed the ultimate betrayal, and Andy wasn't far behind. No, Andy wasn't dating my mom, but he hadn't stopped being friends with Miguel. Mom once told me the whole feud was "the kind of typical pettiness anybody can expect from your father," which I thought was unfair, maybe. If my best friend decided to start dating my girlfriend, I would also be upset. Of course, I did not have a girlfriend—and, let's face it, I never *will* have a girlfriend, not where I am now—but if I *did*, and then my best friend *dated her*, oh man. Plus, to top it all off, our other very close friend decided the situation was okay, and I was simply overreacting? Yikes. Watch out. I would want to break the planet.

"Back, back!" Andy shouted as he walked through the front door, shooing Comrade away from jumping on him. Several plastic grocery bags hung from either hand. He kicked the door shut and gave us a little nod as he headed into the kitchen. "Howdy."

"Where have you been?" Dad asked, trailing behind him.

Andy set the bags on the table. "Where do you *think* I've been?"

"Did you go to the bar?"

"What?" Andy sighed, shaking his head. "Kinda shit is this? I go out, do y'all a favor, only for you to grill me? No, I didn't go to the goddamn bar. I went to the goddamn CVS, like you goddamn asked me to." He gestured to the many bags he'd brought in, in case Dad had somehow missed them. "Y'know, you oughta really consider working on your social skills. Lesser men would've clocked you one already."

I stood between Dad and Andy, afraid they were about to physically fight each other in the kitchen. Instead Dad said, "Okay, I'm sorry."

"Are you?" Andy asked.

"I said I was, didn't I?"

Andy stared at him, dead serious, then let out a laugh. "Boy, you two look like shit."

"I know," Dad said, rubbing his belly. "We started . . . bloating."

"We keep farting," I told him.

Which of course only made him laugh again. "You keep *farting*, you say?"

Dad sat at the table, clutching his stomach. "Our bodies are building up all this gas. It's gotta come out some place."

Andy sniffed, then grimaced. "I thought this place somehow smelled worse than when I left."

I strained my own nose, but didn't detect anything noticeably different. It wasn't that I *couldn't* smell. I had simply spent so much time in the odor that it no longer registered as abnormal to my senses. It was what life smelled like now.

"Well, I also got us some breakfast tacos, but I suspect I might be better off eating mine outside. This ain't no place to enjoy a taco."

"You stopped for tacos?"

"Calm down," Andy said. "I got enough for all of us. Had a hell of a time finding a place that sells them this late in the afternoon, too. Which is partially why I was gone so long."

"I don't want any goddamn tacos," Dad said. "Did you get the drops or not?"

"Wow. You know. A simple *thank you* would be nice every once in a while."

"Andy."

He shook the comment off and picked up one of the CVS bags, waving it as he spoke. "Did you know these fuckin' drops cost ten bucks each, *before* tax? And that's the generic ones! What a total scam."

"Did you get them or not?"

"Yeah, but I want you to know I had to dip into my own account, so you owe me another twenty." Andy unloaded the bags' contents on the table, revealing numerous bottles of artificial tears, bandages, various ointments, cans of air freshener, a tube of balm designed to block horrific odors, a small bag of dog food, and several breakfast tacos wrapped in foil, along with a couple cups of green salsa. Dad and I each took a bottle of eye drops and unpeeled the wrapping while Andy scooped up a can of Hawaiian Aloha Febreze and started spraying it throughout the house. "Gonna make this shithole smell like paradise!" he shouted over his shoulder, then fell into a coughing fit as a cloud of fragrance drifted into his open mouth. He grabbed the balm and rubbed it under his nose, then made a screwed-up face like the substance was tickling him.

I tilted my head and squeezed the bottle over me, missing and hitting my cheek several times before finally making contact with my eye.

"It's easier if you hold it against the bridge of your nose," Dad said, demonstrating with his own bottle. He pressed it against his nose, tilted, and the tear dropped directly into his eye. He blinked a couple times, then straightened his neck. "Waste less drops that way," he said, seconds before a thick stream of yellow liquid dripped down his chin. He wiped it with the back of his hand and started scavenging through the rest of Andy's groceries.

"You fellas hungry or what?" Andy said, stomping into the kitchen. Behind him, Comrade snapped her jaws at the falling Febreze mist.

"I don't . . . I don't think so," Dad said, then glanced at me. "What about you?"

I shook my head. There was no possible way I was going to eat something. Not with everything going on with my stomach, and certainly not with a mysterious yellow liquid building up in my mouth every couple minutes.

"When was the last time any of y'all had something to eat?" Andy asked, studying us with one brow raised.

"I don't know," Dad said. "We had Whataburger yesterday. I don't know when."

"For lunch," I said.

"So it's probably been over twenty-four hours since you ate?" Andy said.

Dad shrugged. "Maybe?"

Andy shook his head, disappointed with our answer. "You gotta try, then. Consider it the ultimate test, right? If you're alive, you need to eat."

"The dead can eat, too," I said, and they both frowned at me, waiting for me to elaborate. "Sometimes they eat other people."

"Dylan, for the last goddamn time, we are not zombies," Dad said.

"How do you know that?" I said.

"The boy raises a good point," Andy said. "Y'all definitely fit the profile."

Dad cocked his head at him. "Oh, you think so?"

"I mean, yeah." Andy scratched his chin. "Ain't y'all looked at yourselves recently?"

"Tell you what," Dad said. "Let me take a bite out of you, see if I enjoy the taste."

Andy chuckled. "Only if I get to pick the spot, pardner." He grabbed two tacos and gave one to each of us. "Just try, see what happens."

I took the taco over to the sink and unrolled the foil. Bacon, egg, and cheese wrapped in a cold tortilla. I lifted it to my mouth and hesitated, trying to force myself into being hungry and failing. Any semblance of an appetite had vanished from my system. Bits of egg dropped out of the tortilla and splattered in the sink basin. The cloud of flies around my head increased in size. I opened my mouth and slid the tip of the taco between my lips and bit down. I felt it in my mouth but tasted nothing. I chewed, then realized I couldn't remember how to swallow. I didn't know what to do. I stood over the sink and tried several times, but it wouldn't go down my throat, so I spat it out into the basin, then tossed the rest of the taco into the trash can. The flies waited all of five seconds before swooping down to claim the rejected remains. They did not get to enjoy their trash feast for very long, however, as Comrade stuck her head in and inhaled the tortilla in one massive bite.

Dad hadn't bothered trying his taco. Instead he unwrapped it and gave it to Comrade, too. This one took her two whole bites to finish.

Andy stared at us in disbelief. "Y'all just wasted like four dollars' worth of breakfast tacos."

Dad shrugged, squeezing another round of artificial tears into his eyes. "Told you we weren't hungry."

Andy scooped up the last two untouched tacos and took them outside in the back yard.

"What are you gonna do?" Dad asked, as we followed him. "Feed them to the bodies?"

Andy stopped and laughed, incredulous. "What? I'm gonna feed them *to myself,* if that's okay with you."

"Oh. Yeah. Okay."

"You might not mind the smell," Andy said, gesturing to the open door leading into the kitchen, "but that shit is horrendous. Even with the Febreze—goddamn. I'd like to enjoy my tacos without also consuming specks of decay."

"Fair enough," Dad said, giving him plenty of room.

Comrade was running around the yard with a renewed energy as Dad and I stood in the grass watching Andy eat breakfast tacos. The flies had also followed us outside. They weren't letting us escape that easily.

I refused to look at the covered garden grave. I was afraid of what I'd do. I couldn't stop thinking about you being in that hole. It didn't seem fair that you were down there and I was up here. The fair thing to do would have been to dig you back up and return you to the living room couch until we figured things out, but it wasn't up to me, and for that I was grateful.

Once Andy returned, it didn't take too long for Dad and I to start farting again, which Andy found hysterical. In addition to the other previously mentioned CVS supplies, he had also purchased several tubes of body lotion, and it was while applying this lotion to our perpetually bloating stomachs that our flatulence returned with a vengeance.

"Oh my gawd," Andy said, from across the kitchen. "That sounds like it came from a vampire's asshole."

"Why a vampire?" I asked, thinking *zombie* would've been a more apt comparison—but then again, weren't vampires also undead?

Andy shrugged, clearly not having given it as much consideration as I had. "I don't know. First monster that came to mind."

"We ain't monsters," Dad said, annoyed, and tossed the lotion on the kitchen table. "I don't know what we are, but we ain't no goddamn monsters."

"Tell that to your anus, pal," Andy said.

I nudged Dad, prompting him to look down at me.

"What?" he said, still irritated with Andy's accusation.

"You gonna tell him?" I asked, gesturing to Andy.

Dad frowned, either not understanding the question or acting intentionally ignorant. "Tell him what?"

"Yeah," Andy said, alert, "tell me what?"

"About Mom . . . ?"

"You got a hold of Lori?" Andy said. "Is she okay?"

"No," Dad said.

"*No,* you didn't get a hold of her, or *no* she ain't okay?"

" . . . Both of 'em?" Dad said. "Miguel called while you were gone. Whatever's going on with us, it's . . . maybe it's happening with Lori, too."

"What the fuck do you mean—*maybe*?"

"They're up at the hospital, in Corpus. Lori and Miguel."

"*Miguel,* too?"

"No, he's fine. I mean, yeah, he's there, but more for, uh, support, I guess. He's fine."

"And Lori?"

"Not so fine," Dad said, defeated, shoulders slumped.

"What did she say?"

"I didn't . . . you know, get to talk to her, or anything. I spoke to Miguel. He was the one who called me. She was already in the hospital. They were, uh, in the process of moving her to a private room..."

"Well, do they at least know what's *wrong* with her, for Christ's sake?" Andy asked, pacing. "Because it has to be the same thing, right? It *has* to."

"Nobody knows anything. They're still trying to, uh, you know, figure it out."

"Okay, sure, but what did Miguel say when you told him about you and Dylan? Is he going to pass it on to her doctors? I mean, this shit ain't no coincidence. All three of you. Oh my gawd. Whole goddamn family, rotting together. You got any other kin around these parts you can call up, see if they're blasting ass more often than usual?"

"I didn't tell him about us."

"I'm sorry. You didn't *what*?" He glanced over at me,

jaw dropped in disbelief. "Dylan, I know I haven't been over much lately, so you're gonna have to catch me up to speed here. Has your dad completely lost his fuckin' mind, or what?"

I stood between them, mouth open, tongue drooping out, unsure what to say besides, "Uhh . . . "

"There's no reason for them to know yet," Dad said. "It's better for us to wait it out, see what happens with Lori. One body in the hospital is plenty. They don't need the rest of us. Not yet, at least. There's just no point in it."

Andy stepped forward, squinting like a bad detective. "Why'd you say it like that?"

Dad backed up, all confidence draining. "Why'd I say what like what?"

"*Body*. You said one *body* in the hospital. Not one *person*. One *body*."

"So the fuck what?"

"I don't know. A little suspicious, that's all."

Dad chuckled. "What exactly do you think is going on here?"

Andy shrugged and turned around. "Isn't that what you called me over here to find out?" he asked, then stormed out of the room, lighting another cigarette.

"Okay, I got an idea," Andy said a little over an hour later. We were sitting on the couch, watching *The Simpsons*. He barged in through the front door, scaring not only us but also Comrade, who had returned to intensely sniffing my crotch. The flies above our heads acted a little spooked, as well. We'd long ago abandoned the idea of swatting them away. They'd just return a second later. Moving our arms like that was a waste of good energy. Soaking our clothes with insect repellant spray hadn't proven effective, either.

"An idea about *what*?" Dad said.

"What?" Andy said. "What do you think, motherfucker?"

"What's your idea?" I said, attempting to cut off another ridiculous argument before it could grow any legs. The fact was, all this internal rotting was starting to make the two of us a little cranky.

"The body farm," Andy said, a smug grin across his face.

Dad and I both remained quiet, waiting for him to elaborate, but he seemed satisfied with his answer, as he offered no further explanation.

"What . . . what about the body farm?" Dad finally asked.

"What's a body farm?" I added, although they both predictably ignored me.

"Don't you think they might have some idea what's happenin' to y'all?" Andy said. "I mean, it's their fuckin' *job*, right? Studying dead folks. Figuring out the different ways we decompose. Hell, to be honest, I can't think of anybody *more* qualified to approach about this issue."

"I don't know," Dad said. "That place has always given me the creeps."

"Shit, what do you think y'all's been giving *me* since I got here? This fuckin' house is creep central."

"Oh, come on. It's not that bad," Dad said, not sounding entirely convinced of his own words. He dismissed the thought with a shake of his head. "And, anyway, I know exactly why you want to go down to the body farm, and it has nothing to do with us."

Andy tried to conceal that he was blushing by covering his face with his arm, and in doing so only succeeded in drawing more attention to his cheeks. "I . . . uh, don't know what you're talking about."

"What is a *body farm*?" I said, stressing my voice so it sounded deeper than normal. A new terror attempted to paralyze me. A hundred different images entered my brain, but none of them could have prepared me for the reality of what a body farm actually is.

"It's a place," Dad said, scratching his head, "where scientists study dead people."

"*Real* dead people?" I asked, feeling oddly self-protective.

Andy laughed. "As opposed to what? *Fake* dead people?"

"I . . . I don't know," I said.

"Why don't you explain it then?" Dad said, giving up. "You're the one who's always making deliveries there."

"Yeah, but it's not like I've ever been, like, past the front desk or anything.

"Is it really a farm?" I asked. "Do they . . . *grow* dead people?"

"No, no, no," Andy said, amused, then suddenly serious. "Uh, at least . . . I don't *think* so . . . " He coughed, then lit another cigarette. "The way I understand it is, some people don't want a proper burial when they die—some people, they decide to donate their little corpses to science. To places like the body farm. And scientists take those bodies and . . . I guess study them, or some shit. Do experiments. I don't fuckin' know."

"What are they studying them for?" I said, wondering what kind of studying these body farm scientists might do on myself if presented the opportunity. Or . . . you. The fear that they might find you down in your garden grave and take you far away gripped me with an unexpected intensity. Was this the first time I felt protective of you?

"I don't know, Dylan," Andy said, "but that's one of the things we can ask. Along with, you know, uh . . . what would cause two living humans to suddenly start decomposing? Or maybe why the hell a fella might have a dead doppelgänger buried in his back yard."

"Oh, come on," Dad said. "Do you honestly think they'll have any goddamn clue?"

"Well, we won't know until we ask, right?"

"What do you mean—*we*?"

"Y'all gotta come with, obviously. I ain't compiling some goddamn list of symptoms to read off once I get there. You two know better than anybody how to describe whatever the fuck's going on here. What am I gonna be able to offer, there by myself? Come off it. Be grateful I was kind enough to run your little eye drop errand earlier. Plus, you know, I *did* get breakfast tacos . . . "

"Which we couldn't eat," Dad said.

Andy shrugged, indifferent. "And that's my problem somehow?"

Dad pointed at me, then himself. "Have you fucking *looked* at us lately? I don't exactly think we are in any state to be seen in public—do you?"

"Shit, that ain't no problem," Andy said, dismissing him with a wave of his hand. "That's what disguises are for."

"Disguises?"

Andy nodded. "Damn right—disguises. We get y'all dressed up properly and no one'll be the wiser."

"What about the smell?" I asked.

"The smell?" Andy said, for some reason highly amused by my question. "Kiddo, don't you get it? You and your old man—y'all already smell like you belong there. Ain't no one gonna notice shit out of the ordinary. If anything, the smell's only gonna make you blend in better."

"Why don't you admit why you actually want to drive up there?" Dad said, smirking, which wasn't the easiest facial expression to configure with a tongue constantly drooping out of your mouth. Trust me. I know from experience.

Again, Andy started blushing. "What? To help out one of my closest friends and his son? Wow, what a total bastard I must be!"

"Uh-huh," Dad said. "And I don't suppose Candy happens to be working today?"

"I fail to see how that's really relevant," Andy said, turning away from us.

"I knew it!"

"Who's Candy?" I asked.

"Andy's girlfriend," Dad explained.

"She's not my girlfriend!" Andy said, bright red with embarrassment.

"Well, okay, fine," Dad said. "He *wants* her to be his girlfriend."

"So what?" Andy said. "What's so wrong with that? A man can't like a girl all of a sudden, huh? That some kinda crime now or something?"

"You and I ain't spoke in how long?" Dad said to Andy. "How do you suppose I knew you hadn't made a move yet?"

"Man, you don't know shit," Andy said. "Candy and I talk all the damn time. We have, like, fuckin' *conversations.*"

"When you deliver packages to the farm, or do you also talk other times, too?"

Andy screwed up his face with anger. "So fuckin' what if we talk at her work? We both live busy lives. The farm's just, like, a convenience for us, at this point."

"Do you have her phone number?"

"No, but it's not like she has mine, either."

"Oh, she doesn't?"

"Man, you know I don't give my number out to just anybody. And besides, ain't no way in hell I'd ever have a meaningful—much less *intimate*—conversation via cellular communication. With the NSA listening in? Are you fuckin' nuts, buddy?"

"Is this girl even one of the scientists? Or is she just . . . what, a receptionist?"

"Man, she ain't a fuckin' receptionist. She's an *assistant.* But yeah. Okay. Sure. She's mostly front desk. Admin shit. Still, dude, you don't get it."

"I don't get what?"

"Last couple times we hung out, she—"

"—You mean, the last couple times you delivered a box to her place of employment."

Andy sighed. "I swear to gawd, it's almost as if you don't want my help. Did you honestly call me over here *just* to be a dick, or . . . ?"

MAGGOTS SCREAMING!

"Dad, stop being so mean," I said, not caring if I hurt his feelings. At this point, he was being needlessly cruel.

"What are you—?" Dad stopped himself, wiping a thin stream of yellow liquid from his chin. "Okay. You're right." Back to Andy: "I'm sorry. I'm being an asshole."

"Correct," Andy said.

"Please," Dad said. "Continue, okay? Ignore me."

"All I'm trying to say, goddammit, is not that long ago she promised me a personal tour of the property—if, ya know, I was ever interested in that sort of thing."

"Okay, I take back what I said. It *does* sound like maybe she has a thing for you, after all."

"There's no reason to be a dick, Max."

"I'm not being a dick," Dad said, swatting at a cloud of flies above his head. "I'm serious. Why else would she offer something weird like that?"

"Shit," Andy said, "you really think so?"

"Yes. I really think so," Dad said, trying his best not to make some smartass comment. I admired the effort.

"So, what do you think?" Andy said. "Should we do it or not?"

Dad shrugged, tongue drooping out of his mouth like an absolute idiot. "Sure. Why not?"

To disguise two dead people who are somehow also alive at the same time, here is what you're going to need: big coats, sunglasses, floppy hats, gloves, makeup, an excess of Axe body spray, and several tree-shaped car fresheners hanging around their necks, tucked under their shirt collars. And luck. Lots and lots of luck.

The body farm was a half-hour drive, out in San Marcos, which was where Dad, Andy, and Miguel all worked for

UPS. Dad always talked about wanting to get transferred to a hub closer to his house, but for some reason it never happened. Maybe, despite the way he claimed to have felt about Miguel's "betrayal", he still preferred working with his buddies. Outside of Miguel and Andy, I don't think I'd ever witnessed Dad socialize with anyone.

What do you talk about while driving to a body farm? Trick question, because somehow Andy listened to music louder than Dad. Plus, with the rumbling of his stripped muffler, it was nearly impossible to hear myself think, much less what anybody else might've been saying.

I felt ridiculous in my disguise. Ridiculous and hot. Here we were in Texas, in the middle of *summer,* when the temperature regularly lingered on triple digits—wearing *trench coats.* Big, thick, long coats designed for the kinds of heavy winters that seldom hit this area. I felt extremely hot but the feeling might have existed only in my mind, as I never started sweating while riding in the back of Andy's pickup. Any other kid would've surely expired from extreme heat exposure. But not me. Not actual heat, not like I imagined. Plus, the coldness had mostly disappeared by then, as well. Leaving behind a sensation I struggle to describe even now. Some kind of uncomfortable . . . nothingness? But not quite that, either. It was more similar to the feeling that precedes or follows a limb falling asleep, except it wasn't focused on only one part of my body—the sensation had spread *everywhere,* like a disease.

We'd left Comrade at Dad's house. No sense in taking her with us when we had no idea how long we'd be inside the body farm. It seemed unlikely the scientists would allow a strange dog to invade their work stations. As it was, we pretty much doubted they'd grant *us* permission inside, despite Andy's many reassurances. But we were going along with it, anyway, because what else were we supposed to do? Go down to Corpus with Mom, check ourselves into the hospital? Well, okay, yeah, that *did* sound like the smartest plan, but it wasn't like anybody was letting me make any decisions. I brought the idea up once, but Andy had laughed and rubbed my head—momentarily scaring away a cloud of flies—and suggested it would be a foolish thing to do, willingly offering yourself to the government like that—especially when they already had their greedy mitts on one member of the family—why go easy on them and give them any more? His response sounded a little crazy to me, but Dad had nodded along with him, seemingly in agreement, so maybe this was some greater truth easier to comprehend upon entering adulthood. Or maybe they were both nuts.

Once we got off I-35, we had to cross over a curvy concrete bridge labeled PURGATORY CREEK, which Andy thought was hilarious. "Ain't that some ironic shit!" he shouted over his muffler, pointing at the sign as we passed it.

"What are you talking about?" I asked, struggling to raise my voice. Straining vocal cords was a skill quickly fading from my inventory, among many other things I used to take for granted.

"Purgatory!" Andy shouted again. "Don't you get it?"

I shook my head. Dad also appeared equally puzzled.

"The place between, baby!" Andy said. "Not heaven, not hell, but right smack in the middle. If that ain't ironic, I don't know what is . . . "

"How . . . how is it ironic?" Dad asked.

Andy lowered the radio volume. "Well, c'mon, think about it. How else would you describe what's happening to y'all? You sure as shit ain't dead, but you also ain't exactly alive, are ya? So, what does that make ya then if not *in between?* Buncha purgatory boys crossing Purgatory Creek! Ironic as fuck, if you ask me."

"Oh," Dad said. "I don't know. Maybe. I always get confused. You know. About irony and shit."

"What the hell's so confusing about it?" Andy said, irrationally annoyed as we exited Purgatory Creek. "Don't you remember that song, by Janice whats-her-face?"

"*What* song?"

"Goddammit. The fuckin' ironic song. I don't know what it's called."

"Are you talking about Alanis Morissette?"

Andy grimaced. "*Who*?"

"Alanis Mor—"

"I don't know who that is."

"She sang the ironic song."

"No," Andy said, shaking his head. "I'm telling you, her name was Janice something."

"What's so ironic about it raining at a wedding, anyway?"

"What the fuck is that supposed to mean?"

"Isn't that from the song? Raining on a wedding."

"How—how the hell should I know? You think I go around memorizing every little song I listen to now?"

"You're the one who started talking about the song!"

"Not *that* song," Andy said. "I'm talking about the *ironic* song."

"Me too!"

"Raining at a wedding?" Andy said. "Nah. That ain't irony. That's just a bummer."

"Same with a black fly in someone's Chardonnay."

Andy side-eyed him. "I don't drink that shit and you know it."

"Dude, it's from the song. Oh my god."

But Andy shook his head, disgusted, and raised the volume on his radio again.

A couple minutes later, he started slowing down as we approached a narrow hard-to-spot road to the right. He turned onto it, tapping the brakes several times to avoid swerving into the grass and gravel. To the right of the road's entrance was a white sign marked HENENLOTTER CENTER, and to the left of the road, leaning against a prickly pear cactus, was a large rock someone had graffitied the word *JESUS* on with red, blue, and black spray paint.

"Always turn right at the Jesus rock," Andy told us. "Once you find your way out of Purgatory, of course . . . "

The road we were on was barely wide enough to fit one

vehicle. I got nervous someone would come blasting through the opposite direction and crash into us, but the area thankfully appeared deserted of all other human life. Tall fences and poles followed us down the road on either side, preventing us from entering the true Texas Hill Country. The fences might've once been painted seafoam green, but the structures were now rusty, flaking. The road contained many twists and curves, making it impossible to gain much speed despite Andy's reckless driving. Several hills and drops in the road also cautioned us against going too fast. Otherwise we'd likely flip over, smash into a pole, something idiotic like that.

I was worried Andy didn't know where he was going, that he was as lost as the rest of us but too embarrassed to admit it. But then gates started showing up along the side of the road, spread out every five hundred feet or so, locked with heavy chains and flaunting signs that warned trespassers the premises was under twenty-four-hour surveillance with cameras capable of night-vision abilities. Texas Hill Country poked out from behind the fences, promising adventure beyond the locks. The signs made me paranoid, although I wasn't sure why. It wasn't like we were planning to break the law or anything, right? We wanted to ask a couple questions, get to the bottom of this thing. So who cared if there were cameras? Maybe it was the fact that Andy didn't seem remotely disturbed by them that had my own suspicions going a little haywire. Out of the three of us, Andy should've been the one acting more overly cautious. He was typically against any kind of surveillance, and tried to avoid it at all costs. I remember one time he brought his laptop to Dad's house. He had multiple layers of duct tape wrapped around the top of the screen, where the webcam lens was located. Not only there but also along the side, covering the internal microphone area. "You never know what kinda fuckin' whack job's listenin' in on you," he'd said, after noticing me staring at the tape. Then he winked, although I don't know why.

The truck slowed down and turned right again—this time into a small opening blocked off by a tall gate. Large letters made of pipe stood atop the archway, spelling out HENENLOTTER RANCH.

"It's locked!" I cried, as if nobody else had already noticed. "Now what are we going to do?"

"Would you get your panties out of a wad?" Andy asked. "I got it taken care of, okay?"

"Hey," Dad said. "Don't talk about my son's panties that way."

"I don't have panties, you guys!" I shouted, despising how much like a baby I sounded.

Fortunately they ignored my outburst and the truck crept closer to the gate, stopping next to a call box. Andy poked his head through the driver's side window and pressed a red button. Several seconds passed, then a woman's voice crackled out of the speaker box: "Good evening. May I ask you to please state your business?"

"Candy?" Andy asked. "It's me. Andy. From, um, UPS?"

He sounded nervous, like he was afraid she wouldn't recognize him, that she'd respond with one, simple, crippling, *Who?*

Instead she said, "Oh, shucks! Andy? I didn't recognize your vehicle."

I glanced around the area again and spotted another security camera, this one at the top of the gate, hidden under the second "H" in HENENLOTTER RANCH.

"Yeah," Andy said. "It's my personal truck. Not, uh, UPS's."

"Oh. I see." She paused, then said, "I didn't realize we had a package scheduled for today."

"No package today. Just me. I'm off the clock."

"You're off the . . . ?"

"Off the clock, yup. Here on my own, uh, freewill—so to speak."

"Your own freewill, huh?" she said, audibly amused.

"Yeah, that's right," Andy said, regaining his confidence. "I was hoping to take you up on one of those private tours you keep promising me."

Another long pause. I wondered if she was going to answer at all. Then she said, voice hushed, "I'm not so sure now's such a good time. My boss is here, and . . . "

Andy's face practically collapsed into itself. "Oh, I'm sorry. I didn't—"

"And you drove all the way up here . . . for this?"

"Well, yeah." He sucked in a breath, then added, "And, uh, well, to see you, too."

Dad let out a laugh and Andy slugged him in the arm, which somehow triggered another fart from his ever-bloating body.

"What was that—? Sorry, Andy, I'm having a hard time hearing you. Come on down. I'll buzz you in."

And, just like that, the giant gate started creeping open, following along an automatic track.

Andy glanced at us with a look that said, *See? What did I tell ya?* then drove forward, through the open gate and over thick drainage pipes, something my dad had once told me were specifically designed to prevent cattle from escaping farms. Which was what we were entering—a farm. Only, not the kind with cows hanging around—as far as I could tell, at least. This was a farm for corpses. *Human* corpses. As we drove over those drainage pipes, I couldn't help but wonder what, exactly, they didn't want leaving the property. What they didn't want escaping.

We parked in front of a small welcome center. Andy cut the engine and the two of them got out, but I stayed put. I didn't want to leave the truck.

"C'mon, Dylan," Dad said, standing outside my open door, not trying to hide his annoyance with me. "You can't just sit here."

"Why not?" I asked, arms folded across my chest. Pouting like an infant but I didn't care. This place felt like bad news and I wanted nothing to do with it. "What does it matter what I do?"

Andy chuckled, behind Dad, somewhere in the parking lot. "Max, I didn't realize your son had become a goth."

"Would you shut the fuck up?" Dad said over his shoulder, which only prompted another chuckle from the parking lot. Then, to me, he said, "Listen, kiddo— whatever's going on with us, with your mom, I know . . . I know it's scary. But someone might actually *know* something here. I doubt it, but who's to say for sure, right? We won't know until we know. So, why don't we go find out? At the very least, cross this idea off the list so we can explore others."

He made a good point. Plus, the idea of sitting out here all by myself didn't exactly sound the most appealing. What if someone stopped by and started questioning me? *What are you doing out here all by yourself? Why are you wearing such a big coat? Say . . . what's that smell? How come you aren't blinking?* It'd be safer to stick with grownups—to be by Andy and my dad, who could do all the talking instead of me.

I'm not sure what I expected, driving up there originally, but nothing about the welcome center screamed *body farm!* to me. It was a standard brick building. Minimal windows. Zero advertisement. And inside, through the door, it was like any doctor's office lobby I'd ever visited. Big front desk, a side-door leading who-knew- where, several chairs, tables with magazines, a small television set hanging from the corner of the room with the local news playing one decibel away from mute.

The woman behind the front desk—Candy—had faded pink bubblegum hair, and I wondered what came first: the dye, or her name. She peered her head over a desktop and smiled at Andy, then frowned once she noticed me and Dad standing next to him.

"Uh, hi," she said. Was she more disappointed that Andy wasn't alone, or confused over our ridiculous disguises? If I had to guess, probably a mixture of both. "What—what's going on?"

"Hi, Candy," Andy said, smiling and blushing all at once. "It's nice to see you again."

"Yes . . . you too," she said, not taking her eyes off me. She looked like she was a second away from calling security, assuming body farms *had* security. And, if they did, what would their job be, exactly? Who would body farm security officers be assigned to protect? The dead, or the living?

Andy cleared his throat, realizing how awkward the situation had become, and gestured at the two of us. "Uhh . . . this is my friend, Max, and his son, Dylan."

Dad and I waved and said, "Hey."

She waved back. "Hi?" Enunciated it like a question, like she didn't understand what we were all doing here.

Andy cleared his throat a second time. It sounded wet and disgusting. "So, uh, the thing is, I was wondering—you know, about the tour you're always teasing me about. See, Dylan here—he, uh, he has a science project due on Monday. On . . . well, you know, corpses and whatnot. How shit decomposes or whatever, that kinda thing. So, we were hoping maybe you could show him around, answer some questions."

"School?" Candy said, frowning. "Isn't school out? It's July."

Andy gulped, then gave me a playful slap on the back, nearly knocked off my sunglasses. "Yeah, but he's dumb as shit, so they're making him do summer school."

Dad turned toward Andy like he was going to attack him. Instead all he said was, "Are you serious?"

"Hey," Andy said, "ain't nothing to be ashamed of. I got stuck doing summer school bullshit twice when I was a kid, and now I own my own truck." He winked at Candy and gestured behind us, at the front door. "That's right. You know that truck you saw me pull up in? All mine, a hundred percent. No more monthly payments or nothin'."

"Oh," she said, sounding the opposite of impressed. "Wow."

"So what do you think?" Andy said. "Can you help this poor child pass summer school, or what?"

"Um, well . . . " Candy cleared her throat. "I suppose I—"

"—Unfortunately," said another woman, standing next to the open side-door across the room, "Ms. Candace's occupational duties require her to remain behind this front desk, unless her supervisor requests her to assist on a project." The woman stepped forward, letting the side-door shut behind her. "And, as fate would have it, I happen to be Ms. Candace's aforementioned supervisor. In fact, I happen to run this entire facility. And, as far as I can recall, I have not granted any such permission to abandon her post. Have I, Ms. Candace?"

"Doctor Winzenread," Candy said, nervous. "I was just about to tell him that. I—I swear."

"Now, now, there's no need for that kind of erratic blabbering, Ms. Candace. You're fine. All is well, all is well." She smiled, wide, and held out her hand for one or all three of us to shake. I instantly distrusted it. Anybody who wanted to shake your hand undoubtedly had something nefarious hidden up their sleeve. And this woman—Doctor Winzenread—was wearing a white lab coat, which was the second-best type of sleeve to conceal something under— the absolute best being, of course, a magician's cloak. "Now, why don't you introduce me to your very interestingly-dressed friends?" she said.

Candy's brain seemed to skip a beat, her reaction delayed like a video game lagging, then snapped back to reality. "Oh, yeah, of course, Doctor Winzenread. Of course. That's . . . uh . . . that's Andy. He works with UPS?"

"Oh? Did we receive a package?" The doctor studied Andy, frowning. "You don't appear to be dressed in the proper attire typically found on the United Parcel Service's delivery drivers. And it couldn't be casual Friday, considering Friday was *yesterday*—at least, according to most standard calendars."

"He's off duty, Doctor Winzenread," Candy explained. "His friend's son needs help with a science project. For summer school."

"Hmm," Doctor Winzenread said, eyes on me. "And I suppose you are the young man in question, yes?"

I refused to respond until Dad flicked me, then I blurted out, "Uh, yes, ma'am."

"What might your name be, then?" She smiled again. This close, I was unfortunately able to get a better look at her teeth, which were more yellow than white.

"His name is Dylan," Dad said, then shook her hand. "And I'm Max."

"Doctor Winzenread," the doctor said, shaking his hand longer than anybody had ever shaken someone's hand, "as I'm sure you've already managed to gather from Ms. Candace over there. I am the head anthropologist at this little facility you find yourselves in today."

"It's, um, a pleasure to meet you," Dad said, yanking his hand free.

"Your son is quite shy, isn't he?" she asked, then leaned toward me again. "You're quite shy—aren't you, Mr. Dylan?"

"I don't know," I mumbled. "Maybe. I guess so."

"Tell me something, Mr. Dylan," the doctor said, straightening her spine. "Are you cold?" She glanced at Dad. "And you, Mr. Max? Are you cold, as well?"

"Uh," Dad said, "I'm all right."

"Then could you perhaps explain why the two of you are dressed like a pair of scopophiliacs?"

"What?" Dad said, stammering.

"Peeping toms, Mr. Max. Good old-fashioned *voyeurs*. It's July. What's the cause for such heavy coats? Is this some sort of bizarre fashion statement?"

"Uh," Dad said again, utterly useless.

"They got shitty skin," Andy said, trying to save the day.

"Beg your pardon?" Doctor Winzenread said, returning her gaze to Andy.

"They got, you know, one of those skin conditions. Too much contact with the sun will fuck them up."

"What?" Candy said from behind the front desk. "Like vampires?"

Andy snapped his fingers, ecstatic. "*Exactly* like vampires!" He hesitated, backtracking. "Well, I mean, not *exactly*, okay. They ain't, you know, un*dead* or anything like that. That would . . . that would be crazy. Right?"

"Andy," Dad said, trying to get him to shut up without having to say it.

Another yellow-toothed smile from the strange doctor. "Tell you folks what. While Ms. Candace here may not be able to leave this office and show you around, there's no reason *I* can't."

"Y-you?" Andy said, poorly hiding his disappointment.

The doctor clapped her hands and rubbed them together, giddy. "Yes, *me!* Why not *me?* I am, after all, the head researcher at this facility, am I not? You do not need to answer that, because I already know the answer. *Yes,* I am. I very much am!"

"Uh, well, we were kinda hoping—"

She raised her pointer finger toward the ceiling, cutting Andy off like a feared school teacher silencing a classroom. "And *also* considering Ms. Candace has not been properly trained or prepared to answer the sort of questions Mr. Dylan here might need answered, I honestly cannot imagine a more perfect guide than *me*. Can you?"

"Well," Andy said. "Um."

"Yes," Dad said, stepping in front of Andy. "We would appreciate your help. Thank you so much for the kind offer."

No joke. That was the politest I'd ever heard my father speak to anybody. It left me and Andy a little dumbstruck.

MAGGOTS SCREAMING!

The tone certainly worked its charm over Doctor Winzenread, who showed us her hideous teeth again. If I was still able to smell anything beyond my own rotten odor, I'm confident her breath would have been strong enough to force another dose of mystery liquid out of my mouth.

"Now *that* is how a proper gentleman communicates with a member of the opposite sex," she said, then winked.

Oh my god, I realized, was she *flirting* with him?

Doctor Winzenread clicked her tongue. "Okay, how about this? Mr. Andrew, why don't you stick around here and keep my Ms. Candace company?" She turned to Candy. "Now, that's not to mean I am giving you an excuse to slack off, Ms. Candace. But, seeing as we are nearing the end of a workday—a workday which has been particularly slow at that—I cannot imagine you have much left to accomplish before closing. Plus, you and Mr. Andrew already seem like good friends, so if you wish to socialize while finishing your tasks up, what kind of heartless boss would I be to stop you? This is not a sweatshop, after all. This is not Amazon dot com. We are a simple facility with simple functions. We treat our staff not like *employees* but like *family*. Would you say that's true, Ms. Candace?"

"Uh . . . yes, Doctor Winzenread. That's . . . that's true."

The doctor turned to Andy. "And is this agreeable with you, Mr. Andrew?"

"Sure, I don't see why not."

"Then it's settled!" Doctor Winzenread said, clapping her hands again. "Mr. Andrew will stay with Ms. Candace, and Mr. Max and Mr. Dylan will accompany me on a brief tour of the premises. We will then reconvene here in this very office, and then who knows where fate will take us? Go grab some dinner, perhaps? A cup of hot, steaming coffee? The day is young—is it not?"

The question didn't seem to be directed at anybody in particular, so when nobody answered she followed up with another clap and exclaimed, "All right! Let's proceed!"

123

Before we could enter the actual farm, Doctor Winzenread told us, first we had to undergo some safety precautions. She led us down a long, narrow hallway over-lit with excessive fluorescent bulbs. Posters were hung up on either side of the hallway—and, as we would come to discover, all throughout the facility. Not just any posters but *motivational* posters. They were also all themed around NBC's *The Office* for some reason. One read:

> **Would I rather be feared or loved?**
> **Easy, both.**

I want people to be afraid of how much they love me.

—Michael Scott

And another read:

C·O·M·M·I·T·M·E·N·T

IF AT FIRST YOU DON'T SUCCEED,
TRY TO SOLVE THE SITUATION WITH A SPUD GUN.

The second one included a picture of Dwight Schrute sitting over a plate of jello. Dad also noticed, as he giggled nervously and asked, "Uh, what's with these posters?"

The anthropologist shrugged. "We inherited them from the college. *Evidently,* the drama department printed too many copies and didn't know what to do with them. One day I come to work, find several boxes of these posters at the front door. What am I supposed to do, throw them away? I think not, Mr. Max! Here at the body farm, we waste nothing, not even unnecessary television propaganda."

"Prop-propaganda?"

She turned and eyed him cautiously. "How else would you label these?"

"Are you guys, like, an educational thing or something?" Dad asked.

"We are connected to Texas State University, yes, as part of the Forensic Anthropology Center." Doctor Winzenread pointed in what felt like a random direction. "The college is about seven, eight miles that way. Personally, I try to avoid it. The professors who roam those halls do not always tend to see eye-to-eye with me. Meaning, they are fools. They are scoundrels who simply clock in for the paycheck and lengthy summer vacation. How utterly pathetic. How completely pedestrian!" She clapped her hands, spooking both of us. "Come! We are wasting time! I can talk and walk just fine. But the question is, Mr. Max and Mr. Dylan, can you *listen* and walk?"

"Uh, sure, yeah," Dad said. "I suppose so."

She clapped again, and somehow neither of us had been ready for it. "Excellent! Into the preparation room we go!" We continued down the impossibly long hallway, passing dozens of *The Office*-themed motivational posters. "Now, before anybody is allowed out on the farm—especially guests such as yourselves—they must first go through the proper safety precautions. Which isn't as strenuous as it sounds, so don't worry. We simply must wash our hands and put on the protective gear for our hands and feet."

We entered the preparation room by pushing through two large doors that could swing either direction. The inside reminded me of how morgues look in movies. Several gurneys with white sheets were on either side of us. They were all empty.

Doctor Winzenread studied us, curious. "I'm surprised neither of you seem to be reacting to the smell. Typically, guests start gagging almost immediately. I would have warned you ahead of time, but to be truthful, Mr. Max and Mr. Dylan, I sort of enjoy witnessing the reaction."

We didn't pick up on whatever she was talking about. Either we'd lost our sense of smell, or we'd spent so much time basking in our decomposition at the house that we'd simply gotten used to the odor. It occurred to me then that we'd lucked out. The only reason this anthropologist hadn't detected a strange smell on *us* was because the entire premises shared the same scent. It was the perfect camouflage.

"Oh," Dad said, realizing she wasn't going to stop looking at us until we provided some kind of an answer. "Well, I don't know, I guess we aren't easily disgusted."

Doctor Winzenread showed us her teeth again. "One of the finest attributes a man can have. Tell me, Mr. Max, have you ever seen a dead body before?" She glanced down at me. "And you, Mr. Dylan?"

"Uh," Dad and I both said in unison, which the anthropologist thankfully accepted as a response, and led us across the room to an elaborate washing station surrounded by cabinets and various other storage units.

"Typically," Doctor Winzenread said, "I make our students strip and thoroughly wash their bodies. I despise the idea of outside contamination somehow leaving a footprint in my research. *However,* seeing as neither of you are students, and you won't be *touching* anything important, I don't think conducting a strip-clean is entirely necessary. I also have to factor in the age of your son, Mr. Max. He is clearly a youth, and I am not entirely certain of the legalities in that area. Would I be arrested? That's one question we could ask. Could an American penitentiary successfully keep me imprisoned for any respectable length of time? An even better question! Let's not answer either today. Please put these on."

She handed each of us a pair of rubber gloves and rubber booties, then turned around to give us privacy, probably more out of routine from overseeing the terrifying "strip-cleans" she had mentioned. Or was that *threatened?* It was hard to tell from the way she spoke.

MAGGOTS SCREAMING!

Every word out of her mouth sounded at least a *little bit* menacing.

At first I tried pulling the rubber gloves *over* the cotton winter gloves we were already wearing, but obviously I don't need to tell you how little success I had. Anybody with half a brain—rotten or not—should've been able to guess that. Despite her back facing us, I felt the need to turn my own back on her before delicately pulling off the cotton gloves. I realized far too late that part of my skin had gotten a little too attached to the inside of the cotton, and when I tried pulling off the gloves the movement also yanked the top of my hand forward. I paused, resisting the urge to scream, and carefully maneuvered the rest of the cotton gloves off. The skin, blissfully, remained on my hands, although now it all felt . . . *loose*. Like it could slip off the bones at the slightest altercation. I peeked over at Dad for some guidance, but he was focused on his own hands, looking equally disturbed. This was not good. What the hell was happening to us? Could skin really slip off your hands like that? And what would the anthropologist do if it happened in front of her?

I forced the rubber gloves over the loose flesh of my hands, then rolled the booties over my shoes. Dad was already finished and waiting on me. I looked at him as if to ask, *What are we going to do?* and he shrugged, as if to answer, *How the fuck should I know?* It probably didn't help that we were both wearing sunglasses and couldn't exactly see each other's drying eyes.

"Okay," Dad said. "We're ready."

She took us out through a back door and we all piled into one of the several golf carts parked near the grass. *THE WIZ* was spray-painted along the front hood, and it took me a full thirty seconds to connect it to Doctor Winzenread's name.

"Where are we going?" Dad asked, nervous.

"I thought you wanted to see the farm?" the anthropologist said.

"I guess I thought it was right here."

She laughed. "Oh, Mr. Max, you are quite the humorous fellow!" And with that, she stomped on the gas. The golf cart shot out of the parking spot and onto a dirt road like a very slow bullet. My floppy hat immediately blew off and disappeared somewhere behind us. I became paranoid that, like my hands, my scalp had already loosened to the point of slipping off my skull. I reached up and gave my head a little pat. Everything still felt somewhat intact.

We drove for five minutes or so, passing numerous hay barns and small wooden houses the anthropologist explained belonged to the ranch manager, and finally stopped at a pair of fences with locked gates.

"Okay, Mr. Dylan and Mr. Max, from here we walk." She cut the engine and hopped out of the golf cart, then hustled over to the gates to unlock them. "Come on!" She waved for us to hurry. "Respect the dead's time and move it, fellas!"

"Dad," I whispered, "what are we doing here?"

"I . . . am not sure," Dad said, and we joined the bizarre anthropologist at the gates to the body farm.

She led us through the opening, further down the dirt path, until she paused and examined us once more. "Excuse me, but it only now occurs to me that I have no idea what this science report is supposed to be out."

She was looking directly at me, but fortunately Dad answered instead, since I didn't know what to say. "Just, you know," he said, "the general process of . . . .uh, body decomposition, I guess?"

"And this is an assignment for a summer school class?"

I slowly nodded, terrified of this woman catching me in a lie. She didn't seem like the kind of person who would react well to deception.

"What teacher is this?" Doctor Winzenread asked. "What school is this?"

"Uh."

"I find it curious that some nitwit would dare assign such a project without first seeking me for consultation. In fact, strike the *curious* from my last sentence. I find it downright insulting!"

"I'm sorry," I said.

"Well, it's not your fault, Mr. Dylan. Personally, I blame the state of education in Texas. It's not exactly—how would you say it?—*competent*. You wouldn't believe some of the students who come my way. In addition to conducting my own research, I also guide plenty of college kids in their own forensic ambitions—hence the Texas State University connection I mentioned earlier—and the majority of them can barely spell the word 'anthropology' without first having to look it up on their cellular devices. I hate to say this, but so many of them are simply lost causes at this point, and would provide more use in the ground than above it. At least then I would have a greater source of bodies to study, rather than sentient bags of meat more concerned with their little penises and Instagram followers than real, legitimate *science*." She gasped, out of breath, and shrugged. "But alas, dear Mr. Dylan, we are not talking about the students of TSU. We are talking about *you,* and I have a good feeling about you."

"You—you do?" I asked, genuinely surprised.

"Mmm-hmm," she said, grinning. "I can't quite place it, but there's something about you—about *both* of you, in fact—that I have registered as instantly charming. That's why I agreed to give you this brief tour—which, by the way, we really should start if we want any chance of finishing before the sun goes down. So, shall we?" She took two steps then stopped again, remembering one last detail. "Oh, and I should have probably mentioned this in the lobby, but what we're about to encounter can be considered quite graphic and disturbing to certain people—mostly cowards, if I'm being honest, and I am *always* honest, except for when I am not. However, you two do not strike me as cowards, especially considering you already took the initiative to drive down here in the first place, so I assume this will not be a problem for either of you."

We told her it was fine. She got excited and clapped again, then continued leading us down the dirt trail.

The Henenlotter Ranch was located deep in the heart of Texas Hill Country, and the Forensic Anthropology Center had opted to leave the natural landscape mostly untouched. Which meant we soon found ourselves stepping over various weeds and wildflowers. The greenery out here was less *green* and more *yellow*. Dried out. That's what happened when it didn't rain for a couple weeks and the sun was allowed free rein upon the land. It cooked the planet.

I don't know how I would have reacted to the bodies she showed us if I hadn't already encountered you and the other impossible corpses back home. So, I guess for that, I am grateful.

The first body we came across, the anthropologist kept glancing our way like she was expecting one of us to vomit, but neither Dad nor myself expressed much of a reaction at all. Maybe this also had something to do with the fact that we were also dead not just inside but also outside. Our faces were not exactly the most animated anymore. In retrospect, this was also probably why she had taken such an initial interest in our presence in the lobby of the research facility. The longer we talked, the more it became apparent that she preferred the dead over the living.

The body we stood over was stripped naked, and male. A metal cage had been built over him. When Dad asked about it, Doctor Winzenread explained it was meant to prevent wildlife from eating the remains. "Vultures are quite adventurous out here. If you aren't too careful, they'll pick these bones clean." Then she snapped her fingers, excited. "However, *with that said,* there are plenty of specimens out here who we monitor *unprotected,* for the specific purpose of studying how they decompose with the predatory element present. Sometimes the findings are extremely fascinating. For instance, did you know a vulture will scatter the bones of a musician farther than the bones of a cartoonist? Why is that, do you think? I don't know! A former researcher here once speculated certain musical notes, if played enough times, can leave a sort of *imprint* in the instrument-wielder's skeleton, and the vultures can still feel the melodious vibrations in their beaks as they slurp off the remaining fat, which is apparently an enjoyable sensation for them, hence why they prefer to spend more time with these specific bones than the bones of someone who simply doodled obscene genitalia or traced over coloring books. Notice I described her as a *former* researcher. She was a raging alcoholic who often took long naps curled up next to the specimens out here. Sometimes she wrote them poems and refused to let any of us read them. We simply could not trust her."

"What happened to her?" I asked.

The anthropologist gazed out into the distance, seemingly lost in her thoughts, before saying, "Nobody knows."

"What, uh, exactly is the purpose of all this?" Dad asked, gesturing at the caged corpse. It was a pretty good question. I'd been wondering the same thing.

"Of this particular specimen or the entire facility?" the anthropologist said, already sounding offended.

"The whole thing, I guess?"

"Well, Mr. Max, this is a body farm." She performed a little twirl next to the caged corpse, like a ballerina. "It is not the only one in the country, but it *is* the largest, which I suppose has something to do with Texas's incessant desire to make everything bigger here than anywhere else. Usually I find that mindset immature and pathetic. But, in the case of this specific anthropology research facility, I am grateful, as that means extra acreage for additional experiments. The entirety of Henenlotter Ranch is, I believe, forty-two-hundred acres, and twenty-six of them are reserved solely for the body farm. Oh, and another difference you'll find with us compared to other similar facilities is everybody else refuses to use that label. *Body farm.* They feel the term is too macabre. Too morbid. Too dark. Personally I feel they are all cowards, and we should call it exactly what it is. A body farm. There's also a novel by Patricia Cornwell titled *The Body Farm,* although it's terrible and not worth anyone's time, if you want to hear my honest opinion about it. It's been several years since I read the book, mind you, but if I remember correctly only one, maybe *two* chapters in total take place at the actual farm. The rest of the plot is about something else. That, Mr. Max, is what I would call a con job. You cannot title a book *The Body Farm* and then not spend the rest of the book exploring it. Readers will revolt!"

"Okay," Dad said, probably thinking the same thing I was, that she hadn't exactly answered his question. "But, I guess what I mean is, what's the . . . uh, *purpose* of these . . . experiments?"

"I suppose that's a complicated question."

"It is?"

"It's a complicated answer, at least."

"Oh. I'm . . . I'm sorry?"

"Allow me to say this, Mr. Max." The anthropologist cleared her throat and glanced around the field, as if searching for potential eavesdroppers. "The very kind-hearted people who fund our programs, they hold certain expectations. Primarily, they view forensic science as a method for capturing 'the bad guys'," she said, making the finger-quote gesture.

"What bad guys?" I asked, paranoid she was referring to Dad and myself. Ever since our inexplicable decomposing, I had started considering ourselves *guilty* of something, although I couldn't quite place what.

She did finger-quotes again as she said, "'Criminals',

Mr. Dylan. Those who have broken the law. Murderers, mostly. Our research serves many functions, and one of those—the most important one, in the eyes of the government and, of course, our financiers—involves determining a person's time of death. If police detectives know the exact day—and, sometimes, even the *hour*—when someone was killed, then that helps narrow down their list of suspects."

"How do you do that?"

"Well, Mr. Dylan, that's also a complicated answer, but the simple explanation is every human being goes through a somewhat predictable pattern of decomposition."

"Uh," Dad said, "we don't need to talk about this."

"Yes we do," I said, elbowing him in the stomach, which forced a massive fart out of him.

"Oh," he said, clutching his bloated gut, "I'm sorry."

The anthropologist stared at us, then giggled. "You two are a lot of fun. A regular barrel of monkeys. You ought to consider visiting more often."

"Decomposition?" I said, prompting her to continue.

"Ah, yes! Decomposition!" Doctor Winzenread motioned for us to follow her through the field. We stumbled upon several other caged corpses in various states of decay. "So, decomposition—as I hope you are both already aware—is the beautiful, natural process of organic matter breaking down after it ceases living. Everything alive will eventually decompose. Fruits, vegetables, trees, animals, humans. In the grand scheme of things, we are all heading toward the same fate. The planet gives us life, and that life gets recycled back into the planet. It is simply inevitable. A lot of my students seem surprised by this at first, but after a person dies and releases the many juices typically found in a body, our purge fluids will annihilate pretty much any living wildlife nearby—grass, flowers, you name it—mostly thanks to the ammonia that accompanies the decay. *However,* give the area about a year, and the grass will have grown back like you've never seen before.

The purge fluids really enrich the soil unlike any other fertilizer I've ever encountered. Isn't that marvelous, Mr. Dylan? Wait, shouldn't you be taking notes?"

"Pu-purge fluids?" I said, thinking of the mysterious yellow liquid that insisted on randomly dripping out of my mouth.

Dad slapped me on the shoulder, jolting a fart of my own to wiggle out of me, and said, "Don't worry, this kid's memory is damn-near supernatural."

The anthropologist sighed. "I would prefer you did not use such language in my presence, Mr. Max."

"Um—"

"*Supernatural* implies something unexplainable, which implies *laziness*. Everything has an explanation if you know how to search for it. People place the supernatural label on things they simply don't feel like investigating, and such carelessness is not welcomed here. Do we understand each other?"

"Uh, yes," Dad said. "I'm sorry, I didn't mean—"

"Quite okay, Mr. Max! Now that we are on the same page, allow me to continue." The anthropologist directed our attention to a corpse that looked more asleep than dead. She explained that human decomposition consisted of four stages. "Although," she said, a little annoyed, "walk into a forensic convention and expect to have a difficult time getting anybody to agree on the exact terminology of these stages, and sometimes—if they want to be really frustrating—they'll argue about the *number* of stages. Some professionals insist on five, even *six* stages, which I view as a perfect example of stereotypical American exorbitance. Four is an appropriate number of stages. Anything beyond four is—if you'll pardon the morbid pun—overkill."

"Nice," Dad said.

"Thank you, Mr. Max. I appreciate the compliment. Guests seldom appreciate my jokes, and that is because they are cowards."

MAGGOTS SCREAMING!

"What are the stages?" I asked, somehow the only one who remembered why we were here in the first place.

"Right! The stages!" She nodded at the caged corpse at our feet. "As you'll notice, the specimen before us hardly looks deceased. Dress him up in pajamas and slip him in bed and you might never notice the truth. Well, *I* would notice, but that is because I am not a complete imbecile. *Anyway*, this particular stage of decomposition is the first stage, the *freshest* stage. When the person first dies and the body begins its journey of breaking down its organic material. This stage is called *autolysis*, although you'll encounter plenty of simple-minded anthropologists who have settled on labeling it *fresh*. Don't you find that a little . . . cringeworthy, though? I certainly do. *Autolysis,* now at least there's some respect in a name like that. But *fresh*? What is this? *Subway*?"

Doctor Winzenread paused and waited for one of us to answer.

"Uh, no?" Dad said.

"Correct!" She clapped. "This is definitely not Subway. In fact, if we were to set up a condiment display and offer to prepare long rolls split lengthwise packed with various meats, we would not be Subway, because that is a trademarked name and nobody here has the budget to pay the franchising fees required to grant us the right to operate a business with that title. We would instead have to come up with an original name that has nothing to do with Subway. Something like Body Farm Hoagies, or . . . Carrion Carry-Out? I do not know. I am merely spitballing here. Besides, this is all a rather big hypothetical situation we are finding ourselves in here, considering no health inspector would ever consider approving our facility for sandwich operations. And that is because health inspectors are—"

"—Cowards?" Dad said.

The anthropologist blushed. "Yes, exactly that!" She stared at Dad without saying anything long enough to

135

make both of us uncomfortable, then continued our tour to a corpse with a familiar fat stomach. "Now, the next stage of decomposition is probably the most universally-agreed upon name, and that is the *bloat* stage. I do not think I need to get into a detailed explanation here, as it's pretty self-explanatory. All the gases found in a human body begin excreting as tissues are self-digested, causing . . . well, a rather obvious *bloating* to occur. Actually, quite a few neat tricks begin popping up around this stage, as you can see from the specimen before us. Bloat is when we will first notice maggots hatching, along with the awesome arrival of purge fluids and skin slippage."

"Skin slippage?" I asked, subconsciously hiding my hands behind my back.

"How do you get the goddamn bugs to leave you alone?" Dad said, swiping around a cloud of flies forming over his head. "Seems like there oughta be a way to stop 'em from . . . hatching eggs and shit in you like that." We were all studying the multiple sheets of maggots writhing on the bloated corpse. His face, bellybutton, and genitals were all covered with them. Wherever there was some kind of orifice. I thought about the hole in my arm from where Comrade had bit me. I hadn't looked at it since putting on a jacket at Dad's house. I was terrified of what I would find once I removed the disguise.

Doctor Winzenread appeared genuinely depressed by the question. "But, Mr. Max, why would anyone want to *stop* them from such a beautiful act of nature? This is what they do. This is what they were *designed* to do, just as *we* were designed to be eaten by them. It is the order of the universe."

"Oh, yeah, I get that," Dad said, sounding doubtful, "but I was wondering, like what if you wanted to get rid of them, anyway? I think that's one of the questions my son has to answer for his project. Ain't that right, Dylan?"

"Uh," I said.

The anthropologist grimaced. "This school of yours

sounds more and more horrible by the minute. But, I suppose, if you really needed to kill a group of maggots—which, by the way, is called a *wriggling*—pouring boiling water over them is a surefire way to get the job done. Salt also works pretty well. *However,* I cannot recommend ever trying this yourself, unless it becomes absolutely necessary, although I cannot fathom how such a situation would arise. Maggots are wonderful creatures. They're also *babies,* in case you need to be reminded. Fly larvae. The beginning of an exciting life. They mean nobody any harm. All they wish to do is feed until they are strong enough to continue their metamorphosis—which, I might add, is what we are all trying to do, is it not?"

"Yeah," Dad said, "we know—"

"You ever hear of maggot therapy, Mr. Max?" She glanced down at me, somehow knowing I would take particular interest. "Mr. Dylan?"

"Maggot . . . therapy?" I said, trying to make sense of the phrase. I imagined one maggot sitting on a comfortable recliner, legs crossed, taking notes while listening to another, depressed maggot cry about its mother while sprawled out on a tiny maggot-sized couch. Surely that couldn't have been what she was talking about, but *what if?*

"It's a form of healing," she said. "Considered primitive by most cultures nowadays, but I've heard tell of some societies continuing to practice it. Personally I think it's pretty neat, and the only reason it's fallen by the wayside is because, statistically, modern Homo sapiens are cowards."

"What . . . what is it?" Dad asked, stealing the question from my lips before it could fully form.

"Well, maggots can't properly digest living things, and sometimes this proves helpful when necrotic flesh needs to be cleaned off of soft-tissue wounds. Once they get what they're after, they move on, leaving the rest of you unbothered."

"Unless all of you is dead," I said, unable to stop myself.

"Exactly," she said, nodding at the bloated corpse. "Then they'll just keep feasting until there's nothing left." She clapped her hands and led us deeper into the field, toward another caged corpse. "If the specimen we saw was in the bloat stage—which he definitely was, as you could tell from how, well, bloated he looked—then the next stage involves all of those gases and liquids and fats finally purging from the body. This is stage three, which we tend to label as *active decay*."

"Active—"

"—*decay*, yes," she said. "It's everything inside the body further breaking down, this time at a more advanced level. Things really get cooking around here, everything except for hair and bone beginning to slowly liquify. Skin blackens. It's really cool stuff." She nodded at the new corpse at our feet.

If the previous example of bloating had resembled a blown-up balloon, then this next specimen was that same balloon after someone had popped it with a pin. The body had *deflated*. Flattened, almost. The chest was caved in and bones poked out of its deteriorating flesh. Before coming to this farm, I had seen dead bodies. You and the rest of your doppelgänger family had made sure of that. But what you hadn't prepared me for was what would eventually happen to you—no, not just *you*. What would happen to *me*. Because I was decomposing right along with you, wasn't I? We were in this together, and it didn't appear either of us had much choice in the matter. This was our shared fate, if we didn't figure out a way to stop it in time.

"When does this happen?" I asked.

The anthropologist seemed confused at first, not expecting the question. "When does—this stage happen?"

I nodded.

"It typically takes a couple weeks, maybe a month, for the liquefying to begin."

A month. That didn't sound so bad. We were in the second stage already—*bloat*—so surely we could crack the case before progressing into the next stage. There was plenty of time.

"Wait," Dad said, and we both looked up at him, forgetting he was here. "How long does it take for . . . uh, the other stage? How much time passes between stage one and two?"

I understood immediately why he'd asked the question. A new fear sprouted inside me.

"I would say there's a good three to five days before bloating becomes noticeable."

Three to five days? For us, everything had started *last night,* and we were already on stage two.

As if reading my mind, the anthropologist added, "Sometimes decomposition can be sped up or delayed depending on the weather."

"Could a body start bloating within twenty-four hours?" Dad asked.

She shrugged. "It's not likely. I don't think I've ever seen it happen or read about it occurring so soon. Bodies *do* tend to decompose faster under hotter elements, *but—*"

"You mean like Texas," Dad said.

"Yes, indeed, Mr. Max. I've worked in many different states and countries, and Texas by far exhibits the most extreme heat. In fact, sometimes if the remains are left out with direct prolonged contact with the sun, the final stage of decomposition—skeletonization—fails to occur. Instead the body will enter an *alternative* stage. Would any of you like to guess what stage that might be?"

Dad and I stared at her through our big sunglasses, too afraid to respond.

"Mummification!" Doctor Winzenread said, startling us with another clapping of her hands.

"What do you—what are you talking about?" Dad said. "Mummies?"

The anthropologist was giddier than anybody I'd ever

encountered before. "Oh, I'm sorry, Mr. Max, did you think they only existed in movies?"

"No, I just . . . "

"Mummification is not as uncommon as you might think. Come, fellas, and I will show you!"

She led us to a clearing in the field where there were no trees around to offer shade. A single body waited for us in the middle of the opening, vertical instead of horizontal. It took me a moment to realize how it was upright, then I paid better attention to the lower half of the body. It was buried up to its stomach in dirt. The skin was intact, but dried out, making it look like someone had dressed the corpse in a suit of old leather. Its mouth hung wide open, as if caught in an infinite scream. Without the context of the body farm, the specimen might've passed for somebody's bizarre art project. A sculpture of some kind.

"It's screaming," I said, thinking about you at Dad's house, wondering if you were doing the same.

"It sure looks like it, doesn't it?" Doctor Winzenread said, clapping me on the back. "That's what skin shrinkage will do to a person. The same reason it always looks like your hair and fingernails are growing after you die. Everything else shrinks."

The way she'd phrased that—after *you* die—would've probably sent a chill down my spine, were I capable of experiencing chills down my spine.

"This is one creepy-ass lookin' mummy," Dad said, and I had to agree with that. The corpse did not in any way look like how mummies are usually represented in media.

One time, when I was younger, Dad wrapped my entire body with toilet paper. I'm talking *head to toe*. Leaving enough room at my eyes so I could see and my mouth so I could breathe. It wasn't Halloween or anything like that. Just a day I had off from school and a day he had off from work. Only the two of us were at the house. Mom was working a shift at her job. I don't remember what job it was back then. She's had so many over the years. But anyway.

He thought it'd be a funny idea to turn me into a mummy, and I agreed. Once it was all finished, he spun me around in front of the mirror and exclaimed, "Voila! You're a mummy now!" I looked at my reflection for a couple minutes, impressed with my dad's handiwork, then asked him what we were supposed to do. He got real excited, then frowned, and admitted that he wasn't sure, that he hadn't thought much past the idea of turning me into a mummy. Then Mom came home and got mad at Dad for wasting several rolls of toilet paper and they spent the rest of the evening yelling at each other while I pretended to read *Captain Underpants* in my bedroom.

Looking at the body farm mummy made me think of that day, which reminded me that somewhere in Corpus my mom was going through the same weird decomposing process we were going through, only she was probably more confused than any of us. After all, at least we were aware of you and the other corpses in our back yard. Not that y'all were much of an explanation. If anything, you only succeeded in further complicating things. It might've been for the best that she had no idea you existed. What would she have done with the information besides panic like the rest of us?

"But, like I said," Doctor Winzenread continued, "mummification is only an alternative final stage, occurring when the remains experiences extreme heat without any protection from the sun. If you come with me over here, I'll show you the proper final stage of decomposition, which should be the most self-explanatory of them all: *skeletonization.*"

She was correct. Nothing further about this stage really needed elaborating. The caged corpse was all bones and nothing else. A skeleton but not like the ones in movies. The bones weren't connected or complete. Everything was falling apart. Everything was disintegrating.

"Will the bones go away, too?" I asked.

"Nothing lasts forever, Mr. Dylan," the anthropologist

said cheerfully. "Bones do decay at a significantly slower pace than the rest of the remains. It also varies. Some break down over the course of several decades. Some last millions of years. But eventually, one way or the other, the earth will collect its debt." She cleared her throat. "Anyway, these are just the specimens we keep protected in cages. How would you like to see some *really* interesting dead people?"

"Uh," Dad said.

To properly study how human beings decompose, Doctor Winzenread explained, the anthropology research facility needed to observe their donations under every possible circumstance a person might meet their end.

"*Donations?*" Dad said, disgusted by the word.

"Well, of course, Mr. Max. How else do you think we've managed to obtain hundreds of cadavers since opening our doors in two thousand eight? Many people around this area sign up to have their bodies donated upon death. They've come to the correct conclusion that rotting in an overpriced coffin benefits nobody except for huckster funeral directors. But when you are taken here, to our facility, we treat you with respect. It's one of the few ways a person can continue being useful after they cease to live. Because now you are a part of real, genuine science. You are helping us learn and discover new truths about the world every day. And, at the end, your final *final* remains will be absorbed back into the soil, anyway, only not with some obnoxious *box* getting in the way. It will be you and the dirt, as it was always meant to be." She snapped her fingers, like she remembered one last detail. "If you want, after we're finished with our little tour here, I can show you the paperwork for donating, if either of you were interested. Mr. Dylan, normally we don't allow children to fill it out, but seeing as your father is here, I don't see why we couldn't make an exception provided he grants us his permission."

"Uh," Dad said, "I'll have to ask his mother."

The anthropologist frowned. "Are you married, Mr. Max?"

"No. Not, uh, not anymore."

This seemed to please her.

We explored deeper into the farm. None of us bothered slapping away the insects. It was already understood that they'd keep coming no matter what we did. Their desire to screw with us was far stronger than our desire to remain unscrewed. And, besides, considering the last twenty-four hours, we'd grown plenty accustomed to bugs landing on our faces. What were a couple hundred more?

As promised, the next bodies she showed us were exposed to the elements, and—as a result—missing limbs and other sections of the body.

"Vultures," Doctor Winzenread told us. "They pick away at everything out here. Scatter the bodies all over the place. Without the many monitors recording the premises twenty-four-seven, we'd probably never know where anything is."

Some of the bodies were sprawled out in the grass and dirt like how anybody would imagine normal bodies to be presented, but others were displayed a bit more creatively. One specimen was half-submerged in a manmade pond. Several were wrapped in plastic bags. Another was locked in the trunk of an old car. Rust had practically consumed the outside paint. Its tires were hidden by wildflowers that had grown against it. There weren't any tire tracks anywhere near the car, either. It must've been parked here for a long time.

"Wait a second," Dad said. "Why is it locked?"

"Excuse me?" the anthropologist said.

"You said the trunk is locked?"

"Yes, of course it's locked."

"But . . . why? Is there any threat of the body . . . somehow . . . I don't know . . . escaping?"

She looked at Dad like he was an absolute lunatic. "Mr. Max, all trunks lock when you close them. It is an automatic function. It is no more of a choice than getting wet after twisting the shower knob. That is simply what happens."

"Oh, okay," Dad said.

"But why the trunk?" I asked, feeling stupid for not being able to figure it out.

"Because, Mr. Dylan, that is where homicide victims are often discovered."

Another body we came upon sat under a tree, back leaning against the bark. It appeared to be a man in the fresh stage of decomposition. Unlike most of the other corpses we had seen, this one was dressed. He wore a green fedora, a *Boondock Saints* T-shirt, cargo shorts, and crocs with socks on.

Someone had propped a small cardboard sign in his lap that read: I'M A PIECE OF SHIT.

"All right, hold on," Dad said. "What's going on with this guy?"

"Oh, him?" Doctor Winzenread said. "That's Zach. He's terrible."

"What do you mean?"

She shrugged. "The sign is rather self-explanatory, I thought. He's a piece of shit."

"But . . . he's dead?"

"Even the dead can suck, Mr. Max." Then, in a whisper: "Actually, we're conducting a new experiment that I devised several weeks ago. Do humans decompose differently if they are constantly insulted and ridiculed?"

"You mean, after they've died?" Dad said.

"Yes, of course, silly!" The anthropologist nudged Dad against the shoulder. "It's not like we can decompose while we're *alive*. Although, imagine the possibilities I could explore . . . the knowledge I could discover, simply by *asking* a specimen a question and letting them *answer* me with *language*. It might not be as fun as watching their decaying remains shift over the course of several months, but who said science was always fun?"

"Is that possible, though?" Dad asked.

"Is *what* possible, Mr. Max?"

"Could someone . . . you know, decompose while alive?"

" . . . In a way, yes, I suppose they could. If they were suffering from necrosis, maybe."

"Ne-*what*?"

"Ne*crosis*, Mr. Max. The premature death of cells and tissue. The afflicted section begins to rot. Typically caused by burns or black recluse spider bites. Those aren't the only causes, but probably the two most popular, if I had to guess."

"What—what do you do for it?" Dad said. "How do you *fix* it?"

"Necrosis cannot exactly be *cured*. You cannot bring dead tissue back to life. So, the best-case scenario then becomes *cleaning* the area of infection. The necrotic tissue must be *removed,* otherwise nothing will ever properly heal. Remember the maggot therapy I was telling you about earlier?"

"But what if it's the whole body?" Dad said. "What if it isn't just one area?"

The anthropologist frowned. "Then you would no longer be living."

Whatever was going on with us, it was more complicated than necrosis. Maybe a super version of it. I don't know. But nowhere in that description did Doctor Winzenread include any information about additional lookalike bodies rotting together in unison, and I feel if that *was* a part of necrosis it wouldn't have been a detail she'd easily omit. Which prompted my follow-up question.

"Could a body *never* decompose? Like . . . after the person was dead?"

"Ah," she said, nodding, "you're thinking of *embalming*, which is an extraordinarily vile procedure practiced by funeral homes around the nation. A chemical solution is pumped into a cadaver which supposedly preserves the organs and prevents the body from decomposing. It's a *little* more complicated than that, but that's the basic gist." She shivered. "Nothing on this earth upsets me greater than thinking about those hacks. Why would anyone want to disrupt the natural rhythm of the universe? And besides, the process only half-works, anyway."

"What do you mean?" Dad said.

"Funeral homes love to make fake promises, is what I mean!" the anthropologist shouted. "They guarantee their grief-stricken customers that embalming is a permanent service, but in reality? The preservation only lasts long enough for an open-casket funeral. A couple months after they've been buried in the ground, try digging them up again, and you'll see how *fresh* they look!" She took a deep breath, cheeks red with rage. "Some of these—pardon my language—*bozos* will go as far as pretending the act of embalming is required by law, which couldn't be further from the truth. It's all a con. I am telling you right here and now, Mr. Max and Mr. Dylan, never agree to an embalming. In fact, why bother with a cemetery at all? Like I was telling you, up at the office I have plenty of paperwork—"

"Wait," I said, not wanting to hear another sales pitch about donating ourselves to the body farm, "what if they *weren't* embalmed? What if they died and then . . . nothing happened?"

"Yeah, exactly," Dad said. "How would something like that be possible?"

The anthropologist sighed and rubbed the bridge of her nose. "Well, it *wouldn't* be possible. What you're describing is something called *incorruptibility*."

"What the hell is that?" Dad said.

"I am not exactly positive on all the details," she said. "I am a woman of science, and incorruptibility belongs to religion, meaning it is fantastical and not worth my mental or physical energy. But . . . yes, certain religions—I think

MAGGOTS SCREAMING!

Catholics? Protestants? something like that, there's so many of these cults nowadays, who can keep track anymore?—they believe that when a body fails to decompose, or displays a severely delayed decomposition, that might be a sign of incorruptibility, which would lead them to suspect the body belonged to a saint. Again, none of this has ever been scientifically proven. It is merely another scheme out of infinite other schemes the church will use to bamboozle their brainwashed flock into coughing up their hard-earned paychecks."

Our family had never been very religious, although we'd never acted *anti*-religious, either. In Texas everybody believed in God. Some people believed more than others. We never went to church, or prayed, or anything like that. It was understood that somewhere God existed, and they were watching over us. Other kids in my school talked about going to church every Sunday and saying grace before eating meals. I think the most we ever acknowledged God was mindlessly staring at the ONE NATION UNDER GOD INDIVISIBLE decal found on Whataburger drive-thru windows.

"What's up with that one?" Dad asked, pointing at another specimen displayed across the next clearing.

We approached the body. The sex wasn't clear with this one. Based on the information the anthropologist had told us earlier, they were probably somewhere at the end of stage three of decomposition. *Active decay.* For some reason, they had this body propped up in a sitting position on an office chair, leaning forward with their head resting on top of a wooden desk. On the desk was a big desktop monitor, a keyboard, mouse, and several folders of paperwork. Also on the desk, and around it, were several large birds pecking away at the body's remaining flesh. *Vultures.*

"Well," Doctor Winzenread said, "we were curious how the common office worker decays if, in death, they still cannot escape their miserable nine-to-five."

147

"And what did you find out?"

"Not much, to be honest, except that vultures tend to favor them over the other bodies."

Living in Texas, it wasn't uncommon to see these birds circling roadkill, preparing to feast, but I'd never been so close to one before. They were far bigger than I'd ever imagined. We could hear the skin and muscle being slurped off the body's bones. It made me think of people eating ribs at a barbecue buffet, which prompted me to spit out another helping of yellow liquid. *Purge fluid* was what the anthropologist had called it. Might as well have called it *bird* fluid, though, for how fast those vultures spun their bald heads our direction. Their necks were longer than expected, almost like swimming pool noodles. One of them let out a screech, which was followed by the rest of them imitating the noise.

They started moving toward us in short, chaotic hops.

"Uh," Dad said, "what are they doing?"

The anthropologist stepped back. "I . . . do not know."

"Should we run?"

"They usually leave the living alone. It's the dead they want."

"Fuck," Dad said.

We turned around to run, but it was useless. The vultures swooped down on our backs before we had a chance to gain any speed. One moment I was on my feet, and the next I was hitting the grass—hard. Claws dug between my shoulders and beaks investigated the crevices in my neck. The noise they made sounded like someone continuously pulling a lawnmower cord. Blasting it straight in my ear. I tried to roll away from them, but there were too many on me. They had my body pinned to the grass. Somewhere nearby I could hear Dad struggling just as much. They were going to eat us. They were going to peck us clean, oblivious to our gargled screams, and there wasn't a thing either of us could do about it. Because, together, the vultures were stronger than we were. Because Dad and

Maggots Screaming!

I, we were nothing. We were powerless to stop the thing that happened to everybody sooner or later. These vultures eating us would have been as natural as the sun rising and falling.

Except . . . they didn't get a chance, thanks to Doctor Winzenread.

"No violence without my permission!" she screamed, then scooped up two of the birds by their hind legs and swung them against several other vultures still fixated on devouring our rotting flesh. The vultures yelped and tried to fly away. The anthropologist chased after them, still holding two of the vultures by their legs, swinging them as awkward weapons. "This is a place of science! If you cannot conduct yourself professionally, then there is no room for you here!"

Later, once she'd calmed down, she returned to the scene of the crime and helped both of us up.

"I apologize for what just occurred," she said. "Usually the vultures are far more behaved."

"It's okay," Dad said. "It happens."

She raised her eyebrow and leaned forward, lips twisted in a repulsive grin. "It does?"

"Sure. Sometimes. I guess."

"Interesting," she said. "Very interesting."

On the ride back to the anthropology facility, Doctor Winzenread asked if she'd answered all of the questions I had for my summer school project.

"Yes," I said, freaked out about the vulture attack, "thank you."

"Not all of them," Dad said, shaking his head. "I think there was one more."

"Oh? And what's that, Mr. Max?"

"Have you ever . . . like . . . I don't know, heard about someone finding a corpse that looked exactly like them?"

149

"Are you referring to a facsimile? A *doppelgänger*?"

"I don't know. Maybe?"

"And you're asking if someone's ever discovered their own doppelgänger, *already* deceased?"

"Yeah, I guess so."

The anthropologist took an alarmingly long time to respond, then said, "No. That sounds crazy."

The anthropologist tried convincing us to join her for dinner afterward, but Dad was smart enough to come up with a lie about having to get me to Mom's house. She and Candy—or, *Ms. Candace*—told us goodbye, welcoming us back any time, and the three of us headed toward the truck. Before starting the engine, Andy grinned and held out his finger to Dad's nose.

"Dude, smell this," he said.

Dad paused, then said, "I can't smell anything."

"What? Seriously?" Andy sniffed his finger and shook his head, confused. "You can't smell that?"

"What the hell is it you expect me to smell?"

"Candy."

"*What* candy?"

"*Candy* Candy," Andy said, waiting for us to get the joke.

Dad grimaced. "Are you serious?"

"Thanks for distracting the boss so long, man," Andy said. "I really appreciate that."

"You're disgusting."

"Disgusting and in love!"

"What are you talking about?" I asked, and an uncomfortable silence followed.

"Y'all want to learn a little trick?" Andy said. "Next time you get the opportunity to finger a woman, quietly hum the theme song from *Beverly Hills Cop*—'Axel F'?—and move your fingers to the beat. Never fails to make 'em squirt."

"Can . . . can we please go?" Dad said.

Finally Andy coughed and started the truck, then pulled out of the parking lot and onto the road. "Oh yeah," he said after a while, "I got y'all a little present, too."

He shifted and wrestled out a plastic bottle of pink liquid from his front pocket. Dad took it from him, examining the label. "How did you get this?"

"Well, I fuckin' stole it, obviously."

"What is it?" I said, taking the bottle from Dad.

The label read: **EMBALMER? I HARDLY KNOW HER!**

"Is this . . . ?"

"Embalming fluid, baby!" Andy said. "It might be just the shit y'all need."

"And you found it back . . . *there*?" Dad asked.

Andy chuckled. "Shit, where else? Taco Bell? Speaking of, that sounds pretty good . . . y'all care if I make a quick stop?"

"That doctor went on the longest rant at the farm about how much she hates this shit," Dad said.

"Maybe they gotta have a couple bottles laying around, for liability purposes or something."

"Liability purposes?" Dad said, unconvinced.

"Who knows?" Andy shrugged. "At least I was able to get it."

"What are we supposed to do with it, though?"

"Don't you know anything? It's *embalming fluid*. What do you *think*?"

"I know what it is," Dad said. "But I don't know how to use it. Do you?"

Andy blew a cloud of smoke out the truck window and shook his head. "No, but that's why the internet exists. You want to embalm someone? Search that shit up. On a secure browser, obviously. Eat my entire asshole, *Google Chrome*."

"Dad," I said, resting the bottle of embalming fluid between my legs, "can you call Mom and see if she's okay?"

"Yeah, good idea, I was planning on it anyway."

He took out his cell phone and called, but it went to voicemail.

"What about Miguel?" Andy said. "Ain't he the one who updated you last time?"

Dad hesitated, then sighed and dialed a new number. Waited.

No answer.

"They must be inside the hospital," Dad said. "He already told me there wasn't much of a signal."

"That's weird," Andy said. "You'd think they'd have, like, WiFi and shit in there, right?"

"I don't know, man. That's what he told us."

Andy nudged me. "And you heard this, too?"

"What?" I said.

"Do you not believe me?" Dad asked, incredulous.

"I just want to know if he also heard it," Andy said. "What's the problem with that? I'm not allowed to ask him questions?"

"Why would I make it up?"

"Who said you made it up?"

"That's what you're implying," Dad said, "and you know it."

"Well?" Andy elbowed me again. "Did you hear Miguel say all this or not?"

"Yes," I said. "I heard him."

"There. That wasn't too hard, was it?" Andy said. "I drive y'all down here, steal goddamn embalming fluid and everything, I think the least y'all can do is answer my questions when I ask them, right? Right? Now does anyone want Taco Bell or not?"

"We're not hungry," Dad said, answering for both of us.

"Well, then suit yourself." Andy turned into the drive-thru. "I'm about to go nuts on this value menu, y'all. Just you fuckin' watch."

Maggots Screaming!

By the time we made it back to Dad's house the sun was already down. We stumbled inside with hardly any more information than when we'd left earlier that afternoon, except now we had embalming fluid and Taco Bell, which some would argue were the same thing. The back door was wide open. Andy explained he had opened it before we left, to give Comrade the freedom to pee whenever she needed to go.

"Plus," he added, "maybe y'all can't smell what it's like in here, but trust me, this shit *reeks*. A nice airing out was exactly what you needed."

But Dad wasn't too concerned about the smell. "Do you have any idea how much AC was wasted because of this?"

"Oh, would you relax?" Andy laughed, taking a bite out of his chalupa. Lettuce sprinkled down to the floor, and Comrade was on top of it within seconds.

I was the first one to notice that she was covered in dirt. "She's filthy," I said.

Andy inspected her, then shrugged. "Probably out there digging holes again. You know how she likes to scavenge."

A silence filled the kitchen, as realization hit all three of us at the same time.

Digging holes . . .

We ran into the yard. It was dark out, yes, but the light from the kitchen blasting through the open door was bright enough for us to see what we'd already feared had happened.

Comrade had dug up the garden grave.

And staring at us, from the dirt, were the three of you.

A little chewed from Andy's dog, and—like Dad and I— bloated beyond belief. Swarms of flies were partying down there with you. And the eggs they'd planted in you had already hatched.

It was like you had been waiting for us to get home, knowing we would bring you inside.

Knowing we couldn't get rid of you, no matter how hard we tried.

MAGGOTS SCREAM.

I didn't know that until I started decomposing. Maybe it's not a commonly known fact, but it's true all the same.

Maggots scream.

It's hard to hear unless you get really close to them. That's what I had to do. I don't know why I did it, not exactly. Something about them was calling to me.

Later, once we'd gotten you and the other bodies out of the garden grave and into the living room, Dad made me go into the bathroom to wash up a little bit, and it was in there that I finally took off my jacket and properly examined the wound on my arm again.

I hadn't paid any attention to it since we left for the body farm earlier that evening. My first thought was, *Oh, it's healing!* quickly followed by, *No, wait.* Because that new layer of discolored white skin over the wound wasn't a layer of skin at all. And if you've paid attention to the first half of this story, I'm sure you can already guess what it was.

Maggots.

They'd packed themselves into my dog bite until they were bursting out of the hole. Falling out of my arm and splattering at my feet. My wound had reached maximum capacity.

A normal person might have panicked and tried washing them out, like I'd done the last time this started happening. But I was beyond the point of normalcy. Vultures had attacked me at a body farm and we'd removed our lookalike corpses from a grave for the *second time* in one weekend. There was nothing normal about anything anymore.

157

So I did the only thing that made sense, and I lifted my arm and lowered my head so my ear was facing the wound and I closed my eyes and submerged myself into a deep state of concentration, and what I heard were the screams of a hundred, a thousand, infinite maggots wriggling against each other as they feasted on a buffet of necrotic tissue.

Wet, *sticky* screams.

Screams that sounded like a casserole baking in the oven.

Screams that sounded like milk pouring over Rice Krispies.

Screams that sounded like babies begging for their mothers, for their fathers.

Am I their father? Am I their mother? I wondered in one insane moment, but the moment kept stretching itself, like elastic, and the question repeated in my head over and over—an echo pinballing around a black hole, traveling through all of time simultaneously. I desperately wanted to protect these maggots at all costs—because, like it or not, they belonged to me. They were my responsibility. Once they screamed for you, that was it. They'd never trust anyone else again.

We tried searching online for how to embalm ourselves, but all the guides sounded overly complicated. Most articles said we'd need a machine specifically designed for embalming, which we did not have, plus we'd have to make incisions at "vein breaking points"—whatever that meant—and insert the fluid through special arteries. It became obvious very quickly the process wouldn't be as simple as "swiping a bottle of embalming fluid from a body farm" and that we were all in way over our heads.

"This is some bullshit, man," Andy said, squinting at a wikiHow article on his laptop titled "How to Embalm (with Pictures)," then grunted and slammed it shut. "More instructions than a goddamn IKEA bookshelf."

"What does it matter, anyway?" Dad said. "As long as it's *in* our bodies, right?"

Without waiting on a response, he took off for a cabinet across the kitchen and pulled out two shot glasses layered in dust.

"I don't think drinking it is the way to go here, pardner," Andy said, although there was something in his tone that seemed to suggest he wanted nothing more than to watch us drink it. A sick curiosity to know what would occur. He wasn't the only one in the kitchen feeling that way.

Dad washed out the shot glasses and set them on the table. "Just think about it a second, would you?" Dad said, as the three of us stared at the experiment-waiting-to-happen. "Regardless of whether it enters through the vein or down our throats . . . it's all going the same place, right? It's going inside us. Wouldn't it still accomplish the same thing?"

"Then why wouldn't they always drink it, if that were the case?"

"Because," Dad said, tapping his forehead like a man who believed he was far more brilliant than he was, "most dead people can't drink liquids."

"And you can?" Andy said.

"Of course we can!" Dad gripped my shoulder. "You can drink, can't you?"

"We couldn't drink water earlier," I said.

"Well that's different. Water's bullshit."

"Oh."

I couldn't remember the last time I'd successfully drank something. Time seems to operate differently when you are dead. Everything moves like it has a slow internet connection. Slowly buffering, and periodically needing to reboot.

"See?" Dad said to Andy. "He can drink. We both can. We can drink just fine."

He unscrewed the cap off the bottle of embalming fluid and poured each glass full to the brim. The liquid was thick and pink, like Pepto-Bismol. Dad pushed one toward me and picked up the other, then said, "I knew you and I would share a shot together one day, but I figured it wouldn't be until your sixteenth birthday, and—if I had to guess—we would've been drinking Jack Daniel's . . . not . . . uh . . . this, but hey! At least we're doing something together that doesn't involve watching TV, right? Your mom would be proud."

"Umm," Andy said, and we looked up, waiting for him to finish his thought, but he didn't seem to have anything else to say, so he shrugged and stepped back a little, giving us more room.

"Okay," Dad said. "On the count of three. Ready?"

I held the glass close to my nose, trying to give it a sniff, but my sense of smell hadn't returned—and, spoiler alert, it still hasn't. Later, Andy would tell us the stuff smelled nearly worse than we did. The scent was powerful, impossible to ignore. *But what did it smell like?* we'd ask, and he'd pause, thinking carefully, before saying, *Pickles*. So maybe it was a good thing I couldn't smell it, because there's no way I would have willfully guzzled a pink beverage that smelled like pickles.

Although, to be fair—and, again, this is another spoiler alert—it's not like the embalming fluid *helped us*. Even after the additional shots. One after another. Dad and I sitting across from each other at the kitchen table, sloshing glasses together and saying *Cheers!* while Andy stood against the sink, shaking his head disapprovingly while nibbling on the rest of his Taco Bell. Comrade bouncing around between us, indecisive about whose dinner she wanted to steal the most. In the end, she wasn't able to get her paws on either, and she curled up in the corner of the room facing the wall, which was her way of throwing a dog temper tantrum. She probably wouldn't have been so depressed if she'd known how much food awaited her future. More food than the luckiest, richest dog in the universe.

Of course, that wouldn't come until later.

But not that much later.

Maggots Screaming!

Last year, for science, we had to research and write a report on something that grows in nature. At first we were allowed to pick our own topics, but it quickly became apparent that everybody planned on writing something centered on bluebonnets, since they're the state flower and even the stupidest kid in school already knows a *little bit* about them, so our teacher decided it would only be fair if she devised a list herself and then assigned us which plants to research.

Somehow I ended up with the corpse flower, AKA the *Amorphophallus titanum,* rooted from the Greek words for "shapeless", "penis", and "huge". Yeah, I also giggled when I discovered that. I couldn't believe the school was letting me write a report about something with the word "penis" in its name. Although, in retrospect, maybe the whole thing had been a trick, because suddenly I went from not caring in the slightest about the project to finding myself fully invested in learning everything I could about this plant—which is nicknamed "the corpse flower" due to the rotting dead body odor it emits.

In order for the corpse flower to pollinate, it has to have—at the base of the spadix—a band of cream male flowers above a ring of the larger female flowers. When they are ready, the spadix emits this *rotting dead bodies* smell to attract nearby insects. Mostly large carrion beetles easily lured by the delectable stank of decaying flesh, as well as other nocturnal insects that usually lay eggs in rotting meat. Insects that neither of us are strangers to at this point, right? The kind of insects we might as well consider *family*, if we're being honest. The only true family we have left, anyway.

So much about this flower is unknown, especially what compounds are present in creating its iconic death odor. Sulfurous chemicals—the chemicals responsible for the smell of rotten eggs—are definitely there, as well as the two compounds cadaverine and putrescine, which are produced during the breaking down of flesh.

Let me say that again, in case you're having a little trouble hearing.

The.

Breaking.

Down.

Of.

Flesh.

Does that not also define *autolysis*, AKA the first stage of decomposition?

And, although they're mostly found in Sumatra, that doesn't mean people haven't tried growing them in the United States. Even in Texas. I remember, while researching corpse flowers, reading about one that had recently bloomed at the Moody Gardens Rainforest Pyramid in Galveston. They'd named the flower Morticia. Although I'd missed the livestream by a couple years, the website had a time lapse video of the blooming available, and I remember sitting in front of the school computer watching it over and over, the whole clip lasting barely over a minute. The way it slowly peeled apart, like a jaw unhinging. The word that came to mind then and the word that comes to mind now is the same:

Majestic.

So tell me something, then.

If birds are known to feast on these corpse flowers and later scatter their seeds, is it really *that* insane to imagine a few of these seeds landing in our back yard? Not just our back yard but *right in the same section* my mom had planted her garden? Improbable, maybe, but *impossible*? And, since so much is unknown about these things, who's to say what might happen if corpse flower seeds mixed with certain soil, or certain *other* plants? Nobody knows anything, not really. But thinking about these corpse flowers and thinking about *you* and the rest of your dead family in that garden grave, thinking about the way Dad and I reeked like dead rotting meat despite being alive—or, at least, *somewhat* alive—I couldn't help but wonder if there was something to this theory.

Because if not *this,* then what else?

What else could have possibly caused this?

That's what I'm asking you, yes, but it's also what I asked my dad.

This was a few hours after we'd finished off the pink bottle together. Andy was complaining about the way we all smelled, and at some point he used the phrase "rotting meat" and suddenly all I could think about was the science report I'd written about corpse flowers.

"What if?" I said, after spitting out year-old school research at them. "What if that's the thing causing all of this?"

"What if birds scattered *corpse flower* seeds in our back yard?" Dad said, the tone in his voice suggesting he was waiting on a punch line that didn't exist.

"Yeah," I said, nodding, excited. "Doesn't it make *sense*?"

And he'd looked at me for a long time, not saying anything, before sighing and taking away my shot glass. "Boy," he finally replied, "I think you've gone and gotten your ass drunk off embalming fluid."

"Besides," Dad said, "I already know what caused this, and it wasn't no corpse flower bullshit."

"Oh, is that so?" Andy said, cracking open another of Dad's beers. "You mind enlightening us so we can all stop wasting our fuckin' time, then?"

"Of course." Dad tried to crack his knuckles, but only succeeded in repositioning the loose skin around his fingers. Everybody grimaced and he hid his hands under the kitchen table, embarrassed. Then he continued to tell us about the "ecosystem" he accidentally created last summer, which would've been his first summer alone after the divorce.

"The fuck you talkin' about?" Andy asked, cigarette dangling from his mouth. "What *eco*system?"

"Well, if you'd give me a chance to explain, I'd tell you."

"Okay, shit, pardon me. Please, by all means . . . "

Dad hesitated, waiting to see if Andy was going to interrupt him again, then went on to explain that really, if we wanted to get technical, all this shit was the HOA's fault. "Personally," he said, "I don't understand what the big goddamn deal is with having a short lawn. Everybody's so *precious* about having the best-looking yard. Who cares? What does it matter? Let it grow! It's *Mother Nature!* The planet's worked perfectly fine for the last billion and a half years with grass being able to grow as high as it wants."

"I think the planet's older than a billion and a half years," I said. "I think it's almost five billion."

"Okay, so then five billion. That further proves my point."

"Well, actually," Andy said, "the number's irrelevant, if you accept the simulation theory."

"Oh here we fucking go."

They were already moving too fast for me to catch up. "What's the sim . . . sim . . . "

"The simulation theory!" Andy said. "It's like *The Matrix*, but with less trench coats."

"I don't . . . "

"The planet's not real, basically," Andy said. "In fact, *none* of this bullshit's real. It's all computer trickery. An artificial simulation. This so-called *Earth* might be zero days old, you know what I mean? Memories are programmed. Yesterday? Never fucking happened." He cleared his throat, took another drag of his cigarette. "Assuming, again, y'all buy into that shit. Personally? I don't know, man. I just don't know. But it certainly makes you *think,* don't it? Which, in retrospect, might be the most dangerous trap of them all."

Dad held up the empty bottle of embalming fluid. "Did you sneak a shot of this, too? Because you sound insane. Like, more than usual, I mean."

"Insane with the truth, brother," Andy said, and winked.

"What happened with the HOA?" I asked, afraid we'd never get back on topic with Andy present.

"The HOA?" Dad said. "I'll tell you what happened with the goddamn HOA."

"Okay," I said, when he didn't continue after half a minute.

Dad glanced around the room like he'd forgotten where he was, then said, "So there I was, right? Minding my own goddamn business. Not bothering anybody whatsoever—or so I *thought*, until I get this email from the HOA with a picture of my front yard, telling me some stupid crap like my grass is too tall and it's upsetting my neighbors, and if I don't cut it they're gonna fine me every month until I do. Imagine being so fragile that tall grass upsets you! What a goddamn joke, man. Some people, they ain't got no lives, I'm telling you."

"You ever read Bentley Little?" Andy asked. "He has this book—*The Association*, I think? Read that shit and you'll never live anywhere near where an HOA's in charge again. They're some evil-ass motherfuckers, man. No doubt."

"So what happened?" I asked, confused why I'd never heard anything about this before. It was true I no longer lived there, but I still *visited* every other weekend.

"What happened?" Dad said. "What happened was I mowed the yard."

"Gotta say." Andy popped open another beer and foam slowly erupted from the top. "This story is pretty goddamn thrilling."

"Well, what happened *after* I mowed is when it gets more interesting."

"Maybe you should've skipped to that to begin with."

165

"*Any*way," Dad said, "after I finished up, I did what I always do, and dumped all the pulverized grass into a small trash can. But it was almost a week until garbage day, meaning I couldn't drag it out to the curb yet, so I said screw it, left it on the side of the house next to our fence gate, figured I'd come get it in a couple days. Except, come garbage day, I completely blanked on the small trash can full of grass. And then it rained for, like, five days straight. Directly into that can jam-packed with cut grass. And I forgot about it some more, giving plenty of time for all that rainwater to fully soak in. When I finally *did* remember the trash can, it was because of the smell. I'll never forget that smell. You have no idea."

Andy motioned around the kitchen. "Uh, I think maybe I do have some idea, actually . . . "

Dad held up his index, middle, and ring fingers. "Three words: rotting, primordial ooze."

I wanted to ask him what *primordial* meant but he seemed to be too deep in the zone to be interrupted. Whatever it was, it sounded terrifying.

He continued: "The kind of smell that makes you start gagging immediately. I'd never smelled anything like it before in my life. To get close, I had to first go inside and wrap a bandana around my nose and mouth."

"Oh, shit," Andy said, "that's a great idea. Do you still have it?"

"Do I have what?"

"The bandana."

Dad gestured over at a kitchen drawer.

Andy eagerly pulled the drawer open and scavenged through its contents. "Got it!" he said, excited, and held up an old red bandana. Then he brought it closer to his face and grimaced. "Goddammit, it smells *just like* you guys. You've contaminated everything inside this house." He dropped the bandana in the drawer and slammed it shut with his hip.

"What did the can look like, Dad?" I asked.

Maggots Screaming!

"Well, it was the oddest thing," he said. "Because, if you remember, the bottom of that specific trash can has a crack along the bottom, meaning you'd think all the water would have . . . you know, *drained* out. Except, I guess all the grass, bunched up like that, it created this sort of wall, this *sponge* that soaked all the rain up, filling the can to the brim with this dirty, brown water. But that wasn't even the most disgusting part, right? No. Because *also* in this can, on top of the waterlogged grass, were all these *insects*. I'm talking, like, *sowbugs* and *pillbugs* and *maggots* and anything else that, uh, *feeds*. All of them grouped together like they were at church or something. Like they'd established an entire society in my little trash can."

"What did you do?" I asked, trying to disguise how hurt I was feeling while hearing all of this. Why hadn't he ever shown me? I would have *loved* to see it.

"My first thought was to drag it out to the curb and let the garbage people take care of it."

"*Garbage* people?" Andy said. "Wow, that's a psychopathic way to describe another human being."

"What are you talking about? That's what they are. Garbage people."

"I think the only garbage person here is you, sir."

"Would you shut up?" Dad said. "Anyway. Two things were wrong with this idea. One, I didn't think the gar—the people who work with the trash company—would empty it into their truck. Don't they have some kinda rule about liquids? And two, I couldn't, uh, pick it up?" At me only, he asked, "You remember that time our washing machine broke mid-cycle, and we had to wrestle all the clothes into a trash bag and take it to the laundromat because they were soaked with soapy water? Remember how much *heavier* the clothes were with all that water in them? Well, it was like that, only instead of clothes it was grass, and a *lot* of it. Filled to the very top. Any time I tried nudging it a little, the stuff would start spilling everywhere, which maybe sounds like a good thing, sure, but let me remind you how much it all *smelled*. I didn't want that shit all over my yard, reeking up the place." He pointed at Andy. "And before you say anything, yes, I already know the current state of things. You don't need to remind me."

"It's really bad, man."

"What do you want me to do about it?"

Andy considered, then shrugged. "I don't honestly know if there *is* a solution beyond nuking the place from orbit."

"Helpful feedback," Dad said. "Thank you."

"Any time."

Dad went on to tell us that since he couldn't move it, he decided to leave it there in his yard for a couple days, let the sun dry it out until the weight loosened a little. "Except," he said, irritated, "the goddamn water only got muddier, *thicker*, and the insects multiplied. The moment you stepped within five feet of the goddamn trash can, flies started swarming your face. Sound familiar?" He gestured vaguely around us at the flying insects I'd almost forgotten had taken over the kitchen. At that point, only Comrade seemed to pay them any attention. We'd lost count of how many of them she'd eaten already. Dad continued: "So, I finally decided fuck it. Wasn't like I had many options at that point, right? I grabbed the can by the edge and started dragging it across the yard, brown muddy bug water splashing on my hands, my shoes . . . it wasn't a pretty sight. At one point, I cut my goddamn hand on the can, a place where the plastic's been cracked from the heat, and I start bleeding everywhere, but do I stop and go inside to take care of my wound? Of course not. I got a job to do and I intend on carrying it out to the very end. I keep pulling the can until I get to my destination. Anyone want to guess where that was?"

Neither of us had to speak the answer to know it was true.

Mom's garden.

He'd dumped the can in Mom's garden.

"Wait," Andy said, blowing a cloud of smoke at the flies, "why would something like that have caused . . . well, you know?"

"Ain't you listening, goddammit?" Dad said. "I *told* you, the stuff in that can, it had turned into something *weird*. It was a goddamn *ecosystem*. Don't you find it a little odd that I unload it there and then—"

"But that doesn't explain why it . . . what? *Replicated* you guys . . . "

"But it does!" Dad said, excited. "Don't you get it? I cut myself. I *bled* into the goddamn can! It had my DNA. It could have used the blood and . . . I don't know! Isn't that how they make clones in movies? All it takes is a small, little itty-bitty speck of a person to make a whole new person. Right? Plus, Dylan came from me, right? He's got my DNA. Who knows what crazy alien shit was in that can? What kinda technology it might've had . . . and plus! Think about this, okay? This happened last year, right? How long do you think it properly takes to grow a human?"

"Uh, nine months," Andy said. "I'm pretty sure that's been heavily documented."

"But that's just a baby. I'm talking about the bodies we found in our garden. They were fully formed, right? Two adults, one kid. Makes sense it'd take a little bit longer than nine months, right? About a year, yeah, that sounds right. Especially if they're growing in some weird ecosystem from another world, or whatever the hell that was exactly I dumped out of the trash can."

"Nah," Andy said, still not buying it. "Because what about Lori, then? Did you forget about her all of a sudden? As far as I know, you and her don't share DNA—not the kind that makes up a person's biology, at least. Unless y'all been brother and sister this whole time. In which case, I got some PornHub videos to show you later that you might enjoy."

Dad settled in his seat, disappointed. "I guess I hadn't thought of that."

"Unless . . . " Andy held up his finger like a great idea had suddenly struck him. "Dylan, block your ears." Then, before I had a chance to comprehend what he told me to do, he said to Dad, "Now, don't get offended by this question or anything, okay? But, back when you and Lori were together . . . did you two ever, you know, fuck during her period? More importantly, did you ever *eat her out* during it? Because I have a theory."

Dad stared at him for nearly a full minute before saying, "I think perhaps it's about time you went home."

Later, after we finally convinced Andy to leave, I said to Dad, "What if both of our ideas are right?" And I could tell from the way he looked at me that he had no idea what I was talking about, so I elaborated: "What if you dumped the ecosystem in the garden, and *then* birds scattered corpse flower seeds in it? What if, combined, that's what it takes to grow some bodies? What if we both did it, together?"

What if we're both responsible? I wanted to ask, but didn't.

With Andy gone, it was just the two of us again. Well, I guess, to be more accurate, the *five* of us. Me, Dad, plus you, Dead Dad, and Dead Mom. The whole dang family, in the living room together, watching television. Plus Comrade, since Andy had left her here. Didn't ask if we would babysit her or anything. Assumed we didn't have a problem with her staying—which we didn't, of course. Comrade is the best dog I've ever known. I often wished she had always lived with us. She spent most of her time that evening in the kitchen, smashing her head against the glass of the back door in an attempt to kill flies and eat their corpses. She was having the time of her life.

MAGGOTS SCREAMING!

We were on season six of our annual rewatch of *The Simpsons*. Dad owned the first twenty seasons on DVD. The entire series could be found on streaming websites, but Dad insisted we use discs as much as possible, since he'd paid good money for those first twenty DVD collections. After season twenty, the production company had decided to stop releasing physical media, which pissed Dad off to no end. And me, too, if we're being honest. I love sitting on the floor, legs folded beneath me, flipping through those booklets that come with every boxset. Reading the episode guides. The little jokes they'd managed to squeeze into the artwork.

Plus, most of the DVDs contained special features, like commentaries and deleted scenes and all other types of cool stuff, and Dad and I often went through them all after finishing our annual rewatch of each season. Streaming websites never offered any cool bonus material. Not only that, but they also automatically minimized and fast-forwarded through the credits. Dad said this was because the world had gotten lazier. Nobody was interested in how anything was made anymore, he told me. They just wanted more more more without taking the time to appreciate the creators.

I still remember the day we watched a newer episode on a streaming site and it provided us with the option to skip the introduction, AKA one of the best parts of any *Simpsons* episode. Dad got so mad I thought he was going to throw the remote through the TV. Instead he walked outside and paced around the front yard for a couple minutes, then came inside and drank a shot of whiskey before agreeing to continue the show.

Since we could no longer sleep, and leaving the house seemed pretty risky, we figured marathoning *The Simpsons* would be a good way to pass the time. Without Andy here, the constant talking had died down. What more did Dad and I have to say to each other at that point? Not much. When we talked all we had to say were questions, and nobody had any answers, so why not watch cartoons instead? What *else* was there to do?

Season six, episode six of *The Simpsons* is one of my favorite episodes of all time, so when we finally made it there I was probably as excited as any undead thirteen-year-old boy could possibly be, given the circumstances. It was a Halloween episode—*Treehouse of Horror V*—not *VI*, because the Halloween specials didn't begin until season two. I remember, either last year or the year before, our teacher referencing something related to Roman numerals, and I was the only kid who understood what she meant. For a brief minute, the whole class was impressed, including our teacher. And what did I have to thank for that? *The Simpsons*. But also? My dad. If not for him, would I know what *The Simpsons* was?

Treehouse of Horror V, like all of their Halloween specials, is split into three sections, with two bookends at the beginning and end of the episode. I know you've seen it at least once, since you were there in the living room with us that night, but in case you need a quick refresher, here you go:

It starts with Marge walking out behind a red curtain and waving at the screen. She tries to introduce the show, only to be handed a letter announcing the episode is *so scary* that Congress won't let them broadcast it. As an alternative, Congress suggests playing "the 1947 classic Glenn Ford movie, *200 Miles to Oregon,*" and the screen cuts to an old black-and-white clip of horses dragging carriages in the desert.

Dad and I once tried finding *200 Miles to Oregon* but, after investigating Wikipedia, we concluded it doesn't exist. Glenn Ford was apparently a real actor, but nowhere in his credits is *200 Miles to Oregon* listed. The writers of *The Simpsons* must've made it up. But then what movie did they show us? Like most mysteries, I'll probably never figure it out, and that's okay, because what other choice do I have? I either accept the lack of knowledge or allow it to eat me from the inside out.

And speaking of "inside out," let's continue . . .

MAGGOTS SCREAMING!

The fake *200 Miles to Oregon* movie doesn't last long before Bart somehow intercepts the signal and resumes the legitimate programming, and we get into our first story, which is a parody of *The Shining*, except here it's called "The Shinning" (shh! you want to get sued?), followed by a story where Homer discovers his toaster is a time machine, then it concludes with the school segment about the teachers eating all of their students, which—thanks to this episode—was a real fear of mine during my first couple years of going to school.

The second bookend of this *Treehouse of Horror* begins with Bart waking up to Marge standing above him, offering reassurance that everything we've witnessed has been nothing more than a terrible nightmare. "You're back with your family now, where there's nothing to be afraid of," she comforts him, before adding, "except that *fog* that turns people inside out."

A green gas quickly enters through Bart's window ("stupid cheap weather stripping!") and forces its way into each of the Simpsons, promptly reversing their flesh in one of the most disturbing sequences of animation I've ever witnessed. Even Marge's hair gets turned into weird pink flesh, which has always made me wonder how long her skull really is under all that blue dye.

Inside out, the Simpsons family reserves a period of calm introspection to examine their new bodies, but not *too* long, as music starts playing, and someone or some*thing* offscreen flings top hats and canes toward them, and they're *dancing* and *singing* and despite the fact that their biologies have been forever manipulated, they seem to be having a pretty good time together—including when the family dog digs into Bart's intestines and drags him offstage.

I've watched this episode probably more times than any other episode of *The Simpsons*, but that night it struck a different chord than previous viewings. In the past, I'd always cringed during the fog epilogue. It's disturbing and creepy and all kinds of wrong. Nothing about it is *natural*—or, honestly, *funny*. It's just *scary*. Even with the accompanying song and dance. It's *ghoulish*.

Except when we watched it with you and the other corpses. Something changed. It's hard to describe, but as we all sat together in the living room watching it, as one big undead family, I couldn't help but feel strangely optimistic. Because here was this family, turned completely inside out from a mysterious fog, and what did they do? They didn't sit around complaining about their lives. They didn't constantly ask each other *why do you think the fog turns us inside out?* or *how can we turn ourselves inside in again?* They got up and danced and sang and acted like everything was perfectly fine, and in that brief moment I truly believed everything *was* fine.

If they could continue on, despite their bizarre condition, then why couldn't we?

Of course, the answer is simple.

The Simpsons is a cartoon.

It's not real.

But what about the stuff happening to us? Is that real? How are we supposed to determine what is reality and what is a cartoon? And what if there isn't any difference, after all? What if everything and nothing are simultaneously real and make-believe? And what if discovering the answers to any of these questions doesn't change a darn thing?

At some point in the middle of the night, Dad's phone started ringing, and Mom's face filled the screen. Some photo he'd taken of her from back when they were married. In the picture she's smiling and staring at the photographer—Dad—like she still loves him. This was before they'd had me, and I wonder if she ever looked at him like that once I was alive. Somehow I already know the answer.

MAGGOTS SCREAMING!

I paused the current episode of *The Simpsons* we were on and leaned closer so I could hear her once he finally answered, except there was something wrong with his phone. Every time he tried swiping the screen, nothing happened. It refused to recognize his thumb. He used his other fingers and received the same lackluster result.

"What the fuck?" he said, swiping harder. "*What the fuck?*"

"Why won't it answer?" I asked.

"Does it look like I know, Dylan?"

"But . . . it's Mom! She's calling!"

He looked up from the phone like he wanted to break it over my head. "Would you be quiet and let me think?" The phone had been ringing for a while. Any second it'd go to his voicemail and we'd miss our chance to talk to her. He tried swiping again, failed, then thrust the device out to me. "Here, quick, you try."

I took it from him, but it was no use. The screen didn't recognize me, either. "What's going on?" I said. "Is it broken?"

The phone stopped ringing.

Dad held both his hands out, palms toward him, fingers spread and arched inward. Several minutes passed before he said, "Phones don't respond to dead skin."

"Maybe if I had a cell phone . . . "

"Oh, would you knock it off?" Dad said. "If you had one, we'd be encountering the same issue. It wouldn't change a thing."

"I'm just saying."

"I know what you're saying."

The phone beeped and a NEW VOICEMAIL! notification generated on the screen. We weren't able to navigate to that, either. The whole thing was useless when operated by one of us. Dad took it from me and tossed it on the coffee table, then told me to click PLAY so we could resume *The Simpsons*.

I held the remote out, hesitating. "What do you think she wanted to tell us?"

"I don't know."

"Do you think she's okay?"

"I think she's as okay as we are."

"Oh," I said, then: "Are we okay?"

"I don't think so."

"Do you think she's still in the hospital?"

"I don't know where she is."

"Should we drive down there?" I asked. "To Corpus Christi?"

"It's probably not a good idea."

"Why not?"

"Are you gonna hit PLAY or not?"

"I'm worried about Mom."

"I know you are. I am, too."

"What are we going to do?"

"We're going to watch *The Simpsons* until Andy comes back tomorrow, then we're going to have him unlock my phone so we can listen to the voicemail. I don't know what we'll do after that. I guess it depends on what she has to say."

"Oh," I said, thinking that wasn't the worst plan I'd ever heard. "Okay then."

I clicked PLAY and we resumed our annual *Simpsons* rewatch.

It didn't occur to me until later in the night that neither of us were laughing at the jokes we usually found hilarious. The gags that we often quoted to each other around the house. They felt different. Two dimensional, kinda. Hollow. I guess it's hard to focus on much of anything when you're rotting away to nothing. But then again, I guess you already know that.

Morning came and we weren't close to finishing the series rewatch, so we kept going, because what else were we supposed to do? We couldn't sleep. We couldn't go anywhere. We were stuck until Andy showed up. Stranded on Purgatory Creek.

At noon, he finally called, but of course we couldn't answer it, so it went to voicemail. Then a series of texts from him generated on Dad's screen, none of them saying anything important besides *CALL ME BACK* and *ARE YOU OKAY?*

"What do you think he's doing? Why isn't he here?" I asked, as we stared at the phone neither of us could operate. In addition to flies, the kitchen had recently greeted its share of yellowjackets and wasps. Sometimes they landed on us, but we didn't seem to care that much. If they wanted to hang out, then they could hang out. Who were we to stop them?

"I don't know," Dad said. "Probably chickened out on us or something."

"What are we going to do if he doesn't come back?"

"I guess we'll have to figure this shit out by ourselves. Which, honestly, might be for the best anyway."

"But we need his help to listen to Mom's voicemail."

"I am definitely starting to see the flaws in modern technology." Dad tossed the phone on the coffee table. "You ask me, the future is pretty goddamn retarded."

"Dad," I said, "don't say that word."

"Oh, shut up. What does it matter? We're dead! We can say anything we want."

"I don't know . . . "

He leaned forward, face animated with a new excitement. "You think I care if you start saying shit and fuck and dick? You might as well get them out of your system while we got a chance."

"What?" I said. "Do you think—?"

"—I don't know what I *think*, I just know what I *feel*, and what I feel is . . . fucking nothing. I don't know about you, son. But I imagine a regular person would be scared shitless right about now. Not me, though. Something in my chemistry . . . it's changing. Like this is the new me, you know? Like maybe this is how we go on with life. Undead. A couple of ghouls. So, if you want to curse, why the fuck not, right? Ain't we beyond the boundaries of a normal father-and-son relationship?" He paused, thinking it over. "Okay, that last sentence sounded a little creepy, but you know what I mean. It's not like I'm gonna fuckin' *ground* you, right? You can't ground what ain't alive! And you, baby boy, are no longer alive. And neither am I! So yes, go ahead. Say fuck. Do it. Scream it!"

"I don't really want to," I said, truthful.

"Not even a shit? Or a dick?"

" . . . Maybe later, okay?"

He slumped his shoulders, disappointed. "Yeah, okay. Maybe later."

"Do you think we're going to become skeletons?" I asked.

"What?"

"Skeletons. Like at the farm. The last stage of decomposition."

"Yeah," he said, without much hesitation, "yeah, we probably will."

"Are we gonna be able to move around and talk?"

"Why wouldn't we?"

I thought he might've been joking with me, but he seemed genuinely confused by the question. "Because won't our lungs go away?"

"What? Where would they go?"

"I thought maybe they melted out of you . . . with all the other purge fluid?"

"Please don't say purge fluid," Dad said.

"I thought you said I could say anything I wanted."

"I know, but not that. It's too gross."

"But that's what the lady at the farm called it."

"Yeah," Dad said, "but that lady was nuts."

"She was?"

"Uh, yeah. She thinks she's a wizard."

"A wizard?"

"Didn't you see her little golf cart? She spray-painted THE WIZ on it. What kind of sane person thinks they're a wizard?"

"I thought it was because of her name."

"What are you talking about?"

"Doctor . . . Winzenread?"

Dad stared at me so long without responding I started suspecting something inside him had shut down. Then he said, "Wait, do you need lungs to talk? I thought they were for breathing."

"I don't know," I said. "I don't know what we need."

"Shit, Dylan, don't they teach you health in school?"

"I don't know. I guess so."

"And what have they taught you?"

I tried to think of anything besides corpse flower statistics and failed, so to change the subject I told him his stomach didn't look so fat anymore, which was true.

"Yeah, same with you," he said, and I followed his gaze to my own gut. Or lack of a gut, maybe. I lifted my shirt up and felt around my stomach, which hadn't so much shrunk as *deflated*. The extra skin was there, but it was loose, like I could grab a handful and readjust its positioning if the desire struck.

Inspecting our bodies led to us discovering a copious amount of purge fluid had leaked from our orifices since the last time we'd checked. Trails of slime seemed to follow us around the house. Looking at Dad, *really* looking at him, I determined the only accurate word to describe him was *wet*. And the same word applied to myself. Our inner liquids had spilled everywhere, adding weight to our clothing and sticking everything against our loose skin. Skin so fragile I was convinced most of it would peel off my skeleton if I pulled hard enough. I bounced between wanting to see what that might look like and never, ever wanting to find out.

"Your mom always got on my ass about losing weight," Dad said. "Who would've thought it would be this easy? All this time, all I had to do was decompose. You think maybe we could start some kinda diet program? Get a book published. Schedule regular decay meetups at the local gym. Might be an easy way to get rich. I don't know."

"How would the other people also decompose?" I asked.

"Hmm," Dad said, thinking it over. "I guess we'd have to kill them, wouldn't we?"

"How would you kill them?"

"That's a good question, son. I've never killed anybody before. What about you?"

"I've never killed anybody, either," I said, shaking my head and trying not to think about frogs.

Dad paused for a second, thinking something over, then reached into his mouth and started digging around his teeth like he had popcorn stuck in there. But instead of a kernel, he pulled out a little maggot. He grimaced and flicked it across the kitchen. Comrade followed the trajectory and licked it up before the five-second rule could be broken. "I'm never gonna get used to these goddamn things."

"They're not so bad." I held up my left arm, showing off the open bite wound. The maggots inside wriggled in greeting. Dad took one look at them and stepped back, thoroughly disgusted.

"Dylan . . . that . . . oh man. You gotta wash those out."

"I like them."

"You *like* them?"

"They're not hurting me."

"Dylan, they're literally eating you."

"That's okay. I don't mind."

"You don't *mind*? No. I don't think so. Here, let me see that again."

This time, when I showed him my arm, he grabbed it with one hand and scooped up the salt shaker on the table with his other hand. Before I could comprehend the situation, he started sprinkling salt into my open wound. I wrestled away from him and said, "What are you *doing*?"

MAGGOTS SCREAMING!

"Isn't that what the body farm lady said to do? To get rid of maggots? You gotta salt them. Salt . . . or . . . or . . . boiling water? Yeah, let's boil some water. Cook these little bastards alive."

"No, Dad!" I said, and stormed down the hallway into my bedroom. I slammed the door shut and hid under my blanket, expecting him to follow, but he never did. Maybe he was just trying to scare me. Either way, I discovered it was sort of nice being covered up like that. Shielded by darkness. The same way we'd been covering the three of you on the living room couch. I felt connected to you in a way I hadn't previously. I could have stayed under the blanket forever.

I held my left arm up and pressed my ear against the wound and listened to the maggots screaming for attention. Like babies crying in their cribs. Begging to be fed. Begging to be held. Begging not to be abandoned. This was a frightening, confusing world they'd hatched into. Of course they were scared.

"It's going to be okay," I whispered. "It's going to be okay . . . "

And they responded.

I *heard* them. They *spoke* to me.

But what they said is something I'll never confess. Not even to you.

This one's my little secret.

Later that evening, when the front door swung open and Andy rushed inside, nobody reacted. *The Simpsons* was playing, but I'm not sure either of us were really watching it at that point. Looking at the screen, yes, but it was getting harder and harder to concentrate on television, to make sense of the audio and visuals. Characters were moving and talking, but I wouldn't have been able to say what they were *doing* or talking *about,* not even for a million dollars—

181

although, let's be honest, what good is money when you're dead?

"What the hell's going on in here?" Andy asked, sweaty and scared. Comrade wagged her tail from the couch. Not by *you*, but by *me*. I gave her a little pat on the head for choosing wisely, then brushed her away when she started gnawing on my fingers.

"Oh, hey," Dad said, offering a lazy wave. "We're watching *The Simpsons* if you want to join."

"Yeah," I said, "it's our annual rewatch."

Andy closed the door and flipped on the living room light. "I've been calling you all goddamn day."

"I can't answer my phone."

"What are you talking about?"

Dad held up his hand, as if that would explain everything. "It doesn't recognize me anymore. Him, either." He jabbed a thumb toward me. "We've become obsolete."

"Where were you?" I asked.

"Me?" Andy asked, as if it was a ridiculous question. "I was at *work*, which is where both your dad and I were supposed to be today." He side-eyed Dad. "But don't worry. I covered for you. Told them you picked up some kinda bug."

A repulsive snorting noise erupted from Dad's throat, then he reached into his mouth and pulled out the fattest maggot I'd ever seen in my life (and non-life). He raised it over his head and waved it around like a tiny flag. "Well, you weren't wrong . . . "

He flicked the maggot across the room and Comrade slurped it up. She sat and stared at Dad, wagging her tail, as she waited for another helping. He scavenged a handful out of his gums and tossed them on the carpet. Comrade went to town on the greatest buffet in the world.

"Man, don't feed her that shit," Andy said, disgusted. "She's gonna get sick." Andy lingered at the closed front door, studying all of us in the living room—Me, Dad, you,

Dead Dad, and Dead Mom, then sighed. "Where am I supposed to sit? There's nowhere to sit in here. This is ridiculous"

"So, you were at work, huh?" Dad said. "That's where you were?"

"Oh, come on. Can't we go in the kitchen or something? It's too creepy being this close to them."

Dad glanced at you and the other corpses with surprise, like he'd forgotten you were with us.

"Dad," I said, wondering if he'd forgotten about something else, as well. "Are you gonna ask him about the voicemail?"

"Oh, yeah." Dad pointed at the coffee table. "Lori called last night and left a message."

"What? Are you serious? What did she say?"

"Well, we was hoping you'd fill us in on that, considering I already goddamn told you I can't use the thing anymore."

We took the phone to the kitchen. At first, I wasn't sure why it mattered, then it dawned on me: Dad didn't want you or the other two corpses hearing what my mom had to say. And I agreed. At that point, we were uncertain how much you could hear or comprehend, but it was probably smart not to take any unnecessary chances. After all, how were we supposed to know if you were friends or enemies?

I mean, come on, even now I don't really know the answer to that one.

And I don't think you do, either.

Anyway, I'm sure it's safe to tell you about the voicemail. It's not like we learned much from it. And if we had, what exactly would you do with the information? It's a bit too late, don't you think?

You *do* think, don't you?

At least a little bit.

You must.

But the question is: are your thoughts different than my own, or do we share the same cloud?

183

It wasn't even Mom who had left the message, anyway. It was Miguel.

"Hey, man, it's me again. Calling from Lori's phone since mine's about to die. Soooo . . . a little update on the situation over here. Things have gotten a little, uh, dicey, I'd say. Some fuckin' government suits rolled up and quarantined the ward they have her staying in. Won't let me go in. Won't answer any of my goddamn questions. Won't do anything. The only reason I have her phone is she'd left it in my car—which is where I'm sitting, out in the parking lot, just . . . waiting, I guess? Waiting on what, I don't even know. But I sure as hell ain't gonna leave her here. Call me back when you can. I would suggest you and Dylan coming out here but, honestly, I don't know what good it'd do. They're not letting anybody in to see her. I don't know if she's got something contagious or what the fuck. I don't know goddamn anything. These fuckers . . . Anyway, listen, I know you and I, we ain't exactly on the best of terms these days, but I hope you can put our feud on hold until this is over with. We both want the same thing, after all. For Lori to recover, right? From . . . from whatever the hell is going on. Jesus Christ. Don't tell Dylan I said this, but before they kicked me out, she wasn't looking too good. Her skin was . . . well . . . let's just say it was weird. I would be lying if I said I wasn't scared. Anyway. Fuck it. Call me or text me or whatever. I don't know who else to talk to right now."

After the voicemail ended, Andy said, "Don't know who else to talk to? Shit, I guess I'm just some asshole the both of you have to deal with, is that it?"

"Should we go down there?" I asked.

"I don't know," Dad said, then to Andy: "Call him back and put it on speaker."

Andy pressed Mom's name on Dad's phone and placed it screen-up on the kitchen table between us. Instead of ringing, it transferred us directly to her voicemail, the way it would if she was on the phone with someone else, or if the battery had died.

"Lori? Miguel?" Dad said into the phone. "Please call back when you can. I think we need to talk."

"I'm here, too," Andy said, "if that means anything to you, of course." He ended the call, leaving the phone on the table. We all studied it, waiting for it to start vibrating again with a new call, but after ten minutes of inactivity we decided if a watched pot never boiled, then surely that meant a watched phone never rang. "Well shit," Andy said, cracking his knuckles against his skull, "now what?"

"I don't know," Dad said. "I was hoping you might have some ideas. We've just been watching *The Simpsons* since you left."

"Which seasons?"

"All of them."

Andy grimaced. "Goddamn. That's rough."

"Hey," I said, "I like the new seasons."

"That's because you are a dumb child who hasn't developed good taste yet," Andy said. "You think everything's good."

And, before I realized what was coming out of my mouth, I responded, "Fuck you. They're funny."

Andy gasped and glanced toward Dad for help. Dad shrugged and said, "I told him that he can say fuck now, considering the situation we're in."

"Oh," Andy said, nodding like it made perfect sense, "that was pretty cool of you to do."

"Thanks," Dad said. "I thought so, too."

"Well, in that case," Andy said, focused on me again, "Fuck you, too, you little piece of shit."

It was the most he and I had ever bonded.

"Anyway," Andy said, "it's a good thing I'm here, isn't it?"

"Is it?" Dad asked, and Andy frowned.

"Hey, fuck you too, pardner. You and your goddamn kid. Treating me like that, I oughta go home and let you fend for yourselves. And to think, I even brought y'all some special supplies on the way over here."

"What kinda supplies?"

"Why don't you ask nicely and I'll tell you?"

"What kinda fuckin' supplies?"

Andy laughed and wiped sweat from his lip. "You know, I've said this before, but I'm gonna say it again. This house reeks. Seriously. Y'all should be goddamn embarrassed."

"Andy," Dad said, "what did you bring?"

He grinned. "Some pretty cool shit, if I do say so myself."

Andy went out to his truck and returned with a duffel bag, which he unloaded on the living room floor. Once Comrade realized the bag didn't contain any treats, she returned to her attempts of gnawing on my calves.

"So," Andy said, kneeling over the bag, "the way I see it, these fuckers you found in the back yard are clearly dead. They look like you, and they're rotting the same way, but where y'all seem to differ is the fact that they can't get up and move around or anything like that. And also? They can't communicate. I ain't heard a goddamn peep out of 'em since I've been here. Have you?"

"No," Dad said. "They aren't talking."

"Right, exactly, so I was thinking about that today, while out on my route, and I got to thinking maybe because they aren't talking, it doesn't mean they *can't*. Maybe we just ain't . . . you know, *listening* the right way. Hence . . . "

He removed his laptop from the bag and opened it with the screen facing us.

On the browser, a video resumed playing at the midway point, which consisted of several men and women, all of them nude and in various states of arousal. Loud moans filled the living room. Comrade scrambled into the kitchen, terrified by the sudden noise intrusion.

"What the hell are you doing?" Dad asked, trying to block my eyes with his loose-skinned arm.

Andy panicked and spun the laptop around toward him and exited out of the browser. "Uh, sorry about that." He clicked a couple more times, then said, "Okay, here, look at this."

He rotated the laptop again, showing us a different webpage. Another wikiHow article. This one was titled "How to Talk to the Dead: 10 Steps (with Pictures)."

"Is that real?" I asked, already wondering what questions I would ask you if given the chance.

"Of course not," Dad said.

"Wait, why are you so quick to dismiss it?" Andy asked. "Why not give it a chance? You never know . . . "

"Because it's ridiculous."

"As ridiculous as hanging out here with a set of freaky deaky doppelgängers? Brother, don't you think we've exceeded the realm of criticizing what is and ain't ridiculous?"

Dad responded, a little quieter, "Okay, so what are we trying to do, exactly? Isn't shit like this usually used for . . . spirits? Not, like, actual physical bodies?"

"Sure, maybe, but who knows?" Andy said. "Who's to say there ain't also spirits or whatever in this very room, attached to the bodies, and we can't see them? Hell, I ain't even saying spirits are *real*. If you'd asked me a couple days ago I would've laughed in your goddamn face. But now? I guess we'd be morons if we didn't at least give it a shot."

"Fine, I suppose . . . I suppose you got a point. What's the first step?"

MAX BOOTH III

The first step in wikiHow's "How to Talk to the Dead: 10 Steps (with Pictures)" suggested shifting our focus to a "higher realm" if simply focusing on the image of our dead loved ones wasn't sufficient enough to form a connection.

"See, this is already dumb," Dad said. "For one thing, who says we love these . . . these *things*?" He nodded at you and the other two corpses on the couch. "Plus, obviously we can see them. They're *here*. So why the hell would we need to 'focus on the image' of them. All's we gotta do is look at 'em."

Hunched over the laptop, Andy said, "It says here we gotta make ourselves, uh, 'consciously aware' of what it's like to be, uh, ourselves? Like, in the present moment."

"What the fuck does that mean?"

"Hell if I know. What's it like to be yourself right now?"

"Well," Dad said, "I gotta say, it's not fucking great. In case you haven't been paying attention, I'm kinda decomposing over here."

"What about you, Dylan? What's it like to be you?"

The question alarmed me in a way I had not expected. "I don't know," I blurted out.

"It wants us to take note of where we are, what time it is, and what our feelings are like. Evidently if we don't do this, we might experience some trouble returning to our sense afterward."

"This all seems pretty redundant," Dad said.

"Once our physical awareness declines, we're supposed to focus on the other energy."

"What *other* energy?"

"I guess, like, the energy surrounding us in the living room. But we ain't supposed to search for it, otherwise we won't find it. We just gotta, like, be open to the idea of there being other energy. And if we feel anything, like a spirit or whatever, then we can ask it some questions. But it says

188

here that sometimes they don't always respond with words, but with emotions."

"*Emotions*?" Dad said. "What kinda emotions?"

Andy shrugged. "It doesn't say."

The second step in wikiHow's "How to Talk to the Dead: 10 Steps (with Pictures)" introduced the possibility of talking through the power of our minds. We pushed the coffee table against the wall and sat on the carpet in the middle of the living room, with our legs folded Indian-style, which isn't the easiest position to accomplish while physically deteriorating. Comrade kept trying to investigate by sticking her snout in our crotches, but Andy convinced her to leave us alone after coughing up a couple milk bones from his duffel bag.

"Okay," Andy said. "Next we're supposed to close our eyes and empty our minds of anxiety and thought."

Dad glanced over like he wanted to attack him. "Did you just say empty my mind of thought?"

"That's what the article said."

"And how the hell does someone do that, exactly?"

"I don't know. It didn't specify."

"You want to know what happens if I start trying to empty my mind of thought?" Dad asked. "I start thinking about not thinking, which is just another thought. And then I think, 'Oh no, now I'm thinking about not thinking,' and suddenly I'm thinking about the fact that I'm thinking about not thinking, and the panic never ends. It only multiplies. Only assholes can empty their mind of thought."

"And corpses," I added, not taking my eyes off you up there on the couch. I hadn't seen you move yet, but I wasn't convinced you wouldn't.

"Dylan has a point," Andy said.

"What are you talking about?" Dad asked.

189

"If you're having such a hard time not thinking, then maybe that means you aren't as dead as you thought."

"Then what are we?"

Andy shrugged. "Something else?"

"Something else like what?"

"I don't know. Something . . . something weird." He leaned over and read the laptop again, then said, "Okay, it wants us to fix an image of our deceased loved one in our—"

"Again," Dad said, "this article is making a lot of bizarre assumptions."

"Wouldn't it be more bizarre if it assumed the physical corpses were in the room with us?"

"Not to me!" Dad said.

"Okay, fair enough," Andy said. "Then let's stare at the bodies instead, since we got 'em here with us."

"Stare and do what?"

"Well, the article says we oughta ask our deceased loved one—or whoever, I guess, it don't gotta be a loved one, I suppose—anyway, we oughta ask them a question once we've held that person's image in our mind long enough. Or, stared at them long enough, in our case? And then we wait for them to answer. Sometimes they might answer, uh, telepathically, I guess. Like, in our minds? But we gotta be careful and not get too anxious for a reply, otherwise we might imagine they're saying something. Patience, the article says, is essen—"

"Hey, you," Dad said, staring at his own corpse. "Dead Me. Yeah, I'm talking to you, you piece of shit. What the hell's going on here? What are you? Why is this happening? Answer me, goddammit."

Dead Dad remained motionless on the couch, his lifeless eyes focused on something in the corner of the room as maggots treated his exposed bellybutton like a fast-food ball pit.

"Well, there you have it," Dad said. "They're not talking."

"Of course not," Andy said. "You're talking to them like

a goddamn jerk. Would you engage somebody in conversation if they spoke to you like that?"

"I'd probably break their jaw," Dad said. "Not just . . . sit there and take it, like a coward."

Andy chuckled. "Dude, I've seen you fight. You ain't breaking nobody's jaw."

"I'll break my jaw against your jaw, you want to test me."

"Are you . . . are you threatening to violently kiss me?"

"What?" Dad said. "What are you talking about?"

"Why would your jaw break my jaw? Unless you're trying to kiss me? But, like, in a really weird, psychotic way?"

"I never said anything about kissing you. I was talking about headbutting."

"Who headbutts with their jaw?"

"Maybe I do, okay? You ever think about that?"

"I don't . . . I don't think that's how you're supposed to headbutt."

"How about I headbutt how I want, and you headbutt how you want?"

"Now I'm afraid you're going to headbutt me," Andy said.

"Wait a second," I said, troubled by the implications of their conversation, "do heads really have butts?"

The third step in wikiHow's "How to Talk to the Dead: 10 Steps (with Pictures)" was remarkably similar to the second step, except it wanted us to ask basic yes-and-no questions, while also specifying how they should respond. For example, the article told us, the most common methods used were flashlights or knocking.

"What do you mean, knocking?" Dad said. "Who knocks?"

"Well, ideally, the person we're trying to talk to. Like, we tell them knock once for yes, or twice for no."

"But they can't knock."

"We don't know that."

Dad shook his head. "If they could knock, they would've fuckin' knocked. They would have shown *some* type of movement. Have you seen them move?" He glanced down at me. "Have you?"

"No," I said, disappointed. "I haven't."

"Well there you have it. They can't move."

"What about flashlights?" Andy asked.

"What *about* flashlights?"

"That's another way of getting them to talk."

"What? *How?* Like, shining it in their eyes until they tell us to leave them alone?"

"No, you don't *shine it into their eyes.* That's you being a jerk again."

"Okay, then what?"

"You gotta get a flashlight with a button on the end, one that can easily be turned on and off, then you power it on, unscrew the front of it so the light kinda dims down, and set it down on the floor. You give instructions to the spirit to tap the button once for yes, twice for no."

"Andy," Dad said, "if they can't knock, what the hell makes you think they're gonna be able to operate a flashlight?"

"Maybe their spirits can operate a flashlight."

"My spirit is going to shove a flashlight up your ass."

Andy sighed. "Somehow I don't think you're taking this seriously."

"Okay," Dad said, "I think that's enough wikiHow bullshit for one day."

"But we haven't finished all the steps," Andy said, almost whining.

"Why don't you tell me what the rest are first? Because so far . . . let's say I'm not exactly impressed."

"Of course you're not impressed," Andy said. "You're a corpse! Not much is going to impress you at this point."

"I thought we weren't corpses," I said, "because we can think about not thinking."

"Yeah," Dad said, "what about what he just said?"

Andy sighed and rubbed the bridge of his nose. "We gotta skip the next step, anyway, if that makes you feel better."

"Why? What's wrong with it?" Dad asked.

"It wants us to hire a medium."

"What's that?" I asked.

"Some kinda psychic huckster," Dad explained.

"I looked up prices online last night," Andy said. "Because some of them will Skype in to you. But holy crap. None of us can afford something like that. Not on UPS salaries. Same with step five, which wanted us to buy a buncha EVP shit. Like what those ghost hunter shows use. You know how much that shit costs?"

"Well, then how much is step six?" Dad asked, sounding as sarcastic as a dead-but-not-quite-dead person could sound.

"About twenty bucks," Andy responded, then removed another item from the duffel bag.

An ouija board.

Brand new, by the look of it. The box was wrapped in plastic, with a big Walmart price tag sticker flattened along the bottom corner. It'd cost him $18.59, plus whatever tax made it out to be.

The front of the box presented two sets of children's hands maneuvering a planchette over a wooden spirit board. Above the hands, in simple font, it read:

Ouija®
BOARD

And below the hands:

MYSTIFYING ORACLE®

To the left of the bottom subtitle, the board claimed to be appropriate for anybody eight years of age or older, and to the right of the bottom subtitle, it read: *Sturdy Wood Board with Original Graphics!*

"You gotta be fuckin' kidding me," Dad said.

"I mean, we might as well give it a try, right?" Andy asked. "Considering I already bought it and all."

"I cannot believe you purchased an ouija board," Dad said. "Of all the weird shit I've seen at your place, somehow this surprises me the most."

"Typically I'd say these things are full of shit," Andy said. "Another scam conceived by Lady Capitalism." He held up his finger. "However, I think we've reached a point in our investigation where we might as well *try*. I'm about out of other ideas. What about you?"

Dad threw up his hands, defeated. "Fine, okay, I guess we're gonna really do this, then. That all right with you, Dylan?"

I was caught off guard at first. They hadn't exactly been asking my opinion on anything else they'd tried today. "Uhhh," I said, which was evidently all the permission they needed to proceed.

"Let's do this shit!" Andy said, tearing apart the game's wrapping and opening the box.

I'm not sure how we settled on using you for the planchette operator, instead of the other two corpses. Maybe it simply boiled down to who weighed the least. Andy scooped you up and propped you on the carpet next to us, leaning against the couch. You did not seem annoyed or fazed whatsoever by the disturbance. Your head swung down, chin digging into your chest, and several handfuls of maggots dropped out of your eyes, nose, and mouth— but, other than that, you didn't move. Andy brushed the maggots off your lap and I reached out to stop him. There was no point in discarding them like that. They belonged with you, just as my maggots belonged with me, and Dad's maggots belonged with him. Andy kept gagging at the sight of them. He didn't understand the connection we had all started forming with our individual insects. But that was okay. He didn't need to understand. This wasn't about him.

We set up the ouija board on the floor next to your right thigh, and guided your arm down to it, rotted fingers touching one end of the planchette while Andy sat across from you and operated the opposite side.

"Shouldn't he be doing this by himself?" Dad asked. He and I stood above you and Andy, watching like nervous spectators.

Andy shook his head. "Ain't you ever seen a movie? You can't do this shit with one person. It just doesn't work like that."

"Maybe Dylan should do it," Dad said, "since it's . . . uh . . . his."

My *what*? I wanted to ask. My *corpse*?

"I'm doing it," Andy said.

"Why?"

"Because I'm already down here and getting up hurts my knees. What should we ask? What do we want to know more than anything?"

"Does a girl really do the voice for Bart Simpson?" I blurted out.

"How many times do I gotta tell you that's true before you believe me?" Dad asked. "We don't need the dead to answer a question like that. You can google it, if you don't believe me."

Andy cleared his throat and gave us an annoyed look, then refocused on the ouija board. "Are you human?"

The planchette didn't move, so he continued with further questioning.

"Are you . . . from another planet?"

No response.

"Are you from . . . another point in time? Like, are you fuckin' . . . time travelers or something?"

No response.

"Do you know who we are?"

No response.

"Are you here to hurt us?"

No response.

"Are you here to protect us?"

No response.

"Did the FBI assassinate Martin Luther King Jr.?"

No response.

"This is useless," Dad said. "You wasted your money on this thing."

"Actually, I wasted your money," Andy said.

"What?"

"I may have swiped your debit card before leaving yesterday."

"Are you serious?"

"What does it matter to you? It's not like you're going shopping any time soon."

"I fully expect you to reim—"

"Shh, shut up!" Andy whispered, frantic.

"What?"

"Something . . . something's moving."

We leaned closer to the ouija board and realized he was telling the truth. The planchette had started wobbling.

"What's it doing?" I asked, seconds before it slid toward the letter I, dragging both Andy's and your hand along with it.

"Holy shit," Dad said, and neither of us said another word, instead witnessing in silence as the planchette continuing slithering around the board, from I to M to P to O to S to—

I kicked the ouija board.

The planchette flew across the living room.

I don't know why I did it, but I did. I'm the one who interrupted it. I'm the one who kicked it. It wasn't an action I planned out. It was purely instincts. Suddenly, as we watched the ouija board do its magic, I was hit with an overwhelming fear. A fear of what, I'm not quite sure, but

Maggots Screaming!

I was positive I did not want to find out what word was being spelled.

Afterward, once Andy and Dad had fully observed what happened, they looked up at me and asked what the hell my problem was.

"I don't know," I said. "I'm sorry."

"You're *sorry*?" Andy said. "What the hell is that supposed to mean?"

"Calm down," Dad said.

"How can I calm down? How can you be calm? We finally almost get some kind of message from these dead fuckers, and your son goes and ruins it."

"I'm sure it was an accident."

"An *accident*?" Andy let out a laugh. "He straight up kicked it across the room like a goddamn soccer ball."

"Why did you do that, Dylan?" Dad asked.

"It didn't feel right," I said. "It felt . . . it felt wrong."

"It felt *wrong*?" Andy said. "And what has everything up until now felt, then? Fine? Hunky-dory? Little dude, this shit has felt wrong from the getgo. So what?"

"What was it saying?" Dad asked.

"I don't know. It didn't get to finish." Andy surveyed the living room until he found a black Sharpie on the coffee table, then hurried over to an empty wall next to the kitchen entrance and wrote out the letters previously spelled out on the ouija board:

I M P O S

"That's as far as we got before Dylan got kick-happy."

"How many words could that spell?" Dad asked.

"I don't know, but we're going to find out."

IMPOSSIBLE
IMPOSTER
IMPOSE

197

MAX BOOTH III

IMPOST
IMPOSITION
IMPOSTHUME

After an hour of brainstorming and internet browsing, we narrowed down the possible spelling to six words. Some of them made more sense than others. Andy wrote each one on the wall in huge capital letters, ignoring Dad's requests to use a sheet of paper like a normal person.

The first two words—**IMPOSSIBLE** and **IMPOSTER**—were easy enough to understand, but the rest we felt obligated to research on Merriam-Webster dot com.

IMPOSE meant to "to force into the company or on the attention of another," which felt relevant to our situation, so we didn't rule it out.

IMPOST could've meant a couple things. An "impost" could be a tax of some kind, or it could also be considered a "a block, capital, or molding from which an arch springs." None of us could figure out why you would have been warning us about architecture, but the "tax" definition didn't feel entirely unrelated. Were you telling us we needed to pay a tribute? Had you and the other two corpses come here to collect on a debt we owed?

IMPOSITION was pretty much the same as the last word, except the wording on Merriam-Webster dot com sounded a little bit more sinister in this instance: "an excessive or uncalled-for requirement or burden." Yikes.

IMPOSTHUME was labeled *archaic*, and linked to the definition for ABSCESS, which was defined as "a localized collection of pus surrounded by inflamed tissue."

"Puss?" I said, hovering over Andy's shoulder as he clicked on the dictionary link. "Like from pimples?"

Andy snorted a laugh. "Did you just say puss?"

"That's what it says!" I pointed at the screen, as if he couldn't somehow see it right in front of him.

"What?" Dad said, rushing over to the laptop. Andy

was too busy cracking up to respond. A second later Dad was joining him, but at least he was nice enough to tell me it's pronounced *pus* not *puss*.

"Oh," I said.

"A local collection of *puss* is something very different," Andy said. "Maybe if y'all get out of this in one piece, I'll take you to one."

"Um," Dad said, "no you won't."

"We'll talk about it later." He stood in front of the list he'd written on our wall, hands on his hips, admiring his handiwork. "Shit. All of these words make sense for what's going on here."

"Which one do you think it is?" I asked.

"Well, I have my suspicions . . . "

"It's none of them," Dad said. "This is stupid. The corpse didn't try spelling something."

"Then how do you explain what we saw?"

"You were clearly guiding it."

Andy tossed his marker on the coffee table and cocked his head. "What are you trying to say?"

"I'm saying that ouija boards are bullshit, and you were the one moving the planchette. Intentionally? That I don't know. But I wouldn't be surprised."

"What the fuck's your problem, man?"

"What's my problem?" Dad said. "I don't know. Why don't you tell us where you really were today?"

"What are you talking about?"

"You went to work? At UPS? You think I don't know what day it is all of a sudden? Since when do you deliver packages on a Sunday? Since when has *any* of us?"

"Oh my gawd," Andy said. "Would you listen to yourself? You sound like a fuckin' nerd."

Despite his anger, Dad laughed. "What? That's your response? I'm a *nerd*?"

"Yup. You got it, pardner. A great big fuckin' nerd. Why don't you go marry your calendar, you love it so much?"

"Where were you?"

"Maybe it's none of your business. You ever consider that?"

"No," Dad said. "Screw that. You're afraid to tell us for a reason, and I want to know why."

Andy nodded, slowly, in a deliberate motion that made me afraid physical violence was on the verge of erupting between the two of them. Then some of the tension in his body loosened, and he slumped his head and said, "I was on a date, okay?"

"A date?"

"Yeah, with Candy. From, uh, the body farm?"

"With everything going on over here, you decided to leave and go have sex?"

"Now, wait a second. No one said we've had sex yet. Some hand stuff, sure. But—"

"You told her, didn't you?"

"What?"

"That's why you were keeping it a secret," Dad said. "You told her about us. About what's happening."

"I—I may have mentioned a few details."

"Goddammit. What did she say?"

"What the fuck are you so cranky about? It's Candy. We can trust her."

"Why can we trust her? Because she jerked you off?"

"Well, for one thing, it was a mutual jerking off, so why don't you—"

"I thought we could trust you."

"You *can* trust me," he said. "Candy promised to keep it a secret. Hell, you want my honest opinion, I don't even think she believed me. But I had to tell *somebody*, man. Don't you understand how fucking crazy all this is? Are you so used to it that it all seems normal? Well let me break the news to you. This shit ain't normal! It's fuckin' weird! Now if you'll excuse me . . . " He pointed at the wall of IMPOS words. " . . . I have a puzzle to crack. If you want to help, great. If not, then shut up and let me think."

"You want to waste your time?" Dad said. "Go for it.

MAGGOTS SCREAMING!

Dylan and I have plenty of *Simpsons* episodes to watch. All this other crap, it's just a distraction. A waste of time. I'm done with it."

Andy grinned. "Just you wait. I'm gonna solve this fuckin' retarded mystery and make you eat your words."

Dad shrugged and collapsed on the loveseat, fumbling for the remote and clicking play on *The Simpsons*. I stood between them, trying to figure out what I was supposed to do, but Andy didn't seem to require my assistance, either, so I gave up and returned my attention to the television, where everything was predictable, where everything was calm.

I don't think either of us realized what Andy was doing until after he finished. By then he had been muttering a lot of crazy stuff, and we'd learned to mostly tune him out. The ouija board incident had messed with his head big time. After writing the IMPOS word choices on the wall, he pretty much spent the rest of the evening pacing around in front of it, taking the time to thoroughly examine every letter.

Dad and I kept exchanging glances, asking each other silent questions with our eyes, like *Should we maybe give him some space and go do something in the kitchen?* But neither of us budged, and I can't say for sure what Dad's motives were for staying in the living room, although I suspect we were probably operating along similar wavelengths, because you were why I didn't want to leave. You and the other two. I didn't know what Andy would do if we left him alone with you. He was freaking out in a way I'd never witnessed another human being behave before.

Something in his brain had shifted, or distorted, or *something*. Once, a while back, we'd accidentally forgotten a lithium-ion battery outside, and it sat there on our porch for two whole days before anybody remembered. Two days in the middle of *summer*. The battery had undergone a bizarre transformation. Its innards were bulging out of its swollen sides, acid and other sticky substances bleeding from various cracks. Yes, in a way, that's a good description for our bodies as we all decomposed together. But also? That's how I started picturing Andy's brain after the ouija board incident. Swollen and leaking dangerous liquids.

So we stayed in the living room, half-paying attention to *The Simpsons*, half-paying attention to Andy's increasingly troubled muttering. Of course, we weren't *that* concerned, considering how easily he conned us into sitting in the two kitchen chairs he dragged into the living room, in front of the couch where we had previously pushed the coffee table out of the way.

To be honest, I'm not sure where he produced the rope from. His truck? I like to think one of us would have observed him leaving the house, but who knows how much goes unnoticed when you're slowly rotting away to nothing? It's likelier the rope had been stored in his duffel bag. The same bag he'd used to conceal the ouija board. Which only makes me further wonder if the rope had been part of the plan from the beginning. Otherwise why pack it? Same with the ouija board. Before he returned to the house that afternoon, he already knew he'd be utilizing both items. He had already made up his mind. Except, the way things unfolded, it felt like one item's purpose had solely served as the reaction to another item. Without the ouija board's presence, there wouldn't have been any rope.

At least, that was my logic when he tied Dad and me up in the living room. But now I realize the truth, that this was a false conclusion on my part. Without the ouija board, there would still be a rope. There would always be a rope. The plan had *always* been to restrain us. I don't know if the plan originated before or after he departed Saturday night. If I had to guess, the idea planted itself in his head like a seed when he saw you on the couch for the first time on Friday, but it didn't start to fully blossom until he went home the following night, and was alone enough to let his paranoid brain wander without interruption. So then why bring the ouija board at all? Not only *bring* it but first go to Walmart and *purchase* one? Who, exactly, was he trying to convince with it? Us, or himself?

"I've gone over it a thousand times," Andy said, after double-checking the knots around our wrists, "and the only word that makes sense—the only word the ouija board could've realistically been spelling—is IMPOSTERS."

"You don't know that," Dad said.

"I'm fairly certain."

"You're guessing."

"Then you tell me what other word feels more appropriate. The *only* other one I can sorta see is IMPOSSIBLE, but don't you think that's, you know, a little *redundant*? No *shit* this feels like an impossible situation. We've already done *established* that. So what's the point in bringing it up again? If a ouija board's got somethin' to say—and if it actually *says* it—then goddamn it better be somethin' important, don't you think? It's not gonna just, you know, *waste* our time on something as useless as IMPOSSIBLE."

"All of the words fit. We already established that, Andy. What are you talking about?"

"Nah," Andy said, shaking his head, because he'd made up his mind and now there was no changing it, no matter what Dad said. "It's gotta be IMPOSTERS."

"Okay," Dad said, no longer trying to break free of his restraints. "Let's say you're right and it *is* IMPOSTERS. What does that mean in this context?"

"You know damn well what it means."

"Enlighten us, anyway."

"It's not like the word contains that many different definitions, Max."

"If you really believed I was an imposter, then you wouldn't be calling me by that name."

"It's not like you've introduced an alternative."

"That's because there ain't one."

"At least not one my feeble human mind would be able to comprehend experiencing in your true language, right?"

"What? What the hell are you *talking* about? Tell me exactly what you think is going on here. Seriously. Walk me through it—step by step—so I can tell you why you're being so goddamn stupid."

"Does IMPOSTER mean we aren't real?" I asked, having almost forgotten I also possessed the ability to speak.

"Do you feel real?" Dad said.

"I don't know," I answered, with a hundred percent honesty.

"Ah-ha!" Andy shouted, and pointed an accusatory finger at me. "You fuckers don't even know if you ain't actually imposters, do you? You don't know shit!"

"And neither do you," Dad said.

"I know enough to question this entire goddamn mysterious corpse charade y'all tried pawning off on me."

"What fuckin' charade?" Dad jerked his head toward the couch. "They're right fuckin' there. Don't believe me? Go touch them!"

"I didn't say they weren't real," Andy said. "I'm sayin' the *circumstances* in which they supposedly were discovered is awfully suspect."

"In what way?"

"In every goddamn way!"

"You want to try being a little bit more specific?"

"You want me to be specific? Sure, I can be specific. I can be real fuckin' specific." Andy wiped drool from his mouth and increased the frantic speed of his pacing around the living room. It was impressive he didn't trip or knock anything over. "How's this for specific? Friday night—*late* Friday night—I get a call from someone who hasn't spoken to me in at least a year, someone who works for the same goddamn company as me—and if that ain't dedication to being an asshole, I don't know what is. So this guy, this real fuckin' prick, he gives me a ring—*out of the fuckin' blue*—and asks me to come over. Asks if I can come right away. Says it's urgent. He needs a favor and no it can't wait 'til morning. Remind you, this is all comin' from the same guy who's been doin' nothin' but treating me like shit because of why? Because I refused to pick sides once our other best friend started dating his ex-wife? Because I'm a grown-ass man and I'm not gonna allow myself to get sucked into some kinda sad, pathetic high school soap opera bullshit? I never did a goddamn thing to nobody, and I get treated like that? Nah. Fuck off. This world, this fuckin' *planet*, man, it don't matter what you do, does it? There's no winning. There's no escaping the petty drama forever fabricated by some dickhead's broken heart."

"Andy, I—"

"And *this* is the kind of fuckin' guy asking me for a favor. Should I have helped him? Of course not. Should I have answered the phone when I saw his name on the caller ID? Hell no. But of course I did. Because, despite everything that's happened, I like to believe I'm a pretty good fuckin' friend."

"You've tied us up in our own living room," Dad said.

"I'm getting to that."

"Oh, you're *getting* to that, okay, my bad."

"Would you cool it with the sarcasm? I mean, seriously."

"Okay. I'm sorry," Dad said. "*Proceed.*"

"Now imagine my surprise—seriously, put yourself in my point-of-view, if your species is capable of that level of empathy—imagine my utter *shock* once I walked through that front door Friday night, and saw what I saw. Hell, it's the same shit I'm seeing right now, if we're being honest—and we *are* being honest, aren't we?"

"I haven't lied to you about any of this," Dad said.

"What did I see?" Andy said, not waiting for either of us to respond. "I'll tell you what I saw. I saw my old buddy Max, and his little boy Dylan, and his ex-wife Lori, and the three of 'em were displayed out on the couch—just as they are now—dead as anything I've ever seen. Killed by some unknown cause. And what else did I see? Both of ya—standing there, covered in dirt, hands in your pockets, trying your best not to look guilty as fuck."

"Guilty of what?" Dad asked, which Andy was fully prepared to answer.

"Guilty of being imposters."

"So you're saying . . . you're *really* saying you honestly believe me and Dylan ain't the real me and Dylan?"

"I'm saying it's starting to sound more plausible by the second, yes."

"Okay, then who . . . exactly . . . do you think we are? Besides imposters. I want you to be more specific. Tell us who we are, if I'm not me and Dylan ain't Dylan."

"I'm not me?" I asked, alarmed and confused. I no longer knew what was true anymore. The longer this interrogation continued, the less confident I remained about anything concerning reality.

"It's not who you are," Andy said, "but *what*."

"What?"

"Exactly."

"What are we?" I asked, catching on before Dad.

"Well," Andy said, "that's what I'm aiming to find out."

"Oh, Jesus Christ," Dad said. "What do you *think* we are?"

"I don't know exactly. Obviously you ain't from Earth. Your technology is far superior than any bullshit we got here. So that makes you extraterrestrials of some kind. Little green men. Greys. Motherfuckin' reptiloids. Goddamn invasion of the fuckin' body snatchers. You know what I mean? You ever see that movie? Any of you? Because I have. And I know your goddamn tricks. I know what you do. You fuckin' pod people dipshits. Go ahead and try convincing me there ain't a replica of myself somewhere out in that back yard in the process of morphing into its final form with the goal of replacing me.

MAGGOTS SCREAMING!

Replacing me like you replaced those poor sons of bitches on the couch. Like you replaced my *friend*. Well I ain't gonna let it happen. You hear me? I ain't your fuckin' crab shell. I know what you are and I know what's out there and I'm gonna find it and I'm gonna kill it and then you're gonna tell me every goddamn thing you know and pray to whatever fuckin' stupid retarded god you got on your bizarro planet that I spare you some motherfuckin' mercy. Are we crystal, fellas? Are we goddamn clear?"

He didn't hang around for a response. Instead he marched out into the back yard, leaving us in the living room tied to the kitchen chairs.

"What—what is he doing out there?" I asked. "Is he really digging more holes?"

"Sure sounds like it."

Rhythmic grunts filtered in through the open back door. From where we were tied up in the living room, neither of us could see exactly what Andy was doing, but he was making plenty of noises to paint a clear enough picture.

I wondered what Dad's neighbors must've been thinking about all of this. Not just from Andy's frantic digging, but also from all the other insane sounds they surely picked up on throughout the weekend. My father and I in particular had partaken in our fair share of screaming. Which is understandable, I think. Decomposing is not for the quiet. Were any of our neighbors *concerned*? What did they think was going on over here? We weren't throwing a party—well, not a normal one, at least. A corpse party, maybe. But would they be concerned enough to call the cops? They would've already rolled up, if so. Yesterday morning would've made the most sense for authorities to get involved, when we woke up paralyzed, screaming in the purest agony any creature on this planet has ever experienced. But now? A man was simply digging holes in a back yard. Where was the crime in that?

"Do you think he's going to find anything?" I asked.

"What?" Dad said, snapping out of some daydream I wasn't privy to.

"Outside, in the yard. Do you think there are other bodies?"

"*What* other bodies?"

"I don't know . . . "

"Who else would be buried here?"

"Maybe there's one of Andy, too—or Comrade."

At the sound of her name, Comrade came trotting into the house, abandoning her master out in the harsh Texas heat.

"There's nobody else out there," Dad said, with an unsettling confidence.

"But how do you know?"

"Because why would there be?"

It was so frustrating that he couldn't see the flaw in his own logic. "But why would *we* be there? Why would we have been buried out there and not other people, too?"

"Because," Dad said, matter-of-factly, "it's my property."

Behind the chair, where Andy had tied my wrists together, something tugged violently at my arm. I tried glancing over my shoulder but failed to locate the source of the disturbance. Regardless, it didn't take a genius to decipher Comrade's wet snarls and growls.

Dad eyed me with suspicion. "Hell's the matter with you? You got ants in your pants or something?"

"Comrade's biting me."

"She's *what*?"

"She's trying to eat my arm."

"Oh." He didn't seem that concerned about what I'd told him—but, to be fair, neither did I. "Uh, does it hurt?"

"Not really. It kind of . . . tickles, I guess."

"Like in a pleasant way?"

"I don't know. Not in an . . . *unpleasant* way."

"Son, this better not turn into some kinda bizarre fetish."

"Some kinda what?"

Dad chuckled. "Nothing. I was making a joke."

"What does it mean?"

"You don't need to know. The joke wasn't for you."

An uncomfortable silence passed as I went over his words in my head. "Wait. Who was it for?"

"Nobody. It's not important."

He didn't need to tell me. I already suspected the real answer. He had made the joke for himself—his *other* self. Dead Dad. The way Dad was tied up, he was forced to face the couch where you guys were lounging. How long had he been forced to stare at his dead shirtless doppelgänger without taking a break? He couldn't get up. And, if he was like me, he couldn't close his eyes. Which meant he'd had a lot of time to study his own corpse.

"You're talking to the bodies, aren't you?" I asked. "You're trying to make them laugh."

"Don't be silly," Dad said, nervous. "The dead can't laugh."

"How do you know they can't?"

"Because . . . we'd know about it, if they could. It'd be all over the news. This just in: corpses love jokes!"

"But how do you know *these* bodies can't laugh? They aren't like regular dead people, right?"

"Good point," Dad said, then, to his other self on the couch: "Hey, you! Hey, fatso! It's me, you! I mean it's you, me! You know what I mean. Or is that *I* know what *you* mean? Anyway, Dylan here thinks you can laugh. Me, though? I call bullshit on that."

"Dad, you sound crazy," I said, but he didn't seem to hear me.

"So I thought we'd do a little test. See which one of us is correct. A laughing test, we'll call it. How does that sound? Don't answer that. Just listen. I want to talk about something no human being on this planet can find unfunny, unless you're already dead and incapable of laughter, which you definitely are, and we're wasting our time here even entertaining this test, but let's give it a go, anyway—you know, to satisfy the boy."

"Dad . . . "

"So," Dad said, to the corpse, "I don't know about you, but when I want to be put in a better mood, there's one thing that never fails to—wait, what am I saying? 'I don't know about you'? Of course I know about you! I know *all* about you! I know more about you than anyone else on this whole goddamn planet. You *are* me, right? And I'm you. So, if that's true, then that must mean you've already heard the story I'm about to tell you—but that shouldn't prevent you from laughing—that is, if you're capable of laughing. I've told this story to dozens of idiots over the years— friends, family, strangers—and it's never *not* made me laugh. And I'm sure Dylan has already guessed what I'm talking about."

He was correct. I knew exactly what story he was building up to telling. Most of the time when he brought this up, I left the room or plugged my ears. Now I couldn't choose either of these escape routes. I'd be forced to sit there and listen to him embarrass me in front of not only you, but also your dead mother and your dead father. Plus Comrade, who had yet to abandon her dreams of eating me one limb at a time.

"They can't hear you," I said. "They can't laugh. They can't talk." The words tasted repugnant as they left my mouth. If I couldn't convince myself, how was I going to convince someone else?

Dad continued without bothering to acknowledge my weak response. All attention focused on his deceased counterpart. "Now this must've been about seven years ago, which would have made Dylan . . . what? Six years old? Something like that. This is in that final stretch of

MAGGOTS SCREAMING!

Blockbusters still existing, too. A couple months after this story ends, I think the rest of them shut down for good. Except for that one in Alaska—the one they're always talking about on the internet. But who could give a shit about Alaska? Especially at a time like this? What *matters* is we were at a Blockbuster—in *Texas*. The whole family. Lori went in to return some DVDs and pick up whatever looked interesting on the newly-arrived shelves, and Dylan and me stayed in the car, listening to Duncan kick ass on the radio. This was also when we had that stupid van. I don't know if you remember it, but it was god awful. Hated that thing. Lori's idea, obviously. So we're out there in the parking lot, waiting, Dylan's sitting at the back of the van like he always did. He liked the privacy or something. I don't know. And this lady walks out of the video store, she gets in her car which is parked to the right of us, and pulls out only to then immediately swing into the spot to the left of our van. And I'm thinking, *What the hell? Is this lady drunk or something?* And she rolls down her window, then gestures for me to do the same, so I entertain her and I roll it down and I ask how I can help her, and by gawd . . . I swear I'll never forget how she responded. Verbatim, this lady, she says, 'I don't know if you're aware of this, mister, but your son was just flipping me the bird back there!' Then she drove away, not so much as waiting for an apology. I remember being impressed by what she had said—largely because nobody had ever called me 'mister' like that before. It made me feel fancy, like in an old-timey sort of way. I liked it."

Despite seven years having passed, I could remember this incident clear as day. Yes, it was true, I had given her the middle finger, but I didn't think she'd *seen* me. I thought I was being *sneaky* about the whole thing. But then, when she pulled into the other parking spot, I knew it was all over. I was busted. A tremendous fear seized me, gripped my heart and tried squeezing it dry.

"Now," Dad continued, "Dylan had obviously

overheard what the lady had said, because the instant I turned around in my seat and made eye contact with him, what did he do?"

"Dad, please," I said, hating this part of the story the most.

"He started crying!" Dad told his motionless, decomposing doppelgänger. "I didn't have to say *nothing*. Not a single word. Suddenly he was . . . *bawling*. The kind of heavy sobs that smear snot all over your face and shit. I was like, 'Dylan? What the hell?' And he started apologizing, shouting how sorry he was and begging me not to tell his mother. And I promised him I wouldn't. It wasn't *that* big of a deal. It wasn't like he'd fuckin' *killed* somebody or something, right? Lori would've probably never known, either, except Dylan can't keep a secret for shit. That boy emerged from the womb looking guilty, I swear. 'What's wrong?' Lori asked the silent van after getting back, and Dylan lasted all of three seconds before busting out the waterworks again. Then she turned to me, gave me a look like *I* was the one who had done something to *him*, and said, 'What the hell is going on here?' But I couldn't tell her, right? Because I had made a promise. So I said, 'You'll have to ask him,' and drove out of the Blockbuster parking lot without another word."

Comrade whined behind me. My arm tugged again. I wondered how much of it was left at this point.

"Later on we learned the whole story," Dad said to his corpse. "Dylan broke down and told us everything when we got home. That not only had he flipped off the lady at Blockbuster, but he had been flipping off strangers everywhere we went, whenever he had the chance. He couldn't help himself, he said. He'd tried to stop but the urge was too strong. Which meant anytime we had driven anywhere, around that time, Dylan would've been in the back of the van, flashing his little middle finger to any person we passed. Imagine that. You're going on about your day, minding your own business, when suddenly a random child is saying fuck you. It'd wreck the rest of your evening! Psychologically, you'd be ruined. Of course, when we asked Dylan, he claimed he had no idea what it meant, that he'd seen Jim Carrey do it in that fuckin' *Liar Liar* movie and thought it looked funny."

This was only half true. I had indeed seen it in *Liar Liar*, but I also knew exactly what it meant.

"Then Lori asked him if he ever did this at school, and Dylan said . . . oh gawd, I'll never forget this, either . . . he said, 'Not to other people.' And Lori and I both looked at each other like *what the fuck does that mean?* And what we found out was . . . well, every day at school—*multiple* times a day—he was excusing himself to the bathroom so he could stand in front of the mirror and flip himself off."

Dad paused, since this was usually the part where—if they hadn't laughed already—they busted a gut. Except his audience wasn't making any noise. In fact, they weren't reacting at all. It was true, what he had told them. When I was younger—for a short spell—I was irrationally addicted to giving myself the middle finger. It wasn't a habit I personally found funny or cool. Instead I was deeply ashamed, and terrified somebody would catch me. At least when I was flipping someone else off, that was partially explainable. But if someone had caught me doing it in front of a mirror . . . I didn't know what I would say. I would have probably run away. And yet, I had told my mom and dad as soon as the tiniest ounce of pressure was laid upon me. I spilled everything. And afterward, neither parent had known what to say. They just stared at me, emotionless, until one of them burst out laughing, followed by the other—although, when I think about it, I cannot recall which one of them laughed first.

Regardless, none of the corpses on the couch betrayed me by also laughing. Including you, fortunately. I don't know what I would have done if you had laughed. Maybe you were just as embarrassed as I was about the situation.

I can't help but wonder if there's a hidden deeper

meaning behind my childhood middle finger addiction. Back then I was obsessed with saying fuck you to my reflection. I craved the inexplicable hatred. I wanted more and more and more. How different is a doppelgänger from a reflection? They aren't exactly the same, but there's an undeniable similarity.

"Oh well," Dad said. "Tough crowd, I guess."

"Dad," I said, barely a whisper.

"What?"

"I—" I stopped, and whatever I was about to tell him was lost, as Comrade chose right then to retreat from her hiding spot behind us, trotting around our chairs and finding a spot on the carpet to stretch.

I don't know how long we stared at her before I realized she had half my arm in her mouth.

The hand—the *severed* hand—was balled into a fist.

Except for the middle finger.

It was pointing straight up.

And, I swear to god, in that moment I heard maggots laughing. The few remaining ones lingering inside my decayed carcass, yes, but also any others still adventurous enough to be hanging around our house. Forgotten, abandoned, whatever. They were here and they were deeply, disgustingly amused. For the longest time I'd mistakenly assumed that this *casserole-crackling-in-an-oven* noise was what maggots sounded like when they were screaming. When they were in *pain*. Agony.

But I'd been wrong.

They'd never been screaming.

All this time, they were laughing.

Howling with joy.

Because this was all a joke to them.

And they were loving every second of it.

Only then did my brain register that the rope was no longer restraining my wrists together. I brought my arms around, hoping it wasn't true, but of course it was. My left arm was missing—chewed off a couple inches below my elbow. Not a single drop of blood poured out. Some of that yellow liquid—the purge fluid—yes, but no blood. Purge fluid and maggots. More maggots than I could possibly count. Tumbling out of my exposed wound like an unstable cheerleader pyramid. It didn't hurt. None of it hurt. In the beginning of our transformation, earlier this weekend, there had been pain—immense pain—but now the sensation was different. Like I had tried explaining to Dad: it tickled. Not in a pleasant way—but also not in an *unpleasant* way.

"Dad," I said, repositioning my elbow to prevent further maggots from spilling out, overcome with a strong need to protect them, "Comrade took my arm."

"I see that," he said. "Are you okay?"

"I don't know."

"Are you able to untie me?"

"I don't know."

"Well, you think you might want to give it a shot?"

I don't want to talk about what happened next. You were there, too. In the same room as the rest of us. So what's the point in bringing this up again? Do you really want to hear it? Because I sure don't—and if you're me, and I'm you, shouldn't we want the same things?

Okay, fair, maybe that's wishful thinking on my part. But still. You have to understand why I don't want to linger too long here. None of this would have happened if I hadn't untied Dad. I didn't make him do what he did, but I absolutely helped him. I assisted. It doesn't matter that I didn't know what the outcome would be. The universe doesn't care about our inability to predict the future. It holds us accountable all the same.

I did it. I untied him. It took some doing, considering I was working with one hand. Untangling a knot with only five fingers is not the easiest task, although it's not impossible.

"Stay here," Dad said, shambling through the kitchen and out the door.

He didn't need to tell me twice. I stood in the living room and watched Comrade gnaw on my arm. She looked like she was in heaven. Existence no longer extended beyond herself and her new chew toy. She had gotten what she wanted. She was content. I considered what I wanted, what object would give me a similar satisfaction, and failed to conceive of anything worthwhile. I didn't want my arm back. Far as I was concerned, Comrade could keep it.

Out in the yard Dad and Andy started arguing. I couldn't make out what they were saying. They sounded angry. They sounded unpredictable. I sat on the floor next to the couch and grabbed your hand, which was dangling off the armrest. I would like to say that you squeezed my hand back, but maybe I had imagined it. I don't know. I think maybe you really squeezed. Let's say you did, okay? Just this one time, we can pretend.

A new noise erupted in the yard, drowning out their yelling. A machine noise. It took me a second to recognize the sound, but once I did, it was indisputable.

Someone had turned on the hedge trimmer.

I'd forgotten all about it. We must've left it in the yard after discovering you in the garden.

And now it'd been rediscovered.

I didn't need to guess which one of them had found it.

Andy's angry shouts transformed into a gargled scream, then the hedge trimmer cut off and the yard was once again occupied by silence.

A couple minutes later Dad entered the house and shut the door. The front side of him was covered in fresh blood. From someone who could still bleed.

"Well?" he said, after catching me staring at him.

"Wh-what?"

"Are we going to continue our *Simpsons* marathon or not?"

A COUPLE YEARS AGO—before the big divorce, before the great decomposing—the three of us went out for dinner somewhere, I forget where. Probably that Italian place next to the comic book shop, if I had to guess. Where we ate isn't relevant to the story. What's important is afterward we stopped at Walgreens. I don't remember what we needed. Cigarettes, probably. All three of us got out of the car, but only *one* of us remained biologically connected to the car.

I'm pretty sure, if someone is given enough time on earth, they will eventually slam their finger in a car door. Which is what happened to me that night. The door swallowed the entirety of my thumb. It didn't bounce back like you'd expect it to do after connecting with a human finger. Instead, the door came to a close, clicking in place and everything.

Followed by the sound of my dad pressing the automatic lock button on his car keys.

The pain was instantaneous.

I tried pulling away, and nothing gave. I tried opening the door, already knowing it was locked, and nothing opened. So what other choice did I have but to scream? So I screamed. And screamed. And screamed. And my parents panicked. It took them what felt like at least two full minutes to figure out what was happening to me, and then another minute to remember the car was locked.

By the time my hand was free again, I no longer had a thumbnail. It'd been ripped clean off, leaving behind a layer of mucus-textured blood matching the same dimensions as the exiled nail. I tried to scream again but no sound emitted from my mouth. Dad dragged me into Walgreens in search of bandages. Blood dripped off my finger and left a trail on the marble floor of the medical supplies aisle. The ability to cry returned while standing at the checkout register. The noise coming out of me was so piercing, I remember the cashier pressing both hands against her ears and grimacing.

The nail grew back, over the course of several months, but not the way it used to look. It was different. It formed with a deep ridge along the center, resembling something like the half-pipes at skateboard parks. A couple years later it still hadn't smoothed out. It always grew wrong. It was *corrupt.*

And I couldn't stop thinking about that. How sometimes, when you lose something, even if it grows back, it never really returns the way you remember it.

Sometimes things change, and there's nothing you or I or anybody can do to make them go back to how they used to be.

Things started getting weird after Andy died. Well, weirder than they already were. Dad forbade me from setting foot in the yard. The kitchen table was dragged across the room and placed in front of the door to prevent me from exiting. He told me Andy had decided to go home, that he no longer wanted anything to do with us, that we were alone again.

"What about Comrade?" I asked.

"He said we can keep her," Dad replied. "You know. For good luck."

"But what about his truck? It's still out front."

"Wouldn't you know it? He gave that to us, too."

I didn't believe a single word of what he was saying. Andy loved only two things in this world, and both of them were on our property. He never would have given them to us. Not as gifts. Not as anything. As far as I'd been able to gather over the weekend, he hardly *liked* my father that much anymore. Could they still be considered friends? Maybe so, otherwise Andy would've never come out here on Friday night when we needed him the most. But *good* friends? Once upon a time, yeah, totally—before everything that happened between them and Miguel and Mom. Now, though, there was *something* present in their friendship, but it wasn't as strong as it used to be, and it *certainly* wasn't at the sort of level where it'd make sense for him to randomly give us his dog and truck. I don't think their friendship had *ever* reached that stage.

Plus, I had heard the noises outside. The screaming. The hedge trimmer. The silence.

If Dad didn't want to tell me what he'd done, then fine. He could keep it as his little secret. Maybe he was too ashamed to admit the truth. And maybe I was too afraid to fully embrace the idea that my father had murdered another human being with a hedge trimmer. Neither of us spoke about the kitchen table he pushed in front of the door. After all, if Andy had gone home, then what was Dad preventing me from seeing?

After she finished gnawing on my dismembered arm, Comrade camped out beneath the table, scratching at the door. As if she somehow knew what had happened—and maybe she did know. Dogs are smart. They pick up on things. They sense when a new danger's in the air. They *worry*.

Dad and I ignored her the best we could.

Which was easier for Dad than it was for me.

Dad had other things to obsess over. There was no room in his mental energy to stress out about a dog concerned for her master.

"I have a theory," Dad said, not too long after forbidding me from the back yard.

We were in the living room, sharing the loveseat again, watching *The Simpsons* with the volume on low. Dead Dad and Dead Mom still leaned against each other on the couch. You sat on the carpet, next to your parents' legs, one hand brushing against the ouija board. Were you *clutching* it, like the board game was a personal possession? Maybe that was my brain melting into jelly. Something I've learned is that, while decomposing into nothing, it's often difficult to separate fantasy from reality. As chemicals break down and organs liquefy, something in your mind snaps, and the definition of rationality is the first to rot. The reason for this is simple. There is no difference between fantasy or reality. The things we perceive as "unreal" are only disregarded as such because we don't know how to properly process what we're seeing without going insane. Fortunately, one of the many benefits of decomposition is embracing total madness.

Back to Dad's theory, which he was about to explain: "What was it that body farm psycho was saying about saints?"

"Saints?" I said, the word not making any sense in my head.

"They're *incorruptible*," Dad said. "Remember what she said back on her golf cart? Sometimes when a dead body doesn't decompose right away, that might mean the body belonged to a saint."

"I thought she said religious people made that up."

"But what if they were right?" Dad asked. "What if there *are* saints and what if they really are incorruptible?"

I tried to consider his question, then realized I needed several questions of my own answered first. Like, "What does being a saint mean?"

"What are you talking about?" was Dad's response.

"I don't know what saints are."

"Of course you do."

"I do?"

"They're, like . . . religious superheroes, or something. Like . . . celebrities in heaven, holy people who never sinned, or whatever the hell."

"What do they do?"

"What do you mean, 'what do they do'?"

"Are they . . . guards? Do they patrol things in heaven? What do saints have to do?"

"They don't have to do anything. They're saints."

"Are they guardian angels?"

"Guardian angels don't exist," Dad said, with confidence.

"But saints do?"

"I don't know, Dylan. I'm speculating."

"Are we saints?" I pointed at you and your parents. "Or are *they* saints?"

"What?" Dad sounded disgusted. "Why would they be saints?"

"They were dead first."

"Who's to say they were ever alive in the first place?"

Which was a question neither of us had posed before. Before we found you in the garden grave, had there been a time when you weren't dead? If someone is never actually alive, can they be classified as dead, or are they something else?

"Have you ever sinned?" I asked.

"Sinned?"

"You said saints have never—"

"I know what I said."

"Well, have you?"

"I don't know," Dad said. "If I have, it's not like they were *big* sins, or anything."

"What's a big sin?" I asked, thinking about why the kitchen door was suddenly blocked off. "Murder?"

"Listen, I don't know if we're saints, okay? It was just a fuckin' theory, so why don't you get off my case?"

"I'm sorry," I said.

"Jesus Christ. It's like I'm talking to your mother."

"Do you think she's—?"

"No," he said, cutting me off. "I don't think she's any more okay than we are. I think she's very much not okay, actually."

"Oh."

"I'm sorry to break the news to you, kid, but we're pretty much fucked."

"Can we go see her?"

"Where? In Corpus?"

"Yeah."

"I don't know," he said, after a while. "Maybe later."

Dad turned up the TV and we watched *The Simpsons* without continuing the conversation. He didn't bring up saints again, and I stopped asking if he thought my mom was going to be okay.

We ran out of *Simpsons* episodes to watch, so Dad suggested we pass the time by playing video games. I reminded him that I only had one arm, thanks to Comrade. He asked me so what? I said so how am I supposed to use a controller? He shrugged, like I was trying to create an excuse not to play. "Just use your stub," he said. "You only need it to guide the left joystick, right? Most of the action comes from the other hand, anyway." I couldn't argue with that. It sure beat having to think too hard about our current situation. Well, that's what I assumed, anyway—until Dad inserted the disc for *Zombies Ate My Neighbors* into our PlayStation 4. Something about playing a game featuring the undead felt wrong. Like we were belittling ourselves. When I voiced this concern, Dad dismissed me with a scoff and said, "We ain't zombies, goddammit! Grab your controller."

"Then what are we?" I asked, retrieving the second-player controller from the system.

"What are we?" Dad said, like he didn't understand the question. "You're my son, and I'm your dad. That's what the heck we are."

Zombies Ate My Neighbors wasn't a game I'd ever heard of until Dad introduced me to it a couple months after the divorce finalized. Probably the first weekend where he seemed to be in a genuine good mood. Before then, whenever it was his turn to have me, our time together was usually spent with me watching him get drunk and bawl his eyes out. Don't get me wrong. Those intoxicated crying sessions never officially stopped, but they did start occurring less frequently the day his online order of *Zombies Ate My Neighbors* arrived.

When he first told me the title, I asked him what he was talking about, convinced he'd gotten it mixed up with some other game. It wouldn't have been the first time. Memories of him accidentally muttering *Fortcraft* and *Farm Birds* were constant jokes in our family, before . . . well, *before*. So it didn't seem too far outside the realm of reality that *Zombies Ate My Neighbors* was another unique butchering of several different popular games.

Turned out to be a game from *his* childhood, which automatically made me suspicious of it being any good. No offense to him, but in my experience most of the video games from when Dad was my age are pretty boring, especially compared to newer games. So imagine my surprise when *Zombies Ate My Neighbors* ended up kicking ass. He'd ordered it from a retro gaming company that re-released both *Zombies* and its inferior sequel, *Ghoul Patrol*, together in one package.

That weekend it arrived, we played it in co-op mode for the first time, fell in love, then every other weekend afterward we tried to play it again at least once. This was over a year ago, and we still hadn't managed to beat it. The game was sometimes frustratingly difficult, and also a little stupid due to its lack of save options. If you lost all your lives, or turned the game off, you had to start at level one again. I watched a couple videos on YouTube of people managing to reach the end, but I was convinced they'd cheated somehow. There was no way they'd pulled that off on skill alone.

The premise of *Zombies Ate My Neighbors* is not complicated. You have the choice of two characters, both of them kids around my age: Zeke or Julie. They're brother and sister. Or maybe they're best friends? It's never explained too well. Zeke wears weird 3-D glasses for reasons I've never been able to understand. Julie wears a baseball hat and a white tank top that makes me feel uncomfortable whenever I stare for too long. Somehow they are the only ones capable of fighting the numerous monsters destroying the world. Zombies, yes, but as you progress into higher levels you start encountering all kinds of cool creatures, such as vampires, relentless chainsaw-wielding maniacs, mummies, evil dolls, lizard men, blobs, giant ants, and forty-feet-tall babies. It's up to the player to save as many terrified neighbors as possible before they get eaten up. You begin in a standard suburban neighborhood and work your way through pyramids, grocery stories, spooky castles, and so on—utilizing a variety of creative weapons, like uzi water guns, bazookas, weed whackers, explosive soda cans, ice pops, tomatoes, silverware, dishes, crucifixes, flamethrowers, fire extinguishers, and Martian bubble guns.

While playing the game this time, after our *Simpsons* marathon, it was the weed whacker that captured my attention the most. In the game its primary function is to destroy toxic alien fungi spreading throughout the neighborhoods. Anytime one of us operated it, I couldn't help but be reminded of the hedge trimmer we'd left out in our back yard. The one I'd used to destroy Mom's garden. The one Dad had used to silence Andy. While playing the game, I kept losing focus as I wondered what the hedge trimmer might've looked like, if the blade was covered in blood or if Dad had thought to wipe it off before coming inside. That was one reason I kept dying. The other was it's a lot harder to maneuver a joystick using a stump than Dad made it out to be. Maybe if I had an actual stump, with a closed end, things would've been different. But I didn't have that. My wound never healed. Never even *thought* about healing. Instead it remained wide open. Drier than it was wet. Bits of gnawed flesh dangling out of me like those flaps you drive through at a car wash. Rather than simply guide the joystick with a properly-healed stump, the only way I could move it involved pressing my arm down until the joystick popped into my wound, essentially merging us together. I like to think the few maggots lingering in that specific area helped a little, too, clutching onto the joystick with their tiny maggot hands.

No, I thought, *not a joystick.*

A joystump.

"Hey," Dad said, after I died for the seventh time in a row, "what's the matter with you? You tryin' to lose on purpose?"

"I'm sorry."

"It's okay. It's just I can't save all these neighbors by myself. Not without your help."

"I'll try harder."

"Attaboy."

But it was Dad who died next, a couple levels later, when we encountered a series of monsters both of us had evidently forgotten. In addition to the creatures I'd previously mentioned—zombies, vampires, kaiju babies, etc—there was another one I should've probably included.

They emerged from plants, sporting an identical resemblance to our two characters.

Pod people.

Clones.

Evil lookalikes.

Dad paused—not the game, but his movement. Let his character stand there in the middle of the neighborhood while a dozen alien doppelgängers ganged up and gleefully slaughtered him. My own character didn't fare much better, either.

Instead of restarting, he switched off the PlayStation 4 and said, "Okay, that does it."

"That does . . . what?" I asked.

"I can't . . . " He jabbed a thumb toward his own lookalike sitting on the other side of the living room. " . . . I can't be around . . . this . . . this *thing* anymore."

Without saying another word, he got up from the loveseat and stomped toward the couch. I almost expected Dead Dad to flinch or try to retreat, but he remained motionless as Living Dad retrieved the sheet from the carpet and threw it over him. A part of me was tempted to cut out eyeholes on the sheet to make him look like a ghost, but I don't think my father would have appreciated that, under the circumstances. Some other time he would have found it hilarious, I'm sure.

"What do you want to do with yours?" he asked.

"With my . . . what?"

"Your . . . your *thing*. It can't stay here like this. I can cover it up or we can move it. You decide."

"Can we move him?"

"Move it where?"

"My room?"

"Okay." Dad nodded. "But after this, that's where it's staying. I'm not moving it again."

"Him."

"What?"

"Him, not it."

"Dylan, they aren't real people."

"We don't know that."

I thought he was going to continue arguing, but he sighed and said, "You're gonna need to help me. I'm not as strong as I was last time we carried these fuckers."

I couldn't offer much support with only the one arm, but I tried my best. Dad took each of your wrists and I grabbed one of your ankles and slowly, awkwardly, we dragged you down the hall into my room. He tried to leave you near the doorway, but I stopped him and asked if we could lift you into my bed.

"That's disgusting," he said.

"He's been on the floor since the ouija board," I said. "Don't you think that's long enough?"

"It's your bed. What do I care?"

Together, we managed to pick you up and drop you on

my mattress. The springs beneath clashed at the new weight, then settled as your head lolled to the side, motionless.

Afterward, he said, "Okay, next you're gonna help me move the other one to my room."

"I thought you already covered him with a sheet."

"Not that one," he said, and I swear I could hear the shame in his voice.

It took significantly longer, but over the next hour or so we managed to transport Dead Mom from the couch to Dad's bed. He didn't act disgusted by the idea of her corpse rotting in his sheets like he'd been when I wanted to put you in my bed. Maybe he'd come around on the idea. Or maybe it felt different to him, since he used to be married to her. Well, a *version* of her.

"What are we going to do?" I asked, once she was tucked under his blankets. We stood over her, not *panting* exactly, since we weren't capable of being out of breath anymore, but still feeling *weighed down* from the exercise.

"I think I'm going to lay down for a little bit."

"You can *sleep*?"

"No. I don't know. I don't think so." He rubbed his dried-out eyes. By then we had both given up on moisturizing them with artificial tears. "I just want to lay down and be alone."

I tried looking at Dead Mom in bed, but he stepped around me and blocked my path. "You can entertain yourself for a while, can't you?"

"I . . . I guess so." Minus a couple bathroom breaks, we hadn't been separated since he picked me up Friday morning. Suddenly the thought of us not being together felt terrifying. I didn't want to be alone. Not in this house. Not while we were rotting. Decomposing together had somehow seemed manageable. But alone? No way. Impossible.

"Maybe later tonight we'll play some dice or something," he said, and closed the door.

I remained standing on the other side, listening against the wood as the mattress adjusted against Dad's weight. A moment later, I heard him whisper, "I'm sorry, I'm so sorry, I love you, I love you so much. What do I do? What the fuck do I do?"

I decided maybe it was best we had some alone time, after all.

I went to my room and shut the door. You hadn't moved since we left you here. Of course you hadn't. Against everything I had witnessed since digging up the garden grave, I was convinced you were capable of doing more than just lying still, that maybe you could get up and walk around when nobody else was watching. *Toy Story* logic.

I sat on the edge of the bed and said, "Well, now what?"

And you stared back at me, stubborn as ever.

"Should we go outside and ask a neighbor to call the police? Tell them we're rotting and my dad's gone crazy? That he's killed his friend and left his body outside?"

You didn't seem to agree or disagree with this plan.

"But what would happen then?" I asked. "Would I get taken away? Would they take me to my mom? Did she also go crazy? Am *I* crazy? What does going crazy feel like?" I paused, then let out a dry laugh. "I guess talking to a dead version of myself is pretty crazy."

But it didn't feel that way. Talking to you felt like the most natural thing in the world. Which maybe is another sign that I was—and still very much am—crazy as hell.

The longer I think about it, the more I'm convinced that it doesn't matter. Reality is whatever our individual brains perceive it to be. Sometimes the details line up with others and sometimes they take a different path. In the end they're all heading for the same finish line, anyway. So what did it matter that I spent the rest of the day in my room, talking to you? Would it have been considered more normal to tell these things to a neighbor, or a cop? Nobody would have listened like you listen. They would have waited for me to let something incriminating slip out of my mouth, then tried to arrest my dad and thrown me in some orphanage for the dead.

But you don't judge. You just listen.

And sometimes that's all a person needs.

I only wish I could do the same for you.

I didn't fall asleep, exactly, but I came about as close to it as someone with my condition can. I daydreamed. I zoned out. I forgot where I was and why I was there. I got lost in my thoughts. What was I thinking about? It's hard to remember. I think it was something about Corpus Christi. Fantasizing about what my life would be like if I'd chosen to go with Mom and Miguel instead of sticking around with Dad. Would he have dug up the garden? And if he hadn't, would all this crap have still happened? Something told me no. Life would be normal if we'd left the bodies in the ground. If we hadn't destroyed Mom's plants. If things had stayed the way they were and you had remained undisturbed. I could've gone to Corpus and went boogie boarding in the gulf. We had planned on visiting the aquarium, too, which meant I could've seen real sharks. If I had gone with them. If Dad had controlled his temper. If Mom hadn't tried being sneaky about it. If, if, if . . .

Something loud banged above the house.

Followed by footsteps.

Followed by Comrade barking.

I snapped out of whatever daze I had fallen into and glanced down at you, still next to me in bed, as if to receive confirmation that you had also heard the noise. You didn't look like you'd noticed anything.

More banging above the house.

Something was definitely happening.

I rolled out of bed, slowly, my atrophying muscles trying their best to function. It was amazing I could move at all, to be honest. By then I was more skeleton than flesh. A large chunk of my cheek under my left eye had lost all of its skin. When I touched the area I felt smooth bone. Similar areas could be found all over my body. Under my shirt most of my ribs had managed to poke through what remained of my belly and revealed themselves for anybody to see. The more I thought about it, the more I couldn't keep still, so I tried not to think about it at all, which only resulted in me getting obsessed with the imagery. People weren't supposed to see their own skeletons. That was the deal humans made with life. We lugged around these bones from birth until death and, as reward, we never had to come face-to-face with the secret truth hidden inside us all. But the longer we rotted, the clearer it became that somehow the pact had gotten broken somewhere down the line. Now it was a free-for-all. Skeletons gone wild.

At the end of the hallway the door to our attic was extended down to the carpet, like a giant wooden tongue. Comrade circled the bottom of it, barking at the sudden noises. She was outraged at this new disturbance. I peered up into the darkness and listened to the awkward footsteps above.

"Dad? Is that you?"

The footsteps paused, his face appeared at the opening. The skin on his right cheek had deteriorated, revealing the dirty white of his skull. "Dylan? My gawd, I forgot you was here."

"What are you doing up there?"

"I'm trying to . . . find something."

"Find what?"

"Uh. It's none of your concern."

"Do you need any help?"

He shook his head. "No. Go on back to sleep. Everything's okay."

"Sleep? Dad, I can't—"

"Wait!" His expression morphed into a grotesque eureka. "I remember which box it's in . . . "

He disappeared into the darkness again. More frantic footsteps, followed by the sound of several boxes being pushed and scavenged.

"I knew it!" he shouted from the attic. "I goddamn knew it!"

When he returned to the opening, he was holding something large and white. A dress of some kind, zipped in a plastic protective case. He told me to catch and dropped it into the hallway. It hit my head and fell to the floor. Dad didn't notice, though, as he'd already turned his back on me so he could descend the ancient ladder. Each wooden rung released an alarming *creaking* as his feet connected with them. I thought for sure one would snap, but he made it down without any issues. He'd lost a lot of weight since the start of our great decomposition. Both of us had.

I didn't realize it was a wedding dress until he'd unzipped the plastic and pulled it free.

"Is that Mom's?" I asked, following him as he dragged it down the hallway toward his bedroom.

"She never bothered taking it with her when she moved out. Either she forgot about it or didn't give a shit. Honestly, I'm not sure which one's worse."

"But why do you have it?"

"What was I supposed to do with it? Throw it away?"

"No, I mean—why do you have it *now*?"

"Oh. I thought that was obvious."

We made it into his room. Dead Mom was still in his bed, except she didn't have any clothes on. The first thing I noticed were her breasts, and how much they had rotted away since we first carried her out of the garden grave. I turned away, a little too quick, and almost lost my balance. I could no longer blush but that didn't mean I couldn't feel embarrassed.

"Why is she naked?" I asked.

"You ever see someone with regular clothes on also wearing a wedding dress? Of course not. It'd look ridiculous."

"You're gonna put the dress on her?" I asked. The idea sounded insane. I couldn't make sense of it.

"Mm-hmm." He proceeded to nod for at least a full minute without saying another word, then added, "It's what she would've wanted."

I had no idea what he meant by that. I wasn't entirely sure he knew, either.

"C'mon," he said. "You gonna help or what?"

Now that I only had the one arm, it was difficult to offer much assistance, but I tried my best, and together we managed to wrestle my naked dead mother into her old wedding dress—veil and all.

The weirdest thing about it was the dress looked brand-new. I felt bad about letting its pristine cleanliness make contact with her decomposing dirt-stained body. I hoped my real mom—the one being held in a Corpus Christi hospital—would understand how little choice I'd been given in the matter. Then again, if she really cared about the dress, she probably wouldn't have left it in Dad's attic when we moved out. In her head it undoubtedly served as this painful reminder of my parents' marriage. She probably never wanted to see it again.

I wondered what she would say if she came over and caught this imposter wearing it. Would she want her to take it off, or would she say, "It looks good on you. Keep it."?

To be more realistic, her reaction would likely consist of a scream, followed by several questions, such as, "What the hell is going on here?" and, "Why does that dead body look exactly like me?" It was hard to remind myself that Dad and I had plenty of time to cope with this new lifestyle. Outsiders, such as my mother, might not accept you and the other corpses so quickly. Down in Corpus, we already knew Mom was experiencing similar symptoms, but never once did it cross my mind that she had somehow confronted *another* set of lookalike bodies. No. You, and Dead Mom, and Dead Dad, this whole situation felt unique to this specific area.

After Dead Mom was situated in the wedding dress, we both stood above her, admiring her in bed. I had to admit, once the task was complete, I was glad we'd done it. She looked beautiful.

My parents had gotten married before I was born, which meant up until that day in Dad's bedroom, I'd never seen my mother in this dress besides in old photographs. It was different, in person—even if she wasn't the *same* person. They were same *enough*. With the wedding dress on, her various states of decay no longer looked that bad. If anything, the rot complemented her, such was the power of this dress.

"Wow," I said.

And Dad responded with, "I know."

"I miss her."

"Me too," he said. "With all my heart." Then, in a whisper: "And now I have her back."

"Do you think it's time to call someone?" I asked.

He shook his head, never taking his eyes off the bed. "They'd take her away from us."

"Maybe they'd let us keep her."

"Not a chance in hell."

That was the end of the discussion. He turned and, although he didn't physically push me out of his bedroom, he did motion with his hands that he *would* push me out if I didn't leave of my own accord. So I left and he closed the door. I didn't return to my room right away. Instead I explored the house, unsupervised. I could've moved the kitchen table and investigated the yard, but there was no point. I knew what I'd find out there and under no circumstances did I want to see it. I preferred pretending nothing had happened, and everything was fine, and that Andy had simply gone home.

Gone home and left his dog with us.

By then, Comrade had peed and pooped all over the house. I couldn't remember the last time either of us had let her outside. That was okay, though. The house was already a cesspool of disease. A little dog poop wasn't going to cause that much extra damage.

I did feel bad about forgetting to feed and water her. Fortunately neither Dad nor myself ever remembered to close the toilet lid, so she'd had access to water this entire time. Plus, I soon discovered she'd been helping herself to Dead Dad's ankles out in the living room. They were dangling out of the sheet we'd thrown over him. She had enjoyed quite the feast on his spoiled flesh while we isolated ourselves in our individual rooms. He would never walk again, if he'd ever walked in the first place.

Despite this ankle buffet, the dog looked hungry. Her ribs were visible every time she inhaled. The girl needed to eat. I led her into the kitchen and opened the fridge. There was nothing suitable for a dog inside except for some long-expired slices of American cheese, so I closed it and scavenged the cabinets, trying my best not to glance at the table pushed against the door. Comrade kept scratching at the wooden frame below the table. I ignored the noise. Maybe she'd forget about what—*who*—was out there, but I doubted it. How could she? Andy had adopted her when she was a puppy. He was all she'd ever known.

The small bag of dog food Andy had bought her on his drugstore run was already empty. None of us had fed it to her. At some point during our week of decomposition she had ripped the bag open herself and feasted upon its innards.

I found a can of chili in the cabinet above our dish rack. *Perfect*, I thought, up until I attempted to open it and remembered I was minus one limb, and the can was lacking an easy-to-pull tab. The difficulty of this task increased by a thousand percent. I would have probably given up entirely if Comrade hadn't already noticed the can and correctly concluded why I'd taken it out of the cabinet. She was prancing around me, letting out excited howls, as I wandered the kitchen trying to locate something sturdy enough to hold the can in place while I worked Dad's mechanical opener. I'm embarrassed to admit exactly how long it took me to realize I could simply sit down and squeeze the can between my thighs. I'm also hesitant to reveal how much of the contents I accidentally spilled on my crotch while trying to wrestle the opener in a circular motion. If Comrade was impatient or irritated by my slowness, she had nobody but herself to blame. She was the one who ate my other arm.

I poured the chili into a plastic bowl and set it on the floor. I wondered if she would like it, or if I'd need to cook it first, which worried me, because I'd never cooked chili before and my parents had always warned me not to operate the stove without one of them present. Mom was in Corpus and Dad was hiding in his bedroom with Dead Mom. Dead Dad, on the other hand, wasn't *that* far away, so if I had to use the stove, maybe he could function as some sort of loophole. But it didn't matter, anyway. Comrade dug into the cold chili within half a second of it being available. I filled another bowl with water and set it next to her so she wouldn't have to keep drinking out of the toilet. Then I stepped back and admired my ability to get things accomplished when nobody else was around to supervise. I'd never had a dog of my own, and one of the reasons why, according to my mom, was dogs were a huge responsibility, and she wasn't sure I was quite up to the task yet. Well, I wish she could've seen me feeding and watering Comrade. She would have realized what a fool she'd been to say such a thing. I am great with dogs. It doesn't matter if they chew my limbs off or not. I still love them.

MAX BOOTH III

In the living room I stood in front of the couch and stared at the white sheet covering you-know-who and chanted, "Dad, Dad, Dad, Dad, Dad, Dad," but nobody answered.

⬥

I thought maybe you'd be angry that I left you in my bedroom so long without any company. Something I've learned from first-hand experience is it's incredibly lonely to be a corpse.

This must be true for all corpses, especially those buried in cemeteries. Yes, corpses there are surrounded by hundreds of other corpses, but they're still separated *just enough* so they're alone, forever. I wonder if those corpses are conscious enough to understand where they're being imprisoned, if they've managed to retain enough memory to *remember* what a cemetery is, to remind themselves that there are others nearby. Would that knowledge somehow help them cope with their situation? Or would it make things worse?

Imagine being crammed in a coffin, then discarded six feet into the soil, forgotten as the rest of the world continues on as if nothing out of the ordinary has happened. As if we aren't dropping dead every single second. As if we're not all trying to beat the unbeatable. Imagine you're trapped inside this coffin but you don't realize it's a coffin. You don't remember what coffins are anymore. All you know is you can't move, you can't see anything, you can't hear anything. All of your senses are swallowed into a black hole. You are consumed by darkness. And, several feet away from you, on either side, are other corpses, locked in similar boxes, all undergoing the same fate. Would it calm you to be aware of this, or would it instead be better to continue basking in ignorance of existence outside your own?

I don't know. I don't have to deal with that reality. And neither do you. Because I have you, and you have me.

MAGGOTS SCREAMING!

But there are other corpses out there who have nobody.
They will rot in their coffins, alone, forever.
And no one will ever hear their stories.

But you weren't angry. As far as I could tell, you weren't anything. But that's okay, because neither was I. So I crawled into bed next to you and together we lay there for who knows how long. I pretended I wasn't jealous that you had two arms and you pretended you weren't jealous that I could move around and talk. I told you about feeding Comrade a can of chili and I told you about what had happened with Mom's wedding dress and I told you about my growing fear that my father had lost his mind and I told you about how sad I was about Andy and I told you about how worried I was about Mom and you listened to every word without complaint. It was perfect.

Then the doorbell rang, and our lives got exponentially worse.

If I'd known who was waiting behind the door, I wouldn't have hurried out of bed so quickly. But in the heat of the moment, I convinced myself it was Mom. It couldn't be anybody *but* Mom. It sounded unrealistic that other people in the universe besides her existed. Plus, she always rang the bell when she came over to pick me up. I remember the first couple times she did it, the ringing irritated Dad to no end. He said she was doing it on purpose, to intentionally remind him that she no longer lived here, that she considered herself a mere *acquaintance* instead of his wife. "Message read loud and fuckin' clear," he whispered, letting her wait outside another couple minutes before finally opening the door. But over time he got used to the doorbell, or at least he pretended like he got used to it. He stopped complaining to me about it, at least, which was itself a blessing.

I couldn't tell if he heard the doorbell at all. He was too preoccupied with whatever he was doing in his bedroom, with the dead version of my mother, wearing my *real* mother's wedding dress. It was going to be so awkward when I let her inside and she caught him in there. Not my problem. He'd made his decisions. It was time for me to make mine.

Comrade was going nuts at the front door, pawing at the wood, howling at me to hurry up, *there's someone here!* The door wasn't locked, which I found surprising. Given everything going on with us, I thought for sure Dad would have turned the bolt to prevent any intruders from stumbling inside and discovering our little house of rot and decay.

Upon further inspection, I realized not only was the door not locked, it wasn't even *shut.* A strong enough wind could've easily blown it wide open.

The doorbell rang again as I wrapped my hand around the handle. I hesitated, wondering what my mom might look like, if she would be just as grotesque as me and Dad, trying to prepare myself not to react too dramatically, that whatever was waiting for me on the other side of the door, it wasn't my fault. I didn't do this to her. To any of us.

Except it wasn't Mom ringing the doorbell.

Instead, I found two other women waiting on the porch.

One was Andy's new girlfriend—Candy.

And the other wore a white lab coat.

"Hello, Mr. Dylan," Doctor Winzenread said, leaning forward and showing me the same awful smile she'd introduced at the body farm. "Is your lovely father home, by any chance?"

Behind her, Candy gasped and covered her mouth, total shock. "Oh my god, what happened to his arm?"

"Don't be daft, Ms. Candace. Judging by the bite marks surrounding the wound, it's quite clear a canine of some kind has torn it off. And, if I had to make a guess, I would accuse the heeler presently barking in our ears as the culprit. Unless there are other dogs on the premises?"

This last question seemed to be directed toward me, so I shook my head and admitted Comrade was the only one of her kind here.

"Is it also safe to assume that you are not currently in any state of pain? From merely observing your facial expression, you seem to have fallen into some sort of dull acceptance."

"Uh," I said.

Candy coughed and turned away from the front door. "Do you smell that? It smells like . . . "

" . . . work," Doctor Winzenread said, irrationally giddy. Then: "Young Mr. Dylan! May we please obtain your permission to enter your domicile? I believe your acquaintance, Mr. Andrew, is also here, and I must confront him on a most-urgent matter."

"Uh, he isn't here."

Doctor Winzenread cocked her head, curious, trying to figure me out. "If Mr. Andrew isn't here, then why is his truck currently parked in front of your house?"

I glanced around her at the truck. It would be difficult to explain why it was here, but I tried anyway, with a little guidance from my father's previous lies. "Oh," I said. "He gave it to us."

"He gave it to you?" The anthropologist looked doubtful.

"Yes. As a gift."

"There's no way Andy gave y'all his truck," Candy said. "He told me that was his pride and joy."

"It's true," I said. "He said we could have it and then he went home."

Doctor Winzenread raised her eyebrow. "He went home? As in, his current residence?" She recited his address, which I did not know, but it sounded like a place someone might live, so I nodded.

"How'd he get there without his truck, huh?" Candy asked.

"He took a cab," I said, already anticipating this question.

"I call bullshit," Candy said. "Why would he do that? What reason would he have to give you his truck?"

"It was a birthday gift."

"Whose birthday?"

"My dad's."

"That's a pretty nice birthday gift for someone Andy don't even like that much," Candy said.

"What are you talking about?" I asked, then added, "What are you doing here?"

Candy stepped forward, hands balled into fists. "What the fuck do you think we're—"

Doctor Winzenread lifted her hand and pushed Candy away. "That's enough, Ms. Candace." To me, she said, "I think it's clear that we are aware of your little predicament, Mr. Dylan. Hence our casual reaction to your missing limb, not to mention the fact that you quite clearly find yourself undergoing a peculiar sort of skeletonization. Otherwise we would have expressed a greater concern for your wellbeing."

"How do you . . . ?"

"Andy told me," Candy said.

"Which Ms. Candace reported directly to me," Doctor Winzenread said.

"Oh," I said. I wondered what would happen if I shut the door and pretended like they weren't on the porch. Would they leave or bust their way inside? If they'd gone through the trouble of coming down here from the body farm, it didn't sound likely that they'd surrender so easily. They were here to do whatever it was they'd set out to do.

"Are you here to help, or . . . ?" I asked, unable to comprehend what they wanted.

Doctor Winzenread did not bother trying to conceal her impatience. "I think it would be wise if you stepped aside, Mr. Dylan."

"Okay," I said, and did as she requested.

The two women entered our house.

Neither of them acted too horrified by the state of the living room. Instead they looked excited.

And as the anthropologist gave herself a tour of the house, she never stopped smiling. She had a bizarre gleam in her eyes that I couldn't decipher. Not then, anyway. It took me a while to realize it, but now I understand the truth: the anthropologist was thrilled to be here, because what was happening in our house was something she'd been searching for her entire life. Not the *specific* scenario, no, but the same level of *weirdness*. Since she was a little girl, Doctor Winzenread had been on the hunt for the Strange, and she'd tried her best to unearth it up at her body farm, but it wasn't until she stepped through our front door that she legitimately found it.

This was why she didn't call the cops. Not even after she discovered Andy's corpse in the back yard. Candy had tried, but the anthropologist stopped her, practically slapped the cell phone out of her hand. Promised they would loop the authorities into the situation all in due time, once the two of them had properly processed everything going on here. I don't know if Candy knew then that the anthropologist was lying, but I caught it right away, and judging by the way Doctor Winzenread glared at me afterward, she understood I knew the truth.

Which only seemed to cause the grin on her face to widen.

I stayed in the living room as Doctor Winzenread and Candy fetched Dad from his bedroom. When they returned, each of them clutching one of his arms, they appeared thoroughly repulsed.

"It ain't what you think," Dad kept telling them, all the while avoiding eye contact with me.

Meanwhile, Comrade had already grown bored with the newcomers, and resumed her quest to consume Dead Dad from the ankles up. Nobody cared enough to stop her. If she was enjoying herself, where was the harm?

They guided us toward the loveseat and forced us to sit. Each of them easily out-powered either of us. By then most of our muscle had deteriorated. We could still move around, but slowly, and not with much strength.

Dad nudged me with his knee and said, "Why the hell did you let them in here?"

"I don't know. I'm sorry."

"If they say anything weird about what I was doing in the bedroom, they're lying, okay? They're making shit up."

"Okay."

"We are not going to talk about what we witnessed, Mr. Max," Doctor Winzenread said. "Such conversations are not legally suitable for a boy his age, at least in the United States." She cleared her throat. "Besides, I do believe we have other, far more important matters to discuss."

"Oh yeah?" Dad said. "Like what?"

The anthropologist giggled. "You are a very adorable specimen."

"I ain't no goddamn specimen."

Candy couldn't take it anymore and slapped the wall. "You killed Andy, you son of a bitch! I loved him!"

"You barely knew him," Dad said. "And I didn't kill nobody. Who the hell told you that?"

"They were in the back yard," I said, voice low.

"What did I tell you about going out there?"

"I didn't. They did."

Dad glared at them. "You ain't got no right. You ain't got no goddamn right."

"Fuck your rights," Candy said, fuming with rage.

"What y'all did was *trespassing*. Here in Texas that's a crime."

"So is murder!"

"I didn't—"

"Hush, Mr. Max. You as well, Ms. Candace." Doctor Winzenread was viewing us all from the side of the room, as if we were encased in some zoo exhibit. She approached the loveseat with a sheet of paper in her hand. "Perhaps we can speed things up a bit. Please, allow me to explain what we are doing here."

"Well, shit," Dad said. "Explain away, then."

"As I already mentioned, your acquaintance, Mr. Andrew, informed my employee here of your rather curious condition. She, of course, reported this information to me, since that is her job, and she is very good at her job."

"Aww," Candy said. "Thanks, Doctor Winzenread."

"Do not gloat, Ms. Candace."

"I'm sorry."

"At first, I was not sure I believed her. I speculated, perhaps, that Mr. Andrew was simply trying to impress my employee with morbid fictions as an attempt to engage in sexual intercourse with her. It would not be the first time. However, the more I thought about our tour of the farm together, the more I started to suspect Mr. Andrew might be telling the truth. If what he told Ms. Candace was factual, then that would not only explain your bizarre appearance, but also why the odor of the facility did not affect either of you. It affects *everybody* who accepts a tour. Additionally, there's the vultures to consider. In all of my years working with the dead, not once have I ever witnessed a vulture attack the living. It is, quite simply, unheard of. Vultures can see through disguises. They can sniff out the dead from miles away. The moment you arrived at our little facility, they understood what you were. To be perfectly honest, I find myself feeling embarrassed that I didn't realize it myself. It is possible I am getting too old for this job. It is also possible I was simply blindsided by your general attractiveness, Mr. Max. I am, after all, only human. I possess certain desires like anybody else. Do I find it troubling that I was aroused by what has turned out to essentially be a walking corpse? No. Not in the slightest. Am I still attracted to you after discovering the truth? Of course. Without a doubt. Would I consider exploring these feelings, with your consent? Not in front of your son. That would be wildly inappropriate."

"Um," Dad said, "what does this have to do with—"

"Excuse me," Doctor Winzenread said. Her cheeks had turned red. "I am getting off topic, and I apologize." She sucked in a deep breath and exhaled. "What's important is this: a couple days after learning of your condition, Ms. Candace approached me again with a new concern. Mr. Andrew had ceased all communication. He no longer answered his phone when she called. He no longer replied to her texts. He had simply vanished from her life. Which is why Ms. Candace came to me for help. She feared something bad might have happened, and was too afraid to go to his house by herself. She asked me if I would accompany her. At first I told her that would go beyond my duties as her employer, but then I realized this might give me a second chance to interact with you and your son, so I agreed. Imagine our reaction when we discovered this note on Mr. Andrew's refrigerator, waiting for us."

She handed Dad the sheet of paper. I leaned forward so I could read over his shoulder. This is what it said:

CANDY,

IF YOU ARE READING THIS THEN THAT MEANS MY FEARS HAVE COME TRUE. MAX IS NOT WHAT HE SAYS HE IS.

MAGGOTS SCREAMING!

PROBABLY NOT HIS SON EITHER. I HAVE RETURNED TO HIS HOUSE TO CONFRONT THEM. I DO NOT KNOW HOW THEY WILL REACT. THEY MIGHT CONTINUE DENYING THE TRUTH OR THEY MIGHT LASH OUT. IF THEY GET VIOLENT I DON'T KNOW WHAT WILL HAPPEN. I HOPE THEY AREN'T WHAT I THINK THEY ARE BUT I WON'T KNOW FOR SURE UNTIL I GO BACK. IF YOU DON'T HEAR FROM ME AGAIN THEN I WAS RIGHT ALL ALONG AND I AM A FOOL FOR WALKING DIRECTLY INTO THEIR TRAP.

DON'T BELIEVE A WORD THEY SAY.

THEY ARE NOT OF THIS WORLD.

I DON'T KNOW EXACTLY WHERE THEY ARE FROM BUT I KNOW FOR DAMN SURE IT AIN'T ANYWHERE NEAR HERE. THEY CAME TO EARTH FOR ONE REASON: TO INTEGRATE THEMSELVES INTO OUR SOCIETY, AND SLOWLY CONQUER THE PLANET ONE SUBURBAN RESIDENCE AT A TIME. I DON'T EVEN KNOW IF MAX IS THE FIRST VICTIM OR ONE OF SEVERAL HUNDRED THOUSAND OTHERS. IT'S POSSIBLE WE ARE ALREADY TOO LATE, AND WE ARE AMONG THE REMAINING FEW LEFT UNVIOLATED.

IT'S ALSO POSSIBLE I AM WRONG, IN WHICH CASE YOU WILL NEVER READ THIS LETTER.

I ALWAYS THOUGHT THIS WOULD HAPPEN BUT I'M STILL SURPRISED THE TIME HAS ACTUALLY COME. WHY DID THEY HAVE TO TAKE DYLAN, TOO? HE'S JUST A BOY. HE NEVER HURT A GODDAMN SOUL IN HIS LIFE.

WELL . . . NOW HE'S ONE OF THEM. SO FUCK HIM, TOO, I GUESS.

I AM SORRY THAT WE WON'T BE SPENDING ANYMORE TIME TOGETHER. I WISH I HAD MUSTERED THE COURAGE TO ASK YOU OUT EARLIER THAN WHEN I DID. THE TRUTH

IS YOU INTIMIDATED ME AND I WAS SCARED. THE TRUTH IS I'M AN IDIOT. THE TRUTH IS I THINK YOU ARE INCREDIBLY CUTE AND I AM BUMMED WE NEVER GOT A CHANCE TO PROPERLY MAKE LOVE. HOWEVER, THE HAND STUFF WE DID TO EACH OTHER WAS NICE WHILE IT LASTED. I AM NOT EVEN UPSET THAT YOUR FINGERNAIL CUT ME. ACTUALLY IT FELT KIND OF NICE. I THINK WE COULD HAVE HAD A GOOD LIFE TOGETHER.

—ANDY

P.S. HERE IS THOSE FUCKERS' ADDRESS. BURN IT TO THE GROUND.

"Don't worry," Doctor Winzenread said, after taking the letter back and handing it to Candy. "Unlike Mr. Andrew, I do not believe you are extraterrestrials."

"We don't know that for sure," Candy said.

"Don't be silly, Ms. Candace. I think we can safely speculate that—" The anthropologist paused, attention caught on the couch. Particularly, on the white sheet covering a large human-shaped object. "Is this . . . ? Is this what I think it is?"

"Depends on what you think it is," Dad said.

"Mr. Andrew told tall tales of doppelgängers."

"Well then yes, that's what you think it is."

She reached forward, then stopped, glanced at Dad. "May I?"

"You actually asking?"

"No, I suppose not."

She pulled the sheet off and dropped it at her feet.

Revealing Dead Dad in all his glory.

For the most part, he had decomposed at the same rate

as Living Dad. Except, thanks to Comrade, this version of my father no longer possessed any feet. Where these feet had disappeared to, none of us were quite sure. Could she have eaten the entire foot of each leg? The bones and all? It didn't sound possible, but then again, it wasn't like we were residing in a house infamous for its logic. Either way, the dog appeared full and content in the corner of the living room, where she had curled up into a ball and fallen into a deep sleep.

But besides the missing feet, Dead Dad and Living Dad remained identical. At this point, both of them had lost a majority of their flesh, leaving behind only thin layers of protection. Bones poked free here and there. Their cheeks had started caving into their skulls. It was not a great sight and I promised myself never to look in a mirror again, which was a useless vow, considering I could have returned to my room and looked at you instead.

"Heilige scheiße," the anthropologist said, unable to take her eyes off the couch.

"How?" Candy said, on the verge of stuttering. "How can—how can this be?"

Doctor Winzenread pointed at me. "And you. There is one of you, too, is there not?"

"He's in my bedroom," I said, feeling oddly guilty for ratting you out.

To Dad, she said, "And what about the one we caught you with? Is there an . . . animated replica floating around here somewhere, like the two of you?"

"What the fuck did you just call us?" Dad said.

"Is there or is there not?" Doctor Winzenread asked.

"His mother? No. She's out of town."

"Where is she?"

"Tell me again how that's any of your business?"

"Mr. Max, do I need to remind you that, presently, you are a walking, talking corpse? And that sitting across from you is an identical version of yourself? I am trying to figure out what is going on here. I am offering my assistance, which—I hope you don't mind me saying—you appear to desperately need."

Dad reclined against the loveseat cushion, sticking out his atrophied chest in a classic act of stubbornness. "We were doing just fine before you got here, and we'll continue doing just fine after you leave. So, if you don't mind, the front door is over there." He offered a little nod toward the door, in case they required visual guidance.

Doctor Winzenread leaned forward, baring her teeth. "Mr. Max, I apologize for misrepresenting the situation, but please, allow me to reassure you: my associate and I do not intend on embarking from the premises any time soon, regardless of your permission. If you wish to report our act of trespassing to the authorities—please, by all means, we will not prevent you from contacting them. However, once they arrive I am sure they will have plenty of other questions for you to answer. Let us not forget what—or, should I say *who*—is currently residing in a hole behind your house."

Dad didn't seem to have much to say about that.

The anthropologist redirected her gaze toward me. "Mr. Dylan, perhaps you can help me. I am curious as to the whereabouts of your mother."

"Don't tell her shit," Dad muttered.

But the answer was already half out of my mouth: "Corpus Christi."

"*The Body of Christ*," she replied, surprised.

"Wh-what?" I said.

She dismissed my question with one of her own. "What is she doing in Corpus Christi?"

"She's on vacation."

"Vacation?" The anthropologist appeared amused. "Without her son?"

"It was my goddamn weekend," Dad said.

"And do we know if she is experiencing similar symptoms?"

Dad and I exchanged glances, trying to mentally communicate with each other how to answer this question.

"Wait a second," the anthropologist said, studying us. "Are you two telepathic? You have to tell me, if you are."

"We ain't telepathic," Dad said. Then he turned to me. "*Are we?*"

"I don't think so," I said.

"Tell me about your mother, Mr. Dylan."

And if I were still capable of tears, I would've broken into a crying fit. Instead I calmly explained the situation with Mom up in the Corpus hospital. Dad helped elaborate on a few details I didn't quite understand. Which led to us telling the anthropologist everything, from the Friday afternoon we dug up the garden grave, until they burst into our living room uninvited.

It was the second time we'd had to recite the story—first, to Andy, except back then the tale had been far shorter.

And I guess, right now, what I'm telling you—this would make the third time I've had to go over it.

The story of how I found you, and everything that followed.

After I'm done here, I hope I never have to tell it again.

Dead or alive, digging up all these memories is exhausting.

"Wait," Candy said, sounding like she was on the verge of crying again, "none of this explains why the hell you had to do what you did to Andy. There was no reason for it. There was no *reason*."

"I've said what I had to say," Dad said.

"He's *dead* because of you. *Dead*."

"You weren't here. He flipped out, went psycho." To me, he said, "Go on. Tell them what happened. How he was behaving."

"He tied us up," I said, which was true. It wasn't like Dad was making up lies about Andy. The day of his death, something had snapped in him. There was no way to predict what he had planned after he grew tired of digging holes in our yard. What if he intended on burying the two of us in them?

Doctor Winzenread retrieved Andy's ropes from the kitchen chairs in the living room and held them up, like they were evidence, which I suppose they were.

"Tied you up with these, I presume?" she said.

"Yes."

"And how did you manage to escape?"

I lifted what remained of my left arm.

"Ah," she said, winking. "Very clever, Mr. Dylan. Very, very clever."

"Uh, thanks."

She tossed the ropes to Candy and said, "I'll hold them down while you secure the knots."

"You'll what?" Dad said.

"Hold you down, Mr. Max," the anthropologist replied, matter-of-factly. "Although, to be perfectly honest, I do not believe I will need to apply much pressure. You do not appear to be in the strongest state at the moment."

"You'll do no such goddamn thing."

"It would be in your best interest not to resist, Mr. Max. I am rather confident I could snap your bones without much difficulty. Perhaps by accident. I don't think either of us would prefer that to happen."

"There's no reason to tie us up," Dad said. "It's unnecessary and . . . and . . . *rude*."

The anthropologist cocked her head, amused with Dad's reasoning. "Mr. Max, do I need to remind you of the fate that befell your acquaintance behind this very residence? A fate that you initiated?"

"I initiated no such goddamn thing."

"We're going to restrain you. I recommend you keep still."

Dad looked like he was about to put up a fight, but once they started tying the ropes around his body, he remained unresponsive. He didn't try to escape, but he certainly didn't go out of his way to make the experience any easier for them.

Next they came for me. There was no use asking them to leave me alone. If they could overpower my father then I stood less of a chance. What good could I do with only one arm? They wrapped the ropes around our shoulders and chests, too, so I couldn't take advantage of my missing limb this time, rendering the amputation pointless.

"Okay," Dad said, "you got us tied up. Congratulations. You did it. Now what?"

"Now?" Doctor Winzenread grinned, as if she'd been waiting for Dad to ask that question. She leaned forward so we could get a better glimpse of her teeth. "Now, Mr. Max, we run some tests."

They spent the rest of the day running various types of tests. Most of them I didn't understand, and they weren't willing to offer many explanations, no matter how many times Dad said, "What the hell are you doing to us?" We had no choice but to sit on the loveseat and let them do what they were going to do. They also transported both you and Dead Mom back to the couch to sit beside Dead Dad. She was still wearing Mom's wedding dress.

First, the anthropologist ordered Candy to go outside and fetch their supplies. This ended up requiring multiple trips since she had to do it by herself. Doctor Winzenread refused to abandon the living room and help. She didn't trust leaving us alone, in case we had any other tricks up our sleeves, which sounded like an unnecessarily cruel accusation to make, considering my current handicap.

They collected pieces of our rotting flesh and studied them under microscopes, jotting down their findings in little notebooks. Comparing our bodies against you and the other two corpses. Sometimes they nodded in approval.

Other times they shook their heads in disgust. Muttering silently to themselves. Doctor Winzenread giving Candy directions with a unique form of sign language they'd probably naturally created together while working at the body farm. All Dad and I could do was watch. He gave up asking them what they were doing. It was useless. They weren't interested in answering our questions. It was hard to accept at first. But it was true. The house had acquired a new presence, and they were the ones in charge. It'd happened so quickly, so unexpectedly. One minute Dad and I were rotting together while rewatching *The Simpsons*. The next, we're tied up on the loveseat while a mad scientist studied every inch of our bodies. That was life, I guess. Sometimes these things happened. Not often, but not never.

It happened to me, after all.

And it happened to you.

When the anthropologist pulled out a hammer from their body farm supplies, I assumed she'd decided to finally obliterate us and move on with her life. Assumed and hoped. The whole process of them running tests on us had quickly become exhausting. Most of the studies they'd conducted on us made little sense. The suspense of whether or not they'd share their findings with us evaporated within the first couple of hours. It might've been the first time since we'd started decomposing that I felt bored.

But the hammer wasn't for putting us out of our misery. I doubted we *could* be, anyway. Instead the anthropologist crouched next to the loveseat and lightly tapped the hammer against my knee cap, waited a couple seconds, then tapped it again.

"How does that feel?" Doctor Winzenread asked, glancing up at me.

"Don't tell her shit," Dad said. "If they can't answer our questions, then why should we cooperate?"

"Mr. Dylan," the anthropologist said, and tapped me a third time with the hammer. "How does that feel?"

"I don't know," I said, which was the truth. "It doesn't really feel like anything."

"Ah, interesting." Then, in one quick motion, she raised the hammer and swung it with sudden speed toward my face, stopping only an inch or two from making contact. I did not flinch, which is what I suspect she was trying to make me do. Afterward, she tossed the hammer on the floor. "Interesting. Very interesting."

"What are you thinking, Doctor Winzenread?" Candy asked. She was sitting across the living room, petting Comrade. She looked so tired I was pretty sure she would've fallen asleep the moment she stopped stroking the dog.

"What am I thinking?" The anthropologist appeared caught off-guard by the question. She rubbed the bridge of her nose and yawned. "What am I thinking . . . ? I'm thinking . . . I'm thinking I need several helpings of alcohol, that is what I am thinking." To Dad, she said, "I am assuming a man of your stature possesses an adequate stock of alcoholic beverages somewhere upon his property."

"Don't you dare lay a finger upon my booze, you maggot-lovin' bitch."

"Oh, Mr. Max," Doctor Winzenread said, a little giddy. "Save the pillow talk for later."

It took them all of two minutes to locate Dad's whiskey. Probably because Andy had left it out on the kitchen counter and none of us had bothered to return it to its cupboard. Comrade followed them into the kitchen in case Candy felt the need to continue petting her. We listened from the loveseat as they each poured a glass of liquor and vented about the situation they'd forced themselves into. I overheard things like *I've never seen anything like this before in my life,* and *This goes against everything we know to be true about human bodies,* and *I don't know what to do,* and *Should we call for help?,* and *Under no circumstances.*

When they returned to the living room, both were remarkably drunker than before they left us. They each took a seat on the kitchen chairs Andy had previously used to tie us up on. They'd also refilled their glasses.

"First of all," Doctor Winzenread said, "I would like to apologize for consuming a depressant while on the job. However, it is not like any of us will be receiving a paycheck for the work we are doing here. Perhaps one day, deep into the future, we will be recognized for our bravery and our willingness to investigate the bizarre and unrecognizable. I suppose that will depend on what, exactly, we conclude. Because, right now, our findings are not looking the most promising. None of this makes sense, which I am sure you both also know."

"We gave up trying to figure it out," Dad said.

"Well, that does not surprise me, as you do not strike me as a man of science. I, on the other hand, have dedicated my entire life to science."

"And yet you're no closer to cracking this mystery, either."

"Mr. Max, I do not say this lightly, but that kind of attitude is not as attractive as you might think it is." Doctor Winzenread sipped from her glass of brown liquor. "So then share with us what information you've managed to gather before our arrival. If you had to speculate as to why this is happening, or what *is* happening, what would you say?"

"Don't you understand?" Dad said. "It doesn't fucking matter why it's happening. Not now, anyway. Whatever's going on, it's way too late to put a stop to it. I mean, fuckin' *look at us.* We're skeletons. You think our flesh is just gonna magically grow back and everything's going to be nice and peachy again?"

Doctor Winzenread ignored Dad's response and redirected her attention over to me. "What about you, Mr. Dylan?"

"Corpse flowers," I blurted out.

"Corpse flowers?" she said, curious.

"Oh my god," Dad said. "Enough with the corpse flower shit."

"Wait a minute." Doctor Winzenread held up her palm to shush him. "I want to hear what Mr. Dylan has to say."

I told her my theory about the seeds from a corpse flower plant being relocated by birds and dropped in Mom's garden.

"Oh, I see," she said. "And have you collected any further evidence indicating this theory's likelihood?"

"Uh, no?"

She nodded. "Yeah, that sounds like nonsense."

"Are corpse flowers . . . real?" Candy asked, once again providing Comrade with lots of love and attention.

"Of course they're real," Doctor Winzenread said. "However, they probably aren't what you are imagining. They don't . . . *grow* corpses, as Mr. Dylan here has loosely implied."

"Then why are they called that?"

"The odor they emit while blossoming is similar to a body decomposing."

"Oh," Candy said, "that's pretty cool."

"Yes," Doctor Winzenread said. "It's *very* cool. It's also not relevant to the situation. I don't believe these flowers grow in Texas."

"Yes they do," I said. "There was one in Galveston a couple years ago. It was named Morticia."

"Equally irrelevant," the anthropologist said. "In case you've forgotten, Mr. Dylan, we are not in Galveston. We are in San Antonio. And it is not a couple years ago. It is now. The only detail of merit you've given me is the plant's name. Morticia is perfect for a corpse flower. Whoever named it that should be awarded a prize of some kind.

Nothing too ambitious, but something subtle, to let them know their naming-techniques have not gone unadmired."

Regardless of their reaction, I felt my theory was substantial enough not to disregard, but I kept quiet after that, too afraid of further ridicule.

"Andy's alien idea makes more sense than corpse flowers," Dad said. "And I don't even believe in goddamn aliens."

Doctor Winzenread turned away from us and kneeled next to Dead Dad on the couch across the living room. "What about you, then?" she said, almost in a whisper. "What do you suspect is happening here?"

Dead Dad did not answer, and neither did Dead Mom, and neither did you. Y'all remained perfectly calm, seated on the couch, most of your flesh long rotted away to nothing. "Why should I answer that?" Living Dad finally replied. "Why should I bother saying a goddamn thing to you?"

"Because, Mr. Max, you are left with very little choice. Whether you wish to accept it or not, I am the only help you're going to receive. It's either us, or the authorities, and do you honestly expect Texas police to treat this situation delicately?"

"Why do you want to help so much?"

The anthropologist stepped back, like Dad's question had physically punched her. "Why do I want to help? Because I am a *scientist*. When will I ever get another chance to study decomposition under these specific circumstances again?"

"Haven't you *studied* us enough already?"

"Oh, Mr. Max," she shook her head and leaned forward, "we haven't even started yet."

"Wait," Candy said behind her. "I thought we started, like, hours ago."

The anthropologist straightened her spine and sighed. "I was attempting to be dramatic, Ms. Candace."

"Oh," Candy said, visibly embarrassed. "I'm sorry."

MAGGOTS SCREAMING!

Somehow they got Dad to reveal his secret theory, and once he started talking I couldn't believe the words that came out of his mouth.

"It's all his mother's fault," he said, nodding toward me on the loveseat next to him.

"His mother?" Doctor Winzenread said. "Alternatively known as your ex-wife?"

We all shared a moment of silence as we glanced at Dead Mom on the couch.

Still wearing the wedding dress. Of course she was. It wasn't like any of us were going to take it off. Now that she had it on, it belonged to her. Just as my DON'T HAVE A COW, MAN T-shirt belonged to you.

"Mom didn't do this," I said. "She isn't even here."

"It was her garden, wasn't it?" Dad said, asking a question that didn't need to be asked. We all knew it was her garden. It was the one thing we *did* know.

The anthropologist gulped down the rest of her liquor and stumbled around the living room. She seemed to be enjoying herself. "So, what exactly are you attempting to imply here? Yes, it was your ex-wife's garden. Are you speculating that she knew what was underneath?"

"Why wouldn't she have known?" Dad said. "It'd be weirder if she didn't know. Too much of a coincidence, to plant something in the same exact place we'd end up finding . . . what we found."

"A coincidence, yes, I would agree with that. A rather strong one."

"She knew what was down there. That's why she never gave me shit about me keeping the house. She couldn't have been more eager to move out when we separated. Like she knew exactly what was growing in that ground, and she wanted no part of it."

"So you suspect she personally planted these . . . specimen?"

"Of course she planted them. Who else would've? *Dylan*?"

"I didn't plant them," I said, choosing to omit the fact that I *did* help my mother originally plant her garden. We certainly hadn't buried anything resembling *human*, but I didn't want to give them any further ammo. The way this conversation was heading felt dangerous. Unpredictable.

"Well then, there you have it," Dad said to the anthropologist. "His mother planted them."

"Your ex-wife," Doctor Winzenread added.

"Why do you keep saying that?"

"Scientists are required to reconfirm facts, in case they were somehow fed false information."

"What false information?"

"Are you two legally divorced?"

"Why would I lie about that?"

Doctor Winzenread shrugged. "Perhaps you were hoping to trick me into bed."

Despite his face having mostly rotted away by then, Dad managed to form an expression of absolute disgust. "What is wrong with you?"

"I'll have you know, Mr. Max, that scientists have feelings, too."

"Wait," Candy said, working on finishing her liquor. "I don't get it. How do you, like, plant another human being, though?"

"With human beans," I whispered, trying not to laugh and realizing I couldn't remember how to, anyway. It didn't matter. No one seemed to hear me—or, if they did, they were choosing to ignore my hilarious joke.

"Witchcraft, maybe," Dad said.

No one laughed at his joke, either—except, it turned out he wasn't joking.

"As a scientist," Doctor Winzenread said, "I am typically opposed to all serious discussions of the supernatural. However, under the current circumstances, I am willing to entertain this theory a little further."

"Oh," Dad said, "well, I guess I don't exactly know what I mean by that. I don't know shit about that kinda stuff. But maybe she did, right? Maybe she was secretly into witch crap. And, I don't know, maybe she plucked our hairs when we were asleep, or something, and buried them under her garden."

"Your hairs?" the anthropologist said.

"Well, sure, isn't that what those witches always do in movies?"

"Which witches?" Candy said.

Doctor Winzenread turned to her assistant. "Witch witches?"

"Are you asking me?" Candy said. "I don't know which witches." She pointed at Dad. "He's the one who brought it up."

"But why are you pronouncing it like that?"

"Pronouncing it like what?"

"Like you've suddenly developed a stutter."

"I don't have a stutter."

"Say it again," the anthropologist said.

"What? Witches?"

"There," she said, "you're getting the hang of it."

"My mom isn't a witch," I said. I would've known if she was. She would've told me. We had a special relationship. She didn't keep secrets like that from me.

"Just like that fuckin' movie," Dad said. "Dylan, you remember? The fuckin' bathroom movie we watched a while back? With the tornado?"

I knew exactly what movie he was talking about, but I chose not to respond.

"There's some witchy shit in that one, too," Dad continued. "They do these spells with, like, a tongue or something, and the world goes apeshit. Or maybe something else caused the end of the world. The movie never really explains it too well."

"Oh, yeah, I saw that one," Candy said. "The ending was terrible."

"Yup," Dad said. "It just . . . ends, like, abruptly, for no reason at all. Goddamn, that movie sucked."

"Wait a second," the anthropologist said. "Are you referring to the motion picture about the bathroom that opens outward rather than inward?"

"That's the one."

She shivered. "I couldn't stomach the architectural inaccuracies."

"The least they could've done was show us what was happening outside the bathroom," Candy said. "I hate it when movies leave mysteries open-ended like that."

"It's lazy writing, is what it is," Dad said.

Doctor Winzenread cleared her throat. "Suppose this witchcraft theory holds some merit. What reason would your ex-wife have for conducting such a bizarre spell?"

"Hell if I know," Dad said. "Maybe she's crazy. Honestly, her being a nutcase explains a lot of things."

"Like why she left you?" Candy asked.

"Who says I didn't leave her?"

She glanced down at Dead Mom in the wedding dress.

"Okay," he said. "That's fair."

"Perhaps," Doctor Winzenread said, "your ex-wife was planning on replacing her family. You two, specifically."

"But why make one of herself, too?" Candy asked. "Wait, scratch that. It would be pretty cool to have a clone. I'd make her do all the stupid shit I don't want to do while I hang out at home watching Netflix all day."

"If I had a clone of myself," the anthropologist said, "I would get twice as much science done. Together, we would be unstoppable. Other scientists would hear about my productivity and tremble in their inferior boots."

Doctor Winzenread drifted her attention away from the loveseat and approached the couch again where the three of you were seated. She knelt so she was eye level with everybody and didn't say anything for an uncomfortable length of time.

Candy stumbled into the kitchen, then returned with

both of their glasses refilled. She handed one of them to Doctor Winzenread, who accepted it without breaking her concentrated gaze away from the corpse couch.

Nobody said anything. The atmosphere felt too thick with tension. Neither Dad nor myself could predict what this drunk body farm operator would do next. I was also beginning to doubt *she* knew what she was going to do, either. At a certain point, their actions came off as improvised, like they were mostly winging things to see what would stick.

Which would explain what happened next.

If not for Comrade, I don't think the anthropologist would have ever gotten the idea to do what she did. Where would that leave us then? I don't know exactly, but I imagine far fewer people would have ended up dead. Except that's not what happened, so why bother losing ourselves in the what-ifs? Because Comrade *was* there, and the anthropologist *did* take a keen interest in her presence.

"I never had a dog of my own," she told us later that evening, on her third or fourth refill of Dad's liquor. "Not even as a young child growing up in . . . well, you don't need to know where I was raised. But not even then. My mother and father forbade it. Not because they were cruel parents, mind you. Cruel, no, but cowards? Absolutely."

"How were they cowards?" I asked, always a sucker for talking about animals—dogs being a particular weakness of mine.

"Well, Mr. Dylan, they were afraid of what I might do to a pet were they to give me one. You see, I expressed an interest in science from an exceptionally young age—and I took the job very seriously, unlike the other children in my class, who were all far too busy stacking blocks and soiling diapers. My mother and father understood that this was not some little-kid phase I found myself in. They recognized I was fortunate enough to discover my true calling in life. And that terrified them, because anything remotely scientific represented itself as an impossible puzzle from their perspective. However, there are a few things even the dimmest brain on this planet can understand when it comes to science, and one of those is eventually a scientist will require living specimens to continue her studies. They assumed—perhaps rightfully so—that if they were to gift me a canine, it would only be a matter of time before I conducted experiments on the animal."

"What kind of experiments?" I asked.

"Oh, I don't know anything specific," Doctor Winzenread said, then paused, said, "Except . . . " and sipped from her glass again before continuing, " . . . except, come to think about it, there *was* one particular experiment that had always fascinated me. One that involved a dog—*two* dogs, in fact. I'd read about it as a little girl, and now, all these years later, those details maintain a permanent residence deep inside me. As today's youth would phrase the phenomenon, it resides rent-free in my head."

On the other side of the room, Candy let out a groan.

The anthropologist ignored her assistant's disapproval and continued. "There was a scientist. Vladimir Demikhov. A Soviet, naturally. A true pioneer in transplantology. I'm sure you've all heard of him."

Crickets in the room.

"Are you serious? Not a single one of you know who Vladimir Demikhov is?"

The crickets grew bolder.

She glanced over at Candy and said, "Now I *know* I am being bamboozled, Ms. Candace, if you are claiming to have never heard the name of Vladimir Demikhov. I only am constantly referring to his many accomplishments. In fact, I can't imagine a single day on the facility has ever passed without me having made at least one comment about Vladimir Demikhov. After all, he is my hero."

"Oh wait." Candy snapped her fingers, like how people do in movies when they've suddenly remembered something. "Is that the two-headed dog guy?"

Doctor Winzenread was quiet for a second, digesting Candy's disrespectful response. "If by 'two-headed dog guy' you mean 'the genius who successfully performed a transplantation consisting of one dog's head onto the body of another dog', then yes, that is who I am referring to, that is exactly correct."

"What the fuck are you talking about?" Dad asked, which was the same question on the tip of my tongue.

"I thought you made that up," Candy said. "He really did that? That's pretty gnarly."

Doctor Winzenread patted her chest, either offended or trying to fight off a heart attack. "You thought I *made up* Vladimir Demikhov?"

"No. I didn't think you made the person up. I just thought the . . . you know, the dog thing wasn't true."

"Do you realize what you are doing, Ms. Candace?" Doctor Winzenread asked. "You are embarrassing me in front of our test subjects. You are demonstrating that they no longer have to respect me. That they can doubt my knowledge and tactics and there will be zero consequences."

"I am . . . ? Geez, Doctor Winzenread, I'm sorry. I didn't mean to do that."

"Hold the fuckin' phone, ladies," Dad said. "Are you trying to say this guy put a dog's head on another dog?"

The anthropologist grinned, seemingly pleased by my father's response. "Yes, Mr. Max, that is precisely what I am saying."

"But . . . why? And . . . *how?* What . . . what happened to it?"

"Did it live?" I asked, which felt like the only question that mattered.

"My, my, my, so much interrogation! I love it." The anthropologist took another swig of my father's alcohol.

"To answer your wonderful questions, one at a time, let's begin with why. Why would Vladimir Demikhov create a two-headed dog? Much like myself, he lived and breathed science. Everything he did was for the betterment of mankind. His motives were pure. He didn't *just* experiment with heads, mind you. He was also the first to perform heart and lung transplants on animals. And why would he do *that?* Because, Mr. Max and Mr. Dylan, once we have perfected a surgical procedural on an animal, we can then safely transition our experience and knowledge onto human test subjects. Although, if you were to ask my opinion on the matter, I would suggest there is little difference between the two, except for the fact that humans defecate in toilets and animals embrace the freedom of relieving themselves wherever they please."

"Cats can use toilets," I said, the words spilling out of my mouth before I could stop them.

"Cats?" Doctor Winzenread said, physically appalled. "Operating a porcelain commode? In *this* climate? I find that highly unlikely!"

"It's true. I saw a video on YouTube. Someone trained their cat to do it."

"You are telling lies, Mr. Dylan. You are sitting there lying straight to my face. Me! An elder! I do not appreciate that magnitude of impertinence, sir. Do you think we drove all the way down here to entertain such blatant fantasy?"

I wasn't making this up, and I was fully prepared to continue arguing until she believed me, but Dad decided right then was the perfect time to cut in:

"It's not toilets that separates us, ya goddamn idiots. It's thumbs."

Every eye in the room directed toward my father, including Comrade's.

"Thumbs?" Doctor Winzenread said.

"Yes. *Thumbs.* Humans are the only ones who have them. That's why we've survived so long, as a species. We can protect our shelters with door knobs and animals aren't equipped with the physical *attributes* to turn them. Because they ain't got any goddamn *thumbs*. Same reason we can use guns and hitchhike on the highway."

"Don't monkeys have thumbs?" Candy said.

"Uhhh . . . yeah," Dad said, "but so what? Aren't monkeys basically dumb humans, anyway? Isn't that what they teach you in school nowadays? All that Stephen Hawking evolution bullshit?"

"Opossums also have thumbs," Doctor Winzenread said.

"No they fuckin' don't."

"I would be extremely curious to hear if you've ever laid eyes upon an opossum, Mr. Max."

"I mean . . . not like a *clear* look, or anything, but I've seen plenty splattered on the road."

"But you have never gotten out of your automobile and closely inspected whether or not one of these corpses possessed an opposable thumb?"

"Why the hell would I have done that?"

"I just assumed you must have, considering the substantial level of authority you're exhibiting about the subject."

"All I'm saying is, if possums or *oh*-possums or whatever the hell had thumbs, that's something I would've heard before. It would be common knowledge."

"Pandas have opposable thumbs, too," the anthropologist said.

"Oh fuck off," Dad said. "So you know more about thumbs than I do. Who cares?"

She smirked, proud of having gotten my father all riled up about thumbs. "Now, the *how* part of your dog experiment question is where things get a bit complicated—"

"You don't know?" Dad said, trying to challenge her.

"Of course *I* know, you decomposing dimwit. But do I know how to explain it in simple enough terms for a man of your abysmal intelligence to accurately comprehend? That, Mr. Max, is where I begin to doubt my capabilities."

"Where did he get the dogs?" I asked. It was around then that I first started getting worried about Comrade being in the presence of the anthropologist and her assistant. Andy had left her in our possession—willingly or not—and by doing so she had become our responsibility. What kind of mature, caring dog owner would I be if I allowed the very first mad scientist to come along perform a bunch of depraved experiments on her? Despite my setbacks—one-armed, tied up, mostly a skeleton—I silently vowed not to let anything bad happen to Comrade.

"If I recall correctly," Doctor Winzenread said, "I believe they were strays him and his team apprehended in the streets of Moscow."

"So they belonged to other families?" I asked.

"Families that were not properly equipped to raise and shelter an animal, yes! That's always a possibility when one is picking up strays for scientific purposes."

"Have you ever picked up strays?"

"No, Mr. Dylan, I have never owned an animal—neither with scientific nor leisurely agendas. As I already mentioned, my mother and father prohibited it. They had no reason to fear, however—at least, not when it came to pet ownership. Even at a young age I understood that within me existed zero interest in experimenting on the living. No, what caught my eye—and continues to catch it—is the very same reason why I was drawn to your lovely residence earlier today. It is the same reason why I have not left, and refuse to do so until I've learned everything there is to learn on this property. There is death here, and not any ordinary kind of death. This is an *unknowable* death—which means, dear Mr. Dylan, that I will do whatever it takes to *know* it. Otherwise, what was the point of everything else in my life preceding this moment?"

I strangely felt bad for the anthropologist. No child should be deprived of a pet. I knew that from first-hand experience. But at least there was always Comrade for me to play with, although not as often as I would have preferred—especially after the divorce, when everybody stopped speaking to each other. Except for me. I would have spoken to anyone. I didn't care.

"Did it work?" Dad said. "Did the dogs live . . . once . . . you know . . . the second head was attached?"

"Yes and no," Doctor Winzenread said, finishing off her second glass of alcohol and shoving it in Candy's hands for a refill. "They attempted the surgery a little over twenty times. Twenty-five, I want to say, but I would not place any money on it—mostly because gambling is for cowards. Some results showed more promise than others. One of the most successful experiments lasted only four days, although it's speculated they would have lived much longer had a vein in one of their necks not been damaged."

"Why is he your hero?" I asked. It seemed like a good question at that point, after hearing what we'd heard.

"Because, dear Mr. Dylan, he was the man who made me realize how exciting and mysterious science can be, that it can transcend a textbook, that it can be raw and transgressive and potentially change the world. And that is exactly what I aim to prove here in this domicile, with all of you as my witness." To Dead Dad, she added, "Including you, regardless of whether or not you possess an inkling of what's happening here." She hesitated, then stepped closer to the couch, raising her voice. "Can you hear me? Is the language emitting from my vocal cords forming any sort of comprehension?" To you and Dead Mom: "For *any* of you?"

No answer. No sign whatever that y'all understood anything she was saying. She made a wet sighing noise like maybe she was drowning and grabbed her glass from Candy, refilled again. She drank and thought and the rest of us had little choice but to watch and wait for whatever was going to happen to happen.

Of course, we both know what happened, don't we? We were there, after all. We witnessed the experiment firsthand. Whether you want to admit it or not—you were there, and you saw the same things as I did.

"Okay, I have an idea," the anthropologist finally whispered, calmer, the alcohol doing its job—but from the tone of her voice I couldn't help but wonder if maybe this idea wasn't as fresh and spontaneous as she was selling it, that maybe she'd long been trying to figure out a natural way to transition into this specific conversation.

Why else would she have brought up Vladimir Demikhov and his two-headed dog?

The anthropologist was good and drunk when she confidently said, "The procedure shouldn't be as difficult as it sounds. I don't see why I wouldn't be able to pull it off."

"Because you're not a trained surgeon?" Candy said.

"Ms. Candace, forgive my shaky memory, but is it within your job description to doubt my capabilities?"

"No. I don't think so."

"Then maybe bite your tongue next time you do not have anything productive to contribute, hmm?"

"Yes, Doctor Winzenread."

"Good, now be a dear and fetch me some extra supplies at the farm." She handed Candy a sheet of paper she'd scribbled a list out on.

Candy glanced at the items and snorted. "Doctor Winzenread, I promise I'm not trying to doubt you or behave . . . uh, argumentative, but are you sure all of these supplies are at work?"

"Indeed they are, Ms. Candace. You will find the majority of them in my office, hidden deep in the closet with the Dunder Mifflin poster on the door. The rest you will find in our examination room."

"But . . . but why do you have some of this stuff?"

"Because a good scientist is always prepared."

"Wait," she said. "Are you sure I should be driving? I'm kinda toasted."

"If you can walk in a straight line, you're capable of driving."

"You want me to walk in a straight line?"

"Indeed I do, Ms. Candace."

"Uh. Okay. I'll give it a shot."

Candy took two steps forward and tripped over her own feet. On the floor, she erupted into laughter.

"There, see!" Doctor Winzenread said, also amused by her assistant's collapse. "You're fit as a fiddle. Now skedaddle! Time is wasting."

After Candy left the house, Doctor Winzenread stumbled into the kitchen and returned with the bottle of brown alcohol, no longer bothering to pour it into a glass. Instead she wrapped her lips around the neck of the bottle and let it spill down her cheeks as she guzzled.

"What kind of supplies is she getting?" Dad asked. "What are you planning on doing?"

"Tell me, Mr. Max, do you think Vladimir Demikhov informed his canines of his intentions before carrying out his experiments?"

"Wh-what?"

"Leave Comrade alone!" I shouted.

"Comrade? You mean . . . her?" She petted Comrade on the head. "I would never lay a malicious finger on this beautiful beast. Haven't you two been paying attention to a word I've said? I have no interest in experimenting on the living—and certainly not dogs."

"Then what the fuck are you talking about?" Dad said.

"Isn't it obvious?" Doctor Winzenread said, swinging the near-empty bottle of liquor as she spoke. "I'm going to create the world's first two-headed man!"

Later, she clarified: "To be fair, many humans have been born with two heads before. Think of conjoined twins. *However,* no one has ever transplanted one human head

271

onto another human's body. Which is what I'm going to do tonight, as soon as my assistant returns with the necessary supplies."

And much, much later, Dad finally replied, "Uh, I don't think you should do that."

Unfortunately, the anthropologist didn't seem to be interested in considering any feedback from us. And why would she? In her eyes, we weren't people. Not really. We were bodies waiting to be studied. We were homework. And judging from the way she danced around the living room as we waited for Candy to return, she was on a tight deadline.

The alcohol hit Doctor Winzenread like a brick. "Oh," she said, legs wobbly, words slurring, and crashed onto the carpet next to the loveseat. Between my father's legs. Resting the back of her head against his crotch and staring up at the ceiling. "Tell me something, Mr. Max, is the room suddenly spinning?"

"Please don't vomit on me," Dad said.

"I would never do such a thing," she promised, then winked and added, "not without your consent, of course."

"You know, you don't need to do this. It's not too late to change your mind."

For some reason, the anthropologist found this hysterical. "Let me tell you something, Mr. Max," she said, recovering from her giggling fit. "Let me tell you something wonderful."

"Uh, okay?"

"You see all these flies?" She waved in a vague direction. It didn't matter. Flies could be found in any area of the house. "You see all of these beautiful, majestic dipterans?"

"Dip *what*—?"

"Do you think they are here simply by chance? Do you

think they are not aware of the generous gift you and your son have offered them?"

"I don't think they *think* at all," Dad said. "They're fuckin' flies. Who cares?"

"Who *cares*?" Doctor Winzenread pressed herself away from my father's crotch and glared at him over her shoulder. "Is what you said? Who *cares*?"

"Yeah," Dad said.

"Sometimes you can be a heartless bastard, Mr. Max. Are you aware of this?"

"Now you sound like my ex-wife."

"I once read a study conducted by Bill Bass and Bill Rodriguez."

"They were both named Bill?"

"Many people are named Bill. It's a common name," the anthropologist said. "Bass, as I'm sure you already know, is the genius who founded the original body farm over in Tennessee. Him and Rodriguez, one day while conducting various insect studies, decided to do something a little unorthodox. Unorthodox if you're a coward, I mean."

"Of course," Dad said. "That goes without saying at this point."

The anthropologist giggled again and leaned her head against my father's crotch. Facing the ceiling as she continued speaking. "This experiment the two Bills set out to perform originated from the desire to determine how far away flies could smell death. Were the same insects returning every day to feed on these bodies? That was the question. So what did they do, Mr. Max? Utilizing a net, they captured several specimens from a decomposing body, transported them several miles away, marked the thorax of each fly with orange paint, and released them to the wild. The next day, the Bills returned to the body, and what did they find? Flies hovering over the corpse. Not just *any* flies but flies with orange paint. They came back for the body. Despite the odds, they found it again, and if that isn't the most romantic thing you've ever heard in your life, then I'm sorry, I'm afraid you do not have a heart."

"You know," the anthropologist said, smacking her lips and studying the near-empty bottle of liquor in her hands, "there's over twenty thousand cemeteries in this country of yours. Twenty *thousand*. And those are just the *official* ones. The ones documented and reported. Of course there are others. Consider the Civil War. Consider Native Americans. Since humans set foot on earth, we've been burying ourselves beneath it. We were given a finite amount of space and we have tried our hardest to fill it as quickly as possible. Do you know how many people have ever lived? In all of history?" If she was directing these questions toward us, she wasn't waiting for a response. "A little over one hundred billion. Presently there's maybe eight billion people alive, which tells us what? That there's . . . fourteen or so dead people to every one person still living? We are surrounded by the dead, Mr. Max and Mr. Dylan, and their numbers only grow larger every day. Do you think we will always have the room to bury them? To bury *you* or *me*? The planet's capacities are limited. Soon there will be no spaces available for anyone, and then what? What will we do with our dead? Cremation? Always a choice. A wasteful choice, but a choice. Except, most modern cowardly religions explicitly forbid desecration of the body. Will they cave in and allow it, risking exile from their fantastical holy lands? You have any idea what those 'ashes' are, Mr. Max and Mr. Dylan? The ones family members carry around in prized urns? Because they aren't *ashes*, at least not in the sense that most people understand the definition of the word. No, what's in those urns . . . it's your skeleton. It's your crushed bone fragments. The bits that never disappear. Because try as we might, as a human race, we are here to stay. As bone fragments, as memories, as destroyers of nature, we are here forever." Her lips started trembling and I thought for a second she was about to cry, then she wiped her face and took another drink and refused to make eye contact with any of us. "Some countries have already started embracing grave rentals. Meaning loved ones pay an ongoing lease for a certain amount of time, and when the lease expires, you're dug back up and flung in the trash to make room for the next corpse eager to rot in an overpriced box. Meanwhile, science facilities all around the planet are in desperate need of new donations to continue their studies, and do you know what it costs the donors? Absolutely nothing. Compare that to a coffin, which averages between two and five thousand dollars, and does not include the cost of the funeral itself, which can add another five to seven thousand. The average cost of a funeral in the United States is nine thousand dollars. Nine *thousand*. Do you think cremation is any more affordable? It certainly isn't as expensive as a standard burial, but if you think it's cheap, you have another thing coming. Cremations average between four and seven thousand. In Texas, minimum wage is seven dollars and twenty-five cents, meaning someone working forty hours a week with a minimum wage job can, at the most, expect to bring in fifteen thousand dollars in one year. And that's *before* the government decides to gleefully drain you further into poverty by collecting taxes—not from the wealthy, mind you. Do you think Bezos pays taxes? Or any of these billionaire savages who can afford to be buried on the moon? No. They come for *you*. Because they know you don't have any other choice. So, Mr. Max and Mr. Dylan, let me ask you this: in this country, in this lifetime, can you or anyone else really, truly afford to die? Is that a luxury we have at this point?"

Candy returned a little over two hours later.

"It's about time, Ms. Candace!" Doctor Winzenread said when her assistant walked through the door. "I was beginning to fear you had abandoned your employment."

"I'm sorry, Doctor Winzenread," Candy said, dragging in several tote bags full of medical supplies. "I-35 is a graveyard this time of day. Everybody coming home from work. Especially between New Braunfels and San Marcos, where all the construction is."

The anthropologist giggled. "We were *just* discussing graveyards, were we not?" She glanced over at us for confirmation, which we refused to offer. Neither of us had said a word to her since her drunken ramblings about burial plots. I think we were too afraid to hear what else she had to say.

"I think I found everything you wanted," Candy said, out of breath. "There's a couple more bags out in the trunk I need to get. Are we doing this . . . this procedure tonight, or . . . ?"

"I fail to see another appropriate time, Ms. Candace. Do you?"

"It's just that, neither of us have eaten dinner yet, and we've both had a lot to drink today, so maybe it'd be better to wait until tomorrow, when we've rested and had a chance to sober up?"

"Nonsense," the anthropologist said. "Do you think Vladimir Demikhov would have held up science because he'd knocked back a couple drinks? In those glorious times, everybody operated drunk off their asses. If anything, I imagine the alcohol only improved his skills as a champion of transplantology."

"Oh, okay," Candy said, sounding doubtful. "If you say so, Doctor Winzenread."

"I *did* say so, Ms. Candace. If you were listening properly, you would know that's exactly what I said."

"Yes, ma'am."

"Now, are we going to change the world forever, or are

we going to stand around second-guessing ourselves all night?"

They decided to conduct the procedure in Dad's bedroom, since a master bed was the next best thing to a surgical table. Plus, by then the living room had started feeling awfully packed—considering how many bodies, both living and dead, occupied it: myself, Dad, Dead Dad, Dead Mom, Candy, Doctor Winzenread, Comrade, and—of course— you. There was simply no space there to transplant a head onto another body. Dad suggested this might've been a sign not to do the surgery at all, and Doctor Winzenread responded by laughing louder than any person had ever laughed before, then she unscrewed the lid from another bottle of liquor Candy scavenged from the kitchen. After helping herself to a generous chug, she made a screwed-up face and belched, then nodded down the hall. "Let's get started."

We were left restrained on the loveseat as the two of them ventured down into Dad's bedroom and began reorganizing it in the way Doctor Winzenread envisioned. Once in a while stepping out to retrieve another bag of supplies they'd set down in the living room. Sometimes we could hear arguing, sometimes we could hear laughter. Dad and I said nothing as we waited. Time passed. Maybe an hour. They returned to the living room, drenched in sweat. They were ready.

I wasn't needed, as it turned out—but you already knew that, because you weren't needed, either. They only wanted the two dads. Did it feel more ghoulish to create a two-headed boy compared to a two-headed man? I imagine so. If they were busted trying to attach a grown man's head to another grown man, they'd have plenty of concerning questions to answer, but if they were caught attaching a child's head to another child? They'd be shot on sight.

Everything was safer with adults. That's why they left us in the living room while they did what they did. You, me, Dead Mom, and Comrade. None of us were invited to witness scientific history being made—which, honestly, was fine by me. Nothing about the experiment sounded appealing. What kid wanted to see their father in such a state? Okay, maybe lots of kids. But not me. That was the last thing I wanted to lay eyes upon.

They took Dead Dad into the bedroom first, since he was the least likely to put up a fight. Doctor Winzenread took his shoulders and Candy grabbed his ankles. We never did dress him in a T-shirt, and I regretted not arguing for one when we originally brought them into the living room. His chest had caved in and his stomach had eaten itself. Blackened bone poked out of bits of flesh. The maggots had long abandoned their post, having helped themselves to anything worthy of salvage. I wondered if, under my own shirt, something similar was going on with my body. Surely the answer was yes. Our decomposition had been a shared experience—a gross, sacrilegious weekend of gonzo simultaneity. Why would our mutual rot suddenly stop? It wouldn't. We'd be together, linked by some unknowable curse, until the very end.

Next they came for Dad, who told them to get fucked. Unfortunately, he was tied up, so there wasn't much he could do to defend himself as they dragged his carcass down the hallway. The last thing I heard him say before they shut the bedroom door was something about the anthropologist being crazy, which I don't think anybody exactly disagreed with, including the anthropologist herself.

Someone turned on music in the bedroom. Loud and abrupt. It scared not only me but also Comrade, who jumped from her sleeping spot and started barking at the wall. It took me a second to recognize the song. I hadn't seen *The Office* in a long time, not since Mom and I binged every season a couple Christmas breaks ago. But it was impossible to forget the show's theme song, and that's exactly what they were blasting in Dad's bedroom as they performed the surgery. It didn't play once, either, but continuously, as if edited on a loop. From the living room, I grew sick of the noise within three minutes, but at least I was lucky enough to have the rest of the house to muffle it a bit. In the bedroom, however, I imagined the song was pure torture.

"Turn it off!" I heard Dad scream after so long. "Please, god, turn it off!"

But I didn't know if he was talking about the *Office* theme song, or the sudden machinery noises that had also announced themselves down the hallway.

Both sounded equally terrifying.

We didn't have any clocks in the living room. There used to be this nice, antique grandfather clock across from the television, but Mom took that with her in the divorce. Dad didn't care. What use did he have with time? He could check his cell phone if he got desperate, like a normal person. That's what he told me when I asked him about it. Whenever that had been. Soon after the divorce, I guess.

So, realistically, I had no way to track how much time passed during the surgery. Well, not a *traditional* method. Because, to be fair, I did have the theme song from *The Office* playing . . . nonstop . . . over and over. And that theme song is, at the most, thirty seconds long. Meaning every thirty seconds the music would die down, offering this false sense of hope that maybe, just maybe it was finally over, only for the pianos to come bursting through the speakers again, and again, and again, in these half-minute howls of madness. Like if someone were to insert a knife into my ear and twist, only to pause every thirty seconds and start pulling it out, then suddenly jam it back in. Sometimes I blissfully forgot it was playing, but the amnesia didn't last for long. The specific notes of the song are too jarring to simply tune out for any extended length of time. Nothing about it is relaxing. It's the kind of song that feels like it's aware of the pain it's causing, and it's reveling in the agony of it all. I wanted to kill it. I wanted to reach through time and prevent *The Office* from ever airing. I wanted to do this more than anything else. More than fixing our decomposition issue. More than trying to save Mom. I wanted to murder *The Office*. I wanted to erase it from existence. I wanted it gone, forever.

Comrade never calmed down, either. She despised the music as much as I did. Running up and down the hallway, growling and barking. If the song had been a person she would've ripped its throat out. Instead she was left with no other choice but to bask in frustration.

They were in the bedroom for a little over four hundred *The Office* theme songs, which I *think* translated to about three hours? *Office* math is difficult. They don't teach that in school—and, to be clear, they shouldn't. Nobody should practice *Office* math unless they're stuck in a similar situation as I was, then I suppose it does come in handy, but still. Avoid it if possible.

The bedroom door opened and Candy came down the hallway, looking utterly exhausted. She sat on the loveseat next to me and leaned her head back. Comrade ran over for some attention but the assistant was too tired to offer any. The anthropologist remained in the bedroom, but I couldn't hear what she was doing over the sound of the *Office* theme song.

"Did it work?" I asked, unable to decide what I wanted the answer to be.

"Of course it didn't work," Candy whispered. "It was never going to." She yawned and glanced down the hallway. It was empty. "She's lost her fucking mind."

"Why . . . why are you guys listening to that song over and over?"

MAGGOTS SCREAMING!

She gave me a look like *why do you think?* and said nothing more about it. Then she turned and untied me. "There's no reason for you to be like that. You're just a kid."

"Thank you."

"Are you going to run away?"

I shrugged. "I don't think so." I studied the rotten stump of my left arm. It had turned black. "I don't know where I would go."

"To the police, maybe?"

"Dad said no police."

"Your dad murdered my boyfriend."

"He didn't mean to."

"Are you so sure about that?"

Then, from the bedroom, the *Office* theme song shut off and the anthropologist screamed, "*It's aliiiive!*"

Candy and I hurried down the hallway with Comrade in quick pursuit behind us. On the floor, next to the bed, was Dead Dad. Except now his head was missing. The other dad—*my* dad—was sitting up on the mattress, looking dazed. Behind him, at the top of his shoulders, attached to his spine, was the second head. It hung sideways, with his eyes facing the ceiling. His eyes, which were open, yes, but also *looking around*. And his mouth was opening and closing, trying to talk but only succeeding in making strange, wet animal noises. And Dad—*my* dad—trembling and saying, over and over, "What . . . what . . . what . . . what . . . what . . . "

Meanwhile, Doctor Winzenread stood in front of the bed, eyes darkened with exhaustion and lunacy, grinning wide enough to devour a village. "I did it!" she shouted. "I did it! I did it! I did it!"

Comrade squeezed between me and Candy, took one look at the two-headed dad, then let out a loud whine and fled the way she'd come.

As it turned out, she was the only smart one.

The second head—the one attached to Dad's spine—reminded me of a fish discarded on dry land, gasping for breath he didn't know how to accept. The mouth kept opening and closing in wide, drawn-out gasps. He was *wheezing*. Like he still had lungs. Which couldn't be true, right? Because he was just a head. A head attached to the back of my father.

"Oh my god," Candy said. "How . . . how did . . . how is it . . . ?"

"Dad?" I said. "Dad, are you okay?"

"I can feel it," he said. He hadn't looked this afraid since we first found you guys in the garden. "I can *feel* it trying to talk."

"The mouth is moving."

"No," he said. "That's not what I mean."

"Tell us," the anthropologist said. "Tell us everything you're feeling."

"Like a bad thought," he said. "Like a thought you don't want to have but it keeps trying to break through. Like an impulse. Like an urge. What is this? What *is* this? What did you *do*?"

"What is the thought saying, Mr. Max?"

"It's saying everything. It's saying *everything*."

"What does that mean?" Candy said.

"Dad, what do you want me to do?" I asked.

"Whatever happens," he said, finally looking at me, "don't let them do this to you . . . whatever this is . . . don't let them do it."

"Don't be silly," Doctor Winzenread said. "I would never—"

"*Oh gawd oh shit oh fuck*," Dad screamed. "I thought we couldn't feel pain anymore. I thought we couldn't—"

"*Shut . . . up . . .*" another voice said, from behind him. The head dangling from the top of his shoulders. Surgically attached to his spinal cord and who knew what else. "Please . . . shut . . . *up* . . . " The voice sounded like gravel.

"It's talking!" Candy shouted. "Holy shit it's talking!"

We had spent so much time since digging y'all up from your garden grave trying to get you to talk or give *some* kind of indication that you were conscious or *aware* of what was happening—anything to debunk the increasingly probable theory that the three of you were simply strange bags of insentient meat—that we never stopped and wondered if the idea of you guys talking was a good idea in the first place. Because if you talked, that implied you had something to say. And what could someone in a situation like yours or Dead Dad's possibly have to say? Nothing uplifting. Nothing optimistic. Nothing *good*.

"Talk . . . talk . . . talk," the second head said, pupils rolling around the room as Dad trembled on the bed. "You *talk* and *talk* and *talk*. Nothing productive. Sounds . . . *voices*. Soak it *up*, soak it *up*, soak it—"

"Hello!" the anthropologist said, leaning over the mattress and meeting the second head face-to-face. "My name is Doctor Winzenread! It is a pleasure to—"

"We *know* who you are . . . we *know* what you are," the second head said, then spit a glob of something black into her face. She nearly fell down as she scrambled away, using the collar of her white jacket to clean the saliva-like substance from her cheek. "We *know* who *all* of you are. Listening. Listening, *talk*, listening, *talk*, listening—"

"Who *are* you?" Dad asked in a pained scream. "Who the fuck *are* you?"

"No," the second head said. "That mouth . . . that mouth *no speak*."

"How is this—" Dad started to say, then stopped and choked on something thick and wet sounding. His own head sagged down, but the rest of his body remained active—still on the bed, but fidgety, squirmy.

The second head had taken control.

"There," he said. "Isn't that better?"

283

"What did you do to my dad?" I asked, somehow the only one capable of speaking. Everybody else was either incapacitated or too shocked to say anything. "Is he—"

"Alive?" The second head tried to laugh but he ended up sounding like a failing car engine. "Is that what . . . you ask?" Black spit sprayed from his mouth as he pronounced the last word. Everybody in the room flinched, which only seemed to amuse the head.

"Are you an alien?" Candy asked, loud and sudden.

"Alien to what? To *you?* Maybe . . . you are . . . alien . . . to *us*."

Doctor Winzenread stepped closer to the bed, confidence returned. "Do you know what you are? Do you have any idea what's happening here?"

The second head smacked his disgusting lips. Black spit trickled down his cheeks. Then, as if he'd already forgotten what the anthropologist asked, the head said, "Earlier . . . you were . . . *talking* . . . the differences . . . humans . . . animals. Not see . . . *you don't see* . . . the one . . . true . . . separation."

"And what would that be, Mr . . . uh . . . Mr. Head?"

Dad crawled forward to the edge of the bed. His own head was limp, but the second head attached to his spine was active and drooling, like it was piloting my father's body. "Humans . . . only creatures . . . on planet . . . understand . . . one day . . . they *die*," he whispered to the anthropologist, "and nothing . . . in this world . . . or other . . . that can stop it."

Then, without waiting for a response, Dad's body sprung forward, and the head attached to his spine opened his jaws and sunk his teeth into Doctor Winzenread's face.

When he jerked away, he kept his mouth clenched shut, tearing off a chunk of her flesh.

Revealing pulsating red tissue plastered over the front of her skull. Nerves and veins and everything else nobody's ever supposed to see.

But there it was.

Almost like she was wearing a Halloween mask.

MAGGOTS SCREAMING!

I'd never seen eyeballs so white before. They glowed against the contrast of her face's sudden redness. Like white cue balls submerged into lasagna.

"Hey now," the anthropologist managed to mutter, before collapsing to the floor.

Candy was the first and only one to scream. Maybe because none of the rest of us in the room were still alive. Fear seemed to impact the dead differently than the living. It was harder to surprise us. And when such an emotion *did* strike, the physical act of expressing it with appearance or sound often did not feel worth the effort. Meaning, while Candy screamed and ran down the hallway, I simply stood next to the door, silent. Watching.

The anthropologist twitched on the floor a couple times before going motionless. Her impossibly white eyes remained wide open. The front of her exposed skull cried red. The lab coat she'd been wearing since we met her had lost its impeccable cleanliness.

On the bed, the second head gnawed on Doctor Winzenread's detached face. It looked like a loose flap of fried chicken skin dangling from his lips. But he never swallowed. Because he couldn't. He could only chew and prepare it for someone else. Someone like my father.

When the second head spit the mangled face onto the bed, Dad jolted awake again. He looked around, confused, mumbling something unintelligible before focusing on the pile of soggy skin beneath him.

"*Eat*," the second head whispered. "*Eeeaaat iiiit . . .* "

Without hesitating, Dad leaned down and pushed his eager mouth into the wet sloppy mess and started feasting, swallowing the anthropologist's face bit by bit.

The second head attached to my father's spine moaned in bliss with each helping. "Yes!" he shouted. "More! More! *More!*"

After the face was gone, the dad creature crawled off the bed and began working his way through the rest of Doctor Winzenread.

I could only watch them go at it for so long before leaving the bedroom.

This wasn't my father. This was something else. If our bodies had been going through a transformation, then this was the final form. Something about combining the two bodies— the *alive* version and the *dead* version—that was the key in completing whatever bizarre atrocity we were experiencing. Maybe that was my dad's body in there, but it was no longer *my dad*. It was something different. Something . . . something what, exactly? Something bad. Something real bad.

I found Candy in the kitchen, going through our drawers and collecting as many knives as she could find. Comrade followed her every movement, perhaps hopeful she would get another helping of canned chili.

"What are you doing here?" I asked.

The sound of my voice prompted Candy to scream again. She spun around and dropped several knives. Comrade hopped away as the blades scattered along the linoleum floor.

"Get away from me!" she shouted, face smeared with tears and snot. She waved the only knife she'd managed not to drop.

"You should leave," I said, and meant it. I did not fear for myself. The idea of being in danger at this point felt laughable. But Candy? She had things to lose. She wasn't safe here. This wasn't a house for the living anymore.

"I *can't*."

"She's already dead," I told her, thinking she was afraid to abandon her boss.

"My keys and phone . . . " She gestured the knife toward the hallway.

"Oh," I said. "Uh, maybe you should just run?"

"Where am I going to go?"

"Anywhere away from here."

But it was too late.

Loud, frantic movement crescendoed down the hallway. The dad creature, on all fours, burst into the kitchen with the bottom head (*my father*) licking leftover globs of gore from his lips. The top head (*imposter*) drooled black sludge and moaned, "*Hungry . . . sooo hungry . . .*"

Candy let out another scream and dropped the last knife.

"You," the second head said. "*You . . .*"

"I'm sorry," Candy cried out. "It wasn't me. I didn't do anything."

"*You . . . help . . . us . . .*"

"Help?"

"*Come . . .*"

The dad creature crawled out into the living room, leaving me and Candy alone in the kitchen. Comrade was nowhere in sight. Hiding somewhere.

"What do I do?" Candy asked me.

"I think it wants you to follow it."

"But *why*?"

"I don't know."

In the living room, we found the dad creature crouched next to the couch, studying Dead Mom in her wedding dress. Both of the heads were giving their complete devotion to her presence. Like they were worshipping her at an altar. The scene looked oddly sad.

"Her too," the second head whispered. "*Fix her too.*"

"Fix . . . ?" Candy said, shaking her head. "What do you mean . . . ?"

"Like you did us," the dad creature told her. "Fix her like you fixed us."

Candy backed away until she walked into a wall. "I . . . I can't. I'm not . . . I don't know how . . ."

The dad creature spun around and caught her trying to flee. The bottom head growled while the top head screamed, "*Fix our bride or we will take your face.*"

Crying again, she pointed down the hallway. "You killed her! She knew how to do this, not me!"

"You . . . know . . . enough . . . " With each word, the dad creature crawled closer. "We need our bride. *We need her.*"

"I don't know where she is!"

The top head was so close to Candy's mouth he could've kissed her if he wanted to. "*Corpus,*" he whispered. "*Corpus Christi.*"

LOOKING BACK, I don't think the dad creature ever said a word to me while he was in our house. I suspect he didn't so much as *glance* at me, to tell you the truth. As far as he was concerned, I didn't exist.

After the dad creature and Candy departed in the anthropologist's van, I wondered why they hadn't made me join them on their journey. Why they'd left me all alone in this house of death. I wasn't needed. I wasn't wanted. And neither were you. They left you in this house just as they'd left me. The whole reason they went to Corpus Christi is because my mother wasn't here to have the other head attached to her. But you and me? We were in the house the whole time, weren't we? They could have easily connected us if our dads had any interest in preserving his sons. But he didn't care. He only wanted his bride—he only wanted our mom.

Which, if we're being honest, helped confirm my longest-held theory. And perhaps yours, too. That without me getting in the way of things, maybe Mom and Dad would have never gotten divorced. There was a reason they didn't take us with them. We were a distraction. We were an infection. Without us around, the dad creature believed he had a chance of saving his marriage. And you know what? Maybe he wasn't wrong.

I don't know how long I stood in the living room looking out the window after the van left. Andy's pickup was still in the driveway. So was my dad's. But what use were they to me? Even if I did know how to drive, I was missing my left arm. How much could I accomplish in my current state?

On the road that ran in front of our house, cars passed from both directions, oblivious to the events that had transpired here over the weekend. If a single vehicle was aware of what had been going on in here, would they have stopped to lend a hand? I wondered what my own father or mother would have done if forced into such a situation. If they were told, *Hey, you know that house you're about to pass on your way to wherever you're going? Well, some truly heinous activity is taking place, and a little boy sure could use your help. Two little boys, in fact. One of them can't move or talk, and the other one, he's missing his left arm. What are you going to do?*

I knew what they would have done. They would have kept driving. They would have said this wasn't any of their business, and they would have been correct. All those cars that passed our house, it wasn't their responsibility to help us. They had their own lives to live. Who knew what kind of issues they were currently facing with their individual families? Everybody had baggage. Everybody had drama. Sometimes someone's problems were more severe than others', but that didn't make them any less unique, any less important. I was rotting away to a skeleton with my doppelgänger, and my father had transformed into a two-headed monster and was on his way to Corpus Christi with a kidnapped anthropologist's assistant. In some other house, something similar or one-hundred percent worse could have been unfolding, and I had no way of knowing about it, just as they had no way of knowing about what was happening in our house.

If someone *did* want to help, what realistically could they have done at this point? There was no reversing what had already occurred. My flesh wasn't going to grow back. I was dead. We were all dead and there was no fixing that. This family, this household, we'd embarked on a downward spiral the moment we dug y'all up from the garden. There was no climbing back from something like this.

So where did that leave me? It left me alone, with you and Comrade. She was getting hungry again. I could tell by the way she kept nipping at my ankles as I wandered the house. I gave her another can of chili and a bowl of water and that seemed to calm her down some. Piles of feces and puddles of urine were scattered throughout the kitchen and living room. We hadn't let her outside since Dad killed Andy. I didn't want her to see her owner in such a state. It didn't seem fair. She was just a dog. She wouldn't have understood why Dad had to do what he had to do. I hardly understood, myself.

I mean. Deep down I knew the truth. I knew that it wasn't something Dad *had* to do, not at all. He'd *wanted* to kill Andy. Because even back then he had something monstrous inside him. Long before Doctor Winzenread surgically attached the other head to his spine. There had been a desire to kill. To destroy. And the first chance he was given, out in the yard when it was only him and Andy, he'd taken it, hadn't he? How many more people would he kill now that his transformation was complete? How many bodies would be eaten, ripped open, desecrated?

What I couldn't understand, though, was that the transformation my father had gone through—I was experiencing the same build-up. Nobody had physically connected you and I, but still. If my dad had wanted to kill before the head attachment, then where was that desire in me? Why didn't I feel the same way? I didn't want anybody to die. I didn't want anybody to get hurt. I didn't want anything bad to happen to anyone. I just wanted everything to go back to normal. The way it had been before he'd shown up at Mom's door Friday morning, demanding his custody rights. But that was no longer an option, and it hadn't been for quite some time.

So what did I do? What did *we* do? We turned on *The Simpsons*. Season one, the beginning. The first episode to ever air, which was a Christmas special. When the family adopts Santa's Little Helper. Since our parents were no longer present, I sat on the couch next to you, with Comrade curled up between us, chewing on your hand—your left one, which was the same hand she'd already taken from me. You didn't seem to mind. Even if you could have said anything, I don't think you would have complained. Sometimes it felt nice to be wanted. Especially by a dog.

And we would have probably stayed that way, plowing through another marathon of *The Simpsons*, Comrade subtly trying to consume both of our bodies, if the kitchen door leading to the back yard hadn't swung open halfway through the season one finale.

Followed by Comrade's former master.

"Hey," Andy said, upon noticing us in the living room. Comrade had already bolted off the couch and joined him in the doorway, where she was sniffing his legs. "Hey, I got a question for you."

I couldn't tell if he was talking to me or you. The way he was looking at us, it could have been either one.

Finally I said, "Yes?"

"Am I . . . am I dead?" he asked.

And I nodded. "Yeah. I think so. Yeah."

"Mmm. That's what I thought."

It looked like he was wearing leather at first. Then I remembered the corpse Doctor Winzenread had proudly demonstrated during the body farm tour. The one that had been left out in the sun, buried up to its stomach, exposed to the elements without any protection. That one had also been covered in leather—or so it had appeared upon an initial glimpse. Of course, what we had seen at the farm had been the body's own skin, shrunken and dried-out from the harsh, unrelenting Texas sun. Which was exactly what had happened to Andy. Sprawled out in the unearthed garden grave, rotting under the sun, not a spot of shade in sight.

"Holy shit," Andy said from the bathroom down the hallway. Inspecting himself in front of the mirror above the sink. "Am I a goddamn mummy?" He walked out to the living room. Comrade close on his heels. I hadn't gotten off the couch. The thought of moving felt like entirely too much effort.

"Holy shit," Andy said again, gesturing at himself with both thumbs, as if to say *would ya get a load of this?* "I'm a goddamn mummy!"

"How do you feel?" I asked.

Andy started to respond, then paused, further considering the question. "Dry. I feel . . . incredibly, disgustingly dry."

"Well . . . you *are* a mummy."

"Holy shit." Andy shook his head, in shock, but also somehow amused by it all. "A goddamn mummy. Can you believe it? Me? A mummy!"

He scooped up a mostly-empty bottle of liquor Doctor Winzenread had abandoned on the coffee table and took a long chug from the glass neck. The alcohol remained inside him for maybe five seconds before he spewed it all over the carpet. Comrade followed the mist and started licking it up, as if that had been the plan all along.

He sat the bottle on the table and said, "Okay, that's out." He tried to snap his fingers but they must've been too dry to produce sound. "Hey, I know! Y'all got any more of that embalming fluid shit left?"

"No," I said. "We already drank all of that."

"Damn. How did it taste, though?"

"Not too bad, I guess."

"Damn." He glanced around the living room. "Well, what about those eye drops I got y'all from the drugstore?"

"All gone."

"All of 'em? Really?"

"I'm sorry."

"Ah. It's okay." He leaned forward, squinting his hollowed mummy eyes at me. "Hey, you know you're missing an arm?"

"Yeah."

"How'd you manage that one?"

"Comrade ate it."

"Bullshit."

"It's true."

"My dog did not eat your arm."

"Did too."

Andy scratched Comrade behind her ears. "Did you eat Dylan's arm? Did you, you little lunatic?"

Comrade let out an excited squeal, as if to confirm *yes, I certainly did eat Dylan's arm, and it was delicious!*

Andy giggled and said, "Well, I apologize for that. I'll buy you a new arm, if you want."

"A new arm?"

"Sure, why not?"

"What kind of arm?"

"Any arm you want."

"Even a robot arm?"

"Whoa, calm down. How much do you think UPS pays me, anyhow?"

"You said any arm."

"I said any *human* arm."

"No you didn't. You never said human."

"I can't afford to buy you a robot arm," Andy said. "There's just no way."

"That's okay. I guess I don't need a robot arm."

"There, that's the spirit." He paused again, looking around for something he couldn't seem to locate. "Hey, I got another question for you."

"What?"

"Did your dad kill me?"

"Yeah."

He nodded. "I figured as much."

"Are you mad at him?"

"Well, I suppose I ain't too pleased, if you want the truth."

"What are you going to do to him?"

"I don't know. For starters, I reckon a conversation is in order. Talk things out. See where we sit on everything. I mean. He killed me. And now I'm a mummy. These things don't happen every day, you know?"

"He isn't here."

"Who isn't here? Your *dad*? Where the hell did he go?"

"You missed a lot," I said, then tried my best to explain the events that had occurred following his murder. Afterward, he stumbled down the hallway and stuck his head in Dad's bedroom, checking I wasn't lying about the anthropologist's corpse.

"Shit," he said, returning to the living room, "he really ate the hell out of her, didn't he?"

"Yeah."

"But Candy wasn't hurt? She was okay?"

"She was scared."

"But he didn't *do* anything to her?"

I shook my head.

"Man. They really sewed the head to his spine like that?"

"Yeah."

"That's pretty fucked up."

"I know."

"How come they didn't do the same to you?"

"I don't know."

"Probably child labor laws or some such shit."

"Yeah, I guess so."

"Well." Andy adjusted the **OBEY.** cap on his mummified skull. "I reckon there's only one thing we can do now, huh?"

"What's that?" I asked, hoping he'd suggest another episode of *The Simpsons*.

"We gotta head down to Corpus," he said instead, "and stop your old man from doing something truly stupid."

Before we could leave, Andy said there was something we had to take care of first. Something we should've done a long time ago. He went out to his truck and came back with two red plastic canisters of gasoline. I tried to hold one of them but the weight threw me off-balance and I crashed to the floor. Comrade thought we were playing a game and tried leaping on me, but I was too afraid of getting gasoline on her so I shoved her away with my elbow. It's not easy, carrying a full can of gasoline with only one arm. I wouldn't recommend it. Andy didn't seem upset by my failure, though. He picked up both cans and started splashing gasoline all through the house.

"If there's anything you desperately wish to save," he said, "I suggest retrieving it ASAP."

I tried to think of a single possession I cared enough about to collect, but nothing sprung to mind. Maybe our collection of *Simpsons* DVDs, but those felt like too much work to gather. They'd served their purpose. It was time to move on.

But there was one thing we couldn't leave behind.

I pointed at you and said, "He has to come, too."

"I don't know, Dylan. These bodies don't seem to be doing anybody any good. I think maybe we oughta just—"

"We aren't burning him."

"But have you thought about—"

I shook my head. "If he stays, I stay."

"Okay," Andy said. "He can come."

Together, we wrapped you in a sheet and carried you out to his truck, hiding you in the uncovered bed with the rest of his odds and ends.

"What about the doctor?" I asked.

"Nah," Andy said. "Ain't enough of that crazy bitch left to try salvaging."

"Are you really going to set the house on fire?"

"You betcher ass I am, buddy. You ain't scared, are you?"

"No. It's just . . . won't we get in trouble?"

Andy shook his head. "You forget? I'm a mummy. You can't arrest mummies. It's unconstitutional."

"Won't Dad get mad, though? It's his house."

"Eh. Something tells me he doesn't have much use for it anymore."

"Okay," I said, suddenly excited to see some flames. "Let's burn it."

Comrade sat between us in the middle seat. You remained in the bed of the truck, wrapped in a sheet. We drove away with smoke in our rearview windows. Only then did it occur to me to ask Andy how he was walking and talking if my father had murdered him.

After all, there hadn't been an Andy doppelgänger. There was just the one body. And he hadn't died during mysterious circumstances like the rest of us had. He'd been gutted with a hedge trimmer. It felt like a proper way for someone to die. Unlike whatever had happened to me and Dad. With us, there had been no specific incident. No moment in time where we felt death overtake us. Suddenly we were decomposing—a sensation so natural it was almost as if we'd always been in such a morbid state and somehow hadn't noticed it until this weekend. But things were slightly different with Andy. There wasn't an additional body. Plus he had actually been murdered. And now he was back from the dead.

"How?" I asked again. "How are you alive?"

"Well, I don't think I'm *alive*, per se—"

"How are you a mummy?"

"Figured that was obvious," Andy said. "You got yourself a haunted back yard."

"What?"

"Well, okay, the *hole* is haunted at least. Your momma's garden. Haunted as fuck, I'd say."

"It's haunted?" I asked. "By ghosts?"

"Ghosts? What *ghosts*?"

"I thought ghosts haunt things."

"Lots of things can haunt something." Andy raised the volume on his truck radio and increased his speed, then a minute later lowered the knob again. "Okay. Maybe *cursed* is a better word here. You got a *cursed* back yard, okay?"

"How is it cursed?"

"Well, okay. I don't know *how*, not exactly, but c'mon. Look at the . . . you know, look at the fuckin' evidence, right? Where did you guys find the other bodies? In that hole. What happened once you took them out? Both to them and you? Spooky shit, right? Now what happened once your dad *murdered* me to death, and left me to rot in the very same hole? I came back! As a mummy! Sooo . . . at this point, it feels pretty safe to conclude that the common denominator here is the hole itself. Maybe there's something weird in the soil, like some fuckin' redneck witchcraft bullshit, or maybe there's a goddamn Indian burial ground somewhere in your yard, or maybe a thousand other things we could spend all day trying to figure out. Truth is, I don't think the reason matters all that much. Just accept the fact that you got yourself a haunted back yard, and move on with your life."

"I thought you said it was cursed—"

"Haunted, cursed, fuck's the difference?"

"Is the fire going to make it . . . normal again?" I asked, thinking how Andy tossed both canisters into the garden grave before leaving. The cans had been mostly empty at that point, but there was a little liquid splashing around inside when they flew through the air. I kept envisioning the grave bursting in flames, like a pit leading directly into Hell.

"I don't know if it was ever normal to begin with, Dylan."

"Will it still have its powers after it's burned up like that?"

"Powers?" Andy said, thinking it over. "Boy, I sure as fuck hope not. Let me tell you this, okay? That hole? It ain't good news. The wrong kinda people learn about it—like, say, the United States Government, for instance—and we're gonna have a whole lot worse to deal with than your goddamn dad running around with two heads making an ass out of himself. I'm talkin', fuckin', *armies* of ghouls. I mean, come on, who knows what other kinds of freaky monsters that hole can generate? Because that's what it is, right? A bonafide monster hole. You want to be the one responsible for the president genociding some Middle Eastern country with a legion of unstoppable mummies? Or what about little . . . I don't know . . . fuckin' *gargoyles* flying around your property, getting all up in your business? It's bad enough they listen through our cell phones. Now they want to send gargoyles to eavesdrop? I think not, friend."

"Oh," I said, wondering if Andy had forgotten my age during his mummification. "How long does it take to get to Corpus Christi?"

"About two hours and some change," Andy said. "Three, if you drive like a pussy." He punctuated that last sentence by stomping on the gas and swerving around a line of slow cars in the left lane. I wondered what would happen if a cop pulled us over. Was it illegal to operate a moving vehicle while undead? I noticed no difference between Andy's driving as a mummy than when he'd been alive.

"What are we going to do when we get there?" I asked.

"What do you think?"

"Kill him?"

"How can you kill what's already dead?"

"Then what?"

Andy shrugged. "Shit, Dylan. I don't know. We'll figure that out when we get there."

"You ever hear how your mom and dad met?" Andy asked, shouting over the horrendous sound of his truck's muffler.

"No," I said, alarmed I'd never considered the concept of them not knowing each other. In my head they had always been together—until they weren't. But I'd never given much thought to *how* they got together in the first place. Did that make me a bad son?

"It's a pretty funny story," Andy said. "It was the same night your dad got arrested. I'm surprised nobody's ever told you about it before."

"He was arrested?"

"Yeah, but not, like, for anything bad. He was trying to impress your mom, and things got out of hand."

"What did he do?"

"He stole Homer Simpson."

"What does *that* mean?"

Andy laughed. "Goddamn, this would've been what? Ten years ago? Wait, how old are you?"

"Thirteen."

"Goddamn time passes, huh? Even after you're dead. You might stop but time does not. It just keeps on going and going and—anyway, we would've been in our early twenties. At least old enough to buy booze, since the three of us were drunk as hell. The three of us being me, your dad, and Miguel. It was the premiere of *The Simpsons Movie*. We smuggled in a couple six-packs in this big trench coat your dad used to have. I remember the ticket lady giving us these ugly looks like she knew exactly what we was doing. Considering it was the middle of summer in goddamn Texas. But she didn't say nothing. Didn't get paid enough to say nothing. Who really gives a shit if a couple fellas enjoy themselves while watching a movie, right? What does it *matter*?"

"I didn't know you guys saw *The Simpsons Movie* in theaters," I said, a little hurt that my dad had never mentioned this story to me during the numerous times we'd watched it on DVD together.

"Do you know who else saw the movie that day, in the same theater?"

" . . . My mom?"

"Bingo."

"They met while watching *The Simpsons*?" Okay, now I was past merely feeling hurt. I was downright offended.

"If you believe in fate and all that bullshit, then I suppose you could call it fate. But yeah. Her and a couple of her friends were sitting next to us in the theater. It's a miracle they didn't complain to a manager, the amount of noise we were making. In retrospect we were total assholes. I can't stand people who make noise while watching a movie. Yet that's exactly what we were doing. Anyway. Your mom, her and her friends noticed we had extra beers, and asked if they could have some. We were more than happy to oblige. I hope you're not offended by me saying this, Dylan, but back then your mom was hot as fuck. I mean, to be fair, she still is. I probably shouldn't have said that to you. I apologize."

"It's okay."

"So, uh, yeah. The group of us together, we get progressively drunker while watching *The Simpsons Movie*. Then, when it's over, we stumble out into that slanted hallway you can never tell which way to exit from, and right outside our screening there's this huge cutout of Homer fuckin' Simpson with a big ol' pink doughnut in his hand. Like, a promo thing. They wanted you to stick your head in the center of the doughnut and take a picture. Which was weird. I don't think any of us had a smartphone at that point. Were people showing up to theaters with actual cameras? Huh."

"He stole it?" I asked.

"Look at you, getting ahead of the story! Yup, you're goddamn right he stole it. All it took was one innocent little comment from your mother. I believe it was something like, 'It would be hilarious if somebody stole this sign.' Less than five seconds later, your dad had it over his head and was running full-speed out of the theater. I don't know what his plan was, exactly. Hell. Come on. Let's be honest, okay? He didn't *have* a plan. He saw a beautiful pair of tits—again, I'm referring to your mother—and stopped thinking. Let that big dick of his plan out the rest of his actions—which, evidently, involved stealing a promotional cutout of Homer Simpson and fleeing teenage theater employees. Later, we all met up at 7-Eleven—your mom and her friends included—because the store had temporarily redecorated itself as a Kwik-E-Mart to tie into the movie coming out. They were selling shit from the show, like Squishees and Buzz Colas and all that other bullshit."

"Twice the sugar, twice the caffeine!" I shouted.

"Tasted terrible, if I recall correctly," Andy said. "Anyway, we're all at the 7-Eleven—or, uh, the *Kwik-E-Mart*, I mean—waiting to see if your dad's gonna show or not. We'd already agreed to meet up there after the movie. But that was before he'd spontaneously decided to commit a crime. I knew he'd come, though. Especially since your mom already told us at the theater that she was interested in checking out the store with us. And, lo and behold, there he was, emerging from the night like a ghost. Holding that goddamn Homer Simpson over his head. We all stood out in the parking lot and cheered and made him feel like the coolest guy in the world, which probably lasted all of five minutes before a cop pulled up and asked where he got the sign. But by then it was too late. Your mom and dad were helplessly in love. Not even a night in jail and eight weeks of community service would separate them."

"Was he able to keep the sign?"

"The Homer Simpson?"

"Yeah."

"Hell no. That shit was filed away into evidence. It's probably there to this day, rotting away to nothing."

"Just like us," I said.

"Just like us," Andy said, smiling.

We had to stop for gas in Choke Canyon, about an hour outside Corpus Christi. "It's a good thing I have your dad's card," Andy said as he got out of the truck. "Can you imagine me going inside looking the way I do?" He didn't need to tell me not to leave the truck. I already knew things wouldn't go well if people laid eyes upon me in my current state. It wasn't every day someone saw a skeleton boy with one arm. Especially in the summer, when we were months away from Halloween.

He swiped his card and leaned forward, inspecting the dim screen, then said, "You gotta be shitting me."

"What's wrong?" I asked from the passenger seat. He'd been kind enough to leave the windows rolled down.

"Says something went wrong and I gotta see the cashier."

"What are you going to do?"

"Well." He glanced around the empty parking lot. "I guess I'm gonna go see the cashier. Shit. I shouldn't've used up all the gas from the cans."

He left me alone in the truck with Comrade and entered the gas station. I leaned forward, over the dash, watching him interact with the cashier. Waiting for something terrible to happen. I half-expected her to take one look at him and pull out a gun from behind the counter. But she didn't seem to really notice him. Andy returned to the truck and started pumping gas. I stuck my head out the window and asked him what she'd said.

"Nothing really. The card reader isn't working out here, so they're having everybody come in to pay."

"But didn't she say anything about how you look?"

He shook his head as the gas pump spurted out its last drops. "Nah. She didn't say shit."

We got back on I-37 and Andy cranked his music up. Black Sabbath. The same album my dad liked to play. There was a reason the two of them were friends. It saddened me they'd spent so long not talking because of Miguel and my mom. That the only reason they'd reconnected was because of the mystery in our yard. A mystery that would lead to my father murdering someone who had once been one of his best friends. There was nothing good about the garden grave. Not even you, I'm sorry to say. Everything that proceeded our discovery had progressively made everybody's lives worse. There would be no happy outcome for any of us. That much had been clear for a while. Where we were heading, it wouldn't end with a Disney logo. The three of you guys ruined everything. I hate to say it but it's true. I don't blame you, personally, but you have to take some kind of responsibility. You probably didn't mean to cause the damage you caused but nevertheless here we are. I was honored to have helped Andy set it all on fire.

I couldn't stop thinking about the gas station cashier. The way she'd allowed Andy to purchase fuel without freaking out despite him clearly being a mummy. What did that mean for our future? If he could pass as a non-monster, what about me? What would've happened if I'd gone into the gas station, too? Looking the way I did. I kept envisioning the three of us—Andy, Comrade, and I—panhandling on the streets. The only thing sadder than a homeless kid with one arm was a homeless kid with one arm who also had a dog. Living on the streets felt like the only logical fate. I wasn't returning to school in my current state. Andy wasn't going back to UPS. Mummies couldn't deliver packages. There was no way that'd be allowed. He'd lose his home, which would leave us both without a residence. I didn't see a reality with Dad in my life. Not after the transformation. He was something else now. Something we couldn't tame. And Mom? Maybe she'd be okay. Maybe we would save her and she'd join us in our life on the streets as literal monsters begging for spare change. But that didn't feel right. Something deep in my rotting gut told me we were far too late.

A feeling that would only be confirmed upon spotting the police cars and ambulances surrounding the Corpus Christi Medical Center.

MAGGOTS SCREAMING!

The street in front of the hospital was blocked by police barricades. A terrified-looking cop waved us to turn around. Andy ignored the warning and pulled up as far as he could get before the cop furiously blew a whistle at him and stomped toward the truck. Andy rolled down his window and said, "What's going on? Did something happen at the—"

"Get the fuck out of here!" the cop screamed. "It's not safe! Turn around immediately!"

"Wait a second," Andy said. "I think I can—"

"Gah!" The cop backed away from the truck, having finally taken a good look at the person behind the wheel. "What happened to you?" All the color drained from his face and his lips started quivering. "Are you . . . are you another . . . holy shit, are you one of them?"

"One of *what*?" Andy said, although it was obvious what the cop had meant. One of those *monsters*. Because the dad creature had been here—maybe still was here, and the cop had encountered him. He'd seen what the thing was capable of doing. And he wanted no part of it. Which was why he was out here redirecting traffic instead of joining the other cops behind him in the parking lot, who were slowly approaching the front doors with their guns drawn.

"It's okay," I said, and the cop gasped. He hadn't noticed me sitting in the passenger seat. But now he did. And, judging by the face he made, he did not care one bit for the way I looked.

"Jesus Christ!" He took out his gun and pointed it at the truck. "How many of you freaks are there?"

"Would you fucking relax?" Andy said. "You're making my dog nervous."

As if on cue, Comrade let out a bark, prompting the cop to scream and squeeze the trigger.

Shooting Andy directly in the face.

The back of his skull cracked open and bits of brain matter splattered against me.

Suddenly I couldn't stop thinking about that cop who'd shot the squirrel at my friend's birthday party. Everything repeated itself sooner or later. It was unavoidable.

Comrade's barking pumped up to full freakout mode.

"What the hell did you do that for?" Andy asked, touching the new hole in his face. "That was really fucking rude, you know that?"

The cop yelled something unintelligible, dropped his gun, and took off running away from the hospital. I tried restraining Comrade by gripping her collar but she wrestled out of my grip and leapt through the window and started chasing him down the street.

"Are you okay?" I asked.

"I mean, yeah, all things considered," Andy said. "I feel fine."

"Why did he shoot you?"

"Because that's what cops do."

"Are they going to shoot us, too?" I asked, referring to the group of policemen in the parking lot. Instead of approaching the hospital, they were all turned toward us, weapons raised. We were somehow perceived as a bigger threat than whatever was inside the hospital. They were yelling something but I couldn't understand what they were saying. Something about surrendering.

"Shit, what do you think?" Andy said.

"What are we going to do?"

"Well. The way I see it, we came here with a job to do."

"Get my dad?"

"Get your dad."

"But how . . . ?"

"I reckon the same as anyone else: the front doors."

"But—"

"Now might be a good time to buckle up, by the way."

"What about Comrade?" I asked.

MAGGOTS SCREAMING!

Somewhere in the distance, the cop who had shot Andy let out a painful squeal.

Andy laughed. "She seems to be handling herself just fine."

And, with that, he cranked his music back up and slammed on the gas. The truck shot forward and bounced over the grassy median into the parking lot. I tried to buckle my seatbelt but it turns out buckling a seatbelt while sitting in the passenger's seat is extremely difficult when you're missing a left arm. I gave it three attempts before giving up and letting the seatbelt fling behind me. What did I need a seatbelt for, anyway? I was already dead, right?

The cops pointed their guns at us and fired a few shots before realizing Andy had no intention of slowing down or swerving out of the way. They flung themselves to either side of the parking lot as we barreled through. At one point, I'm positive I heard Andy shout, "Yee-haw!"

The automatic front doors managed to separate maybe an inch before we smashed into the glass and slowed to a stop in the middle of the lobby. Outside, cops continued to yell orders at us and we continued to ignore them.

"Goddamn!" Andy said, punching the ceiling of his truck. "Now *that* was fun, wasn't it?"

I was unable to join in on his excitement, as my attention had redirected to the numerous mauled corpses scattered throughout the waiting room.

On the chairs, on the floor.

Ripped in half.

Disemboweled.

Chewed up.

Despite spending the weekend living in a house of death, nothing could have prepared me for the grisly scene awaiting us at the hospital.

Not all of them were dead. Some were crawling around the lobby, entrails hanging from their severed waists, pleading for help. I'm sure they wished they were dead, though. I sure as heck was grateful to no longer be alive.

"Holy shit," Andy said, embracing reality. "You think your old man did all this?"

"Yeah," I said. There was no doubt about it. "He did it."

"Well where the hell did he go then?"

I pointed ahead, where a trail of gore led toward an entryway marked STAIRS. "We follow the blood."

Andy drove his truck around the corpses and backed up against the stairs. This way, he told us, none of those dickhead cops could follow. Personally I didn't see how that would stop them. They could've easily climbed through the interior of the truck like we did to get to the other side. But at that point I didn't care enough to point out the flaws in his logic. If they followed us, then they followed us. I only wanted to find my dad. And my mom, if she was still here. I couldn't let him turn her into what he'd become. It didn't matter if I failed at everything else in life. As long as I succeeded at this one thing—if I could save my mom—I would be okay. Well, not *okay*. But okay *enough*.

I'm sorry we left you in the bed of the truck, wrapped in that sheet, but surely you can understand the situation we found ourselves in. There had simply been no time to figure out a logical method of transporting your body upstairs with us. Besides, you were fine waiting downstairs. Nobody was going to notice you with everything else going on.

The blood trail stretched to the top floor of the hospital and out the door. More corpses awaited us in the hallway. People moaning and releasing their final breaths. The walls were spattered with human innards. Some of the bodies, I noticed, were different compared to the ones in the lobby. A lot of them wore black suits and sunglasses. Firearms were scattered around them. *Men in Black. X-Files.* Those kinda guys. Secret agents? FBI? Something to do with the government. But why so many, and why on this floor specifically? Because of my mom. They were protecting her. Or maybe *guarding* was the more appropriate word. They knew something was unusual about her illness. Something nobody had ever witnessed before. And they didn't want anybody else knowing about it.

We followed the trail of death until it stopped at a door marked **PRIVATE—LEVEL RED CLEARENCE REQUIRED FOR ENTRY.** The keycard lock was smashed in at the knob. Someone else had already done the hard work for us. Andy pushed the door open without exercising too much energy.

I didn't know what I expected us to find in the room, but I somehow wasn't surprised by what *was* there, and neither was Andy. Maybe we'd known the whole time.

There, directly across from the doorway, was my mother. Sitting up in a gurney, naked. No sheet covering her body. But that was okay. She wasn't naked like an *alive* person, because she was no longer alive. By that point, most of her flesh had deteriorated. Her hair remained. And small patches of blackened skin. Still. She was a skeleton. Just as I was a skeleton. Yet we both possessed fully functioning eyeballs, and tongues, and the ability to move and make noise. None of this seemed strange. It felt perfectly, beautifully natural.

On one side of the gurney stood Candy and a man I'd never seen before, but judging by his attire he was a doctor of some sort. A surgeon would've made the most sense. They both stared at my mom like they couldn't believe what they were seeing. Neither of them had noticed our arrival.

On the opposite side of the gurney was something else. The thing we'd driven here to stop. My dad. What used to be my dad. What my dad was now. *Our* dad. The two-headed creature who had brutally slaughtered countless people throughout the Corpus Christi Medical Center. He was on all fours, like an animal. Focused solely on my mother.

Both of his heads were weeping.

Black sludge streamed from his various tear ducts.

"What the fuck is going on here?" Andy asked.

Candy and the surgeon jumped, startled by Andy's voice. Mom didn't react. Neither did the dad creature.

"Andy?" Candy said. "Is that . . . is that you?"

"Of course it's me. Hell else you think it is?"

She rushed toward him, body trembling. "But you're . . . you're . . . "

"A mummy? You betcher ass, baby."

He wrapped his arms around her and squeezed tightly. I stepped past them and observed the hospital room closer, only then realizing what we'd previously missed.

On the floor, next to the gurney's wheels, there was another body.

A skeletal woman in a dirty wedding dress.

There was nothing between her shoulders. Just a rotted stump where her head used to be.

"Oh, no," I whispered, rushing to the gurney. "Mom!"

Then I stopped, at a loss for words. Seeing why my mom was sitting up so awkwardly like that. She couldn't lay down, at least not on her back. Not with the head of her doppelgänger surgically attached to her spine. We were too late. *We were too late.* The second head was attached, and her eyes were open. Black saliva trickled out of her mouth, hungry, confused, psychotic. The wedding veil hung over her face.

I spun around and glared at the surgeon with murder in my eyes.

"What did you do?" I asked. "*What did you do?*"

"I'm sorry . . . " He backed away from the gurney, stammering. The man was drenched in sweat. "I didn't . . . they didn't give me . . . I can't . . . how . . . how is this possible? How is this . . . how is this . . . oh my god how is this—?"

"We're beyond asking that question," Andy shouted from across the room. "It gets us nowhere."

The surgeon turned toward the sound of his voice and gasped. "You're a . . . you're a . . . "

"Yes. A mummy. We've established that, as well."

"Oh my god."

"It's fine. Relax."

The surgeon exhaled deeply and sat down on a stool. He was drenched in sweat and looked like he was on the verge of a heart attack. The man had performed his duty here already. We'd failed to stop him in time. It wasn't like he could reverse it now. Or maybe he could. But who was going to ask him to do that?

The dad creature wept beside the gurney. Crying, yes, but not from sadness. These were tears of happiness. The thing was *overjoyed* that the surgery had worked. That Candy and the Corpus Christi surgeon had successfully attached the doppelgänger's head to my mother's spine.

"Our bride," the dads moaned. "Join us . . . join us . . . please . . . "

My mother's head grunted something unintelligible, then she repositioned herself on the gurney so she was standing on her knees and palms. The second head had taken control of her body, just as the transformation had unfolded with my father.

Somewhere behind us, the surgeon quietly said a prayer.

She glanced around the hospital room, studying each of us with a newborn's curiosity, until finally giving the dad creature her full attention.

"Our bride," he said again. "We love you . . . "

And the head atop my mother laughed.

Laughed and said, "But *we* . . . don't love . . . *you*."

Even the dad creature was struck silent by the response.

"Why are you here?" the mom creature asked. "We don't *need* you. We don't *want* you. We *told* you . . . "

"We . . . we . . . we . . . " It was the first time I'd seem him afraid since the transformation. "We love you. We are meant to be together."

Mom's top head shook back and forth, still amused by what she was hearing. "We are nothing."

"Nothing?" the dads said.

"Oh shit," Andy whispered, grabbing my shirt collar and pulling me back with him and Candy. "This don't look promising."

"What are they going to do?" Candy asked.

But I already knew the answer.

It was what they'd been doing for years.

It was what they did best.

They were going to fight.

The mom creature made the first move. Like a spider, she leapt off the gurney and tackled the dads against the wall. Both bottom heads started nipping at each other. The top heads growled and screamed and thrust forward with violent strikes. They were like two wild dogs fighting to the death.

The surgeon never stood a chance. He was still on the stool when their bodies rolled in his direction and sucked him up like dust in a tornado. Within seconds every ounce of blood stored inside him had splattered against the wall.

Their chaos quickly spread across the room and knocked us to the ground. I fell into a wooden chair. Andy wasn't so lucky. Practically made a dent into the wall, they hit him so hard. It was amazing he didn't explode like the surgeon. Maybe mummies can't explode. I never read much about mummies before. It could've been one of their hidden talents. Candy was smart enough to flee the room before they got close enough to cause any damage. As the only one of us still *alive*, I couldn't blame her for thinking of herself in that instance.

The dad and mom creatures rolled through the doorway and into the hallway leading into the main waiting room of the top floor. They were a ball of gooey energy gathering more heat with every outburst. Andy and I followed behind, but kept our distance, wary of falling into the line of fire again.

MAGGOTS SCREAMING!

The two-headed parents threw each other against waiting room chairs and overfilled trash cans. They snapped their jaws and tried to rip their throats out. They tripped over the corpses the dad creature had already created upon his arrival, succeeding in spreading more gore throughout the hospital. They were destroying everything that came in contact with them, all while screaming things like *We hate you!* and *We love you!*

Candy caught up with us, out of breath. "What are they *doing*?"

"They're gonna fucking kill each other," Andy said.

"What do we do?" I asked. "*What do we do?*"

He shrugged, like I was overreacting, like it wasn't such a big deal. " . . . Let them?"

"We have to help," I said. "We have to."

"And how the hell exactly do you reckon we do that?"

But of course I didn't know. How could I? It wasn't like I'd ever been in this situation before. They'd fought before, sure. But things had never gotten physical. And they'd never fought as two-headed monsters. This was definitely a first. Not just for myself but possibly for any other kid on the planet cursed with a dysfunctional family.

I had gone so long without seeing my mom. I had missed her so badly, and here she was, too busy to even glance at me. Too caught up with how much she despised my father. And the same thing went for Dad. He hadn't noticed we followed him to the hospital. All he cared about was my mother loving him again, when it was obvious she never would. Not even in death. Their marriage was over, forever. They should have saved everybody the trouble and avoided getting married in the first place. The whole relationship had been a waste of time for everybody.

I thought about how they met at *The Simpsons Movie* and wished they'd never gone to the same screening. That they'd married other people and had other children. That they'd done the whole world a favor and lived different lives. Then maybe everybody in this hospital would still be alive, and Andy wouldn't be a mummy, and the garden grave would have never been discovered. So many different realities that we'd never know because both of them just *had* to go see *The Simpsons Movie* at the same time in the same place and wreck everything.

For the first time in my life, I found myself hating *The Simpsons*.

I would have rather watched *The Office*.

"Wait," I said, an insane idea suddenly forming. I turned toward Andy and Candy. We had to shout over the sounds of my parents killing each other. "I know what to do! I know how to fix this!"

Andy chuckled. "Oh yeah? Whatcha thinkin'? Couples therapy?"

"How do you use the intercom?" I gestured to the speakers hanging from every corner of the room. "I want to play something."

"Do you think I work at this hospital? I don't fuckin' know how to use that."

"Over here!" Candy shouted, excited. She motioned us over to a series of computers hidden in the nurses' station. There was a microphone marked INTERCOM on the desk.

"Okay, you found that a little too easily," Andy said.

"I'm excellent at scavenger hunts," Candy said.

"I don't know what the hell good an intercom is going to do. It's not like they're listening to a goddamn word we have to say."

"We aren't going to say anything," I said, and nudged him aside with my shoulder. I sat at the desk and clicked the closest computer out of sleep mode. A password prompt generated across the screen. The three of us stared at it for nearly a full minute while my mother and father continued wreaking havoc on the other side of the room.

"Try *hospital*," Andy suggested.

I typed HOSPITAL—one-handed—and clicked submit. The monitor blinked to life.

"Holy shit," Andy said. "I can't believe that worked."

"Now who's finding things too easily?" Candy asked.

"Maybe we should try a scavenger hunt together sometime. A *sex* scavenger hunt."

"Wait," she said. "What does that mean?"

"I don't know. I imagine there's whipped cream involved, though. We'll figure it out later. After we're done with this bullshit."

I tried to ignore what they were discussing and focused on the computer in front of me. It took less than ten seconds to bring up YouTube, then another twenty seconds—mostly thanks to my lack of a second hand—to search for "simpsons theme song on loop".

The first result was exactly what I was after, a video titled "The Simpsons—10 hours intro".

I clicked play and blared the volume, then grabbed the microphone and enabled the intercom button, holding the mic up against the computer speakers.

The theme song for *The Simpsons* suddenly exploded through the hospital, drowning out all other noise.

The dad and mom creatures stopped fighting and froze in mid-attack upon the arrival of the music. It was like magic almost, how quickly the theme song affected them.

"What the hell?" Andy said. "There's no way this is gonna work, right?"

"Something's different about them," Candy said. "Can't you tell?"

"The fuckin' *Simpsons*, I swear to gawd."

I abandoned Andy and Candy at the nurses' station and cautiously maneuvered across the room, around the corpses, around the gore, toward my parents, or what was left of my parents. They were standing on all fours next to a huge window overlooking the hospital parking lot. The way their bodies were wrapped around each other, a stranger might have mistaken their embrace for a hug or some other act of loving devotion.

The theme song erupted through the intercom speakers at a deafening volume. I had applied a piece of tape to the microphone button to prevent it from shutting off. It would continue for the next ten hours if nobody tampered with it.

"Mom?" I said. "Dad?"

Either they couldn't hear me over the *Simpsons* theme song or they both chose to ignore me. Regardless, neither acknowledged my presence. As I neared, I noticed both of them were crying that bizarre black sludge again. The tears slowly dripped down their skeletal cheeks. Each head maintained eye contact with the other. They were sharing something together but I couldn't tell what. Communicating through telepathy.

The music had triggered something undeniable in them. The memory of how they met, perhaps, so many years ago, at the premiere of *The Simpsons Movie*.

Did it remind them that they hadn't always hated each other?

Did it remind them that they once, indeed, *loved* each other?

"Mom," I said again. "Dad . . . "

And this time, both of them turned toward me. All four heads. Finally, truly looking at me. Black tears down their faces. Mouths curling into sad smiles. They had heard me. They were listening.

"It's going to be okay," I told them, because it sounded like something I would have wanted them to tell me.

And Dad shook his bottom head and said, "No. It's not."

And Mom shook her bottom head and said, "Not okay. Never okay."

"But I'm here," I said. "I'm here to save you."

"You cannot save us," both the moms and the dads said in unison.

"What are you talking about?"

"We aren't . . . " They paused, all four heads now speaking as one. "We cannot be saved. And neither can you."

"What do you—?"

"Mistake. Error. Never again. *Never again.*"

"We can hide," I told them. "We can go somewhere. People can help us."

"No more help."

"But . . . but Mom . . . Dad . . . c'mon . . . we . . . we—"

"—*We belong dead,*" my parents said, and before I could comprehend what they were doing, the two of them—still looped in their bizarre, slimy embrace—lunged toward the window, shattering through the glass and disappearing from view.

I ran toward the opening and looked down at the parking lot below. They must've exploded upon impact. Body parts were scattered all over the cement. None of them moving.

The cops rushed toward the mess with their guns drawn, prepared to plug holes into anything that tried lashing out at them, but they didn't need to worry.

My parents weren't going to get up again.

Not then.

Not ever.

"I think that's our cue to get out of here!" Andy shouted behind me. I could barely hear him over the sound of the *Simpsons* theme song kicking back up through the intercom speakers. I understood enough of what he was saying, though, and couldn't have agreed more.

The three of us hurried down the stairs, careful not to slip on the trail of gore my parents had spread during their final argument. Nobody had touched Andy's truck. Anyone who was still alive must've been too preoccupied trying to make sense of the monster suicide out in the parking lot. I climbed in the bed next to you and Candy slid into the passenger seat beside Andy and he reversed out of the lobby and gunned it through the vandalized hospital entrance.

We made it halfway through the parking lot before Andy slammed on the brakes. I flew against the back window of the truck and would have probably experienced a considerable amount of pain if that were something I could still experience. Instead I mostly felt annoyed. I stood up in the bed and surveyed the scene.

Comrade stood in front of the truck, blood dripping from her jaws. But she didn't appear injured. The blood wasn't hers. It was cop blood.

But she wasn't alone.

Standing next to her was Miguel, holding an iced coffee and a paper bag from Dunkin' Donuts.

"Andy?" he said, head cocked.

Andy got out of the truck and approached them. I remained in the bed, where it felt safer. I wanted nothing to do with Miguel—in that moment, and any other. He had failed to protect my mother.

"Howdy, Miguel," Andy said, grabbing Comrade's collar and guiding her toward the truck.

"What—what what's going on? Are you okay? What's going on with all these cops? Is that Dylan in your truck? *Dylan?* Is that you? What . . . what is *happening?*"

I ducked behind the truck window. Nothing I could say to him would make a lick of sense, so I didn't bother trying.

Andy, on the other hand, was more sympathetic. "Where have you been?"

Miguel held up the bag and iced coffee. "I . . . went to get some lunch."

"Well, pardner, you sure missed a helluva lot."

"What the hell is this?"

"Max and Lori are back together," he said, picking up Comrade and sliding her into the truck next to Candy. "And I'm a goddamn mummy."

MAGGOTS SCREAMING!

"You're a *what*?"

"A mummy, Miguel!" Andy shouted. "I'm a goddamn mummy!" He got in the truck and slammed the door.

We drove away without answering any more of his questions, leaving him alone in the middle of the parking lot with his iced coffee. He and I briefly shared eye contact as the truck sped down the road. He lifted his hand and waved the Dunkin' Donuts bag at me. Either he was telling me goodbye or he was offering me a doughnut. I lifted my remaining hand and waved back at him.

I didn't want a doughnut, anyway.

I wasn't sure where Andy was taking us until I saw the bridge sign for Purgatory Creek.

We were returning to the body farm.

It made sense in a weird way. Where else would we have gone? Dad's house was burned to the ground. The Corpus Christi Medical Center surely had my mother's address in their records. Her house was probably swarming with government agents by then. Plus everybody had seen Andy's truck. At least one person must've written down his license plate—and, if not, one of the numerous cameras on the premises would have recorded it. So that ruled out his place. Meaning we were running dry on options. Except the body farm.

We wouldn't have to worry about Doctor Winzenread, since my father had fortunately eaten her face. The only employee there would be Candy. It was the perfect hideout. I didn't know how long we'd be able to stay there until someone noticed the anthropologist was no longer reporting to work. Would they promote Candy as the head of the facility, or bring someone else in for the job? That was a problem for the future. We'd dealt with enough trauma for one week. We were owed a break. And a break was what we were going to take.

We turned right at the Jesus rock and continued down the long, narrow dirt road until coming upon the archway marked HENENLOTTER RANCH. Andy stuck his arm through the window and punched in a series of numbers. The gates swung open, inviting us inside.

A heavy sense of relief hit me as the gates closed behind us. Like we were returning home from a long, stressful vacation.

That first night on the farm, you stayed in the bed of Andy's truck, and I roamed the property with Comrade checking out the various corpses displayed among the land. Andy and Candy disappeared inside the office and I didn't see them again until the next day. I can take a guess of what they were doing. I don't know *how,* considering Andy's new lifestyle as a mummy, but I didn't particularly want to put too much thought into it.

We spent that next day together, the three of us, playing games on the farm. Driving the golf cart around. Having fun for once. It'd been a while. I missed being a kid.

I'm not sure exactly how much time passed before Andy approached me with Candy's idea. I do know it was Andy who talked to me about it. Candy didn't have the courage to bring it up herself.

I wasn't against the idea. Not entirely. I'm not an idiot. My decomposition hadn't magically *stopped*. Things are progressing, albeit slowly. They will get worse. Someday soon I will be less than a skeleton. I will be nothing. The earth will consume me.

And the same goes for you.

If we are going to act, then we need to make a decision soon.

Which is why we're here now.

At my request.

Sprawled out together in the middle of the body farm, protected from vultures by one of those metal cages.

Just you and me. Alone.

Except for Comrade, who keeps circling our cage, whining. Eager to continue eating us.

MAGGOTS SCREAMING!

I told Andy to give us a couple days to think about it. He was more than happy to oblige. It only meant more time he could spend with Candy. More time to do the things I don't want to picture. Sometimes even the dead can be grossed out.

So here we are.

I've told you the story of how we found you.

Or how you found us.

I've told you everything I know.

You and I, we're equal.

There is nothing between us.

And now we have a tough choice, because Andy wasn't exaggerating. We aren't looking too pretty. I don't know how much longer we will last. There is going to come a point where we are *dead* dead. Or at least unable to move, unable to talk, unable to do anything but think think think. Is that what happened to Mom and Dad? All those pieces, scattered throughout the parking lot—did they remain sentient through it all? Are they somewhere this very second, wondering where I am? Where *we* are?

Okay, we have two options here, the way I see it.

Option one—we do nothing. We stay in this cage and we let nature continue its course. We do what we do best and we rot until there's nothing left to rot.

Or, option two . . .

Well, that's where things get tricky, right?

Candy thinks she can do it. She's witnessed the surgery twice now—and, the second time, she'd practically walked the surgeon through it, told him exactly what to do.

She seems confident about her abilities.

Less confident about what the outcome might end up being.

We saw what happened to our parents.

Is that the life we want?

Of course. There's no way to know the same thing will happen to us. Maybe she attaches you to me and everything works out fine. We live forever, the two of us,

323

best friends for life. Assuming the transformation halts the decomposition like we suspect.

Plus you'd finally be able to talk. I could be the one listening for a change.

That sounds pleasant, doesn't it? I wouldn't mind something like that.

Unless . . .

Unless things go dark.

Unless we get hungry like our father got hungry.

I don't want to kill anyone.

I don't want to be responsible for that kind of violence.

I don't want to be a monster.

But the thing that scares me the most? I can't say for certain whether or not you agree.

You've laid here this whole time listening to our story. Not saying a word. But I know, based from experience with the other bodies, you can understand me.

You *know* what I'm saying.

But I *don't know* what you're thinking.

And I *don't know* if I can let Candy complete our transformation without being one-hundred percent sure that things aren't going to get worse.

So, unless you can tell me right here, right now, that you want to try to make things work, that you want to have a *good* life together, then I'm afraid you already know what my answer will be once Andy returns to our cage tomorrow.

Because, truth be told, lately all I can think about is what our parents told us before leaping out that hospital window. Nothing in this world feels truer than those final words. Nothing makes more sense.

Do you remember what they said?

Of course you do.

You remember it because I remember it.

They said we belong dead.

AUTHOR'S NOTE

I moved to Texas in September 2011. I started this novel nine years later in the summer of 2020 and finished it in November 2021. Before *Maggots*, I had written a few other things that take place in Texas, but the majority of my work has been set in Indiana, which is where I was born and raised. My 2017 novel, *The Nightly Disease,* technically happens in Texas, although I do not consider it a Texas novel. Most of the story occurs inside a hotel. Honestly, the hotel could've been built anywhere and not much would have changed.

Maggots, on the other hand, feels like my first real exploration of this state I've decided to call home. Does it take almost a decade to really know a place? In this instance, I think the answer is yes. This is not a book I could have written when I first moved here.

The genesis of *Maggots* originated the same summer I started writing it. My wife Lori, her son Dylan, and I were digging up an old garden in our back yard. The intention was to plant something new and fresh, since the old plants were pretty dead and obsolete by then. Sometimes I like to spook Dylan by asking him bizarre questions. My most well-known book, *We Need to Do Something,* came to life after I asked him and his sister (while sheltering in our bathroom during a tornado warning), "What would happen if we got stuck in here and nobody came to help us?" Naturally, *Maggots Screaming!* sprouted from a similar hypothetical while we were digging up the old garden: "What if we found a body down here?" Then, after a moment of excitement: "What if the body was *you*?" Dylan was not a fan of this question, which told me everything I needed to know about its potential for a horror story.

So thank you, Dylan, for somehow always inspiring weird, disturbing ideas.

And thank you, Lori, for giving me a home and not leaving me for Miguel (yet).

Major thanks to Danny Wescott of Texas State University, who denied my request for a tour of their Forensic Anthropology Research Facility, implying my presence would be disrespectful to the specimens. I hope I did body farms justice without your assistance.

I researched the hell out of this book, despite sometimes relying on cartoon logic later in the narrative. Some of the books I consulted during the creation of *Maggots Screaming!* include *Stiff: The Curious Lives of Human Cadavers* by Mary Roach, *The American Way of Death Revisited* by Jessica Mitford, *Death's Acre: Inside the Legendary Forensic Lab the Body Farm Where the Dead Do Tell Tales* by William Bass, *Working Stiff: Two Years, 262 Bodies, and the Making of a Medical Examiner* by Judy Melinek, M.D., *The Book of Resting Places: A Personal History of Where We Lay the Dead* by Thomas Mira y Lopez, *Texas Graveyards: A Cultural Legacy* by Terry G. Jordan, and *The Body Farm* by Patricia Cornwell (which, seriously, does not contain enough body farm scenes for a book with that title). This novel also wouldn't exist without Mary Shelley's *Frankenstein*.

Despite *Maggots* being a Texas book, I actually wrote 25,000 words of it in Michigan, on the set of my first movie, *We Need to Do Something*. It's a stereotype to say authors are depressed and miserable when they write. *Maggots* was the opposite. I was probably the happiest I've ever been in my life when I worked on it. Above the soundstage was a mini theater where our editor, Shane Patrick Ford, was cutting the previous day's film. I often hung out with him, desecrating a notebook in the dark while he loaded new footage. So thank you to Shane for keeping me company and inspiring my productivity in a time where I probably wouldn't have written a goddamn word. Also thanks to Colin and Josh, who interrogated me on my work-in-progress while I was down there and expressed genuine excitement for what I had to say.

Corinne Halbert nailed the cover art. I fucking love what she made.

Same goes for Lori Michelle's interior layout and formatting. I haven't actually seen it yet at the time that I am writing this afterword, but I am sure it's going to be awesome, and also I think it would be cool if we got naked later today, so I think this paragraph will help make that happen.

Thanks to my manager, Ryan Lewis, for telling me there was no way a commercial publisher would have touched something like *Maggots Screaming!*. I am not being sarcastic when I say that's probably the best compliment you could have given this book.

This book wouldn't be in its current shape without the help from early readers like Ryan, Thomas, Betty, Pedro, Trevor, Logan, and Lori. Thomas needs an extra bit of acknowledgement, however, as he's the one who came up with my "the family that decays together, stays together" tagline. It's perfect.

Additionally, I need to thank my very good friends— Andrew, Miguel, and Zach—who also agreed to take a look at an early copy of this novel and then never mentioned it again.

Although Zach didn't read it, he did design a really cool title font for the front cover, so I guess he's not completely horrible.

I do have to give Andrew props, however, for suggesting I add an exclamation mark to the title.

Miguel did not contribute anything to this book.

Thanks to Andrew's dog, Comrade, for having a great dog name.

And, speaking of dogs, I honestly don't think I would have been able to write this thing without Jack and Frank. Thank you for keeping my feet warm. Thank you for everything.

—**Max Booth III**
February 7, 2022

ABOUT THE AUTHOR

Max Booth III lives in San Antonio, TX where he studies "worm science" in his back yard. Recently he's adapted to an all-dirt diet. All of his teeth have fallen out. Everything itches. He's written novels and screenplays and other things. He wrote *We Need to Do Something* which was adapted into a feature film starring Pat Healy, Vinessa Shaw, and Sierra McCormick. For some reason Ozzy Osbourne has a voice cameo in it. He hosts a podcast called *Ghoulish*. It's spooky. He co-runs a small press called Ghoulish Books. It's also spooky. Everything is spooky. Especially the stuff that isn't spooky. That's the spookiest of them all. At night he cries loudly because the moon frightens him. Is it the sun or something else? He doesn't understand. Sometimes he sticks his ear against the earth and listens to all the terrible secrets of the universe. He's on Twitter @GiveMeYourTeeth. He has a website. Go to your browser and type www. TalesFromTheBooth.com. He is so tired. Everything hurts. One day the world will consume him and everything will be okay. Until then he hopes you enjoyed this book and he hopes you have a good day.

SPOOKY TALES FROM GHOULISH BOOKS

☐**BELOW | Laurel Hightower**
ISBN: 978-1-943720-69-9 $12.95
A creature feature about a recently divorced woman trying to survive a road trip through the mountains of West Virginia.

☐**MAGGOTS SCREAMING! | Max Booth III**
ISBN: 978-1-943720-68-2 $18.95
On a hot summer weekend in San Antonio, Texas, a father and son bond after discovering three impossible corpses buried in their back yard.

☐**LEECH | John C. Foster**
ISBN: 978-1-943720-70-5 $14.95
Horror / noir mashup about a top secret government agency's most dangerous employee. Doppelgangers, demigods, and revenants, oh my!

☐**ALL THESE SUBTLE DECEITS | C.S. Humble**
ISBN: 978-1-943720-71-2 $14.95
A possessed woman and an exorcist descend into an occult labyrinth of dark forces and oppressive spirits.

☐**RABBITS IN THE GARDEN | Jessica McHugh**
ISBN: 978-1-943720-73-6 $16.95
13-year-old Avery Norton is a crazed killer—according to the staff at Taunton Asylum, anyway. But as she struggles to prove her innocence in the aftermath of gruesome murders spanning the 1950s, Avery discovers there's a darker force keeping her locked away . . . which she calls "Mom."

☐**PERFECT UNION | Cody Goodfellow**
ISBN: 978-1-943720-74-3 $18.95
Three brothers searching the wilderness for their mother instead find a utopian cult that seeks to reinvent society, family . . . humanity

☐**SOFT PLACES | Betty Rocksteady**
ISBN: 978-1-943720-75-0 $14.95
A novella/graphic novel hybrid about a seemingly psychotic
woman who suffers a mysterious head injury.

☐**HARES IN THE HEDGEROW | Jessica McHugh**
ISBN: 978-1-943720-76-7 $21.95
15 years after the events in *Rabbits in the Garden*, Avery
Norton is a ghost. 16-year-old Sophie Dillon doesn't know
anything about the alleged murderer, yet she's haunted
nightly by the same dark urges, which send her on a journey
to uncover her past with the Norton family and to embrace
the future with her spiritual family, the Choir of the Lamb.
But Sophie's devotions can't protect her from the ghosts
waiting in the wings. After all, she's the one they've been
waiting for.

Not all titles available for immediate shipping. All credit card
purchases must be made online at GhoulishBooks.com.
Shipping is 5.80 for one book and an additional dollar for each
additional book. Contact us for international shipping prices.
All checks and money orders should be made payable to
Perpetual Motion Machine Publishing.

Ghoulish Books
PO Box 1104
Cibolo, TX 78108

Ship to:

Name _____

Address _____

City_____State_____Zip _____

Phone Number _____

                              Book Total: $_____

                          Shipping Total: $_____

                            Grand Total: $_____

Patreon:
www.patreon.com/pmmpublishing

Website:
www.PerpetualPublishing.com

Facebook:
www.facebook.com/PerpetualPublishing

Twitter:
@PMMPublishing

Newsletter:
www.PMMPNews.com

Email Us:
Contact@PerpetualPublishing.com

CPSIA information can be obtained
at www.ICGtesting.com
Printed in the USA
BVHW031841240422
635200BV00004B/65

9 781943 720682